Richard Grant White

The Works of William Shakespeare

Vol. III

SALZWASSER
VERLAG

Richard Grant White

The Works of William Shakespeare

Vol. III

Reprint of the original, first published in 1863.

1st Edition 2022 | ISBN: 978-3-37500-307-4

Verlag (Publisher): Salzwasser Verlag GmbH, Zeilweg 44, 60439 Frankfurt, Deutschland
Vertretungsberechtigt (Authorized to represent): E. Roepke, Zeilweg 44, 60439 Frankfurt, Deutschland
Druck (Print): Books on Demand GmbH, In de Tarpen 42, 22848 Norderstedt, Deutschland

SHAKESPEARE'S WORKS.

[WHITE.]

IN TWELVE VOLUMES.

VOLUME III.

COMEDIES.

MEASURE FOR MEASURE.
THE COMEDY OF ERRORS.
MUCH ADO ABOUT NOTHING.
LOVE'S LABOUR'S LOST.

THE WORKS OF

WILLIAM SHAKESPEARE

THE PLAYS EDITED FROM THE FOLIO OF MDCXXIII, WITH VARIOUS READINGS FROM ALL THE EDITIONS AND ALL THE COMMENTATORS, NOTES, INTRODUCTORY REMARKS, A HISTORICAL SKETCH OF THE TEXT, AN ACCOUNT OF THE RISE AND PROGRESS OF THE ENGLISH DRAMA, A MEMOIR OF THE POET, AND AN ESSAY UPON HIS GENIUS

BY RICHARD GRANT WHITE

VOL. III.

BOSTON

1863

MEASURE FOR MEASURE.

Measure for Measure occupies twenty-four pages in the folio of 1623; viz., from p. 61 to p. 84, inclusive, in the division of Comedies. It is there divided into Acts and Scenes and is followed by a list of the Dramatis Personæ under the head, "The names of all the Actors." From this list, however, *Varrius* and the *Justice* are omitted: above it is "*The Scene Vienna.*"

MEASURE FOR MEASURE.

INTRODUCTION.

SHAKESPEARE found the plot and the principal characters of this play made to his hand in the *Promos and Cassandra* of George Whetstone which was published in 1578, but never acted. Whetstone founded his play upon the fifth Novel of the eighth Decade of Giraldi Cinthio's *Hecatommithi*, a collection of tales similar to Boccaccio's *Decamerone*, and in which also Shakespeare found the tale upon which he constructed his *Othello*. The course of the story in Cinthio's novel is indicated with sufficient particularity in its long title, which is as follows: — "*Juriste* is sent by the Emperor Maximilian to Inspruch, where he causes a young man, who has violated a virgin, to be arrested, and condemns him to death: his sister endeavours to free him: *Juriste* holds out hopes to the lady that he will marry her and liberate her brother: she lies with him, and the same night *Juriste* causes the young man's head to be struck off, and sends it to his sister. She complains to the Emperor, who causes *Juriste* to marry the lady; after which he orders him to be put to death: the lady saves him, and lives with him most lovingly." *

Whetstone himself published in 1582 a book of tales similar to that of Cinthio, which he called the *Heptameron of Civil Discourses*, and one of these tales he founded on Cinthio's story of *Juriste*. The following argument, prefixed to his play of *Promos and Cassandra*,† gives a very good description of the course of its

* "Juristo e mandato da Massimiano, Imperadore, in Ispruchi, ove fà prendere un giovane, violatore di una vergine, e condannalo à morte: la sorella cerca di liberarlo: Juriste da speranza alla donna di pigliarla per moglie, e di darle libero il fratello: ella con lui si giace, e la notte istessa Juriste fà tagliar al giovane la testa, e la manda alla sorella. Ella ne fà querela all' Imperadore, il quale fà sposare ad Juriste la donna; poscia lo fà dare ad essere ucciso. La donna lo libera, e con lui si vive amorevolissimamente."

† "The right excellent and famous Historye of Promos and Cassandra, divided into Commical Discourses: In the fyrste Parte is showne the unsufferable

incidents, but is defective in two or three points important to the student of Shakespeare: —

"In the Cytie of Julio (sometime under the dominion of Corvinus, King of Hungarie and Boemia) there was a law, that what man so ever committed Adultery, should lose his head, and the woman offender should weare some disguised apparell, during her life, to make her infamouslye noted. This severe lawe, by the favour of some mercifull magistrate, became little regarded, untill the time of Lord Promos auctority: who, convicting a yong Gentleman named Andrugio of incontinency, condemned both him, and his minion, to the execution of this statute. Andrugio had a very vertuous and beawtiful Gentlewoman to his Sister, named Cassandra: Cassandra, to enlarge her brothers life, submitted an humble petition to the Lord Promos: Promos regarding her good behaviours, and fantasying her great beawtie, was much delighted with the sweete order of her talke: and doying good, that evil might come thereof, for a time he repryved her brother: but, wicked man, tourning his liking unto unlawfull lust, he set downe the spoile of her honour raunsome for her Brothers life: chaste Cassandra, abhorring both him and his sute, by no persuasion would yeald to this raunsome. But, in fine, wonne with the importunitye of her Brother, (pleading for life,) upon these conditions she agreede to Promos. First that he should pardon her brother, and after marry her. Promos as feareless in promisse, as carelesse in performance, with sollemne vowe, sygned her conditions: but worse then any Infydel, his will satisfyed, he performed neither the one nor the other: for to keepe his aucthoritye, unspotted with favour, and to prevent Cassandrae's clamors, he commaunded the Gayler secretly to present Cassandra with her brother's head. The Gayler, [touched] with the outcryes of Andrugio, abhorrying Promos lewdenes, by the providence of God, provyded thus for his safety. He presented Cassandra with a felons head newlie executed, who (being mangled, knew it not from her brother's, by the Gaylor, who was set at libertie) was so agreeved at this trecherye, that at the pointe to kyl herselfe, she spared that stroke to be avenged of Promos. And, devisyng a way, she concluded to make her fortunes knowne unto the kynge. She (executinge this resolution) was so highly favoured of the king, that forthwith he

abuse of a lewdo Magistrate, the vertuous behaviours of a chaste Ladye, the uncontrowled leawdeness of a favoured Curtisan, and the undeserved Estimation of a pernicious Parasyte: In the second Parte is discoursed the perfect Magnanimitye of a noble Kinge, in checking Vice and favouringe Vertue: Wherein is showne the Ruyne and Overthrowe of dishonest Practises, with the Advauncement of upright Dealing."

Both Whetstone's tale and Cinthio's are printed in Collier's *Shakespeare's Library*.

hasted to do justice on Promos: whose judgment was, to marrye Cassandra, to repaire her crased honour: which donne, for his hainous offence he should lose his head. This marryage solempnised, Cassandra, tyed in the greatest bondes of affection to her husband, became an earnest suter for his life: the kinge (tendringe the generall benefit of the common weale, before her special case, although he favoured her much) would not graunt her sute. Andrugio (disguised amonge the company) sorrowing the griefe of his sister, bewrayde his safetye, and craved pardon. The kinge, to renowne the vertues of Cassandra, pardoned both him and Promos. The circumstances of this rare Historye, in action lyvelye followeth."

By this it will be seen that Whetstone improved greatly upon the plot of Cinthio's tale, for dramatic purposes, by causing the brother to be condemned for a far more venial fault than that laid to his charge by the Italian author, and by substituting another prisoner as the victim of the governor's faithless cruelty. Upon Whetstone's plot, Shakespeare again improved by still further mitigating the brother's error, by making the monarch himself the principal agent in working out the denouement, and, above all, by the introduction of another female character, betrothed (which in early times was about the same as married) to the deputy, and whose intervention saves his intended victim from compliance with his conditions, while he is yet made answerable for the same crimes of which he is guilty even in the original Italian story. But Shakespeare not only adopted, with these great improvements, Whetstone's variations from Cinthio's novel: he found in *Promos and Cassandra* another set of characters, the Bawd, the Fantastic, the Clown, and the Constable, which he also introduced but re-created. He followed, too, in some measure, the arrangement of Whetstone's Scenes, and in certain passages of the earlier play we find the germs of others in the later. Thus, for instance, in these lines,

"Justice wyll say thou dost no cryme commit,
For in forst faultes is no intent of yll,"

is the origin of these,

"Our compell'd sins
Stand more for number than accompt."

So this passage, in a soliloquy by *Promos*, after *Cassandra* has yielded to him,

"No force for that my might commaundeth right;
Hir privie maime hir open cryes will staye,

> Or if not so, my frowning will hir fright:
> And thus shall rule conceale my filthy deed,"

is plainly but the counterpart of the following, in *Angelo's* soliloquy, when he supposes himself to be in a similar position with regard to *Isabella*: —

> "But that her tender shame
> Will not proclaim against her maiden loss,
> How might she tongue me! Yet Reason dares her on:
> For my authority here bears up a credent bulk
> That no particular scandal once can touch
> But it confounds the breather."

One of Whetstone's comic characters, too, says, "A holie hood makes not a frier devoute," which is but a slight metrical paraphrase of the Latin saw, "*Cucullus non facit monachum*," which Shakespeare puts in *Lucio's* mouth. These are but a few out of many similar instances; and from all that has gone before, the reader can form his own opinion as to the sort of obligation under which Shakespeare was to Whetstone. He will probably not agree with Mr. Collier, that "Shakespeare was not indebted to Whetstone for a single thought, nor for a casual expression, excepting as far as similarity of situation may be said to have necessarily occasioned corresponding states of feeling and employment of language," but he may safely rest assured that *Promos and Cassandra* is about as much like *Measure for Measure*, as heaps of unshaped clay and pits of sand and lime are like an Elizabethan mansion.

The text of this play is generally well printed in the folio; but it contains several passages which give more trouble to the editor and the reader than any others which occur in that volume. To those not disciplined in the construction of language, and unaccustomed to trace the logical connection of thoughts apparently remote, the style of all the serious parts of *Measure for Measure* is involved and therefore more or less obscure; and hence the necessity for the explanation of passages which are not in any way corrupted, as well as the difficulty which has been found in restoring those that are, and the supposition by many intelligent editors and commentators that corruption existed in many passages, which, upon a closer and more analytical examination, have been found pure. The versification is rugged and irregular; but it seems to be so from design, not carelessness. Conjectural emendation is thrown entirely upon its own resources in restoring some extremely difficult and unquestionably corrupted passages in this play; for it receives no aid from any earlier copy than that of the first folio.

We have no means of determining with great approach to accuracy the time when *Measure for Measure* was written. That it was written in Shakespeare's maturity, its own profound philosophy, strikingly akin to that of *Hamlet,* is sufficient evidence: that it had not been produced in 1597, we may feel quite confident, from the omission of it from the enumeration of its author's works in Meres' *Palladis Tamia:* that it was produced before 1604, we know, from an entry in the accounts of the Revels at Court from October, 1604, to October, 1605, in the following words: —

"By his Ma[tis] Plaiers. On St. Stivens night in the Hall, a Play caled Mesur for Mesur."

In a column of the account devoted to "The Poets which mayd the Plaies," the name of a Mr. "Shaxberd," apparently not so well known then as it is now, is entered. The passage in the first Scene, which contains a flattering allusion to the disposition of King James to deny his subjects access to his person, has been, with some reason, supposed to fix the date of the production of this play after the accession of that monarch; and although it might have been inserted for the special occasion of the performance at court in 1604, and afterward retained, the supposition jumps so well with the character of the play itself and with our knowledge as to the date of the production of other plays, that we may safely conclude, with Mr. Collier, that *Measure for Measure* was written either at the close of 1603, or in the beginning of 1604.

The period of the action of this play, which has been hitherto considered, and even pronounced, to be undeterminable, is clearly defined by the first few lines of the second Scene of the first Act, and by our knowledge of the source of the plot. Whetstone tells us, as we have seen, that the incidents took place "in the city of Julio, sometime under the dominion of Corvinus, King of Hungary and Bohemia," and in his *Heptameron* the tale begins, "At what time Corvinus, the scourge of the Turks, rayned as Kinge of Bohemia, for to well governe the free cities of his realme, he sent divers worthy magistrates," &c.: in the Scene mentioned, *Lucio* says, "If the Duke, with the other dukes, come not to composition with the King of Hungary, why then all the dukes fall upon the King:" to which the reply is, "Heaven grant us its peace, but not the King of Hungary's." Now Corvinus, King of Hungary, was declared King of Bohemia in 1473, and reigned until his death in 1490. He was almost continually at war with the Duke of Austria, Frederic III. (whose court was at Vienna,) and with the Turks. His expeditions were almost always successful against both; and he usually "conquered a peace" by a very bloody victory, so that his enemies might well pray for Heaven's peace, "but not the King of Hungary's." As he marched on Vienna and took it in 1485, the apprehensions expressed by *Lucio* and his acquaintance enable us to determine almost the very year of the supposed action, — an accuracy unattainable with regard to any other of these dramas not founded upon a historical subject. Shakespeare, with his usual tact in adapting his plays to the understanding of his audience, changed Whetstone's unknown city, Julio, to Vienna, a place almost or quite as well known in England then as now. With the place he also changed, of course, the prince whose delegated authority is abused; but he scrupulously retained the costume and all the traits and incidents which marked the period of the story on which he built his comedy, and added two or three allusions not to be found in Whetstone's play or story, as if for the very purpose of giving a local habitation and a time, as well as an air of reality, to this wonderful and admirable creation.* The costume of the characters is

* The reader who is disposed to examine closely the points considered in this Introduction will find them discussed with much greater particularity in *Shakespeare's Scholar*. Mr. Verplanck's excellent Introduction to the play should also receive his thoughtful attention. The following lines are the principal part of what passes between the brother and sister in *Promos and Cassandra*, in the interview corresponding to that between *Claudio* and *Isabella* in *Measure for Measure*, Act III. Sc. 1. By comparing them, a correct idea may be formed of the likeness — and the difference between the two plays.

" *Cassandra.* If thou dost live, I must my honor lose.
Thy raunsome is, to Promos fleshly wyll
That I do yielde: than which I rather chose
With torments sharpe myselfe he first should kyll.
Thus am I bent: thou seest thy death at hand:
O would my life would satisfie his yre,
Cassandra then would cancell soone thy band!
Andrugio. And may it be a judge of his account
Can spot his minde with lawles love or lust?
But more, may he doome any fault with death,
When in such faute he findes himselfe unjust?
Syster, that wise men love we often see,
And where love rules, gainst thornes doth reason spurne.

the Viennese dress of the close of the fifteenth century, some approach to which, at least, may be found in Vecelli's *Habiti Antichi e Moderni*, published at Vienna in 1598.

> But who so loves, if he rejected be,
> His passing love to peevish hate will turne.
> Deare sister then note how my fortune stands:
> That Promos love, the like is oft in use;
> And sith he crave this kindnesse at your hands,
> Think this, if you his pleasure do refuse,
> I, in his rage (poor wretch) shall sing *Peccavi*.
> Here are two evyls, the best harde to digest;
> But whereas things are driven unto necessity,
> There are we byd, of both evyls choose the least.
> *Cassandra*. And of these evils the least, I hold, is death
> To shun whose dart we can no meane devise;
> Yet honor lives when death hath done his worst:
> Thus fame then lyfe is of farre more comprise.
> *Andrugio*. Nay, Cassandra, if thou thy selfe submit,
> To save my life, to Promos fleashly wyll,
> Justice wyll say thou dost no cryme commit,
> For in forst faultes is no intent of yll.
> *Cassandra*. How so th' intent is construed in offence,
> The Proverbe saies that tenne good turnes lye dead,
> And one yll deede tenne tymes beyond pretence
> By envious tongues, report abrode doth spread.
> Andrugio, so my fame shall vallewed bee;
> Dispite will blase my crime, but not the cause;
> And thus, although I fayne would set thee free,
> Poor wench, I feare the grype of slaunder's pawes.
> *Andrugio*. Nay sweete sister, more slaunder would infame
> Your spotles lyfe to reave your brother's breath,
> When you have power for to enlarge the same;
> Once in your handes doth lye my life and death.
> Way that I am the selfe-same flesh you are;
> Thinke, I once gone, our house will goe to wrack:
> Knowe, forced faultes for slaunder neede not care:
> Looke you for blame, if I guaile through your lack.
> Consider well my great extremitie;
> If otherwise this doome I could revoke,
> I would not spare for any jebardye
> To free thee, wench, from this same heavy yoke:
> But ah, I see else no way saves my life,
> And yet his hope may further thy consent;
> He sayde, he maye percase make thee his wyfe,
> And 'tis likelie he cannot be content
> With one night's joye: if love he after seekes;
> And I discharg'd, if thou aloofe then be,
> Before he lose thy selfe that so he leekes,
> No doubt but he to marryage wyll agree."

DRAMATIS PERSONÆ.

VINCENTIO, *the Duke.*
ANGELO, *the Deputy.*
ESCALUS, *an ancient Lord.*
CLAUDIO, *a young Gentleman.*
LUCIO, *a Fantastic.*
Two other like Gentlemen.
VARRIUS, *a Gentleman, Servant to the Duke.*
Provost.
THOMAS, PETER, } Two Friars.
A Justice.
ELBOW, *a simple Constable.*
FROTH, *a foolish Gentleman.*
Clown, *Servant to* Mrs. Over-done.
ABHORSON, *an Executioner.*
BARNARDINE, *a dissolute Prisoner.*

ISABELLA, *sister to* Claudio.
MARIANA, *betrothed to* Angelo.
JULIET, *beloved of* Claudio.
FRANCISCA, *a Nun.*
Mistress OVER-DONE, *a Bawd.*

Lords, Gentlemen, Guards, Officers, *and other* Attendants

SCENE: Vienna.

MEASURE FOR MEASURE.

ACT I.

SCENE I. — An Apartment in the DUKE's Palace.

Enter DUKE, ESCALUS, Lords, *and* Attendants.

Duke.

ESCALUS!
Escalus. My lord.
Duke. Of government the properties to unfold,
Would seem in me t' affect speech and discourse;
Since I am put to know, that your own science
Exceeds, in that, the lists of all advice
My strength can give you; then no more remains
But that, to your sufficiency, — as your worth is able, —
And let them work. The nature of our people,
Our city's institutions, and the terms
For common justice, y' are as pregnant in
As art and practice hath enriched any
That we remember. There is our commission,
From which we would not have you warp. — Call hither,
I say, bid come before us Angelo. —
[*Exit an* Attendant.

What figure of us think you he will bear?
For you must know, we have with special soul
Elected him our absence to supply,
Lent him our terror, drest him with our love,
And given his deputation all the organs
Of our own power. What think you of it?
Escal. If any in Vienna be of worth
To undergo such ample grace and honour,
It is Lord Angelo.

Enter ANGELO.

Duke. Look, where he comes.
Angelo. Always obedient to your Grace's will,
I come to know your pleasure.
Duke. Angelo,
There is a kind of character in thy life,
That, to th' observer, doth thy history
Fully unfold. Thyself and thy belongings
Are not thine own so proper, as to waste
Thyself upon thy virtues, they on thee.
Heaven doth with us as we with torches do,
Not light them for themselves; for if our virtues
Did not go forth of us, 'twere all alike
As if we had them not. Spirits are not finely touch'd,
But to fine issues; nor Nature never lends
The smallest scruple of her excellence,
But, like a thrifty goddess, she determines
Herself the glory of a creditor—
Both thanks and use. But I do bend my speech
To one that can my part in him advertise:
Hold, therefore, Angelo, [our place and power:]
In our remove, be thou at full ourself:
Mortality and mercy in Vienna
Live in thy tongue and heart. Old Escalus,

Though first in question, is thy secondary:
Take thy commission.
Ang. Now, good my lord,
Let there be some more test made of my metal,
Before so noble and so great a figure
Be stamp'd upon it.
Duke. No more evasion:
We have with a leaven'd and prepared choice
Proceeded to you; therefore take your honours.
Our haste from hence is of so quick condition,
That it prefers itself, and leaves unquestion'd
Matters of needful value. We shall write to you,
As time and our concernings shall importune,
How it goes with us; and do look to know
What doth befall you here. So, fare you well:
To th' hopeful execution do I leave you
Of your commissions.
Ang. Yet, give leave, my lord,
That we may bring you something on the way.
Duke. My haste may not admit it;
Nor need you, on mine honour, have to do
With any scruple: your scope is as mine own,
So to enforce or qualify the laws
As to your soul seems good. Give me your hand.
I'll privily away: I love the people,
But do not like to stage me to their eyes.
Though it do well, I do not relish well
Their loud applause, and *aves* vehement;
Nor do I think the man of safe discretion,
That does affect it. Once more, fare you well.
Ang. The Heavens give safety to your purposes!—
Escal. Lead forth, and bring you back in happiness!
Duke. I thank you. Fare you well. [*Exit.*
Escal. I shall desire you, sir, to give me leave

To have free speech with you; and it concerns me
To look into the bottom of my place.
A power I have, but of what strength and nature
I am not yet instructed.

Ang. 'Tis so with me. Let us withdraw together,
And we may soon our satisfaction have
Touching that point.

Escal. I'll wait upon your honour.

[*Exeunt.*

Scene II.

A Street.

Enter Lucio *and two* Gentlemen.

Lucio. If the Duke, with the other dukes, come not to composition with the King of Hungary, why then, all the dukes fall upon the King.

1 *Gentleman.* Heaven grant us its peace, but not the King of Hungary's!

2 *Gent.* Amen.

Lucio. Thou conclud'st like the sanctimonious pirate, that went to sea with the Ten Commandments, but scrap'd one out of the table.

2 *Gent.* "Thou shalt not steal"?

Lucio. Ay, that he raz'd.

1 *Gent.* Why, 'twas a commandment to command the captain and all the rest from their functions: they put forth to steal. There's not a soldier of us all, that, in the thanksgiving before meat, doth relish the petition well that prays for peace.

2 *Gent.* I never heard any soldier dislike it.

Lucio. I believe thee; for I think thou never wast where grace was said.

2 *Gent.* No? a dozen times at least.

1 *Gent.* What, in metre?

Lucio. In any proportion, or in any language.

1 *Gent.* I think, or in any religion.

Lucio. Ay; why not? Grace is grace, despite of all controversy: as for example; thou thyself art a wicked villain, despite of all grace.

1 *Gent.* Well, there went but a pair of shears between us.

Lucio. I grant; as there may between the lists and the velvet: thou art the list.

1 *Gent.* And thou the velvet: thou art good velvet: thou 'rt a three-pil'd piece, I warrant thee. I had as lief be a list of an English kersey as be pil'd, as thou art pil'd, for a French velvet. Do I speak feelingly now?

Lucio. I think thou dost; and, indeed, with most painful feeling of thy speech: I will, out of thine own confession, learn to begin thy health; but, whilst I live, forget to drink after thee.

1 *Gent.* I think I have done myself wrong; have I not?

2 *Gent.* Yes, that thou hast, whether thou art tainted or free.

Lucio. Behold, behold, where Madam Mitigation comes!

1 *Gent.* I have purchas'd as many diseases under her roof as come to —

2 *Gent.* To what, I pray?

Lucio. Judge.

2 *Gent.* To three thousand dolours a-year.

1 *Gent.* Ay, and more.

Lucio. A French crown more.

1 *Gent.* Thou art always figuring diseases in me; but thou art full of error: I am sound.

Lucio. Nay, not as one would say, healthy; but so sound as things that are hollow: thy bones are hollow; impiety has made a feast of thee.

Enter Bawd.

1 *Gent.* How now? Which of your hips has the most profound sciatica?

Bawd. Well, well; there's one yonder arrested and carried to prison, was worth five thousand of you all.

2 *Gent.* Who's that, I pr'ythee?

Bawd. Marry, sir, that's Claudio; Signior Claudio.

1 *Gent.* Claudio to prison! 'tis not so.

Bawd. Nay, but I know, 'tis so: I saw him arrested; saw him carried away; and, which is more, within these three days his head's to be chopp'd off.

Lucio. But, after all this fooling, I would not have it so. Art thou sure of this?

Bawd. I am too sure of it; and it is for getting Madam Julietta with child.

Lucio. Believe me, this may be: he promis'd to meet me two hours since, and he was ever precise in promise-keeping.

2 *Gent.* Besides, you know, it draws something near to the speech we had to such a purpose.

1 *Gent.* But most of all, agreeing with the proclamation.

Lucio. Away; let's go learn the truth of it.

[*Exeunt* LUCIO *and* Gentlemen.

Bawd. Thus, what with the war, what with the sweat, what with the gallows, and what with poverty, I am custom-shrunk. How now? what's the news with you?

Enter Clown.

Clown. Yonder man is carried to prison.

Bawd. Well, what has he done?

Clo. A woman.

Bawd. But what's his offence?

Clo. Groping for trouts in a peculiar river.

Bawd. What, is there a maid with child by him?

Clo. No; but there's a woman with maid by him. You have not heard of the proclamation, have you?

Bawd. What proclamation, man?

Clo. All houses in the suburbs of Vienna must be pluck'd down.

Bawd. And what shall become of those in the city?

Clo. They shall stand for seed: they had gone down, too, but that a wise burgher put in for them.

Bawd. But shall all our houses of resort in the suburbs be pull'd down?

Clo. To the ground, mistress.

Bawd. Why, here's a change, indeed, in the commonwealth! What shall become of me?

Clo. Come; fear not you: good counsellors lack no clients. Though you change your place, you need not change your trade; I'll be your tapster still. Courage! there will be pity taken on you; you that have worn your eyes almost out in the service: you will be considered.

Bawd. What's to do here, Thomas Tapster? Let's withdraw.

Clo. Here comes Signior Claudio, led by the Provost to prison; and there's Madam Juliet. [*Exeunt.*

Scene III.

The Same.

Enter Provost, Claudio, Juliet, *and* Officers; Lucio, *and two* Gentlemen.

Claudio. Fellow, why dost thou show me thus to th' world?
Bear me to prison, where I am committed.

Provost. I do it not in evil disposition,
But from Lord Angelo by special charge.

Claud. Thus can the demi-god, Authority,
Make us pay down for our offence by weight. —
The words of Heaven; — on whom it will, it will;
On whom it will not, so: yet still 'tis just.

Lucio. Why, how now, Claudio? whence comes this restraint?

Claud. From too much liberty, my Lucio, liberty:
As surfeit is the father of much fast,
So every scope by the immoderate use
Turns to restraint. Our natures do pursue,
Like rats that ravin down their proper bane,
A thirsty evil, and when we drink, we die.

Lucio. If I could speak so wisely under an arrest, I would send for certain of my creditors. And yet, to say the truth, I had as lief have the foppery of freedom as the morality of imprisonment. — What's thy offence, Claudio?

Claud. What, but to speak of, would offend again.

Lucio. What is it? murther?

Claud. No.

Lucio. Lechery?

Claud. Call it so.

Prov. Away, sir: you must go.

Claud. One word, good friend. — Lucio, a word with you. [*Takes him aside.*

Lucio. A hundred, if they'll do you any good. — Is lechery so look'd after?

Claud. Thus stands it with me: — Upon a true contract,
I got possession of Julietta's bed:
You know the lady; she is fast my wife,
Save that we do the denunciation lack
Of outward order: this we came not to,
Only for preservation of a dow'r
Remaining in the coffer of her friends,
From whom we thought it meet to hide our love,
Till time had made them for us. But it chances,
The stealth of our most mutual entertainment,
With character too gross, is writ on Juliet.

Lucio. With child, perhaps?

Claud. Unhappily, even so.
And the new deputy now for the Duke, —
Whether it be the fault and glimpse of newness,
Or whether that the body public be
A horse whereon the Governor doth ride,
Who, newly in the seat, that it may know
He can command, lets it straight feel the spur;
Whether the tyranny be in his place,
Or in his eminence that fills it up,
I stagger in; — but this new Governor
Awakes me all the enrolled penalties,
Which have, like unscour'd armour, hung by the wall
So long, that nineteen zodiacs have gone round
And none of them been worn; and, for a name,
Now puts the drowsy and neglected Act
Freshly on me: — 'tis surely, for a name.

Lucio. I warrant it is; and thy head stands so tickle on thy shoulders, that a milk-maid, if she be in love, may sigh it off. Send after the Duke, and appeal to him.

Claud. I have done so, but he's not to be found.
I pr'ythee, Lucio, do me this kind service.
This day my sister should the cloister enter,
And there receive her approbation:
Acquaint her with the danger of my state;
Implore her, in my voice, that she make friends
To the strict deputy: bid herself assay him:
I have great hope in that; for in her youth
There is a prone and speechless dialect,
Such as moves men: beside, she hath prosperous art,
When she will play with reason and discourse,
And well she can persuade.

Lucio. I pray she may: as well for the encouragement of the like, which else would stand under grievous imposition, as for the enjoying of thy life, which I would be sorry should be thus foolishly lost at a game of tick-tack. I'll to her —

Claud. I thank you, good friend Lucio, —

Lucio. — within two hours.

Claud. Come, Officer; away! [*Exeunt.*

Scene IV.

A Monastery.

Enter Duke *and* Friar Thomas.

Duke. No, holy Father; throw away that thought:
Believe not that the dribbling dart of Love
Can pierce a complete bosom. Why I desire thee
To give me secret harbour, hath a purpose
More grave and wrinkled than the aims and ends
Of burning youth

Friar. May your Grace speak of it?
Duke. My holy sir, none better knows than you
How I have ever lov'd the life remov'd;
And held in idle price to haunt assemblies,
Where youth, and cost, and witless bravery keeps.
I have deliver'd to Lord Angelo
(A man of stricture and firm abstinence)
My absolute power and place here in Vienna,
And he supposes me travell'd to Poland;
For so I have strew'd it in the common ear,
And so it is receiv'd. Now, pious sir,
You will demand of me, why I do this?
Fri. Gladly, my lord.
Duke. We have strict statutes, and most biting laws,
(The needful bits and curbs to headstrong steeds,)
Which for this fourteen years we have let sleep,
Even like an o'er-grown lion in a cave,
That goes not out to prey. Now, as fond fathers,
Having bound up the threat'ning twigs of birch
Only to stick it in their children's sight
For terror, not to use, in time the rod
[Becomes] more mock'd than fear'd; so our decrees,
Dead to infliction, to themselves are dead;
And liberty plucks justice by the nose,
The baby beats the nurse, and quite athwart
Goes all decorum.
Fri. It rested in your Grace
To unloose this tied-up justice when you pleas'd,
And it in you more dreadful would have seem'd
Than in Lord Angelo.
Duke. I do fear, too dreadful:
Sith 'twas my fault to give the people scope,
'Twould be my tyranny to strike and gall them
For what I bid them do: for we bid this be done,

When evil deeds have their permissive pass,
And not the punishment. Therefore, indeed, my Father,
I have on Angelo impos'd the office,
Who may, in th' ambush of my name, strike home,
And yet my nature never in the fight,
To do in slander. And to behold his sway,
I will, as 'twere a brother of your order,
Visit both Prince and people: therefore, I pr'ythee,
Supply me with the habit, and instruct me
How I may formally in person bear
Like a true friar. More reasons for this action,
At our more leisure shall I render you;
Only, this one: — Lord Angelo is precise;
Stands at a guard with envy; scarce confesses
That his blood flows, or that his appetite
Is more to bread than stone: hence shall we see,
If power change purpose, what our seemers be.
[*Exeunt.*

SCENE V.

A Nunnery.

Enter ISABELLA *and* FRANCISCA.

Isabella. And have you nuns no farther privileges?
Francisca. Are not these large enough?
Isab. Yes, truly: I speak not as desiring more,
But rather wishing a more strict restraint
Upon the sisterhood, the votarists of St. Clare.
Lucio. [*Within.*] Hoa! Peace be in this place!
Isab. Who's that which calls?
Fran. It is a man's voice. Gentle Isabella,
Turn you the key, and know his business of him:
You may; I may not: you are yet unsworn.

When you have vow'd, you must not speak with men,
But in the presence of the Prioress:
Then, if you speak, you must not show your face;
Or, if you show your face, you must not speak.
He calls again: I pray you, answer him.
[*Exit* FRANCISCA.

Isab. Peace and prosperity! Who is't that calls?

Enter LUCIO.

Lucio. Hail, virgin, if you be,—as those cheek-roses
Proclaim you are no less: Can you so stead me,
As bring me to the sight of Isabella,
A novice of this place, and the fair sister
To her unhappy brother Claudio?

Isab. Why her unhappy brother? Let me ask,
The rather, for I now must make you know
I am that Isabella, and his sister.

Lucio. Gentle and fair, your brother kindly greets you.
Not to be weary with you, he's in prison.

Isab. Woe me! for what?

Lucio. For that, which, if myself might be his judge,
He should receive his punishment in thanks.
He hath got his friend with child.

Isab. Sir, make me not your story.

Lucio. 'Tis true. I would not (though 'tis my familiar sin
With maids to seem the lapwing, and to jest,
Tongue far from heart) play with all virgins so:
I hold you as a thing enski'd, and sainted
By your renouncement,—an immortal spirit,
And to be talked with in sincerity,
As with a saint.

Isab. You do blaspheme the good in mocking me.

Lucio. Do not believe it. Fewness and truth, 'tis thus:
Your brother and his lover have embrac'd:
As those that feed grow full, as blossoming time,
That from the seedness the bare fallow brings
To teeming foison, even so her plenteous womb
Expresseth his full tilth and husbandry.

Isab. Some one with child by him? — My cousin Juliet?

Lucio. Is she your cousin?

Isab. Adoptedly: as school-maids change their names
By vain though apt affection.

Lucio. She it is.

Isab. O! let him marry her.

Lucio. This is the point.
The Duke is very strangely gone from hence;
— Bore many gentlemen, myself being one,
In hand, and hope of action; but we do learn
By those that know the very nerves of state,
His givings-out were of an infinite distance
From his true-meant design. Upon his place,
And with full line of his authority,
Governs Lord Angelo; a man whose blood
Is very snow-broth; one who never feels
The wanton stings and motions of the sense,
But doth rebate and blunt his natural edge
With profits of the mind, study, and fast.
He (to give fear to use and liberty,
Which have, for long, run by the hideous law,
As mice by lions) hath pick'd out an Act,
Under whose heavy sense your brother's life
Falls into forfeit: he arrests him on it,
And follows close the rigour of the statute,

To make him an example. All hope is gone,
Unless you have the grace by your fair prayer
To soften Angelo; and that's my pith
Of business 'twixt you and your poor brother.

Isab. Doth he so seek his life?

Lucio. Has censur'd him
Already; and, as I hear, the Provost hath
A warrant for his execution.

Isab. Alas! what poor ability's in me
To do him good?

Lucio. Assay the power you have.

Isab. My power! Alas! I doubt,—

Lucio. Our doubts are traitors,
And make us lose the good we oft might win,
By fearing to attempt. Go to Lord Angelo,
And let him learn to know, when maidens sue,
Men give like gods; but when they weep and kneel,
All their petitions are as freely theirs
As they themselves would owe them.

Isab. I'll see what I can do.

Lucio. But speedily.

Isab. I will about it straight,
No longer staying but to give the Mother
Notice of my affair. I humbly thank you:
Commend me to my brother: soon at night
I'll send him certain word of my success.

Lucio. I take my leave of you.

Isab. Good sir, adieu.

[*Exeunt.*

ACT II.

Scene I.—A Hall in Angelo's House.

Enter Angelo, Escalus, *a* Justice, Officers, *and other Attendants.*

Angelo.

WE must not make a scare-crow of the law,
Setting it up to fear the birds of prey,
And let it keep one shape, till custom make it
Their perch, and not their terror.

Escal. Ay, but yet
Let us be keen, and rather cut a little,
Than fall and bruise to death. Alas! this gentleman
Whom I would save had a most noble father.
Let but your honour know,
(Whom I believe to be most strait in virtue,)
That, in the working of your own affections,
Had time coher'd with place or place with wishing,
Or that the resolute acting of your blood
Could have attain'd th' effect of your own purpose,
Whether you had not, sometime in your life,
Err'd in this point where now you censure him,
And pull'd the law upon you.

Ang. 'Tis one thing to be tempted, Escalus,
Another thing to fall. I not deny,
The jury, passing on the prisoner's life,
May in the sworn twelve have a thief or two
Guiltier than him they try; what's open made
To justice, that justice seizes: what knows the law,
That thieves do pass on thieves? 'Tis very pregnant,

The jewel that we find, we stoop and take't,
Because we see it; but what we do not see,
We tread upon, and never think of it.
You may not so extenuate his offence
For I have had such faults; but rather tell me,
When I that censure him do so offend,
Let mine own judgment pattern out my death,
And nothing come in partial. Sir, he must die.

Escal. Be it as your wisdom will.

Ang. Where is the Provost?

Enter Provost.

Prov. Here, if it like your honour.

Ang. See that Claudio
Be executed by nine to-morrow morning.
Bring him his confessor, let him be prepar'd,
For that's the utmost of his pilgrimage.

[*Exit* Provost.

Escal. Well, Heaven forgive him, and forgive us all!
Some rise by sin, and some by virtue fall:
Some run from brakes of vice and answer none;
And some condemned for a fault alone.

Enter Elbow, Froth, Clown, Officers, *&c.*

Elbow. Come, bring them away. If these be good people in a common-weal, that do nothing but use their abuses in common houses, I know no law: bring them away.

Ang. How now, sir! What's your name, and what's the matter?

Elb. If it please your honour, I am the poor Duke's constable, and my name is Elbow: I do lean upon justice, sir; and do bring in here before your good honour two notorious benefactors.

Ang. Benefactors! Well; what benefactors are they? are they not malefactors?

Elb. If it please your honour, I know not well what they are; but precise villains they are, that I am sure of, and void of all profanation in the world, that good Christians ought to have.

Escal. This comes off well: here's a wise officer.

Ang. Go to: what quality are they of? Elbow is your name: why dost thou not speak, Elbow?

Clo. He cannot, sir: he's out at elbow.

Ang. What are you, sir?

Elb. He, sir? a tapster, sir — parcel-bawd; one that serves a bad woman, whose house, sir, was, as they say, pluck'd down in the suburbs; and now she professes a hot-house, which, I think, is a very ill house too.

Escal. How know you that?

Elb. My wife, sir, whom I detest before Heaven and your honour, —

Escal. How! thy wife?

Elb. Ay, sir; whom, I thank Heaven, is an honest woman, —

Escal. Dost thou detest her therefore?

Elb. I say, sir, I will detest myself also, as well as she, that this house, if it be not a bawd's house it is pity of her life, for it is a naughty house.

Escal. How dost thou know that, Constable?

Elb. Marry, sir, by my wife; who, if she had been a woman cardinally given, might have been accus'd in fornication, adultery, and all uncleanliness there.

Escal. By the woman's means?

Elb. Ay, sir, by Mistress Over-done's means; but as she spit in his face, so she defi'd him.

Clo. Sir, if it please your honour, this is not so.

Elb. Prove it before these varlets here, thou honourable man; prove it.

Escal. [*To* ANGELO.] Do you hear how he misplaces?

Clo. Sir, she came in great with child, and longing (saving your honour's reverence) for stew'd prunes: sir, we had but two in the house, which at that very distant time stood, as it were, in a fruit-dish, — a dish of some three pence: your honours have seen such dishes; they are not China dishes, but very good dishes.

Escal. Go to, go to: no matter for the dish, sir.

Clo. No, indeed, sir, not of a pin; you are therein in the right; but to the point. As I say, this Mistress Elbow, being, as I say, with child, and being great belly'd, and longing, as I said, for prunes, and having but two in the dish, as I said, Master Froth here, this very man, having eaten the rest, as I said, and, as I say, paying for them very honestly; — for, as you know, Master Froth, I could not give you three pence again.

Froth. No, indeed.

Clo. Very well: you being then, if you be remember'd, cracking the stones of the 'foresaid prunes.

Froth. Ay, so I did, indeed.

Clo. Why, very well: I telling you then, if you be remember'd, that such a one, and such a one, were past cure of the thing you wot of, unless they kept very good diet, as I told you.

Froth. All this is true.

Clo. Why, very well then.

Escal. Come; you are a tedious fool: to the purpose. — What was done to Elbow's wife, that he hath cause to complain of? Come we to what was done to her.

Clo. Sir, your honour cannot come to that yet.

Escal. No, sir, nor I mean it not.

Clo. Sir, but you shall come to it, by your honour's leave. And, I beseech you, look into Master Froth here, sir; a man of fourscore pound a year, whose father died at Hallowmas. — Was't not at Hallowmas, Master Froth?

Froth. All-hallownd eve.

Clo. Why, very well: I hope here be truths. He, sir, sitting, as I say, in a lower chair, sir; — 'twas in the *Bunch of Grapes*, where, indeed, you have a delight to sit, have you not?

Froth. I have so; because it is an open room, and good for winter.

Clo. Why, very well then: I hope here be truths.

Ang. This will last out a night in Russia,
When nights are longest there. I'll take my leave,
And leave you to the hearing of the cause,
Hoping you'll find good cause to whip them all.

Escal. I think no less. Good morrow to your lordship. [*Exit* ANGELO.
Now, sir, come on: what was done to Elbow's wife, once more?

Clo. Once, sir? there was nothing done to her once.

Elb. I beseech you, sir, ask him what this man did to my wife.

Clo. I beseech your honour, ask me.

Escal. Well, sir, what did this gentleman to her?

Clo. I beseech you, sir, look in this gentleman's face. — Good Master Froth, look upon his honour; 'tis for a good purpose. Doth your honour mark his face?

Escal. Ay, sir, very well.

Clo. Nay, I beseech you, mark it well.

Escal. Well, I do so.

Clo. Doth your honour see any harm in his face?

Escal. Why, no.

Clo. I'll be supposed upon a book, his face is the worst thing about him. Good then; if his face be the worst thing about him, how could Master Froth do the constable's wife any harm? I would know that of your honour.

Escal. He's in the right, Constable; what say you to it?

Elb. First, an it like you, the house is a respected house; next, this is a respected fellow, and his mistress is a respected woman.

Clo. By this hand, sir, his wife is a more respected person than any of us all.

Elb. Varlet, thou liest: thou liest, wicked varlet. The time is yet to come that she was ever respected with man, woman, or child.

Clo. Sir, she was respected with him, before he married with her.

Escal. Which is the wiser here? Justice, or Iniquity? — Is this true?

Elb. O thou caitiff! O thou varlet! O thou wicked Hannibal! I respected with her, before I was married to her! — If ever I was respected with her, or she with me, let not your worship think me the poor Duke's officer. — Prove this, thou wicked Hannibal, or I'll have mine action of battery on thee.

Escal. If he took you a box o' th' ear, you might have your action of slander too.

Elb. Marry, I thank your good worship for it. What is't your worship's pleasure I shall do with this wicked caitiff?

Escal. Truly, officer, because he hath some offences in him that thou would'st discover if thou could'st, let him continue in his courses, till thou know'st what they are.

Elb. Marry, I thank your worship for it. — Thou seest, thou wicked varlet now, what's come upon thee: thou art to continue; now, thou varlet, thou art to continue.

Escal. Where were you born, friend?

Froth. Here in Vienna, sir.

Escal. Are you of fourscore pounds a year?

Froth. Yes, an't please you, sir.

Escal. So. — What trade are you of, sir?

Clo. A tapster; a poor widow's tapster.

Escal. Your mistress' name?

Clo. Mistress Over-done.

Escal. Hath she had any more than one husband?

Clo. Nine, sir; Over-done by the last.

Escal. Nine! — Come hither to me, Master Froth. Master Froth, I would not have you acquainted with tapsters; they will draw you, Master Froth, and you will hang them: get you gone, and let me hear no more of you.

Froth. I thank your worship. For mine own part, I never come into any room in a taphouse, but I am drawn in.

Escal. Well; no more of it, Master Froth: farewell. [*Exit* FROTH.] — Come you hither to me, Mr. Tapster. What's your name, Mr. Tapster?

Clo. Pompey.

Escal. What else?

Clo. Bum, sir.

Escal. 'Troth, and your bum is the greatest thing about you; so that, in the beastliest sense, you are Pompey the Great. Pompey, you are partly a bawd, Pompey, howsoever you colour it in being a tapster.

Are you not? come, tell me true: it shall be the better for you.

Clo. Truly, sir, I am a poor fellow that would live.

Escal. How would you live, Pompey? by being a bawd? What do you think of the trade, Pompey? is it a lawful trade?

Clo. If the law would allow it, sir.

Escal. But the law will not allow it, Pompey; nor it shall not be allowed in Vienna.

Clo. Does your worship mean to geld and spay all the youth of the city?

Escal. No, Pompey.

Clo. Truly, sir, in my poor opinion, they will to't then. If your worship will take order for the drabs and the knaves, you need not to fear the bawds.

Escal. There are pretty orders beginning, I can tell you: it is but heading and hanging.

Clo. If you head and hang all that offend that way but for ten year together, you'll be glad to give out a commission for more heads. If this law hold in Vienna ten year, I'll rent the fairest house in it after three pence a day! If you live to see this come to pass, say Pompey told you so.

Escal. Thank you, good Pompey; and, in requital of your prophecy, hark you: — I advise you, let me not find you before me again upon any complaint whatsoever; no, not for dwelling where you do: if I do, Pompey, I shall beat you to your tent, and prove a shrewd Cæsar to you. In plain dealing, Pompey, I shall have you whipp'd. So, for this time, Pompey, fare you well.

Clo. I thank your worship for your good counsel, but I shall follow it, as the flesh and fortune shall better determine.

Whip me? No, no; let carman whip his jade;
The valiant heart's not whipp'd out of his trade.
[*Exit.*

Escal. Come hither to me, Master Elbow; come hither, Master Constable. How long have you been in this place of constable?

Elb. Seven year and a half, sir.

Escal. I thought, by your readiness in the office, you had continued in it some time. You say, seven years together?

Elb. And a half, sir.

Escal. Alas! it hath been great pains to you. They do you wrong to put you so oft upon't. Are there not men in your ward sufficient to serve it?

Elb. 'Faith, sir, few of any wit in such matters. As they are chosen, they are glad to choose me for them: I do it for some piece of money, and go through with all.

Escal. Look you bring me in the names of some six or seven, the most sufficient of your parish.

Elb. To your worship's house, sir?

Escal. To my house. Fare you well.
[*Exit* ELBOW.
What's o'clock, think you?

Justice. Eleven, sir.

Escal. I pray you home to dinner with me.

Just. I humbly thank you.

Escal. It grieves me for the death of Claudio;
But there's no remedy.

Just. Lord Angelo is severe.

Escal. It is but needful:
Mercy is not itself, that oft looks so;
Pardon is still the nurse of second woe.
But yet, poor Claudio! — There is no remedy.
Come, sir. [*Exeunt.*

Scene II.

Another Room in the Same.

Enter Provost *and a* Servant.

Servant. He's hearing of a cause: he will come straight.
I'll tell him of you.

Prov. 'Pray you, do. [*Exit* Servant.] I'll know
His pleasure; may be, he will relent. Alas!
He hath offended but as in a dream:
All sects, all ages smack of this vice, and he
To die for it! —

Enter Angelo.

Ang. Now, what's the matter, Provost?

Prov. Is it your will Claudio shall die to-morrow?

Ang. Did I not tell thee, yea? hadst thou not order?
Why dost thou ask again?

Prov. Lest I might be too rash.
Under your good correction, I have seen
When, after execution, judgment hath
Repented o'er his doom.

Ang. Go to; let that be mine:
Do you your office, or give up your place;
And you shall well be spar'd.

Prov. I crave your honour's pardon.
What shall be done, sir, with the groaning Juliet?
She's very near her hour.

Ang. Dispose of her
To some more fitter place, and that with speed.

Enter Servant.

Serv. Here is the sister of the man condemn'd
Desires access to you.

Ang. Hath he a sister?

Prov. Ay, my good lord; a very virtuous maid,
And to be shortly of a sisterhood,
If not already.

Ang. Well, let her be admitted.
[*Exit* Servant.
See you the fornicatress be remov'd:
Let her have needful but not lavish means;
There shall be order for't.

Enter LUCIO *and* ISABELLA.

Prov. 'Save your honour! [*Offering to retire.*

Ang. Stay a little while. — [*To* ISAB.] Y' are welcome: what's your will?

Isab. I am a woeful suitor to your honour,
'Please but your honour hear me.

Ang. Well, what's your suit?

Isab. There is a vice that most I do abhor,
And most desire should meet the blow of justice,
For which I would not plead, but that I must;
For which I must not plead, but that I am
At war 'twixt will and will not.

Ang. Well; the matter?

Isab. I have a brother is condemn'd to die:
I do beseech you, let it be his fault,
And not my brother.

Prov. [*Aside.*] Heaven give thee moving graces!

Ang. Condemn the fault, and not the actor of it?
Why, every fault's condemn'd ere it be done.
Mine were the very cipher of a function,
To fine the faults whose fine stands in record,
And let go by the actor.

Isab. O just, but severe law!
I had a brother then. — Heaven keep your honour!
[*Retiring.*

Lucio. [*To* ISAB.] Give't not o'er so: to him again, intreat him;
Kneel down before him, hang upon his gown;
You are too cold: if you should need a pin,
You could not with more tame a tongue desire it.
To him, I say.

Isab. Must he needs die?

Ang. Maiden, no remedy.

Isab. Yes; I do think that you might pardon him,
And neither Heaven, nor man, grieve at the mercy.

Ang. I will not do't.

Isab. But can you, if you would?

Ang. Look; what I will not, that I cannot do.

Isab. But might you do't, and do the world no wrong,
If so your heart were touch'd with that remorse
As mine is to him?

Ang. He's sentenc'd: 'tis too late.

Lucio. [*To* ISAB.] You are too cold.

Isab. Too late? why, no; I, that do speak a word,
May call it [back] again: Well, believe this;
No ceremony that to great ones 'longs,
Not the king's crown, nor the deputed sword,
The marshal's truncheon, nor the judge's robe,
Become them with one half so good a grace
As mercy does.
If he had been as you, and you as he,
You would have slipp'd like him; but he like you
Would not have been so stern.

Ang. Pray you, begone.

Isab. I would to Heaven I had your potency,
And you were Isabel! should it then be thus?

No; I would tell what 'twere to be a judge,
And what a prisoner.

Lucio. [*Aside.*] Ay, touch him; there's the vein.

Ang. Your brother is a forfeit of the law,
And you but waste your words.

Isab. Alas! alas!
Why, all the souls that were were forfeit once;
And he that might the vantage best have took
Found out the remedy. How would you be,
If he, which is the top of judgment should
But judge you as you are? O, think on that,
And mercy then will breathe within your lips,
Like man new made!

Ang. Be you content, fair maid.
It is the law, not I, condemns your brother:
Were he my kinsman, brother, or my son,
It should be thus with him: he must die to-morrow.

Isab. To-morrow? O, that's sudden! Spare him, spare him!
He's not prepar'd for death. Even for our kitchens
We kill the fowl of season: shall we serve Heaven
With less respect than we do minister
To our gross selves? Good, good my lord, bethink you:
Who is it that hath di'd for this offence?
There's many have committed it.

Lucio. [*Aside.*] Ay, well said.

Ang. The law hath not been dead, though it hath slept:
Those many had not dar'd to do that evil,
If [but] the first that did th' edict infringe,
Had answer'd for his deed: now, 'tis awake;
Takes note of what is done, and, like a prophet,
Looks in a glass, that shows what future evils
(Either now, or by remissness new-conceiv'd,

And so in progress to be hatch'd and born,)
Are now to have no successive degrees,
But ere they live to end.

Isab. Yet show some pity.

Ang. I show it most of all, when I show justice;
For then I pity those I do not know,
Which a dismiss'd offence would after gall,
And do him right, that, answering one foul wrong,
Lives not to act another. Be satisfied:
Your brother dies to-morrow: be content.

Isab. So you must be the first that gives this sentence,
And he that suffers. O! it is excellent
To have a giant's strength; but it is tyrannous
To use it like a giant.

Lucio. [*Aside.*] That's well said.

Isab. Could great men thunder
As Jove himself does, Jove would ne'er be quiet;
For every pelting, petty officer
Would use his heaven for thunder;
Nothing but thunder. Merciful Heaven!
Thou rather with thy sharp and sulphurous bolt
Split'st the unwedgeable and gnarled oak,
Than the soft myrtle; but man, proud man,
Drest in a little brief authority,
Most ignorant of what he's most assur'd, —
His glassy essence, — like an angry ape,
Plays such fantastic tricks before high Heaven,
As make the angels weep; who, with our spleens,
Would all themselves laugh mortal.

Lucio. [*To* ISAB.] O, to him, to him, wench! He will relent:
He's coming; I perceive't.

Prov. [*Aside.*] 'Pray Heaven, she win him!

Isab. We cannot weigh our brother with ourself:

Great men may jest with saints: 'tis wit in them,
But in the less, foul profanation.

Lucio. [*To* ISAB.] Thou'rt i' the right, girl: more o' that.

Isab. That in the captain's but a choleric word,
Which in the soldier is flat blasphemy.

Lucio. [*Aside.*] Art avis'd o' that? more on't.

Ang. Why do you put these sayings upon me?

Isab. Because authority, though it err like others,
Hath yet a kind of medicine in itself,
That skins the vice o' th' top. Go to your bosom;
Knock there, and ask your heart, what it doth know
That's like my brother's fault: if it confess
A natural guiltiness, such as is his,
Let it not sound a thought upon your tongue
Against my brother's life.

Ang. [*Aside.*] She speaks, and 'tis
Such sense, that my sense breeds with it. [*To her.*] Fare you well.

Isab. Gentle my lord, turn back.

Ang. I will bethink me. — Come again to-morrow.

Isab. Hark, how I'll bribe you. Good my lord, turn back.

Ang. How! bribe me?

Isab. Ay, with such gifts, that Heaven shall share with you.

Lucio. [*Aside.*] You had marr'd all else.

Isab. Not with fond shekels of the tested gold,
Or stones, whose rates are either rich or poor
As fancy values them; but with true prayers,
That shall be up at Heaven, and enter there
Ere sun-rise: prayers from preserved souls,
From fasting maids, whose minds are dedicate
To nothing temporal.

Ang. Well; come to me to-morrow.

Lucio. [*To* ISAB.] Go to; 'tis well: away!
Isab. Heaven keep your honour safe!
Ang. [*Aside.*] Amen:
For I am that way going to temptation,
Where prayers cross.
Isab. At what hour to-morrow
Shall I attend your lordship?
Ang. At any time 'fore noon.
Isab. Save your honour!
[*Exeunt* LUCIO, ISABELLA, *and* Provost.
Ang. From thee: even from thy virtue!—
What's this? what's this? Is this her fault, or mine?
The tempter, or the tempted, who sins most? Ha!
Not she, nor doth she tempt; but it is I,
That lying by the violet in the sun,
Do, as the carrion does, not as the flower,
Corrupt with virtuous season. Can it be,
That modesty may more betray our sense
Than woman's lightness? Having waste ground enough,
Shall we desire to raze the sanctuary,
And pitch our evils there? O, fie, fie, fie!
What dost thou, or what art thou, Angelo?
Dost thou desire her foully for those things
That make her good? O, let her brother live!
Thieves for their robbery have authority,
When judges steal themselves. What! do I love her,
That I desire to hear her speak again,
And feast upon her eyes? What is't I dream on?
O cunning enemy, that, to catch a saint,
With saints dost bait thy hook! Most dangerous
Is that temptation, that doth goad us on
To sin in loving virtue. Never could the strumpet,
With all her double vigour, art and nature,
Once stir my temper; but this virtuous maid

Subdues me quite. — Ever, till now,
When men were fond, I smil'd and wonder'd how.
[*Exit.*

SCENE III.

A Room in a Prison.

Enter DUKE, *habited like a Friar, and* Provost.

Duke. Hail to you, Provost; so I think you are.

Prov. I am the Provost. What's your will, good friar?

Duke. Bound by my charity, and my bless'd order,
I come to visit the afflicted spirits
Here in the prison: do me the common right
To let me see them, and to make me know
The nature of their crimes, that I may minister
To them accordingly.

Prov. I would do more than that, if more were needful.

Enter JULIET.

Look; here comes one: a gentlewoman of mine,
Who, falling in the flames of her own youth,
Hath blister'd her report. She is with child,
And he that got it, sentenc'd — a young man
More fit to do another such offence
Than die for this.

Duke. When must he die?

Prov. As I do think, to-morrow. —
[*To* JULIET.] I have provided for you: stay a while,
And you shall be conducted.

Duke. Repent you, fair one, of the sin you carry?

Juliet. I do, and bear the shame most patiently.

Duke. I'll teach you how you shall arraign your conscience,

And try your penitence, if it be sound,
Or hollowly put on.

Juliet. I'll gladly learn.

Duke. Love you the man that wrong'd you?

Juliet. Yes, as I love the woman that wrong'd him.

Duke. So then, it seems, your most offenceful act
Was mutually committed?

Juliet. Mutually.

Duke. Then was your sin of heavier kind than his.

Juliet. I do confess it, and repent it, Father.

Duke. 'Tis meet so, daughter: but lest you do repent,
As that the sin hath brought you to this shame;
Which sorrow is always toward ourselves, not Heaven,
Showing we would not spare Heaven as we love it,
But as we stand in fear,—

Juliet. I do repent me, as it is an evil,
And take the shame with joy.

Duke. There rest.
Your partner, as I hear, must die to-morrow,
And I am going with instruction to him.
Grace go with you! *Benedicite!* [*Exit.*

Juliet. Must die to-morrow! O, injurious law,
That respites me a life, whose very comfort
Is still a dying horror!

Prov. 'Tis pity of him. [*Exeunt.*

SCENE IV.

A Room in ANGELO'S House.

Enter ANGELO.

Ang. When I would pray and think, I think and pray

To several subjects: Heaven hath my empty words,
Whilst my invention, hearing not my tongue,
Anchors on Isabel: Heaven in my mouth,
As if I did but only chew his name,
And in my heart the strong and swelling evil
Of my conception. The State, whereon I studied,
Is, like a good thing being often read,
Grown sear'd and tedious; yea, my gravity,
Wherein (let no man hear me) I take pride,
Could I, with boot, change for an idle plume
Which the air beats for vain. O place! O form!
How often dost thou with thy case, thy habit,
Wrench awe from fools, and tie the wiser souls
To thy false seeming! Blood, thou art blood:
Let's write good angel on the devil's horn,
'Tis not the devil's crest.

Enter Servant.

How now! who's there?

Serv. One Isabel, a Sister,
Desires access to you.

Ang. Teach her the way. [*Exit* Serv.
O Heavens!
Why does my blood thus muster to my heart,
Making both it unable for itself,
And dispossessing all my other parts
Of necessary fitness?
So play the foolish throngs with one that swoons;
Come all to help him, and so stop the air
By which he should revive: and even so
The general, subject to a well-wish'd King,
Quit their own part, and in obsequious fondness
Crowd to his presence, where their untaught love
Must needs appear offence.

Enter ISABELLA.

How now, fair maid?

Isab. I am come to know your pleasure.

Ang. That you might know it, would much better please me
Than to demand what 'tis. Your brother cannot live.

Isab. Even so. — Heaven keep your honour! [*Retiring.*

Ang. Yet may he live a while; and, it may be,
As long as you, or I: yet he must die.

Isab. Under your sentence?

Ang. Yea.

Isab. When, I beseech you? that in his reprieve,
Longer or shorter, he may be so fitted,
That his soul sicken not.

Ang. Ha! Fie, these filthy vices! It were as good
To pardon him that hath from Nature stolen
A man already made, as to remit
Their saucy sweetness that do coin Heaven's image
In stamps that are forbid. 'Tis all as easy
Falsely to take away a life true made,
As to put metal in restrained means,
To make a false one.

Isab. 'Tis set down so in Heaven, but not in Earth.

Ang. Say you so? then I shall pose you quickly.
Which had you rather, that the most just law
Now took your brother's life, or, to redeem him,
Give up your body to such sweet uncleanness
As she that he hath stain'd?

Isab. Sir, believe this:
I had rather give my body than my soul.

Ang. I talk not of your soul. Our compell'd sins
Stand more for number than for accompt.

Isab. How say you?

Ang. Nay, I'll not warrant that; for I can speak
Against the thing I say. Answer to this: —
I (now the voice of the recorded law)
Pronounce a sentence on your brother's life:
Might there not be a charity in sin,
To save this brother's life?

Isab. Please you to do't,
I'll take it as a peril to my soul:
It is no sin at all, but charity.

Ang. Pleas'd you to do't at peril of your soul,
Were equal poise of sin and charity.

Isab. That I do beg his life, if it be sin,
Heaven, let me bear it! you granting of my suit,
If that be sin, I'll make it my morn-prayer
To have it added to the faults of mine,
And nothing of your answer.

Ang. Nay, but hear me.
Your sense pursues not mine: either you are ignorant,
Or seem so, crafty; and that is not good.

Isab. Let me be ignorant, and in nothing good,
But graciously to know I am no better.

Ang. Thus wisdom wishes to appear most bright
When it doth tax itself: as these black masks
Proclaim an enshield beauty ten times louder
Than beauty could, displayed. — But mark me:
To be received plain, I'll speak more gross.
Your brother is to die.

Isab. So.

Ang. And his offence is so, as it appears
Accountant to the law upon that pain.

Isab. True.

Ang. Admit no other way to save his life,
(As I subscribe not that, nor any other,)
But — in the loss of question — that you, his sister

Finding yourself desir'd of such a person,
Whose credit with the judge, or own great place,
Could fetch your brother from the manacles
Of the all-holding law, and that there were
No earthly mean to save him, but that either
You must lay down the treasures of your body
To this suppos'd, or else to let him suffer,
What would you do?

Isab. As much for my poor brother, as myself:
That is, were I under the terms of death,
Th' impression of keen whips I'd wear as rubies,
And strip myself to death, as to a bed
That longing I've been sick for, ere I'd yield
My body up to shame.

Ang. Then must
Your brother die.

Isab. And 'twere the cheaper way.
Better it were, a brother di'd at once,
Than that a sister, by redeeming him,
Should die for ever.

Ang. Were not you, then, as cruel as the sentence
That you have slander'd so?

Isab. Ignomy in ransom and free pardon
Are of two houses: lawful mercy is
Nothing akin to foul redemption.

Ang. You seem'd of late to make the law a tyrant;
And rather prov'd the sliding of your brother
A merriment, than a vice.

Isab. O, pardon me, my lord! it oft falls out,
To have what we would have, we speak not what
we mean.
I something do excuse the thing I hate,
For his advantage that I dearly love.

Ang. We are all frail.

Isab. Else let my brother die,

If not a feodary but only he
Owe and succeed thy weakness.

Ang. Nay, women are frail too.

Isab. Ay, as the glasses where they view themselves,
Which are as easy broke as they make forms.
Women! — Help Heaven! men their creation mar
In profiting by them. Nay, call us ten times frail;
For we are soft as our complexions are,
And credulous to false prints.

Ang. I think it well;
And from this testimony of your own sex,
(Since, I suppose, we are made to be no stronger,
Than faults may shake our frames,) let me be bold:
I do arrest your words. Be that you are,
That is, a woman; if you be more, you're none;
If you be one, (as you are well express'd
By all external warrants,) show it now,
By putting on the destin'd livery.

Isab. I have no tongue but one: gentle my lord,
Let me entreat you speak the former language.

Ang. Plainly conceive, I love you.

Isab. My brother did love Juliet: and you tell me,
That he shall die for't.

Ang. He shall not, Isabel, if you give me love.

Isab. I know, your virtue hath a license in't,
Which seems a little fouler than it is,
To pluck on others.

Ang. Believe me, on mine honour,
My words express my purpose.

Isab. Ha! little honour to be much believ'd,
And most pernicious purpose! — Seeming, seeming! —
I will proclaim thee, Angelo; look for't:
Sign me a present pardon for my brother,
Or, with an outstretch'd throat, I'll tell the world aloud
What man thou art.

Ang. Who will believe thee, Isabel?
My unsoil'd name, th' austereness of my life,
My vouch against you, and my place i' the State,
Will so your accusation overweigh,
That you shall stifle in your own report,
And smell of calumny. I have begun,
And now I give my sensual race the rein:
Fit thy consent to my sharp appetite:
Lay by all nicety and prolixious blushes
That banish what they sue for; redeem thy brother
By yielding up thy body to my will,
Or else he must not only die the death,
But thy unkindness shall his death draw out
To lingering sufferance. Answer me to-morrow,
Or, by the affection that now guides me most,
I'll prove a tyrant to him. As for you, —
Say what you can, my false o'erweighs your true.
[*Exit*

Isab. To whom should I complain? Did I tell this
Who would believe me? O perilous mouths!
That bear in them one and the self-same tongue,
Either of condemnation or approof,
Bidding the law make court'sy to their will,
Hooking both right and wrong to th' appetite,
To follow as it draws. I'll to my brother:
Though he hath fallen by prompture of the blood,
Yet hath he in him such a mind of honour,
That had he twenty heads to tender down
On twenty bloody blocks, he'd yield them up,
Before his sister should her body stoop
To such abhorr'd pollution.
Then, Isabel, live chaste, and, brother, die:
More than our brother is our chastity.
I'll tell him yet of Angelo's request,
And fit his mind to death, for his soul's rest.
[*Exit.*

ACT III.

Scene I. — A Room in the Prison.

Enter Duke, *as a Friar*, Claudio, *and* Provost.

Duke.

SO then, you hope of pardon from Lord Angelo?
Claud. The miserable have no other medicine,
But only hope.
I've hope to live, and am prepar'd to die.
Duke. Be absolute for death; either death or life
Shall thereby be the sweeter. Reason thus with life: —
If I do lose thee, I do lose a thing
That none but fools would keep: a breath thou art,
Servile to all the skyey influences
That dost this habitation where thou keep'st
Hourly afflict. Merely, thou art Death's Fool;
For him thou labour'st by thy flight to shun,
And yet run'st toward him still: thou art not noble;
For all th' accommodations that thou bear'st,
Are nurs'd by baseness: thou art by no means valiant;
For thou dost fear the soft and tender fork
Of a poor worm: thy best of rest is sleep,
And that thou oft provok'st; yet grossly fear'st
Thy death, which is no more: thou art not thyself;
For thou exist'st on many a thousand grains
That issue out of dust: happy thou art not;
For what thou hast not, still thou striv'st to get,
And what thou hast, forget'st: thou art not certain;
For thy complexion shifts to strange effects,
After the moon: if thou art rich, thou'rt poor;
For, like an ass whose back with ingots bows,

Thou bear'st thy heavy riches but a journey,
And Death unloads thee: friend hast thou none;
For thine own bowels which do call thee sire,
The mere effusion of thy proper loins,
Do curse the gout, serpigo, and the rheum,
For ending thee no sooner: thou hast nor youth nor age,
But, as it were, an after-dinner's sleep,
Dreaming on both; for all thy blessed youth
Becomes as aged, and doth beg the alms
Of palsi'd eld; and when thou art old and rich,
Thou hast neither heat, affection, limb, nor beauty,
To make thy riches pleasant. What's yet in this,
That bears the name of life? Yet in this life
Lie hid more thousand deaths; yet death we fear,
That makes these odds all even.

Claud. I humbly thank you.
To sue to live, I find, I seek to die,
And seeking death, find life: let it come on.

Isab. [*Without.*] What, hoa! Peace here; grace and good company!

Prov. Who's there? come in: the wish deserves a welcome.

Enter ISABELLA.

Duke. Dear sir, ere long I'll visit you again.

Claud. Most holy sir, I thank you.

Isab. My business is a word or two with Claudio.

Prov. And very welcome. Look, signior; here's your sister.

Duke. Provost, a word with you.

Prov. As many as you please.

Duke. Bring me to hear them speak, where I may be conceal'd. [*Exeunt* DUKE *and* Provost.

Claud. Now, sister, what's the comfort?

Isab. Why, as all comforts are; most good, most good indeed.
Lord Angelo, having affairs to Heaven,
Intends you for his swift ambassador,
Where you shall be an everlasting leiger:
Therefore, your best appointment make with speed;
To-morrow you set on.

Claud. Is there no remedy?

Isab. None, but such remedy, as to save a head,
To cleave a heart in twain.

Claud. But is there any?

Isab. Yes, brother, you may live:
There is a devilish mercy in the judge,
If you'll implore it, that will free your life,
But fetter you till death.

Claud. Perpetual durance?

Isab. Ay, just; perpetual durance: a restraint —
Though all the world's vastidity you had —
To a determin'd scope.

Claud. But in what nature?

Isab. In such a one as, you consenting to't,
Would bark your honour from that trunk you bear,
And leave you naked.

Claud. Let me know the point.

Isab. O! I do fear thee, Claudio; and I quake,
Lest thou a feverous life should'st entertain,
And six or seven winters more respect,
Than a perpetual honour. Dar'st thou die?
The sense of death is most in apprehension
And the poor beetle, that we tread upon,
In corporal sufferance finds a pang as great
As when a giant dies.

Claud. Why give you me this shame?
Think you I can a resolution fetch
From flowery tenderness? If I must die,

I will encounter darkness as a bride,
And hug it in mine arms.

Isab. There spake my brother: there my father's grave
Did utter forth a voice. Yes, thou must die:
Thou art too noble to conserve a life
In base appliances. This outward-sainted deputy,
Whose settled visage and deliberate word
Nips youth i' th' head, and follies doth emmew
As falcon doth the fowl, is yet a devil;
His filth within being cast, he would appear
A pond as deep as Hell.

Claud. The priestly Angelo?

Isab. O, 'tis the cunning livery of Hell,
The damned'st body to invest and cover
In priestly guards! Dost thou think, Claudio!
If I would yield him my virginity,
Thou might'st be freed.

Claud. O, Heavens! it cannot be.

Isab. Yes, he would give't thee from this rank offence,
So to offend him still. This night's the time
That I should do what I abhor to name,
Or else thou diest to-morrow.

Claud. Thou shalt not do't.

Isab. O! were it but my life,
I'd throw it down for your deliverance
As frankly as a pin.

Claud. Thanks, dear Isabel.

Isab. Be ready, Claudio, for your death to-morrow.

Claud. Yes. Has he affections in him,
That thus can make him bite the law by th' nose,
When he would force it? Sure, it is no sin;
Or of the deadly seven it is the least.

Isab. Which is the least?

Claud. If it were damnable, he being so wise,
Why would he for the momentary trick
Be perdurably fin'd? — O Isabel!

Isab. What says my brother?

Claud. Death is a fearful thing.

Isab. And shamed life a hateful.

Claud. Ay, but to die, and go we know not where;
To lie in cold obstruction, and to rot;
This sensible warm motion to become
A kneaded clod; and the delighted spirit
To bathe in fiery floods, or to reside
In thrilling region of thick-ribbed ice;
To be imprison'd in the viewless winds
And blown with restless violence round about
The pendent world; or to be, worse than worst,
Of those that lawless and incertain thoughts
Imagine, howling! — 'tis too horrible.
The weariest and most loathed worldly life,
That age, ache, penury, and imprisonment
Can lay on nature, is a paradise
To what we fear of death.

Isab. Alas! alas!

Claud. Sweet sister, let me live.
What sin you do to save a brother's life,
Nature dispenses with the deed so far,
That it becomes a virtue.

Isab. O, you beast!
O, faithless coward! O, dishonest wretch!
Wilt thou be made a man out of my vice?
Is't not a kind of incest to take life
From thine own sister's shame? What should I think?
Heaven shield, my mother play'd my father fair!
For such a warped slip of wilderness

Ne'er issu'd from his blood. Take my defiance:
Die; perish! might but my bending down
Reprieve thee from thy fate, it should proceed.
I'll pray a thousand prayers for thy death,
No word to save thee.

Claud. Nay, hear me, Isabel.

Isab. O, fie, fie, fie!
Thy sin's not accidental, but a trade.
Mercy to thee would prove itself a bawd:
'Tis best that thou diest quickly. [*Going.*

Claud. O hear me, Isabella!

Enter DUKE.

Duke. Vouchsafe a word, young Sister; but one word.

Isab. What is your will?

Duke. Might you dispense with your leisure, I would by and by have some speech with you: the satisfaction I would require is likewise your own benefit.

Isab. I have no superfluous leisure: my stay must be stolen out of other affairs; but I will attend you a while.

Duke. [*To* CLAUDIO.] Son, I have overheard what hath pass'd between you and your sister. Angelo had never the purpose to corrupt her; only he hath made an assay of her virtue, to practise his judgment with the disposition of natures. She, having the truth of honour in her, hath made him that gracious denial which he is most glad to receive: I am confessor to Angelo, and I know this to be true; therefore prepare yourself to death. Do not satisfy your resolution with hopes that are fallible: to-morrow you must die. Go to your knees, and make ready.

Claud. Let me ask my sister pardon. I am so out of love with life, that I will sue to be rid of it.

Duke. Hold you there: farewell. [*Exit* CLAUDIO.

Enter Provost.

Provost, a word with you.

Prov. What's your will, Father?

Duke. That now you are come, you will be gone. Leave me a while with the maid: my mind promises with my habit no loss shall touch her by my company.

Prov. In good time. [*Exit* Provost.

Duke. The hand that hath made you fair hath made you good: the goodness that is cheap in beauty makes beauty brief in goodness; but grace, being the soul of your complexion, shall keep the body of it ever fair. The assault that Angelo hath made to you, fortune hath convey'd to my understanding; and, but that frailty hath examples for his falling, I should wonder at Angelo. How will you do to content this substitute and to save your brother?

Isab. I am now going to resolve him. I had rather my brother die by the law, than my son should be unlawfully born. But O, how much is the good Duke deceiv'd in Angelo! If ever he return, and I can speak to him, I will open my lips in vain, or discover his government.

Duke. That shall not be much amiss; yet, as the matter now stands, he will avoid your accusation:— he made trial of you only. Therefore, fasten your ear on my advisings: to the love I have in doing good, a remedy presents itself. I do make myself believe, that you may most uprighteously do a poor wronged lady a merited benefit, redeem your brother from the angry law, do no stain to your own gracious person, and much please the absent Duke, if, peradventure, he shall ever return to have hearing of this business.

Isab. Let me hear you speak farther. I have spirit to do any thing that appears not foul in the truth of my spirit.

Duke. Virtue is bold, and goodness never fearful. Have you not heard speak of Mariana, the sister of Frederick, the great soldier who miscarried at sea?

Isab. I have heard of the lady, and good words went with her name.

Duke. She should this Angelo have married; was affianced to her by oath, and the nuptial appointed: between which time of the contract and limit of the solemnity, her brother Frederick was wrack'd at sea, having in that perish'd vessel the dowry of his sister. But mark how heavily this befell to the poor gentlewoman: there she lost a noble and renowned brother, in his love toward her ever most kind and natural; with him the portion and sinew of her fortune, her marriage-dowry; with both, her combinate husband, this well-seeming Angelo.

Isab. Can this be so? Did Angelo so leave her?

Duke. Left her in her tears, and dried not one of them with his comfort; swallowed his vows whole, pretending in her discoveries of dishonour: in few, bestow'd her on her own lamentation, which she yet wears for his sake, and he, a marble to her tears, is washed with them, but relents not.

Isab. What a merit were it in death to take this poor maid from the world! What corruption in this life, that it will let this man live! — But how out of this can she avail?

Duke. It is a rupture that you may easily heal;

and the cure of it not only saves your brother, but keeps you from dishonour in doing it.

Isab. Show me how, good Father.

Duke. This fore-named maid hath yet in her the continuance of her first affection: his unjust unkindness, that in all reason should have quenched her love, hath, like an impediment in the current, made it more violent and unruly. Go you to Angelo: answer his requiring with a plausible obedience; agree with his demands to the point: only refer yourself to this advantage, — first, that your stay with him may not be long, that the time may have all shadow and silence in it, and the place answer to convenience. This being granted in course, and now follows all: we shall advise this wronged maid to stead up your appointment, go in your place; if the encounter acknowledge itself hereafter, it may compel him to her recompense; and here by this is your brother saved, your honour untainted, the poor Mariana advantaged, and the corrupt deputy foiled. The maid will I frame, and make fit for his attempt. If you think well to carry this — as you may — the doubleness of the benefit defends the deceit from reproof. What think you of it?

Isab. The image of it gives me content already, and, I trust, it will grow to a most prosperous perfection.

Duke. It lies much in your holding up. Haste you speedily to Angelo: if for this night he entreat you to his bed, give him promise of satisfaction. I will presently to St. Luke's; there, at the Moated Grange, resides this dejected Mariana: at that place call upon me, and dispatch with Angelo, that it may be quickly.

Isab. I thank you for this comfort. Fare you well, good Father. [*Exeunt severally.*

SCENE II.

The Street before the Prison.

Enter DUKE *as a Friar; to him* ELBOW, Clown, *and* Officers.

Elb. Nay, if there be no remedy for it, but that you will needs buy and sell men and women like beasts, we shall have all the world drink brown and white bastard.

Duke. O Heavens! what stuff is here?

Clo. 'Twas never merry world, since, of two usuries, the merriest was put down, and the worser allow'd by order of law a furr'd gown to keep him warm; and furred with fox and lamb-skins too, to signify that craft, being richer than innocency, stands for the facing.

Elb. Come your way, sir.—'Bless you, good Father friar.

Duke. And you, good brother father. What offence hath this man made you, sir?

Elb. Marry, sir, he hath offended the law: and, sir, we take him to be a thief too, sir; for we have found upon him, sir, a strange pick-lock, which we have sent to the Deputy.

Duke. Fie, sirrah: a bawd, a wicked bawd!
The evil that thou causest to be done,
That is thy means to live. Do thou but think
What 'tis to cram a maw, or clothe a back,
From such a filthy vice: say to thyself,
From their abominable and beastly touches
I drink, I eat, array myself, and live.
Canst thou believe thy living is a life,
So stinkingly depending? Go mend, go mend.

Clo. Indeed, it does stink in some sort, sir; but yet, sir, I would prove —

Duke. Nay, if the Devil have given thee proofs for sin,
Thou wilt prove his. Take him to prison, officer:
Correction and instruction must both work,
Ere this rude beast will profit.

Elb. He must before the Deputy, sir; he has given him warning. The Deputy cannot abide a whoremaster: if he be a whoremonger, and comes before him, he were as good go a mile on his errand.

Duke. That we were all, as some would seem to be,
[Free] from our faults, as from faults seeming free!

Enter LUCIO.

Elb. His neck will come to your waist — a cord, sir.

Clo. I spy comfort: I cry bail. Here's a gentleman, and a friend of mine.

Lucio. How now, noble Pompey! What, at the wheels of Cæsar? Art thou led in triumph? What, is there none of Pygmalion's images, newly made woman, to be had now, for putting the hand in the pocket and extracting it clutch'd? What reply? Ha! What say'st thou to this tune, matter, and method? Is't not drown'd i' th' last rain? Ha! What say'st thou, Trot? Is the world as it was, man? Which is the way? Is it sad and few words, or how? The trick of it?

Duke. Still thus, and thus: still worse!

Lucio. How doth my dear morsel, thy mistress? Procures she still? Ha!

Clo. Troth, sir, she hath eaten up all her beef, and she is herself in the tub.

Lucio. Why, 'tis good; it is the right of it; it

must be so: ever your fresh whore and your powder'd bawd: an unshunn'd consequence; it must be so. Art going to prison, Pompey?

Clo. Yes, faith, sir.

Lucio. Why, 'tis not amiss, Pompey. Farewell. Go; say, I sent thee thither. For debt, Pompey, or how?

Elb. For being a bawd, for being a bawd.

Lucio. Well, then imprison him. If imprisonment be the due of a bawd, why, 'tis his right: bawd is he, doubtless, and of antiquity too — bawd-born. Farewell, good Pompey; commend me to the prison, Pompey. You will turn good husband now, Pompey; you will keep the house.

Clo. I hope, sir, your good worship will be my bail.

Lucio. No, indeed will I not, Pompey; it is not the wear. I will pray, Pompey, to increase your bondage: if you take it not patiently, why, your mettle is the more. Adieu, trusty Pompey. — Bless you, Friar.

Duke. And you.

Lucio. Does Bridget paint still, Pompey? Ha!

Elb. Come your ways, sir; come.

Clo. You will not bail me then, sir?

Lucio. Then, Pompey, nor now. — What news abroad, Friar? What news?

Elb. Come your ways, sir; come.

Lucio. Go; to kennel, Pompey, go.

[*Exeunt* ELBOW, Clown, *and* Officers.

What news, Friar, of the Duke?

Duke. I know none. Can you tell me of any?

Lucio. Some say, he is with the Emperor of Russia; other some, he is in Rome: but where is he, think you?

Duke. I know not where; but wheresoever, I wish him well.

Lucio. It was a mad fantastical trick of him, to steal from the State, and usurp the beggary he was never born to. Lord Angelo dukes it well in his absence: he puts transgression to't.

Duke. He does well in't.

Lucio. A little more lenity to lechery would do no harm in him: something too crabbed that way, Friar.

Duke. It is too general a vice, and severity must cure it.

Lucio. Yes, in good sooth, the vice is of a great kindred: it is well allied; but it is impossible to extirp it quite, Friar, till eating and drinking be put down. They say, this Angelo was not made by man and woman, after this downright way of creation: is it true, think you?

Duke. How should he be made then?

Lucio. Some report, a sea-maid spawn'd him: some, that he was begot between two stock-fishes; but it is certain, that when he makes water, his urine is congeal'd ice: that I know to be true; and he is a motion ungenerative, that's infallible.

Duke. You are pleasant, sir, and speak apace.

Lucio. Why, what a ruthless thing is this in him, for the rebellion of a cod-piece to take away the life of a man? Would the Duke that is absent have done this? Ere he would have hang'd a man for the getting a hundred bastards, he would have paid for the nursing a thousand. He had some feeling of the sport: he knew the service, and that instructed him to mercy.

Duke. I never heard the absent Duke much detected for women: he was not inclin'd that way.

Lucio. O, sir! you are deceiv'd.

Duke. 'Tis not possible.

Lucio. Who? not the Duke? yes, your beggar of fifty; and his use was, to put a ducat in her clack-dish. The Duke had crotchets in him: he would be drunk too; that let me inform you.

Duke. You do him wrong, surely.

Lucio. Sir, I was an inward of his. A shy fellow was the Duke; and, I believe, I know the cause of his withdrawing.

Duke. What, I pr'ythee, might be the cause?

Lucio. No,—pardon:—'tis a secret must be lock'd within the teeth and the lips; but this I can let you understand,—the greater file of the subject held the Duke to be wise.

Duke. Wise? why, no question but he was.

Lucio. A very superficial, ignorant, unweighing fellow.

Duke. Either this is envy in you, folly, or mistaking: the very stream of his life, and the business he hath helmed, must, upon a warranted need, give him a better proclamation. Let him be but testimonied in his own bringings forth, and he shall appear to the envious a scholar, a statesman, and a soldier. Therefore, you speak unskilfully; or, if your knowledge be more, it is much darken'd in your malice.

Lucio. Sir, I know him and I love him.

Duke. Love talks with better knowledge, and knowledge with dearer love.

Lucio. Come, sir, I know what I know.

Duke. I can hardly believe that, since you know not what you speak. But, if ever the Duke return, (as our prayers are he may,) let me desire you to make your answer before him: if it be honest you have spoke, you have courage to maintain it. I am bound to call upon you; and, I pray you, your name?

Lucio. Sir, my name is Lucio, well known to the Duke.

Duke. He shall know you better, sir, if I may live to report you.

Lucio. I fear you not.

Duke. O! you hope the Duke will return no more, or you imagine me too unhurtful an opposite. But, indeed, I can do you little harm: you'll forswear this again.

Lucio. I'll be hang'd first: thou art deceiv'd in me, Friar. But no more of this. Canst thou tell if Claudio die to-morrow, or no?

Duke. Why should he die, sir?

Lucio. Why? for filling a bottle with a tun-dish I would the Duke, we talk of, were return'd again. this ungenitur'd agent will unpeople the province with continency; sparrows must not build in his house-eaves, because they are lecherous. The Duke yet would have dark deeds darkly answer'd; he would never bring them to light: would he were return'd! Marry, this Claudio is condemn'd for untrussing. Farewell, good Friar; I pr'ythee, pray for me. The Duke, I say to thee again, would eat mutton on Fri days. He's now past it; yet, and I say to thee, he would mouth with a beggar, though she smelt brown bread and garlic: say that I said so. Farewell.

[*Exit*

Duke. No might nor greatness in mortality
Can censure 'scape: back-wounding calumny
The whitest virtue strikes. What King so strong
Can tie the gall up in the slanderous tongue?
But who comes here?

Enter ESCALUS, Provost, Bawd, *and* Officers.

Escal. Go: away with her to prison!

Bawd. Good my lord, be good to me; your honour is accounted a merciful man, good my lord.

Escal. Double and treble admonition, and still forfeit in the same kind? This would make mercy swear, and play the tyrant.

Prov. A bawd of eleven years' continuance, may it please your honour.

Bawd. My lord, this is one Lucio's information against me. Mistress Kate Keep-down was with child by him in the Duke's time: he promised her marriage; his child is a year and a quarter old, come Philip and Jacob. I have kept it myself, and see how he goes about to abuse me!

Escal. That fellow is a fellow of much license: —let him be call'd before us.—Away with her to prison! Go to; no more words. [*Exeunt* Bawd *and* Officers.] Provost, my brother Angelo will not be alter'd; Claudio must die to-morrow. Let him be furnish'd with divines, and have all charitable preparation: if my brother wrought by my pity, it should not be so with him.

Prov. So please you, this friar hath been with him, and advis'd him for th' entertainment of death.

Escal. Good even, good Father.

Duke. Bliss and goodness on you.

Escal. Of whence are you?

Duke. Not of this country, though my chance is now
To use it for my time: I am a Brother
Of gracious order, late come from the See,
In special business from his Holiness.

Escal. What news abroad i' th' world?

Duke. None, but that there is so great a fever on goodness, that the dissolution of it must cure it: novelty is only in request; and it is as dangerous to be aged in any kind of course, as it is virtuous to be constant in any undertaking. There is scarce truth enough alive to make societies secure, but security enough to make fellowships accurs'd. Much upon this riddle runs the wisdom of the world. This news is old enough, yet it is every day's news. I pray you, sir, of what disposition was the Duke?

Escal. One that, above all other strifes, contended especially to know himself.

Duke. What pleasure was he given to?

Escal. Rather rejoicing to see another merry, than merry at any thing which profess'd to make him rejoice: a gentleman of all temperance. But leave we him to his events, with a prayer they may prove prosperous, and let me desire to know how you find Claudio prepar'd. I am made to understand that you have lent him visitation.

Duke. He professes to have received no sinister measure from his judge, but most willingly humbles himself to the determination of justice; yet had he framed to himself, by the instruction of his frailty, many deceiving promises of life, which I, by my good leisure, have discredited to him; and now is he resolv'd to die.

Escal. You have paid the Heavens your function, and the prisoner the very debt of your calling. I have labour'd for the poor gentleman to the extremest shore of my modesty; but my brother justice have I found so severe, that he hath forc'd me to tell him, he is indeed — Justice.

Duke. If his own life answer the straitness of his

proceeding, it shall become him well; wherein if he chance to fail, he hath sentenc'd himself.

Escal. I am going to visit the prisoner. Fare you well.

Duke. Peace be with you!

[*Exeunt* ESCALUS *and* Provost.

He, who the sword of Heaven will bear,
Should be as holy as severe;
Pattern in himself to know,
Grace to stand, and virtue go;
More nor less to others paying,
Than by self offences weighing.
Shame to him, whose cruel striking
Kills for faults of his own liking!
Twice treble shame on Angelo,
To weed my vice, and let his grow!
O, what may man within him hide,
Though angel on the outward side!
How may likeness wade in crimes,
Making practice on the times,
To draw with idle spiders' strings
Most pond'rous and substantial things!
Craft against vice I must apply.
With Angelo to-night shall lie
His old betrothed, but despised:
So disguise shall, by th' disguised,
Pay with falsehood false exacting,
And perform an old contracting. [*Exit.*

ACT IV.

Scene I.—A Room at the Moated Grange.

Mariana *discovered sitting: a* Boy *singing.*

Song.

Take, O! take those lips away,
That so sweetly were forsworn;
And those eyes, the break of day,
Lights that do mislead the morn:
But my kisses bring again,
bring again,
Seals of love, but seal'd in vain,
seal'd in vain.

Mari. Break off thy song, and haste thee quick away:
Here comes a man of comfort, whose advice
Hath often still'd my brawling discontent.—
[*Exit* Boy.

Enter Duke.

I cry you, mercy, sir, and well could wish
You had not found me here so musical:
Let me excuse me, and believe me so,
My mirth it much displeas'd, but pleas'd my woe.

Duke. 'Tis good: though music oft hath such a charm,
To make bad good, and good provoke to harm.
I pray you, tell me, hath any body inquired for me here to-day? Much upon this time have I promis'd here to meet.

Mari. You have not been inquired after: I have sat here all day.

Enter ISABELLA.

Duke. I do constantly believe you. — The time is come, even now. I shall crave your forbearance a little: may be, I will call upon you anon for some advantage to yourself.

Mari. I am always bound to you. [*Exit.*

Duke. Very well met, and welcome.
What is the news from this good Deputy?

Isab. He hath a garden circummur'd with brick,
Whose western side is with a vineyard back'd;
And to that vineyard is a planched gate,
That makes his opening with this bigger key:
This other doth command a little door,
Which from the vineyard to the garden leads;
There have I made my promise upon the heavy middle of the night to call upon him.

Duke. But shall you on your knowledge find this way?

Isab. I have ta'en a due and wary note upon't:
With whispering and most guilty diligence,
In action all of precept, he did show me
The way twice o'er.

Duke. Are there no other tokens
Between you 'greed, concerning her observance?

Isab. No, none, but only a repair i' th' dark;
And that I have possess'd him my most stay
Can be but brief: for I have made him know,
I have a servant comes with me along,
That stays upon me, whose persuasion is,
I come about my brother.

Duke. 'Tis well borne up.
I have not yet made known to Mariana
A word of this. — What, hoa! within! come forth.

Enter MARIANA.

I pray you, be acquainted with this maid:
She comes to do you good.

Isab. I do desire the like.

Duke. Do you persuade yourself that I respect you?

Mari. Good friar, I know you do, and have found it.

Duke. Take then this your companion by the hand,
Who hath a story ready for your ear.
I shall attend your leisure: but make haste;
The vaporous night approaches.

Mari. Will't please you walk aside?

[*Exeunt* MARIANA *and* ISABELLA.

Duke. O place and greatness! millions of false eyes
Are stuck upon thee. Volumes of report
Run with these false and most contrarious quests
Upon thy doings: thousand escapes of wit
Make thee the father of their idle dream,
And rack thee in their fancies!

Enter MARIANA *and* ISABELLA.

Welcome! How agreed?

Isab. She'll take the enterprise upon her, Father,
If you advise it.

Duke. It is not my consent,
But my entreaty too.

Isab. Little have you to say,
When you depart from him, but, soft and low,
'Remember now my brother.'

Mari. Fear me not.

Duke. Nor, gentle daughter, fear you not at all.
He is your husband on a pre-contract:

To bring you thus together, 'tis no sin,
Sith that the justice of your title to him
Doth flourish the deceit. Come, let us go:
Our corn's to reap, for yet our tilth's to sow.
[*Exeunt.*

SCENE II.

A Room in the Prison.

Enter Provost *and* Clown.

Prov. Come hither, sirrah. Can you cut off a man's head?

Clo. If the man be a bachelor, sir, I can; but if he be a married man, he is his wife's head, and I can never cut off a woman's head.

Prov. Come, sir; leave me your snatches, and yield me a direct answer. To-morrow morning are to die Claudio and Barnardine: here is in our prison a common executioner, who in his office lacks a helper; if you will take it on you to assist him, it shall redeem you from your gyves; if not, you shall have your full time of imprisonment and your deliverance with an unpitied whipping; for you have been a notorious bawd.

Clo. Sir, I have been an unlawful bawd, time out of mind; but yet I will be content to be a lawful hangman. I would be glad to receive some instruction from my fellow-partner.

Prov. What hoa, Abhorson! Where's Abhorson, there?

Enter ABHORSON.

Abhorson. Do you call, sir?

Prov. Sirrah, here's a fellow will help you to-morrow in your execution. If you think it meet, compound with him by the year, and let him abide here with you; if not, use him for the present, and dismiss him. He cannot plead his estimation with you: he hath been a bawd.

Abhor. A bawd, sir? Fie upon him! he will discredit our mystery.

Prov. Go to, sir; you weigh equally: a feather will turn the scale. [*Exit.*

Clo. Pray, sir, by your good favour, (for, surely, sir, a good favour you have, but that you have a hanging look,) do you call, sir, your occupation a mystery?

Abhor. Ay, sir; a mystery.

Clo. Painting, sir, I have heard say, is a mystery; and your whores, sir, being members of my occupation, using painting, do prove my occupation a mystery; but what mystery there should be in hanging, if I should be hang'd, I cannot imagine.

Abhor. Sir, it is a mystery.

Clo. Proof?

Abhor. Every true man's apparel fits your thief.

Clo. If it be too little for your thief, your true man thinks it big enough; if it be too big for your thief, your thief thinks it little enough; so, every true man's apparel fits your thief.

Enter Provost.

Prov. Are you agreed?

Clo. Sir, I will serve him; for I do find your hangman is a more penitent trade than your bawd: he doth oftener ask forgiveness.

Prov. You, sirrah, provide your block and your axe to-morrow, — four o'clock.

Abhor. Come on, bawd; I will instruct thee in my trade: follow.

Clo. I do desire to learn, sir; and, I hope, if you have occasion to use me for your own turn, you shall find me yare; for, truly, sir, for your kindness I owe you a good turn.

Prov. Call hither Barnardine and Claudio:

[*Exeunt* Clown *and* ABHORSON.

Th' one has my pity; not a jot the other,
Being a murtherer, though he were my brother.

Enter CLAUDIO.

Look, here's the warrant, Claudio, for thy death:
'Tis now dead midnight, and by eight to-morrow
Thou must be made immortal. Where's Barnardine?

Claud. As fast lock'd up in sleep as guiltless labour,
When it lies starkly in the traveller's bones:
He will not wake.

Prov. Who can do good on him?
Well, go; prepare yourself. But hark, what noise?

[*Knocking within.*

Heaven give your spirits comfort! — By and by: —

[*Exit* CLAUDIO.

I hope it is some pardon, or reprieve,
For the most gentle Claudio. — Welcome, Father.

Enter DUKE.

Duke. The best and wholesom'st spirits of the night
Envelop you, good Provost! Who call'd here of late?

Prov. None, since the curfew rung.

Duke. Not Isabel?

Prov. No.

Duke. They will, then, ere't be long.

Prov. What comfort is for Claudio?

Duke. There's some in hope.

Prov. It is a bitter Deputy.
Duke. Not so, not so: his life is parallel'd
Even with the stroke and line of his great justice.
He doth with holy abstinence subdue
That in himself which he spurs on his power
To qualify in others: were he meal'd with that
Which he corrects, then were he tyrannous;
[*Knocking within.*
But this being so, he's just. — Now are they come. —
[*Exit* Provost.
This is a gentle Provost: seldom, when
The steeled gaoler is the friend of men. [*Knocking.*
How now! What noise? That spirit's possess'd with haste,
That wounds th' unlisting postern with these strokes.

Enter Provost.

Prov. [*Speaking to one at the door.*] There he must stay, until the officer
Arise to let him in: he is call'd up.
Duke. Have you no countermand for Claudio yet,
But he must die to-morrow?
Prov. None, sir, none.
Duke. As near the dawning, Provost, as it is,
You shall hear more ere morning.
Prov. Happely,
You something know; yet, I believe, there comes
No countermand: no such example have we.
Besides, upon the very siege of justice,
Lord Angelo hath to the public ear
Profess'd the contrary.

Enter a Messenger.

This is his lordship's man.
Duke. And here comes Claudio's pardon.

Messenger. My lord hath sent you this note; and by me this further charge, that you swerve not from the smallest article of it, neither in time, matter, or other circumstance. Good morrow; for, as I take it, it is almost day.

Prov. I shall obey him. [*Exit* Messenger.

Duke. This is his pardon; purchas'd by such sin, [*Aside.*
For which the pardoner himself is in:
Hence hath offence his quick celerity,
When it is borne in high authority.
When vice makes mercy, mercy's so extended,
That for the fault's love is th' offender friended.—
Now, sir, what news?

Prov. I told you: Lord Angelo, belike thinking me remiss in mine office, awakens me with this unwonted putting-on; methinks strangely, for he hath not used it before.

Duke. Pray you, let's hear.

Prov. [Reads.] "*Whatsoever you may hear to the contrary, let Claudio be executed by four of the clock; and, in the afternoon, Barnardine. For my better satisfaction, let me have Claudio's head sent me by five. Let this be duly perform'd; with a thought, that more depends on it than we must yet deliver. Thus fail not to do your office, as you will answer it at your peril.*"—What say you to this, sir?

Duke. What is that Barnardine, who is to be executed in th' afternoon?

Prov. A Bohemian born; but here nurs'd up and bred: one that is a prisoner nine years old.

Duke. How came it that the absent Duke had not either deliver'd him to his liberty, or executed him? I have heard it was ever his manner to do so.

Prov. His friends still wrought reprieves for him:

and, indeed, his fact, till now in the government of Lord Angelo, came not to an undoubtful proof.

Duke. It is now apparent?

Prov. Most manifest, and not denied by himself.

Duke. Hath he borne himself penitently in prison? How seems he to be touch'd?

Prov. A man that apprehends death no more dreadfully but as a drunken sleep; careless, reckless, and fearless of what's past, present, or to come: insensible of mortality, and desperately mortal.

Duke. He wants advice.

Prov. He will hear none. He hath evermore had the liberty of the prison: give him leave to escape hence, he would not: drunk many times a day, if not many days entirely drunk. We have very oft awak'd him, as if to carry him to execution, and show'd him a seeming warrant for it: it hath not moved him at all.

Duke. More of him anon. There is written in your brow, Provost, honesty and constancy: if I read it not truly, my ancient skill beguiles me; but in the boldness of my cunning I will lay myself in hazard. Claudio, whom here you have warrant to execute, is no greater forfeit to the law than Angelo, who hath sentenced him. To make you understand this in a manifested effect, I crave but four days' respite, for the which you are to do me both a present and a dangerous courtesy.

Prov. Pray, sir, in what?

Duke. In the delaying death.

Prov. Alack! how may I do it, having the hour limited, and an express command, under penalty, to deliver his head in the view of Angelo? I may make my case as Claudio's, to cross this in the smallest.

Duke. By the vow of mine order, I warrant you:

if my instructions may be your guide, let this Barnardine be this morning executed, and his head borne to Angelo.

Prov. Angelo hath seen them both, and will discover the favour.

Duke. O! death's a great disguiser, and you may add to it. Shave the head, and dye the beard; and say it was the desire of the penitent to be so bared before his death: you know the course is common. If any thing fall to you upon this, more than thanks and good fortune, by the saint whom I profess, I will plead against it with my life.

Prov. Pardon me, good Father: it is against my oath.

Duke. Were you sworn to the Duke, or to the Deputy?

Prov. To him and to his substitutes.

Duke. You will think you have made no offence, if the Duke avouch the justice of your dealing.

Prov. But what likelihood is in that?

Duke. Not a resemblance, but a certainty. Yet since I see you fearful that neither my coat, integrity, nor my persuasion, can with ease attempt you, I will go farther than I meant, to pluck all fears out of you. Look you, sir; here is the hand and seal of the Duke: you know the character, I doubt not, and the signet is not strange to you.

Prov. I know them both.

Duke. The contents of this is the return of the Duke: you shall anon over-read it at your pleasure, where you shall find, within these two days he will be here. This is a thing that Angelo knows not, for he this very day receives letters of strange tenor; perchance, of the Duke's death; perchance, entering into some monastery; but, by chance, nothing of what is [here] writ. Look, th' unfolding star calls up the shepherd. Put not yourself into amazement how these things should be: all difficulties are but easy when they are known. Call your executioner, and off with Barnardine's head: I will give him a present shrift, and advise him for a better place. Yet you are amazed; but this shall absolutely resolve you. Come away; it is almost clear dawn. [*Exeunt.*

Scene III.

Another Room in the Same.

Enter Clown.

Clo. I am as well acquainted here, as I was in our house of profession: one would think it were Mistress Over-done's own house; for here be many of her old customers. First, here's young Master Rash; he's in for a commodity of brown paper and old ginger, ninescore and seventeen pounds, of which he made five marks, ready money: marry, then, ginger was not much in request, for the old women were all dead. Then is there here one Master Caper, at the suit of Master Three-pile the mercer, for some four suits of peach-colour'd satin, which now peaches him a beggar. Then have we here young Dizzy, and young Master Deep-vow, and Master Copper-spur, and Master Starve-lackey, the rapier-and-dagger-man, and young Drop-heir that kill'd Lusty Pudding, and Master Forthright the tilter, and brave Master Shoe-tie the great traveller, and wild Half-can that stabb'd Pots, and, I think, forty more, all great doers in our trade, and are now for the Lord's sake.

Enter ABHORSON.

Abhor. Sirrah, bring Barnardine hither.

Clo. Mr. Barnardine! you must rise and be hang'd, Mr. Barnardine.

Abhor. What, hoa, Barnardine!

Barnar. [*Within.*] A pox o' your throats! Who makes that noise there? What are you?

Clo. Your friends, sir; the hangman. You must be so good, sir, to rise and be put to death.

Barnar. [*Within.*] Away, you rogue, away! I am sleepy.

Abhor. Tell him, he must awake, and that quickly too.

Clo. Pray, Master Barnardine, awake till you are executed, and sleep afterwards.

Abhor. Go in to him, and fetch him out.

Clo. He is coming, sir, he is coming: I hear his straw rustle.

Enter BARNARDINE.

Abhor. Is the axe upon the block, sirrah?

Clo. Very ready, sir.

Barnar. How now, Abhorson? what's the news with you?

Abhor. Truly, sir, I would desire you to clap into your prayers; for, look you, the warrant's come.

Barnar. You rogue, I have been drinking all night: I am not fitted for't.

Clo. O, the better, sir; for he that drinks all night, and is hang'd betimes in the morning, may sleep the sounder all the next day.

Enter DUKE.

Abhor. Look you, sir; here comes your ghostly father. Do we jest now, think you?

Duke. Sir, induced by my charity, and hearing how hastily you are to depart, I am come to advise you, comfort you, and pray with you.

Barnar. Friar, not I: I have been drinking hard all night, and I will have more time to prepare me, or they shall beat out my brains with billets. I will not consent to die this day, that's certain.

Duke. O, sir, you must; and therefore, I beseech you,
Look forward on the journey you shall go.

Barnar. I swear, I will not die to-day for any man's persuasion.

Duke. But hear you, —

Barnar. Not a word: if you have any thing to say to me, come to my ward; for thence will not I to-day. [*Exit.*

Enter Provost.

Duke. Unfit to live, or die. O, grovelling beast! —
After him, fellows: bring him to the block.
[*Exeunt* Abhorson *and* Clown.

Prov. Now, sir; how do you find the prisoner?

Duke. A creature unprepar'd, unmeet for death;
And to transport him, in the mind he is,
Were damnable.

Prov. Here in the prison, Father,
There died this morning of a cruel fever
One Ragozine, a most notorious pirate,
A man of Claudio's years; his beard and head
Just of his colour. What if we do omit
This reprobate, till he were well inclin'd,
And satisfy the Deputy with the visage
Of Ragozine, more like to Claudio?

Duke. O, 'tis an accident that Heaven provides!
Dispatch it presently: the hour draws on
Prefix'd by Angelo. See this be done,

And sent according to command, whiles I
Persuade this rude wretch willingly to die.

Prov. This shall be done, good Father, presently.
But Barnardine must die this afternoon;
And how shall we continue Claudio,
To save me from the danger that might come,
If he were known alive?

Duke. Let this be done. — Put them in secret holds,
Both Barnardine and Claudio:
Ere twice the sun hath made his journal greeting
To th' under generation, you shall find
Your safety manifested.

Prov. I am your free dependant.

Duke. Quick, dispatch, and send the head to Angelo. [*Exit* Provost.
Now will I write letters to Angelo,
(The Provost, he shall bear them) whose contents
Shall witness to him, I am near at home,
And that, by great injunctions, I am bound
To enter publicly. Him I'll desire
To meet me at the consecrated fount,
A league below the city; and from thence,
By cold gradation and well-balanc'd form,
We shall proceed with Angelo.

Enter Provost.

Prov. Here is the head; I'll carry it myself.

Duke. Convenient is it. Make a swift return,
For I would commune with you of such things,
That want no ear but yours.

Prov. I'll make all speed. [*Exit.*

Isab. [*Within.*] Peace, hoa, be here!

Duke. The tongue of Isabel. — She's come to know,
If yet her brother's pardon be come hither;
But I will keep her ignorant of her good,

To make her heavenly comforts of despair,
When it is least expected.

Enter ISABELLA.

Isab. Hoa! by your leave.

Duke. Good morning to you, fair and gracious daughter.

Isab. The better, given me by so holy a man.
Hath yet the Deputy sent my brother's pardon?

Duke. He hath releas'd him, Isabel, from the world.
His head is off, and sent to Angelo.

Isab. Nay, but it is not so.

Duke. It is no other.
Shew your wisdom, daughter, in your close patience.

Isab. O, I will to him, and pluck out his eyes!

Duke. You shall not be admitted to his sight.

Isab. Unhappy Claudio! Wretched Isabel!
Injurious world! Most damned Angelo!

Duke. This nor hurts him, nor profits you a jot:
Forbear it therefore; give your cause to Heaven.
Mark what I say, which you shall find
By every syllable a faithful verity.
The Duke comes home to-morrow; — nay, dry your eyes:
One of our convent, and his confessor,
Gives me this instance. Already he hath carried
Notice to Escalus and Angelo
Who do prepare to meet him at the gates,
There to give up their power. If you can, pace your wisdom
In that good path that I would wish it go;
And you shall have your bosom on this wretch,
Grace of the Duke, revenges to your heart,
And general honour.

Isab. I am directed by you.

Duke. This letter, then, to Friar Peter give;
'Tis that he sent me of the Duke's return:
Say, by this token, I desire his company
At Mariana's house to-night. Her cause and yours
I'll perfect him withal; and he shall bring you
Before the Duke, and to the head of Angelo
Accuse him home, and home. For my poor self,
I am combined by a sacred vow,
And shall be absent. Wend you with this letter.
Command these fretting waters from your eyes
With a light heart: trust not my holy order,
If I pervert your course. — Who's here?

Enter LUCIO.

Lucio. Good even.
Friar, where is the Provost?

Duke. Not within, sir.

Lucio. O, pretty Isabella, I am pale at mine heart, to see thine eyes so red: thou must be patient. I am fain to dine and sup with water and bran; I dare not, for my head, fill my belly: one fruitful meal would set me to't. But they say the Duke will be here to-morrow. By my troth, Isabel, I lov'd thy brother: if the old fantastical Duke of dark corners had been at home, he had lived. [*Exit* ISABELLA.

Duke. Sir, the Duke is marvellous little beholding to your reports; but the best is, he lives not in them.

Lucio. Friar, thou knowest not the Duke so well as I do: he's a better woodman than thou tak'st him for.

Duke. Well, you'll answer this one day. Fare ye well.

Lucio. Nay, tarry; I'll go along with thee I can tell thee pretty tales of the Duke.

Duke. You have told me too many of him already, sir, if they be true; if not true, none were enough.

Lucio. I was once before him for getting a wench with child.

Duke. Did you such a thing?

Lucio. Yes, marry, did I; but I was fain to forswear it: they would else have married me to the rotten medlar.

Duke. Sir, your company is fairer than honest. Rest you well.

Lucio. By my troth, I'll go with thee to the lane's end. If bawdy talk offend you, we'll have very little of it. Nay, Friar, I am a kind of burr; I shall stick. [*Exeunt.*

Scene IV.

A Room in Angelo's House.

Enter Angelo *and* Escalus.

Escal. Every letter he hath writ hath disvouch'd [the] other.

Ang. In most uneven and distracted manner. His actions show much like to madness: pray Heaven, his wisdom be not tainted! And why meet him at the gates, and re-deliver our authorities there?

Escal. I guess not.

Ang. And why should we proclaim it in an hour before his ent'ring, that if any crave redress of injustice, they should exhibit their petitions in the street?

Escal. He shows his reason for that: to have a dispatch of complaints, and to deliver us from devices hereafter, which shall then have no power to stand against us.

Ang. Well, I beseech you, let it be proclaim'd betimes i' th' morn, I'll call you at your house. Give notice to such men of sort and suit, as are to meet him.

Escal. I shall, sir: fare you well. [*Exit.*

Ang. Good night.—
This deed unshapes me quite, makes me unpregnant,
And dull to all proceedings. A deflowered maid,
And by an eminent body, that enforc'd
The law against it!—But that her tender shame
Will not proclaim against her maiden loss,
How might she tongue me! Yet reason dares her on;
For my authority bears up a credent bulk
That no particular scandal once can touch,
But it confounds the breather. He should have liv'd,
Save that his riotous youth, with dangerous sense,
Might in the times to come have ta'en revenge,
By so receiving a dishonour'd life
With ransom of such shame. Would yet he had liv'd!
Alack! when once our grace we have forgot,
Nothing goes right: we would, and we would not.
[*Exit.*

SCENE V.

Fields without the Town.

Enter DUKE, *in his own habit, and* Friar PETER.

Duke. These letters at fit time deliver me.
The Provost knows our purpose, and our plot.
The matter being afoot, keep your instruction,
And hold you ever to our special drift,
Though sometimes you do blench from this to that,
As cause doth minister. Go, call at Flavius' house,
And tell him where I stay: give the like notice

To Valentius, Rowland, and to Crassus,
And bid them bring the trumpets to the gate;
But send me Flavius first.

Friar Peter. It shall be speeded well.
[*Exit* Friar.

Enter VARRIUS.

Duke. I thank thee, Varrius; thou hast made good haste.
Come, we will walk: there's other of our friends
Will greet us here anon, my gentle Varrius.
[*Exeunt.*

SCENE VI.

Street near the City Gate.

Enter ISABELLA *and* MARIANA.

Isab. To speak so indirectly, I am loath:
I would say the truth; but to accuse him so,
That is your part; yet I'm advis'd to do it,
He says, to veil full purpose.

Mari. Be rul'd by him.

Isab. Besides, he tells me, that if peradventure
He speak against me on the adverse side,
I should not think it strange; for 'tis a physic,
That's bitter to sweet end.

Mari. I would, Friar Peter —

Isab. O, peace! the Friar is come.

Enter Friar PETER.

F. Peter. Come; I have found you out a stand most fit,
Where you may have such vantage on the Duke,
He shall not pass you. Twice have the trumpets sounded:

The generous and gravest citizens
Have hent the gates, and very near upon
The Duke is ent'ring: therefore hence, away.
[*Exeunt.*

ACT V.

SCENE I.—A public Place near the City Gate.

Enter, severally, DUKE, VARRIUS, *and Attendant* Lords, ANGELO, ESCALUS, LUCIO, Provost, Officers, *and* Citizens. *During their interview, enter* MARIANA, (*veiled,*) ISABELLA, *and* Friar PETER, *at a distance.*

DUKE.

MY very worthy cousin, fairly met:—
Our old and faithful friend, we are glad to see you.

Ang. and Escal. Happy return be to your Royal Grace!

Duke. Many and hearty thankings to you both.
We have made inquiry of you; and we hear
Such goodness of your justice, that our soul
Cannot but yield forth to you public thanks,
Forerunning more requital.

Ang. You make my bonds still greater.

Duke. O, your desert speaks loud; and I should wrong it,
To lock it in the wards of covert bosom,
When it deserves with characters of brass
A forted residence 'gainst the tooth of time,
And razure of oblivion. Give me your hand,

And let the subject see, to make them know
That outward courtesies would fain proclaim
Favours that keep within. — Come, Escalus,
You must walk by us on our other hand;
And good supporters are you.

Friar Peter *and* ISABELLA *come forward.*

F. Peter. Now is your time. Speak loud, and kneel before him.

Isab. Justice, O Royal Duke! Vail your regard
Upon a wrong'd, I would fain have said, a maid!
O worthy Prince! dishonour not your eye
By throwing it on any other object,
Till you have heard me in my true complaint,
And given me justice. Justice! justice! justice!

Duke. Relate your wrongs: in what? by whom? Be brief.
Here is Lord Angelo shall give you justice:
Reveal yourself to him.

Isab. O, worthy Duke!
You bid me seek redemption of the Devil.
Hear me yourself; for that which I must speak
Must either punish me, not being believ'd,
Or wring redress from you. Hear me, O, hear me, here!

Ang. My lord, her wits, I fear me, are not firm:
She hath been a suitor to me for her brother,
Cut off by course of justice.

Isab. By course of justice!

Ang. And she will speak most bitterly, and strange.

Isab. Most strange, but yet most truly, will I speak.
That Angelo's forsworn; — is it not strange?
That Angelo's a murtherer; — is't not strange?
That Angelo is an adulterous thief,
An hypocrite, a virgin-violator; —
Is it not strange, and strange?

Duke. Nay, it is ten times strange.
Isab. It is not truer he is Angelo,
Than this is all as true as it is strange:
Nay, it is ten times true; for truth is truth
To th' end of reck'ning.
Duke. Away with her. — Poor soul!
She speaks this in th' infirmity of sense.
Isab. O Prince, I conjure thee, as thou believ'st
There is another comfort than this world,
That thou neglect me not, with that opinion
That I am touch'd with madness: make not impossible
That which but seems unlike. 'Tis not impossible,
But one, the wicked'st caitiff on the ground,
May seem as shy, as grave, as just, as absolute,
As Angelo; even so may Angelo,
In all his dressings, characts, titles, forms,
Be an arch-villain. Believe it, Royal Prince:
If he be less, he's nothing; but he's more,
Had I more name for badness.
Duke. By mine honesty,
If she be mad, as I believe no other,
Her madness hath the oddest frame of sense, —
Such a dependency of thing on thing, —
As e'er I heard in madness.
Isab. O, gracious Duke!
Harp not on that, nor do not banish reason
For inequality; but let your reason serve
To make the truth appear, where it seems hid,
And hide the false seems true.
Duke. Many that are not mad,
Have, sure, more lack of reason. — What would you say?
Isab. I am the sister of one Claudio,
Condemn'd upon the act of fornication

To lose his head; condemn'd by Angelo.
I, in probation of a Sisterhood,
Was sent to by my brother,—one Lucio
As then the messenger—
Lucio. That's I, an't like your Grace.
I came to her from Claudio, and desir'd her
To try her gracious fortune with Lord Angelo,
For her poor brother's pardon.
Isab. That's he, indeed.
Duke. You were not bid to speak.
Lucio. No, my good lord,
Nor wish'd to hold my peace.
Duke. I wish you now, then:
Pray you, take note of it; and when you have
A business for yourself, pray Heaven you then
Be perfect.
Lucio. I warrant your honour.
Duke. The warrant's for yourself: take heed to it.
Isab. This gentleman told somewhat of my tale.
Lucio. Right.
Duke. It may be right; but you are i' the wrong
To speak before your time.—Proceed.
Isab. I went
To this pernicious, caitiff Deputy.
Duke. That's somewhat madly spoken.
Isab. Pardon it:
The phrase is to the matter.
Duke. Mended again: the matter?—Proceed.
Isab. In brief,—to set the needless process by,
How I persuaded, how I pray'd and kneel'd,
How he refell'd me, and how I repli'd,
(For this was of much length,)—the vile conclusion
I now begin with grief and shame to utter.
He would not, but by gift of my chaste body
To his concupiscible intemperate lust,

Release my brother; and, after much debatement,
My sisterly remorse confutes mine honour,
And I did yield to him. But the next morn betimes,
His purpose surfeiting, he sends a warrant
For my poor brother's head.

Duke. This is most likely.

Isab. O, that it were as like as it is true!

Duke. By Heaven, fond wretch! thou know'st not what thou speak'st,
Or else thou art suborn'd against his honour,
In hateful practice. First, his integrity
Stands without blemish; next, it imports no reason,
That with such vehemency he should pursue
Faults proper to himself: if he had so offended,
He would have weigh'd thy brother by himself,
And not have cut him off. Some one hath set you on:
Confess the truth, and say by whose advice
Thou cam'st here to complain.

Isab. And is this all?
Then, O! you blessed ministers above,
Keep me in patience; and, with ripened time,
Unfold the evil which is here wrapp'd up
In countenance! — Heaven shield your Grace from woe,
As I, thus wrong'd, hence unbelieved go!

Duke. I know, you'd fain be gone. — An officer! —
To prison with her! — Shall we thus permit
A blasting and a scandalous breath to fall
On him so near us? This needs must be a practice.
Who knew of your intent, and coming hither?

Isab. One that I would were here, Friar Lodowick.

Duke. A ghostly Father, belike. — Who knows that Lodowick?

Lucio. My lord, I know him: 'tis a meddling friar;

I do not like the man: had he been lay, my lord,
For certain words he spake against your Grace
In your retirement, I had swing'd him soundly.

Duke. Words against me? This ' a good friar, belike!
And to set on this wretched woman here
Against our substitute! — Let this friar be found.

Lucio. But yesternight, my lord, she and that friar —
I saw them at the prison. A saucy friar,
A very scurvy fellow.

F. Peter. Blessed be your Royal Grace!
I have stood by, my lord, and I have heard
Your royal ear abus'd. First, hath this woman
Most wrongfully accus'd your substitute,
Who is as free from touch or soil with her,
As she from one ungot.

Duke. We did believe no less.
Know you that Friar Lodowick, that she speaks of?

F. Peter. I know him for a man divine and holy;
Not scurvy, nor a temporary meddler,
As he's reported by this gentleman;
And, on my trust, a man that never yet
Did, as he vouches, misreport your Grace.

Lucio. My lord, most villainously: believe it.

F. Peter. Well, he in time may come to clear himself,
But at this instant he is sick, my lord,
Of a strange fever. Upon his mere request,
Being come to knowledge that there was complaint
Intended 'gainst Lord Angelo, came I hither,
To speak, as from his mouth, what he doth know
Is true, and false; and what he with his oath,
And all probation, will make up full clear,
Whensoever he's convented. First, for this woman:
To justify this worthy nobleman,

So vulgarly and personally accus'd,
Her shall you hear disproved to her eyes,
Till she herself confess it.

Duke. Good Friar, let's hear it.

[ISABELLA *is carried off guarded; and* MARIANA *comes forward.*

Do you not smile at this, Lord Angelo? —
O Heaven, the vanity of wretched fools! —
Give us some seats. — Come, cousin Angelo;
In this I'll be impartial: be you judge
Of your own cause. — Is this the witness, Friar?
First let her shew her face, and after speak.

Mari. Pardon, my lord, I will not shew my face
Until my husband bid me.

Duke. What, are you married?

Mari. No, my lord.

Duke. Are you a maid?

Mari. No, my lord.

Duke. A widow, then?

Mari. Neither, my lord.

Duke. Why, you
Are nothing, then: neither maid, widow, nor wife?

Lucio. My lord, she may be a punk; for many of them are neither maid, widow, nor wife.

Duke. Silence that fellow: I would he had some cause
To prattle for himself.

Lucio. Well, my lord.

Mari. My lord, I do confess I ne'er was married;
And, I confess, besides, I am no maid:
I have known my husband, yet my husband knows not
That ever he knew me.

Lucio. He was drunk, then, my lord: it can be no better.

Duke. For the benefit of silence, 'would thou wert so too!

Lucio. Well, my lord.

Duke. This is no witness for Lord Angelo.

Mari. Now I come to't, my lord.
She that accuses him of fornication,
In self-same manner doth accuse my husband;
And charges him, my lord, with such a time
When, I'll depose, I had him in mine arms
With all th' effect of love.

Ang. Charges she more than me?

Mari. Not that I know.

Duke. No?—you say your husband?

Mari. Why, just, my lord; and that is Angelo,
Who thinks, he knows that he ne'er knew my body,
But knows, he thinks, that he knows Isabel's.

Ang. This is a strange abuse.—Let's see thy face.

Mari. My husband bids me: now I will unmask.
This is that face, thou cruel Angelo,
Which once, thou swor'st, was worth the looking on:
This is the hand which, with a vow'd contract,
Was fast belock'd in thine: this is the body
That took away the match from Isabel,
And did supply thee at thy garden-house
In her imagin'd person.

Duke. Know you this woman?

Lucio. Carnally, she says.

Duke. Sirrah, no more.

Lucio. Enough, my lord.

Ang. My lord, I must confess I know this woman;
And, five years since, there was some speech of marriage
Betwixt myself and her, which was broke off,
Partly, for that her promised proportions

Came short of composition; but, in chief,
For that her reputation was disvalued
In levity: since which time of five years
I never spake with her, saw her, nor heard from her,
Upon my faith and honour.

Mari. Noble Prince,
As there comes light from heaven, and words from breath,
As there is sense in truth, and truth in virtue,
I am affianc'd this man's wife, as strongly
As words could make up vows: and, my good lord
But Tuesday night last gone, in's garden-house,
He knew me as a wife. As this is true
Let me in safety raise me from my knees,
Or else for ever be confixed here,
A marble monument.

Ang. I did but smile till now:
Now, good my lord, give me the scope of justice;
My patience here is touch'd. I do perceive
These poor informal women are no more
But instruments of some more mightier member,
That sets them on. Let me have way, my lord,
To find this practice out.

Duke. Ay, with my heart;
And punish them [un]to your height of pleasure.—
Thou foolish friar, and thou pernicious woman,
Compact with her that's gone, think'st thou thy oaths,
Though they would swear down each particular saint,
Were testimonies against his worth and credit,
That's sealed in approbation?—You, Lord Escalus,
Sit with my cousin: lend him your kind pains
To find out this abuse, whence 'tis deriv'd.—
There is another friar that set them on:
Let him be sent for.

F. Peter. Would he were here, my lord; for he, indeed,
Hath set the women on to this complaint.
Your Provost knows the place where he abides,
And he may fetch him.

Duke. Go, do it instantly. — [*Exit* Provost.
And you, my noble and well-warranted cousin,
Whom it concerns to hear this matter forth,
Do with your injuries as seems you best,
In any chastisement: I, for a while,
Will leave you; but stir not you, till you have well
Determined upon these slanderers.

Escal. My lord, we'll do it throughly. — [*Exit* DUKE.] Signior Lucio, did not you say, you knew that Friar Lodowick to be a dishonest person?

Lucio. *Cucullus non facit monachum:* honest in nothing, but in his clothes; and one that hath spoke most villainous speeches of the Duke.

Escal. We shall entreat you to abide here till he come, and enforce them against him. We shall find this friar a notable fellow.

Lucio. As any in Vienna, on my word.

Escal. Call that same Isabel here once again: [*To an Attendant.*] I would speak with her. Pray you, my lord, give me leave to question; you shall see how I'll handle her.

Lucio. Not better than he, by her own report.

Escal. Say you?

Lucio. Marry, sir, I think if you handled her privately she would sooner confess: perchance, publicly she'll be asham'd.

Enter Officers, *with* ISABELLA, *the* DUKE, *in a Friar's habit, and* Provost.

Escal. I will go darkly to work with her.

Lucio. That's the way; for women are light at midnight.

Escal. Come on, mistress. [*To* ISABELLA.] Here's a gentlewoman denies all that you have said.

Lucio. My lord, here comes the rascal I spoke of; here, with the Provost.

Escal. In very good time: — speak not you to him, till we call upon you.

Lucio. Mum.

Escal. Come, sir. Did you set these women on to slander Lord Angelo? they have confess'd you did.

Duke. 'Tis false.

Escal. How! know you where you are?

Duke. Respect to your great place! and let the Devil
Be sometime honour'd for his burning throne. —
Where is the Duke? 'tis he should hear me speak.

Escal. The Duke's in us, and we will hear you speak:
Look you speak justly.

Duke. Boldly, at least. — But, O, poor souls!
Come you to seek the lamb here of the fox?
Good night to your redress. Is the Duke gone?
Then is your cause gone too. The Duke's unjust,
Thus to retort your manifest appeal,
And put your trial in the villain's mouth
Which here you come to accuse.

Lucio. This is the rascal: this is he I spoke of.

Escal. Why, thou unreverend and unhallow'd friar!
Is't not enough, thou hast suborn'd these women
To accuse this worthy man, but, in foul mouth,
And in the witness of his proper ear,
To call him villain? and then to glance from him
To th' Duke himself, to tax him with injustice?

Take him hence; to the rack with him: — We'll touze you
Joint by joint but we will know his purpose. —
What! unjust?

Duke. Be not so hot; the Duke dare
No more stretch this finger of mine than he
Dare rack his own: his subject am I not,
Nor here provincial. My business in this State
Made me a looker-on here in Vienna,
Where I have seen corruption boil and bubble
Till it o'er-run the stew: laws for all faults,
But faults so countenanc'd that the strong statutes
Stand, like the forfeits in a barber's shop,
As much in mock as mark.

Escal. Slander to the State! Away with him to prison.

Ang. What can you vouch against him, Signior Lucio?
Is this the man that you did tell us of?

Lucio. 'Tis he, my lord. — Come hither, goodman bald-pate: do you know me?

Duke. I remember you, sir, by the sound of your voice: I met you at the prison, in the absence of the Duke.

Lucio. O! did you so? And do you remember what you said of the Duke?

Duke. Most notedly, sir.

Lucio. Do you so, sir? And was the Duke a flesh-monger, a fool, and a coward, as you then reported him to be?

Duke. You must, sir, change persons with me, ere you make that my report: you, indeed, spoke so of him; and much more, much worse.

Lucio. O, thou damnable fellow! Did not I pluck thee by the nose, for thy speeches?

Duke. I protest, I love the Duke as I love myself.

Ang. Hark how the villain would glose now, after his treasonable abuses.

Escal. Such a fellow is not to be talk'd withal: — Away with him to prison. — Where is the Provost? — Away with him to prison. Lay bolts enough upon him; let him speak no more. — Away with those giglots too, and with the other confederate companion.

[*The* Provost *lays hand on the* DUKE.

Duke. Stay, sir; stay a while.

Ang. What! resists he? Help him, Lucio.

Lucio. Come, sir; come, sir; come, sir; foh! sir. Why, you bald-pated, lying rascal! you must be hooded, must you? Show your knave's visage with a pox to you! shew your sheep-biting face, and be hang'd an hour. Will't not off?

[*Pulls off the Friar's hood.*

Duke. Thou art the first knave, that e'er mad'st a duke. —
First, Provost, let me bail these gentle three. —
Sneak not away, sir; [*To* LUCIO.] for the Friar and you
Must have a word anon. — Lay hold on him.

Lucio. This may prove worse than hanging.

Duke. What you have spoke, I pardon; sit you down. [*To* ESCALUS.
We'll borrow place of him: — Sir, by your leave.

[*The* DUKE *takes* ANGELO'S *seat.*

Hast thou or word, or wit, or impudence,
That yet can do thee office? If thou hast,
Rely upon it till my tale be heard,
And hold no longer out.

Ang. O, my dread lord!
I should be guiltier than my guiltiness,
To think I can be undiscernible,

When I perceive your Grace, like power divine,
Hath look'd upon my passes: Then, good Prince,
No longer session hold upon my shame,
But let my trial be mine own confession:
Immediate sentence then, and sequent death,
Is all the grace I beg.

Duke. Come hither, Mariana.—
Say, wast thou e'er contracted to this woman?

Ang. I was, my lord.

Duke. Go take her hence, and marry her instantly.—
Do you the office, Friar; which consummate,
Return him here again.—Go with him, Provost.

[*Exeunt* ANGELO, MARIANA, Friar PETER, *and* Provost.

Escal. My lord, I am more amaz'd at his dishonour,
Than at the strangeness of it.

Duke. Come hither, Isabel.
Your Friar is now your Prince: as I was then
Advertising and holy to your business,
Not changing heart with habit, I am still
Attorney'd at your service.

Isab. O, give me pardon,
That I, your vassal, have employ'd and pain'd
Your unknown sovereignty!

Duke. You are pardon'd, Isabel:
And now, dear maid, be you as free to us.
Your brother's death, I know, sits at your heart;
And you may marvel why I obscur'd myself,
Labouring to save his life, and would not rather
Make rash remonstrance of my hidden power,
Than let him so be lost. O, most kind maid!
It was the swift celerity of his death,
Which I did think with slower foot came on,

That brain'd my purpose: but, peace be with him!
That life is better life, past fearing death,
Than that which lives to fear. Make it your comfort,
So happy is your brother.

Enter ANGELO, MARIANA, PETER, *and* Provost.

Isab. I do, my lord.

Duke. For this new-married man, approaching here,
Whose salt imagination yet hath wrong'd
Your well-defended honour, you must pardon
For Mariana's sake. But, as he adjudg'd your brother,
(Being criminal, in double violation
Of sacred chastity, and of promise-breach,
Thereon dependent, for your brother's life,)
The very mercy of the law cries out,
Most audible, even from his proper tongue,
'An Angelo for Claudio, death for death!'
Haste still pays haste, and leisure answers leisure,
Like doth quit like, and *Measure*, still, *for Measure.*
Then, Angelo, thy fault's thus manifested,
Which, though thou would'st deny, denies thee vantage.
We do condemn thee to the very block
Where Claudio stoop'd to death, and with like haste.—
Away with him.

Mari. O, my most gracious lord!
I hope you will not mock me with a husband.

Duke. It is your husband mock'd you with a husband.
Consenting to the safeguard of your honour,
I thought your marriage fit; else imputation,

For that he knew you, might reproach your life,
And choke your good to come. For his possessions,
Although by confiscation they are ours,
We do instate and widow you withal,
To buy you a better husband.

Mari. O, my dear lord!
I crave no other, nor no better man.

Duke. Never crave him: we are definitive.

Mari. Gentle my liege,— [*Kneeling.*

Duke. You do but lose your labour.
Away with him to death.—Now, sir, [*to* LUCIO.] to you.

Mari. O, my good lord!—Sweet Isabel, take my part:
Lend me your knees; and, all my life to come,
I'll lend you all my life to do you service.

Duke. Against all sense you do importune her:
Should she kneel down in mercy of this fact,
Her brother's ghost his paved bed would break,
And take her hence in horror.

Mari. Isabel,
Sweet Isabel, do yet but kneel by me:
Hold up your hands: say nothing; I'll speak all.
They say, best men are moulded out of faults,
And, for the most, become much more the better
For being a little bad: so may my husband.
O Isabel! will you not lend a knee?

Duke. He dies for Claudio's death.

Isab. Most bounteous sir, [*Kneeling.*
Look, if it please you, on this man condemn'd,
As if my brother liv'd. I partly think
A due sincerity govern'd his deeds
Till he did look on me: since it is so,

Let him not die. My brother had but justice,
In that he did the thing for which he di'd:
For Angelo,
His act did not o'ertake his bad intent;
And must be buried but as an intent
That perish'd by the way. Thoughts are no subjects —
Intents but merely thoughts.

Mari. Merely, my lord.

Duke. Your suit's unprofitable: stand up, I say. —
I have bethought me of another fault. —
Provost, how came it Claudio was beheaded
At an unusual hour?

Prov. It was commanded so.

Duke. Had you a special warrant for the deed?

Prov. No, my good lord; it was by private message.

Duke. For which I do discharge you of your office:
Give up your keys.

Prov. Pardon me, noble Lord:
I thought it was a fault, but knew it not,
Yet did repent me, after more advice;
For testimony whereof, one in the prison,
That should by private order else have di'd,
I have reserv'd alive.

Duke. What's he?

Prov. His name is Barnardine.

Duke. I would thou hadst done so by Claudio. —
Go, fetch him hither: let me look upon him.

[*Exit* Provost.

Escal. I am sorry one so learned and so wise
As you, Lord Angelo, have still appear'd,
Should slip so grossly, both in the heat of blood
And lack of temper'd judgment afterward.

Ang. I am sorry that such sorrow I procure;
And so deep sticks it in my penitent heart,
That I crave death more willingly than mercy:
'Tis my deserving, and I do entreat it.

Enter Provost, BARNARDINE, CLAUDIO, *and* JULIET.

Duke. Which is that Barnardine?
Prov. This, my lord.
Duke. There was a friar told me of this man.—
Sirrah, thou art said to have a stubborn soul,
That apprehends no farther than this world,
And squar'st thy life according. Thou'rt condemn'd;
But, for those earthly faults, I quit them all,
And pray thee, take this mercy to provide
For better times to come.—Friar, advise him:
I leave him to your hand.—What muffled fellow's that?
Prov. This is another prisoner that I sav'd,
That should have di'd when Claudio lost his head,
As like almost to Claudio as himself.
[*Unmuffles* CLAUDIO.
Duke. If he be like your brother, [*to* ISABELLA.] for his sake
Is he pardon'd; and for your lovely sake
Give me your hand, and say you will be mine:
He is my brother too.—But fitter time for that.
By this Lord Angelo perceives he's safe:
Methinks I see a quick'ning in his eye.—
Well, Angelo, your evil quits you well:
Look that you love your wife; her worth, worth yours.—
I find an apt remission in myself,
And yet here's one in place I cannot pardon.—
You, sirrah, [*to* LUCIO.] that knew me for a fool, a coward,

One all of luxury, an ass, a madman:
Wherein have I so deserved of you,
That you extol me thus?

Lucio. 'Faith, my lord, I spoke it but according to the trick. If you will hang me for it, you may; but I had rather it would please you, I might be whipp'd.

Duke. Whipp'd first, sir, and hang'd after.—
Proclaim it, Provost, round about the city,
If any woman's wrong'd by this lewd fellow,
(As I have heard him swear himself there's one
Whom he begot with child,) let her appear,
And he shall marry her: the nuptial finished,
Let him be whipp'd and hang'd.

Lucio. I beseech your Highness, do not marry me to a whore! Your Highness said even now I made you a duke: good my lord, do not recompense me in making me a cuckold.

Duke. Upon mine honour thou shalt marry her.
Thy slanders I forgive; and therewithal
Remit thy other forfeits.—Take him to prison,
And see our pleasure herein executed.

Lucio. Marrying a punk, my lord, is pressing to death, whipping, and hanging.

Duke. Slandering a Prince deserves it.—
She, Claudio, that you wrong'd, look you restore.—
Joy to you, Mariana!—love her, Angelo:
I have confess'd her, and I know her virtue.—
Thanks, good friend Escalus, for thy much goodness:
There's more behind that is more gratulate.
Thanks, Provost, for thy care, and secrecy;
We shall employ thee in a worthier place.—
Forgive him, Angelo, that brought you home

The head of Ragozine for Claudio's:
Th' offence pardons itself. — Dear Isabel,
I have a motion much imports your good;
Whereto if you'll a willing ear incline,
What's mine is yours, and what is yours is mine. —
So, bring us to our palace; where we'll show
What's yet behind that's meet you all should know.
[*Exeunt.*

NOTES ON MEASURE FOR MEASURE.

ACT FIRST:

Scene I.

p. 13. "Since I am *put* to know": — Since I am constrained to know — must needs know. So, in this play, Act III. Sc. 2: "I am made to understand:" also,

> "Though for possession put to try once more."
> *Paradise Lost*, IV. 942.

The expression can hardly need explanation or illustration.

> "—— then no more remains
> But that, to your sufficiency, — as your worth is able, —
> And let them work."

This is the original text, with the mere substitution of the dash, which we now use for the comma in *quasi* parenthetical passages; and it plainly means, — merely putting the words in their conversational order, and remembering "that," as a relative, to be the emphatic word; — "then, as your worth is able, no more remains to your sufficiency but that;" &c. A paraphrase will remove any difficulty which may yet possibly be found in the sentence: — "then, as your worth is able [i. e., your high character rendering you competent,] no more remains to your sufficiency [i. e., no more is wanting to complete your capacity for the fulfilment of your trust,] but that [i. e., that knowledge of government of which I have just spoken;] and let them [i. e. that knowledge and your worth] work [together]."

This passage has been thought very obscure by most editors and commentators, and by many has been pronounced corrupt; and it must be confessed that the latter supposition would be favored by the redundancy of the second line, were not the versification of this play so exceedingly irregular. But had it not been for confusing changes and comments, the supposed obscurity of the passage would doubtless have long since disappeared; and it would have been seen that the original folio, which has hitherto been departed from by all editors without exception, is correct in placing no point after "remains" and a comma after "that." For the phrase "no more remains to your sufficiency," as meaning 'no more is wanting to, or for, your completeness,' could not have presented the slightest difficulty to any intelligent person acquainted with the English idiom; and as to what the relative "that" refers, there can of course be no dispute.

Rowe, with whom the present editor was inclined to concur before he had carefully examined the original, read, —

"then no more remains:
Put that to your sufficiency," &c.

He was followed by Pope, Theobald, and Warburton. But Theobald thought that a line had been omitted, and proposed to complete the sense, thus: —

"then no more remains
But that to your sufficiency *you add*
Due diligency, as your worth is able," &c.

Hanmer attempted to do the same, in this manner, in his text: —

"then no more remains
But that to your sufficiency *you join*
A will to serve us, as your worth," &c.

Johnson restored "But" of the original, for Rowe's "*Put*," but left his mischief-making colon; and, still thinking the passage corrupt, "suspected" that Shakespeare wrote,

"then no more remains
But that to your sufficien*cies* your worth is *abled*," &c.

Capell did not change the words of the original, but helped to fix the prevailing misconception, by removing the comma after "that" and placing one after "remains." In the *Variorum* Edition (Boswell's *Malone*, 21 vols., 1821,) the original text is given, but in seeming despair, as it is left to be obscured for the reader by the comments *variorum*, — the decision of Malone, Steevens, and Tyrwhitt, that two half lines are lost, being added to the conjectures already enumerated. Mr. Singer reads, "But *thereto* your sufficiency;" Mr. Halliwell, on the authority of an old MS. note, "But *task* to your suffici*ence;*" and various other futile attempts, which need not be particularly referred to, have been made, to amend or explain what, after all, needs no emendation, and little, if any, explanation.

p. 13. "—— the *terms:*" — The "terms for common justice" were the forms and technical phrases of the law. Shakespeare may possibly have had the *Termes de la Ley*, written in Henry VIII.'s time, in his mind, as Blackstone suggests; but that is a mere book of definitions, 438 in number, in English and that distracting hodgepodge, Law French.

p. 14. "There is a kind of character in thy life,
That, to th' observer, doth thy history
Fully unfold."

Notes incomprehensibly from the purpose having been written upon this simple passage by such men as Johnson, Steevens, Mason, &c., one may be pardoned for pointing out that the *Duke* merely says to *Angelo*, 'the character of your present life shows what your past life must have been.'

"—— as to waste
Thyself upon thy virtues, *they* on thee."

This is the original text, which has been hitherto changed by reading "*them* on thee." But the original is an ellipsis for "they [to waste themselves] on thee." The passage is far from being strictly grammatical.

" "—— *nor* Nature *never* lends": — Shakespeare very frequently uses two negatives with the force of one, in spite of the grammatical laws which prevailed no less in his day than in ours; as we learn, for instance, from Sidney's Sonnet upon his mistress saying "No, no," to him.

"But Grammars force with sweet success confirm,
For Grammar sayes (O, this dear *Stella* say!)
For Grammar sayes (to Grammar who sayes nay?)
That in one speech two Negatives affirm."

Astrophel and Stella, 63.

Was Shakespeare consciously following classical precedent?

" "Hold therefore, Angelo, [our place and power:]"

The original has only "Hold, therefore, Angelo:" the efforts to explain which imperfect line have been equally various and futile. Johnson would have it mean 'Continue to be *Angelo*,' an exegesis too absurd to merit further attention. Hanmer and Steevens suppose the *Duke* to tell *Angelo* to take hold of his commission, the former introducing a corresponding stage direction: a conjecture how ludicrous, let every reader determine for himself by imagining the *Duke* to extend a roll of parchment to *Angelo*, crying 'Hold!' — for these plays were written to be played. Tyrwhitt thinks that the *Duke* addresses 'Hold' to himself, and that there should be a full point after 'therefore,' and none after '*Angelo*;' but it will be generally admitted that there is no occasion for what the elder *Mr. Weller* would call such a very "sudden pull up" on the *Duke's* part. Mr. Halliwell would sustain Hanmer and Steevens by quoting *Falstaff's* "Hold, sirrah," when he gives his letters to

Robin (*Merry Wives of Windsor*, Act I. Sc. 3.) But *Falstaff* uses the word there merely as an equivalent to 'stay,' as not only appears by the context, but by the corresponding line in the quarto, where he says, "Stay, sirrah." This intransitive sense (if we except that of 'keep your appointment,' which is hardly an exception) being the only one which the word ever has when used in the imperative mood absolutely and alone, the words to which "Hold" refers have, without a doubt, been lost, as we know is the case with others in both the first and second folios. The sense which those words conveyed is shown by the context; but by the *Duke's* remark to *Friar Thomas*, when, in the next Scene but one, he speaks of the very act performed in this, we may be said to learn what they actually were, from Shakespeare himself. The *Duke* says,

"I have deliver'd to Lord Angelo
(A man of stricture and firm abstinence)
My absolute *power and place* here in Vienna."

It has been necessary in several instances for previous editors to supply lost words, which have been received into the text; but it is submitted that there was never greater need of such emendation than the present, and that there could not be better warrant for the words supplied than there is for those which appear within brackets in the present text.

p. 15. "—— shall im*por*tune": — In this line "importune," like "advertise" a little before, and "contract" shortly after, is accented on the second syllable. It would be tedious and superfluous to point out all similar licenses and variations from modern custom: the reader's ear will detect, and his judgment account for or excuse, them.

Scene II.

p. 17. "—— there went but a pair of shears between us": — i. e., we were both of a piece.

" "—— as be *pil'd*, as thou art *pil'd*, for a *French* velvet": — This is a quibbling allusion to the pile of velvet and losing the hair, or being pil'd, — one of the results of what was in Shakespeare's day called 'the French disease.'

" "I have purchas'd as many diseases," &c.: — This appears as part of *Lucio's* speech in the original, owing to the neglect of the compositor, or perhaps the author or copyist, to prefix the proper name to it. The subsequent dialogue shows plainly both that it does not belong to *Lucio* and that it does belong to the 1*st Gentleman*.

" "—— three thousand *dolours*": — Thus the original,

which it has been the practice to change to '*dollars*,' and thus make explanation necessary for an otherwise patent pun.

p. 17. "A *French crown* more": — Another of those allusions so common with Shakespeare and all our old dramatists, to the effect of that 'French disease' which was yet supposed to have been brought to Europe from the Indians of America.

p. 18. "—— the *sweat*": — The sweating sickness, — a pestilence which prevailed about the time when this play was written.

p. 19. "All houses *in the suburbs*": — So, "trust that little stock of money thou hast gathered to set up a house of Carnality ith' suburbs." *The Noble Stranger*. 1640. I. 2.

"—— *Thomas* Tapster": — A tapster was called 'Thomas,' as an ostler was called 'John.'

Scene III.

p. 20. There is, strictly speaking, no new Scene here. One party merely goes off as the other comes on, which is plain enough from the *Clown's* last speech. But as the division is made in the original and has been preserved for nearly two hundred and fifty years, and as the stage is left vacant and an entirely new interest supervenes, it is better that no change should be made.

"—— the *morality* of imprisonment": — The original has "mor*tal*ity" by a palpable misprint which was corrected by Davenant, in his *Law for Lovers*, — an adaptation of this play.

p. 21. "—— the *denunciation* lack": — Mr. Collier's folio of 1632 substitutes 'pronunciation,' which, though seeming plausible at first, cannot be received, and shows the incompetence and the want of authority of the corrector, and, perhaps, the lateness of his labors. Minsheu, 1617, defines "To denounce *or declare*, — *indicere, con-dicere, indicare*. Cooper, 1578, has "*Denuntiare*, — to shew or tell to another, to give knowledge, to signifie, to denounce," &c. Littleton gives the same definition. The word seems to have been used rather in the sense of 'declaring beforehand,' which is well suited to this place.

"—— for *preservation* of a dower": — The original has *propogation*, which has hitherto been naturally, but too readily, assumed to be 'propagation' with the slight misprint of a letter. But it is impossible to find any appropriate signification for that word in this place. It means 'increasing,' and nothing more or less — its sense of 'begetting,' even, being entirely derivative or accidental, because increase is a concomitant of begetting. But in no way would the secrecy of *Claudio* and *Juliet* increase her dower which was "remaining in the coffer of her friends;" and the intention was, as *Claudio* says, only to keep it there, or to preserve it for her, "until time had made them for," instead of against the lovers. These considerations dispose of Malone's suggestion, "*prorogation*," and the "*procuration*" proposed by Jackson, and found in Mr. Collier's folio of 1632. There were few easier misprints than *propogation* for *preservation* in Shakespeare's time; for the *e* and the *o* were so much alike that they could hardly be distinguished, (see, for instance, 'blooding' or 'bleeding' — nobody can tell which — in the facsimile of a part of Mr. Collier's folio of 1632, published in his *Notes and Emendations*, &c.,) and the *p* and the long *s* might be almost as easily mistaken for each other. Further confirmation of this reading is to be found in the word 'assurance,' substituted for it by Davenant. The object sought was, the *safety* of the dower till time had worked a favorable change of opinion in those who had it in their possession.

p. 22. "—— receive her *approbation*": — i. e., enter upon her probationary term — her noviciate.

" "—— a *prone* and speechless dialect": — Johnson took "prone" in its sense of 'prompt,' 'quick,' 'ready;' but the suggestion of Steevens, that it has its almost primitive meaning 'humble,' is far happier.

" "—— the enjoying of thy life, *which* I would be sorry," &c.: — The original has 'who,' which Collier and Knight, as well as most of the earlier editors, retain; but it is plainly a misprint for 'which.' Shakespeare would not write "the like *which*" and "the life *who*" in the same sentence.

" "—— a game of *tick-tack*": — This was played with the backgammon board, and was sometimes called 'trick-track.' As to his meaning, *Lucio* is his own commentator.

Scene IV.

p. 23. "—— to headstrong *steeds*": — The original has '*weeds*,' which, although retained by Mr. Collier, it were a waste of words to show must be a misprint for 'steeds,' to which it was changed by Theobald. The change of '*slip*' of the original to *sleep* in the next line, first made by Davenant, is of the same nature.

" "[Becomes] more mocked," &c.: — The word in brackets, which, or a not easily discovered equivalent, is required by the sense, is not in the original, and was first supplied by Davenant.

p. 24. "And yet my nature never in the *fight*
To do *in* slander."

This is the original reading, which the preceding line both explains and shows to be correct; but Hanmer changed "fight" to '*sight*' and "in" to '*it*.' "To do in slander" is, of course, 'to perform this office in the face of slander.'

Scene V.

p. 25. "Sir, make me not your story": — Malone most needlessly reads, "*mock* me not: — your story," Davenant, "make me not your *scorn*." But this use of 'me' is the commonest of all archaisms. For instance, "— he steps me to her trencher and steals her capon's leg," (*Two Gentlemen of Verona*, Act IV. Sc. 4;) "A good sherris sack hath a two-fold operation in it: it ascends me into the brain, dries me there all the foolish, and dull and crudy vapours," &c. (*Henry IV.* Part 2, Act IV. Sc. 3.)

p. 26. "That from the *seedness*": — Mr. Verplanck, with much reason, suggests that this word is a misprint for '*seeding*;' but although unique in this place, it has a plain and appropriate meaning, and must not be disturbed.

" "His *givings*-out": — In the original the word is "*giving*," the *s* having accidentally dropped. But Mr. Collier strangely retains this word, and changes "were" to '*was*.'

p. 27. "Of business": — In the folio these words are printed at the end of the preceding line, — a palpable error, which destroys the rhythm by two superfluous feet. The arrangement of the original is here very irregular.

ACT SECOND.

Scene I.

p. 28. "—— the resolute acting of *your* blood": — The original has "*our* blood," — a palpable misprint.

" "—— *where* now you censure him": — The folio has "*which* now," &c., and the editors have retained it, some adding and some understanding the 'for,' which both Malone and Steevens pronounced to be necessary to the sense at the end of the line. But this does not avoid the difficulty. *Angelo* did not censure *Claudio* *for* a point: that is not English, and never was. He might censure him *on* a point; but there has been plainly a misprint, easily made, of 'which' for 'where.'

" "—— what knows the law": — The original has,

"what *knowes* the *Lawes;*" and "To justice," belonging to this line, to which it was restored by Steevens, appears at the end of the previous line.

p. 29. "*For* I have had:" — because I have had, or, on account of my having. See Note on "for catching cold." *Two Gentlemen of Verona*, Act I. Sc. 2.

" "Some run from *brakes* of *vice*": — In the original, "brakes of *Ice*." As Mr. Dyce has remarked upon another passage, the old printers were very apt to blunder on words beginning with *v;* and as in this case a capital would be used, the mistake would be the easier. Rowe made the correction. "Brake" has its common meaning, 'a thicket,' in contradistinction to the solitary fault spoken of in the next line; and "answer" has the equally common sense of 'answer for.' Steevens, however, understood "brake" to mean an instrument of torture, a signification which it undoubtedly had; in which case "and answer none" would mean that the torture failed to elicit any reply. But this is from the purpose: *Escalus* is contrasting the impunity of some great criminals with the rigid accountability to which petty offenders are held. Somebody proposed to read "*breaks* of *ice*"!

p. 30. "—— a tapster, sir — *parcel* bawd": — part tapster, part bawd: 'parcel' being from *pars*.

" "—— a *hot-house*": — a *bagnio*, which used generally to be about the same thing as the sort of house actually kept by the *Clown's* mistress.

p. 31. "Come *we* to what was done": — The folio has "Come *me*," which has been hitherto retained and even quoted as an instance of that use of the pronoun, noticed above in *Isabella's* "make me" and *Falstaff's* "ascends me." But 'come' was not so used, and could not be: "comes me the Prince and Claudio," in *Much Ado about Nothing*, Act I. Sc. 3, is not at all a parallel case. *Escalus* means, 'Let us come to what was done,' 'Let us get at what was done.'

p. 32. "—— in a *lower* chair": — an easy chair.

" "—— the *Bunch of Grapes*": — In Shakespeare's time the larger rooms of inns were named.

p. 33. "Justice, or Iniquity": — referring to allegorical characters commonly found in the old Mysteries and Moralities.

p. 34. "—— no more of it, *Master* Froth. . . . Come you hither to me, *Mr.* Tapster": — Upon Mr. Collier's supposition that in Act IV. Sc. 3, Shakespeare makes the *Clown* distinguish between those who had and those who had not the rank of gentlemen, by calling the first 'Mr.' and the last 'Master,' Mr. Dyce well remarks that "no such distinction was ever dreamed of by Shakespeare," and that "*Mr.* and *Master* were put indiscriminately by transcribers and printers." But Mr. Collier's error was even greater than Mr. Dyce shows it to be; for 'Mr.' — pronounced *Mister* — was at first a degradation of the more formal 'Master,' as 'Mrs.' — pronounced *Missis* — was of 'Mistress;' and neither was used in addressing persons 'of worship' until long after they had been applied to common folk. At last, however, (with 'Miss,' which originally had a very derogatory meaning,) they were raised to their present position. Therefore, although the abbreviated form was used in writing, even as the title of persons of consideration, the distinction of the original text between Master *Froth* and Mister *Tapster* is worthy of respect.

p. 34. "—— your bum is the greatest thing about you": — This refers to the fashion of stuffing out the dress around and behind the hips with horse hair or some like material, which prevailed in the time of Elizabeth and the early years of James: — a fashion too fair-ly and openly followed in our own days to need further explanation.

p. 35. "—— after three pence a *day*": — The original has "a *bay*," by the most palpable and easiest of misprints. The fact that the distance between certain beams in a house was called 'a bay' has caused that word to be retained in most, if not all, editions. But this is one of those instances in which the meaning of the word in the original excludes it from the text, as inconsistent both with the context and the character of the person who uses it. And suppose we admit 'bay': — three pence a bay for how long? The *Clown* means to say he could get houses very cheap; and three pence a day would give us the "fairest house in Vienna" at £4 11*s.* 3*d.*, or, at the present value of money, about one hundred and forty dollars a year. 'Day,' which had been suggested by Mr. Halliwell and by the present editor, was found in Mr. Collier's folio of 1632.

p. 36. "—— by *your* readiness in the office": — The original has, "by *the* readiness," &c.: the result of mistaking y^r for y^e.

SCENE II.

p. 37. "He hath *offended but as* in a dream": — The original has "He hath *but as offended*," &c., — a transposition fatal to the sense of the line, but which has hitherto remained uncorrected.

p. 40. "If [but] the first": — The word in brackets is not in the original; and, as one is necessary, Pope read, "If the first *man*," and was followed by Theobald, Malone, and others. This reading, however, has a prosaic particularity; which is also in a measure true of that adopted by Capell and Tyrwhitt — "If *he*, the first." Angelo means to say that if but the first had been punished, the many would have been deterred.

p. 41. "But *ere* they live": — The original has "*here*," which Malone changed to '*where*,' and this is supported by Mr. Dyce. Hanmer first read 'ere,' which is the only word applicable to evils "in progress to be hatched and born." Mr. Collier retained "here"! but the corrector of his folio of 1632 changed it to 'ere.'

p. 42. "—— fond *shekels*": — The word is spelled "*sickles*" in the original — a not uncommon orthography of old.

p. 43. "Where *prayers cross*": — Were it not that every editor, from Johnson down, had found obscurity in this expression, and made it more obscure by his explanation, it would have been passed here without comment. *Angelo*, distracted between his passion and his sense of duty, is in that way of temptation in which his prayers for preservation from wrong-doing cross those which he utters for the enjoyment of *Isabella*. If explanation be needed, Shakespeare himself puts it into *Angelo's* mouth in the first lines of the next Scene but one: —

"When I would pray and think, I think and pray
To several subjects: Heaven hath my empty words,
Whilst my invention, hearing not my tongue,
Anchors on Isabel," &c.

Scene III.

p. 44. "—— in the *flames* of her own youth": — The original has "*flaws*." The error was corrected by Davenant.

p. 45. "—— but *lest* you do repent": — The folio has "*least*;" but the two words used to be pronounced, and so were often written, alike. There are yet people in New England — not ignorant persons — who pronounce 'lest' thus.

" "—— we would not *spare* Heaven": — we would not spare Heaven our sins. Mr. Collier's folio of 1632 has "*serve* Heaven."

" "O, injurious *law*": — The original has "*love*," which is undeniably wrong, as Monck Mason pointed out, though not clearly. Neither her love nor its consequences had any effect upon her life; but the law in question, declaring, as we learn in the old tale on which the play is founded, that the man who broke it "should lose his head, and the woman offender should ever after be infamously noted," thus *did* respite her "a life whose very comfort" was "a dying misery." Hanmer made the slight though important correction; but most modern editors, including Mr. Collier and Mr. Knight, retain the senseless 'love.'

Scene IV.

p. 46. "Whilst my *invention*":—Warburton was more than probably right in reading '*intention*.' But as 'invention' is used by Shakespeare in other places for 'imagination,' which gives a consistent sense, the original word must stand.

p. 46. "Grown *sear'd* and tedious":—Most copies of the first folio have "*feard;*" but the Earl of Ellesmere's, as Mr. Collier tells us, has *seard*, "as if the letter *s* had been substituted for *f* as the sheet was going through the press." Warburton proposed the obvious correction, which needs no authority to sustain it.

" "Blood, thou art blood":—The pause after the exclamation fills out the line with a rhetorical effect, which, with a finer sense, Pope destroyed, by reading "thou art *but* blood," and Malone, by reading "thou *still* art blood."

" "The *general*":—The general public. So in *Hamlet*, (Act II. Sc. 2,) "'twas caviare to the general."

p. 48. "Let *me* be ignorant":—The first folio omits "me," which is supplied in the second.

" "Admit no other way to save his life,
(As I subscribe not that, nor any other,)
But—in the loss of question—that you," &c.

There is a certain obscurity in this sentence, owing partly to its interwoven parentheses, and partly to the obsolete sense in which "question" is used. "In the loss of question" means 'in the very waste of words,' 'supposing an unsupposable case,' or, as Steevens says, 'in idle supposition.' 'Question' is continually used by Shakespeare in the sense of 'discussion.' In the folio the parenthesis begins at "As" and extends to "question," inclusively, thus making confusion. For, excluding all parenthetical matter, the sentence is, "Admit no other way to save his life, but that you, his sister, finding," &c.; and the "but" must not be shut out of the direct construction. Hanmer saw this, and so enclosed "in the loss of question" within marks of parenthesis, by itself. But in his day our useful, but too much and too vaguely used, dash had not taken its present place in punctuation. All of this speech is in a manner parenthetical, except the first and last lines. The reader will find it analyzed with particularity in *Shakespeare's Scholar*, where, however, a needless change of a word in the text is proposed. Dr. Johnson proposed to read "*toss* of question"!

p. 49. "Of the all-*holding* law":—The folio has "all-*building*," by an evident typographical error, which Rowe corrected. The generally received reading, "all-*binding*," is attributed by Johnson, Steevens, Knight, and Collier to Theobald; but it is to be found neither in his edition of 1733 nor in that of 1740, and he died in 1744. It first appears in Johnson's edition, 1765. Theobald would have been obliged to set at naught his own admirable canon of conjectural criticism in substituting 'all-binding' for 'all-holding,' which is its equivalent in sense and much nearer to the form of the word in the original.

p. 49. "—— *I've* been sick for":—The folio has "That longing *have* been sick for," omitting the pronoun, which some editors have merely inserted. But "have" was a misprint, and a very easy one, for "I've."

" "*Ignomy* in ransom":—An old form of 'ignominy,' which occurs again in *Troilus and Cressida*, Act. V. Sc. 3.

" "Else let my brother die,
If not a feodary but only he
Owe and succeed thy weakness."

This speech is found somewhat obscure, but only on account of the obsolete or peculiar sense in which the three important words in it are used. "Feodary" means 'an associate,' 'a fellow': as in *Cymbeline*, Act III. Sc. 2:—

"Senseless bauble,
Art thou a feodary for this act?" &c.

"Owe" means 'to possess,' as is seen by scores of instances in these plays; and "succeed" means 'to follow,' 'to take after,' as in *All's Well That Ends Well*, Act I. Sc. 1:—

"Be thou blest, Bertram, and succeed thy father
In manners, as in shape."

Isabella's reply is therefore—in the clumsiness of paraphrase—'Otherwise let my brother die, if no companion but he alone be possessed of and take after thy weakness.'

ACT THIRD.

Scene I.

p. 52. "The miserable have," &c.:—The metrical arrangement of this passage is, with a slight variation, that of the original, which was needlessly much changed by Steevens, who has hitherto been inconsiderately followed, except by Knight and Singer.

p. 52. " Servile to all the skyey *influences*
That *dost* this habitation where thou keep'st
Hourly afflict."

This is the original text, which Hanmer changed by reading " that *do*." Upon this emendation, Porson is represented in the Variorum edition as remarking, " The construction is not 'the skiey influences that do,' but 'a breath thou art that dost,' &c. If 'Servile thou art to all the skiey influences' be enclosed in a parenthesis, all the difficulty will vanish." It is not surprising that this suggestion has since been followed; for a critical decision by Porson is to be received with as much deference as is due to one in morals by Dr. Johnson. But still it must be remarked that this construction would, in the words of the text, make the breath hourly afflict its habitation, the body, — an absurd result of his suggestion, which, of course, entirely escaped the attention of Porson. Plainly it is "all the skyey influences" that afflict the body. Yet Hanmer's change is inadmissible; for such disagreements of verbs with nominatives are not uncommon in Shakespeare's writings and those of his contemporaries. It is more than probable, too, that he wrote "influ*ence*," both here and in *The Winter's Tale*, Act I. Sc. 2, as the rhythm in both instances would seem to require. For 'influence' in Shakespeare's time was a word without a plural, and was used, especially when applied to the heavenly bodies, (to which service it was then almost set apart, — see Cotgrave's *Dictionary*, also Richardson's,) in its radical sense of 'in-flowing,' and then in the singular form, even when all those bodies are spoken of. See Milton, who frequently uses the word, but never the plural.

" And happie Constellations on that houre
Shed their selectest influence." *Par. Lost*, VIII. 512.

" and taught the fixt [i. e. stars]
Their influence malignant when to shed." *Ib.* X. 663.

" Unmuffle ye faint stars, and thou fair Moon
. . . . .
Or if your influence be quite damm'd up
With black usurping mists." *Comus*, 330, 335.

" —— thou art *Death's Fool*": — The reference here, as Steevens and Douce have heretofore pointed out, is to the introduction of Death and a Fool in the rude old plays and dumb shows; — the sport being made by Death's endeavors to surprise the Merry Andrew and the finally unsuccessful efforts of the latter to elude them.

p. 53. "What *hoa!*" — In this form the exclamation constantly appears in the original, and also with sufficiently rare exceptions in contemporary authors to show that 'ho,' to which it is universally changed by modern editors, although it gives the sense, does not represent the sound of the word as used between two hundred and fifty and three hundred years ago.

" "Bring *me* to hear *them* speak": — The folio has "Bring *them* to hear *me* speak." Strangely enough, it was left for Steevens to make the required transposition of the pronouns.

p. 54. "—— most good, most good indeed": — The second "most good" has been generally omitted; and it is more than possible that the repetition is due to copyist or compositor. But the emphasis is in place, and Alexandrines are too common in this play to make the redundant foot a sufficient reason for the omission of the words.

" "—— an everlasting *leiger*": — A leiger was a resident ambassador.

" "*Though* all the world's vastidity": — The folio has "*through.*"

p. 55. "The *priestly* Angelo?" — The folio has "*prenzie*" both here and three lines below, — a combination of letters, but not a word. It was changed in the second folio to '*princely*,' a word singularly out of relation to the context, and deserving of no particular attention because it is in that edition. Tieck conjectured that '*precise*' might be the word; and in spite of its destruction of the rhythm of two lines and of its meagre sense, it has been adopted by Knight and Hudson. Mr. Singer reads '*primzie*,' which he says is used by Burns for 'formal,' 'demure,' and quotes an old proverb, 'a primzie damsel makes a laidlie dame.' But Shakespeare was not writing Scotch saws. Is it not plain from *Isabella's* phrases in her previous speech, "this *outward sainted* deputy" who "is yet *a devil*," that priestly guards, i. e., priestly ornaments or facings, were the marks of the livery with which she says Hell invests such as he? Pollok's description of a hypocrite, as

"one who stole the livery of Heaven
To serve the Devil in,"

is the very converse, the counter-proof, of *Isabella's* thought. Warburton first suggested 'priestly,' and it was discovered in Mr. Collier's folio of 1632.

p. 56. "—— the *delighted* spirit": — The obvious sense of this much discussed expression is the proper one. *Claudio* says that the body which is sensible and warm is to become a clod, and that the spirit which is delighted [i. e., enjoys what John Bunyan calls the delight of life] is to suffer the torment of fire or ice, or imprisonment in the winds. Warburton first made the passage the subject of comment, and gave an explanation somewhat like this. Hanmer read '*dilated;*' Johnson proposed '*delinquent,*' and approved '*benighted.*'

p. 56. "—— age, ache, *penury*": — The first folio has "*perjury,*" which was corrected in the second.

" "—— slip of *wilderness*": — a wild slip, not from the true stock: often so used by Shakespeare's contemporaries and immediate successors.

p. 59. "—— was affianced to her *by* oath": — The first folio omits "by," which was supplied in the second.

" "—— her *combinate* husband" — contracted husband. So in Act IV. Sc. 3, "I am combined by a sacred vow."

p. 60. "—— the corrupt deputy *foiled*": — The first folio has "*ſcaled,*" spelled of course with a long *s*, — a very easy misprint. This word has been hitherto retained: Warburton supposed it to mean 'weighed;' but *Angelo* had been already weighed and found wanting, and the *Duke's* proposition involved no further test: others are driven to the fish-market for a definition even less disgusting than ridiculous. The only object of the Friar-*Duke*, as far as *Isabella*, *Claudio*, and *Mariana* were concerned, was to *foil* the corrupt Deputy.

" "—— the *Moated Grange*": — A grange was originally a farm house attached to a monastery: this one was, or had been, attached to that of St. Luke, mentioned just before by the *Duke*. The word finally came to be applied to a country house less pretentious than a Hall, and more so than a cottage.

Scene II.

p. 61. "The Street before the Prison." No change of Scene is indicated in the folio, but *Elbow* and the rest join the *Duke*; — an arrangement plainly the result of the want of scenery on Shakespeare's stage.

" "—— brown and white *bastard*": — a kind of sweet wine, made of raisins.

" "—— good *brother father*": — *Elbow* calls the *Duke* 'father brother (*frère*), and the *Duke* in return calls him 'brother father.'

p. 61. "—— I eat, *array* myself": — The folio has "*away* myself," which to a London exquisite would be hardly even a misprint.

p. 62. "[Free] from our faults, as *from faults* seeming free!"
In the original folio this line is printed without the first word, without an initial capital, and with a transposition, thus: —

"from our faults as *faults from* seeming free."

"*Free*," demanded both by sense and rhythm, was supplied in the second folio; but the other equally needed emendation has not hitherto been made. The *Duke* speaks not of faults, but of men. *Elbow's* eulogy of "the precise Angelo" causes his better informed hearer to wish that all men were as free from faults as some seem to be free from them. The line evidently broke down, as the printers say, and in attempting to set it up again, two words were transposed as well as one omitted.

" "—— extracting *it* clutch'd?" — The folio omits "it." It can hardly be necessary to point out that *Lucio* asks the bawd if there are any women to be had for money.

" "What say'st thou, *Trot?*" — Gray suggested "What say'st thou *to't?*" and Collier, "What say'st thou *troth?*" But the word in the original begins with a capital; and there surely could be no name given to a Bawd's assistant more appropriate than Trot.

" "—— she is herself *in the tub*": — The allusion is to the powdering tub in which beef was powdered, i. e. salted, in order to preserve it from corruption.

p. 64. "—— he is a motion *un*generative": — The original has, "a motion *gen*erative." Theobald made the change, the necessity of which will be apparent to any one who considers *Angelo's* character and what *Lucio* has just said and soon after says of him. Yet Steevens, Knight, and Collier retain 'generative,' which the former explains as 'a masculine puppet.'

p. 65. "—— a ducat in her *clack-dish*": — Beggars used to have a dish for the receipt of alms with a hinged cover which they clacked to attract attention. It is almost needless to say that *Lucio* makes a very poor pun for the sake of a very indecent jest.

" "—— an *inward* of his": — an intimate.

" "—— with *dearer* love": — The folio has "*deare*," the *r* having dropped out.

p. 66. "—— would eat *mutton* on Fridays": — *Lucio's* charge of the violation of a fast day involves also an innuendo, from the application of 'mutton' to prostitutes.

p. 68. "—— and it is as dangerous," &c.: — The folio has "and *as* it is as dangerous," the sentence nevertheless being closed at "undertaking" with a full point, and the next word beginning with a capital. Mr. Collier retained the 'as' and made one sentence of the two, to which the objection is, not only that it is not logical, as Mr. Knight says, but that a semblance of logic is not in place. The *Duke* himself calls what he says a "riddle," i. e., a paradox.

"You have paid the Heavens your function": — Mr. Collier's folio of 1632 has, "You have paid the Heavens *the due of* your function," the corrector having failed to see that 'to pay a function' and 'to discharge a duty' are synonymous.

p. 69. "He, who the sword," &c.: — I more than doubt that this and the following lines are Shakespeare's; and, briefly, for these reasons. — They are not interwoven with the Scene or evolved from it, but appended to it, 'tacked on' it: — they are entirely superfluous, having no dramatic purpose, and uttering no moral truth that has not had infinitely better utterance before; and, so, being sheer surplusage, like all surplusage, might be stricken out with advantage: — their rhythmical expression is entirely inconsistent with their sentiment and with the diction of the serious parts of this play; it was not in Shakespeare to stop the *Duke* and set him off in this octosyllabic canter upon the same road over which he had paced before with such severe and stately dignity: — the lines are a mere succession of couplets, each containing a perfect if not an isolated thought, which is not Shakespeare's manner under any circumstances, and above all in such a soliloquy as the *Duke's*; "*non color, non vultus.*" If we will, we must believe that this soliloquy was written by Shakespeare after those in *Hamlet*. Let who will believe it! — I am quite sure that Shakespeare closed the Act with the *Duke's* "Peace be with you!" and that these lines were added by some one of the versifiers that it was common to have about theatres, and often among the actors, in those days, and one who wrote in the old style. The lines may have been added with Shakespeare's consent; for gentle Will had the kindest heart in the world; and while working, himself, up to the highest requirements of his art, was well content, so long as the audience was pleased and the theatre prosperous, to do any thing to serve or gratify a friend; and the play not having been published until twenty years after it was written, the circumstance of the introduction of such a speech would more than probably be forgotten by Heminge and Condell, even if they thought of the subject. But as this is merely an opinion, unsupported by any authority, no marks implying doubt of the authenticity of the speech are allowed to appear in the text.

p. 69. "Grace to stand, and virtue go;"

Various and futile have been the attempts to make better English of this line without rewriting it: — the reason being that the fault is not in the printer but the author. Coleridge and Mr. Collier's folio of 1632 have suggested,

"Grace to stand, *virtue to* go;"

" "How may likeness *wade* in crimes."

The folio has "*made*." Malone suggested the word in the text, which removes all the "great obscurity" which commentators have found in this passage, except that resulting from the writer's own confused notion of what he wanted to say. "Likeness" has been taken to mean 'comeliness.' Mr. Collier's folio has "Masking practice" in the next line: Malone read "*Mocking* practice;" and various other ineffectual and supererogatory labor has been expended upon the passage.

ACT FOURTH.

Scene I.

p. 70. "*Take, O! take those lips away.*"

This most exquisite of love songs reappears in Beaumont and Fletcher's *Bloody Brother*, first published surreptitiously at London, 1639, an authorized edition having appeared at Oxford, 1640. In the latter play this stanza is accompanied by the following: —

"Hide, oh, hide those hills of snow
Which thy frozen bosom bears,
On whose tops the pinks that grow
Are of those that April wears;
But first set my poor heart free,
Bound in those icy chains by thee."

Both stanzas were published as Shakespeare's in the spurious edition of his Poems, London, 1640, and, from that time to the present, both have been attributed to him, except by some of the critics and commentators who were in doubt to whom to assign them. But this stanza alone is Shakespeare's; the other, almost surely, Fletcher's. The two stanzas in fact will not make one song, except at great violence to both the form and spirit of the first. For that is written so that the music shall repeat the last three syllables of each of the last two lines, which is impossible with the other: they can both be sung to the same music only by suppressing the beautiful and touching repetition in the first: and this was done when it was introduced in *The Bloody Brother*. Besides, the stanza added in that play is palpably addressed to a woman, while this is just as certainly and as clearly, though not just as palpably, addressed to a man. See *Shakespeare's Scholar*, where this is shown and the subject examined in detail. The command to the *Boy*, to break off his song, is but a dramatic contrivance to produce the effect of an intrusion upon *Mariana's* solitude.

p. 71. "—— *planched* gate": — a planked gate. The French *plancher* with the *ch* hard.

" "There have I made my promise," &c.: — These lines are prose, although printed as verse in the folio. By no efforts have they been made to assume more than the mere form of verse. The folio has,

"There have I made my promise, upon the
Heavy middle of the night to call upon him."

Capell and Malone make this bold transposition: —

"There have I made my promise *to call on him*
Upon the heavy middle of the night."

Mr. Collier gives,

"There have I made my promise upon the heavy
Middle of the night to call upon him."

No one will regret such verse; and we have many instances of the first part of a speech in verse with the last in prose; of which, indeed, in the third speech of the *Duke* above, there is one at hand.

p. 73 "—— our *tilth's* to sow": — The folio has "*tithe's*," a typographical error which was corrected by Warburton and in Mr. Collier's folio of 1632.

Scene II.

p. 76. "—— were he *meal'd*": — This word is taken by Johnson to mean 'sprinkled,' as meat is, with the dredging box; Blackstone derives it from '*mesler*,' 'to mingle,' which is better; but there is probably a misprint, though for what, I cannot conjecture.

" "—— th' *unlisting* postern": — the unregarding postern. The folio has "*vnsisting*." The emendation is Monck

Mason's; and as both *s*'s are long in the original, it involves only the correction of the easiest possible misprint. Rowe gave '*unresisting*,' Hanmer '*unresting*,' Steevens suggested '*unlist'ning*,' or '*unshifting*,' Mr. Collier's folio of 1632 has '*resisting*,' — a very plausible correction, — and Blackstone says that 'unsisting' "may mean 'never at rest,' 'always opening.'"

p. 76. "*Happely*": — That is, 'hap-ly,' 'by hap,' formerly spelled '*happe*.' This is the word as it stands in the original, — the old orthography and pronunciation being retained on account of the rhythm, which requires a word of three syllables.

"This is his lordship's man": — In the original folio this speech is assigned to the *Duke*, and the next to the *Provost*; but there can be no doubt that Tyrwhitt was right in suggesting the transposition of the prefixes; for the *Duke* would not know, or, at least, seem to know, his lordship's man; and the *Provost* was far from expecting *Claudio's* pardon, which the *Duke*, on the contrary, looked for every moment. Just before, when the knocking is first heard, he says to himself, "Now are they come," and while the *Provost* reads the letter, "This is his pardon."

p. 78. "—— his fact": — his deed: the radical sense of the word.

p. 79. "—— *dye* the beard": — The folio has "*tie* the beard." Heath is the author of this emendation, which ('dye' and 'die' having been in Shakespeare's day without any distinction of orthography) is not only justified but required by what the *Provost* says in the next Scene about *Ragozine*, "his beard and head just of his colour." As it was customary for men to dye the beard and women the hair, materials could easily be procured.

p. 80. "—— nothing of what is [here] writ": — The folio omits "here," which is necessary to the sense, and was supplied by Warburton.

Scene III.

"—— *Master* Rash": — The original has the abbreviated form "*Mr.*" throughout this speech, except in the case of Three-pile. See Note on "Master Froth," Act II. Sc. I.

"—— a commodity of *brown paper* and *old ginger*": — Usurers in Shakespeare's day, as they do now, made their unfortunate clients take part of their loan in rubbish of some sort or other, which must needs be sold at a great sacrifice. Ginger was then, oddly enough, one of the commodities so used.

p. 80. "—— and are now *for the Lord's sake*": — This is an allusion to the practice of permitting prisoners for debt to ask alms of visitors and passers. It obtained until recently at the Fleet in London. Malone quotes the following pertinent passage from Nashe's *Apology for Pierce Pennilesse*, 1593: "At that time that thy joys were in the fleet-ing, and thus crying 'for the Lord's sake' out at an iron window." Singer also gives the following from Baret's *Alvearie*, 1573: — "then will he turn him [the debtor] to commons into Ludgate; where for his ablative case he shall have a dative cage, craving and crying at the gate 'your worship's charitie for the Lord's sake.'"

p. 81. "*Master* Barnardine": — The Clown who has just said "*Mr.* Barnardine, you must rise and be hanged," now, when he coaxes, says, "Pray, *Master* Barnardine." See Note on "Master Froth," Act II. Sc. 1. This may be accidental; but if so, it is to be classed among "*Gli Inganni Fortunati.*"

p. 82. "O, *grovelling beast!*" — The folio has "O *gravell heart*," which means nothing, although many have tried to persuade themselves and others to receive it for 'O stony heart.' The correction is from Mr. Collier's folio of 1632: the misprint which it supposes is an easy one, and the sense which it gives, most appropriate.

p. 83. "Ere twice the sun": — The metrical arrangement here is that of the original, which was needlessly changed by Steevens, who was followed unthinkingly by almost every subsequent editor. The purpose of Steevens was to accommodate the rhythm to a necessary change in the original text, which has "To *yond* generation." Steevens read,

> "Ere twice
> The sun has made his journal greeting *to*
> *The under* generation."

The error resulted from the compositor's mistaking 'ye und^r' (abbreviated for 'the under') for 'yond;' and 'th' under' does not destroy the rhythm of the line, as 'generation' was used sometimes as a word of four, sometimes of five, syllables. The emendation has been rejected of late years, and indeed was never properly established; but an examination of the meaning of the passage will show that we must read "th' under generation," i. e., the antipodes, and not "yond generation," i. e., the world outside the prison. For, just before, we are told, with some particularity, that it is almost day break; and the *Provost's* justification, if made before the sun had twice greeted the people of Vienna, must have been made that day; but if made before the sun had twice greeted the antipodes, that is, before the second ensuing night, it of course must take place on or before the day after; and so it did, and so the *Duke* declared it would to *Isabella* as well as to the *Provost*.

p. 83. "—— *well* balanc'd form": — The folio has "*weal*-balanc'd:" a palpable misprint for "well-balanc'd," as Heath and Mason pointed out.

p. 85. "—— he's a better *woodman*": — a hunter after deer, and so after *dears*. *Falstaff* asks *Mrs. Ford*, with a similar double meaning, "Am I a woodman?"

Scene IV.

p. 86. "—— hath disvouch'd [the] other": — The article, necessary to the sense, is omitted in the folio.

p. 87. "Yet reason dares her *on*," &c.: — That is, of course. 'Reason is on my side, and dares her to denounce me; for should she do so, my mere reputation and authority would at once confound her.' The folio has "Yet reason dares her *no*," by the most obvious and easy of typographical errors, which yet has hitherto remained uncorrected, while vain efforts have been made to extract sense from the passage. Theobald dropped 'no:' Steevens changed it to 'not': Malone read "Yet reason dares her? — no."

" "—— bears *up* a credent bulk": — This needs no explanation. It is the correction of an easy typographical error in the folio, — "bears *of* a credent bulk," — which has hitherto been endured, or cured by reading "bears *off* a credent bulk" or "*here's* of a credent bulk," or by boldly dropping the particle altogether. *Angelo's* thought is plainly, that his position and reputation will *sustain* his denial of any scandalous story.

Scene V.

p. 87. Dr. Johnson thought, not without some appearance of reason, that this Act should end with Scene IV., "for here is properly a cessation of action, and a night intervenes, and the place is changed, between the passages of this Scene (IV.) and those of the next. The next Act, beginning with the following Scene, (V.,) proceeds without any interruption of time or place." But Shakespeare cared comparatively little for such considerations. By the original division of the Acts, which has been preserved, with Act V. begins a grand and entirely new dramatic interest — that attaching to the exposure of *Angelo*. Up to the conclusion of the next and last Scene of the present Act (IV.) we see the toils of the *Friar-Duke* closing round his victim: after that there is no further plotting, and no disguise, except the momentary one necessary to the complete working out of former designs. A clock and a good memory will preserve the unities of time and place, or detect their violation; but for the preservation of the far more important unity of dramatic interest, it is better to trust to Shakespeare.

Scene VI.

p. 89. "Have *hent*": — taken possession of: from the A. S. '*hentan*,' 'to seize.'

ACT FIFTH.

Scene I.

p. 89. "*Enter, severally*": — The folio directs, "*Enter at several doors*," all entrances being made from doors on Shakespeare's stage, from want of scenery. In the folio, too, *Friar Peter* and *Isabella* are not directed to enter until just as the former says "Now is your time;" but though the play-wright was obliged thus to conform to the limited space on which his characters appeared, we know, from the foregoing Scene, that the poet had in his mind's eye the arrangement indicated in this stage direction.

" "—— yield *forth to you* public thanks": — The folio has "yield *you forth* to" — an evident transposition. The *Duke* yielded *Angelo* forth to no public thanks; but he gave him his own thanks publicly. See the first two lines of his next speech.

p. 91. "—— *characts*": — characters, outward seeming.

" "*As* e'er I heard": — 'As' for 'that': the construction being, — 'Her madness hath the oddest frame of sense that e'er I heard in madness' — the intervening line being interjectional.

" "—— for *inequality*": — for apparent inconsistency; as we say that one part of a story does not *square* with another.

" "—— the false seems true": — 'Which' is understood; but some suppose that "seems true" is a compound word for *vraisemblable*, 'true-seeming.'

p. 92. "How he *refell'd* me": — refuted me.

p. 93. "O, that it were *as like*, as it is true": — That is, 'as likely to be believed.' The *Duke*, throwing doubt upon her assertion, says, ironically, "This is most likely [to be true];" and she, knowing it to be virtually true, and wishing it to be so received, replies, "O, that it were as like, [to be believed] as it is true!" Of course, whether it were all actually true or not, she could not wish that it were at all 'likely *to be true*.'

p. 93. "—— with *ripened* time": — The last syllable of this word is not contracted in the folio: it was pronounced *ripe-ned*, not *ri-pen-ed:* hitherto the editors have contràcted it.

p. 94. "This ' a good friar": — The apostrophe marks the elision of 'is;' as in "What ' fool" for 'what *a* fool.' *Two Gentlemen of Verona*, Act I. Sc. 2.

p. 95. "—— let her shew *her* face": — The folio has "*your*," an easy misprint for 'her,' when *h* had a bow below the line like *y*, and *o* could scarcely be distinguished from *e*.

p. 97. "—— informal women" — ill regulated, distracted women. See Note on "make of him a formal man again." *Comedy of Errors*, Act V. Sc. 1.

" "And punish them [*un*]*to* your height of pleasure." The folio has "to" — an error, as the rhythm shows.

p. 98. "*Cucullus non facit monachum*": — The cowl does not make the monk.

p. 100. "Nor here *provincial*": — of this province, and subject to its civil or ecclesiastical authorities.

" "—— forfeits in a barber's shop": — It is only of late in America, that the fashion of lounging in a barber's shop has entirely gone out; and Dr. Kenrick states, in his *Suffolk Words*, that, in 1750, he saw a metrical list of forfeits in a barber's shop to be enforced against those who meddled with the razors or surgical instruments; for barbers were surgeons of old. We may well believe that these forfeits were "as much in mock as mark."

p. 101. "Hark how the villain would *glose* now": — how he would smooth over his treasonable abuses. The folio has "close," an evident misprint, as the *Duke* shows no intention to close the discussion,— yet hitherto retained.

" "—— *giglots*": — loose girls.

" "—— that e'er *mad'st* a duke": — So the original; generally changed to '*made*.'

p. 102. "—— rash *remonstrance*": — used in its radical sense of 'showing again.' It is only of comparatively late years that this word has come to mean 'expostulation.'

p. 104. "—— by *confiscation*": — The folio has "*confutation*," which was corrected in the second folio — a change that hardly merits notice.

p. 107. "If any *woman's* wrong'd": — In the folio, "any *woman*."

p. 108. "—— *that's* meet you all should know": — The original has "*that meet*."

THE COMEDY OF ERRORS.

The Comedie of Errors occupies sixteen pages in the folio of 1623, viz., from p. 85 to p. 100 inclusive, in the division of Comedies. It is there divided into Acts, but not into Scenes. At the head of the first, third, fourth, and fifth Acts, however, "*Scena Prima*" appears. There is no list of Dramatis Personæ, which was first supplied by Rowe.

THE COMEDY OF ERRORS.

INTRODUCTION.

THERE is no doubt that *The Comedy of Errors* is an imitation of the *Menæchmi* of Plautus; but the question whether the imitation was direct or indirect has not been decided. We know, from the Record of the Revels at Court, that a play called *The History of Error* was in existence in the year 1576–7; for among the entries for that year is the following: —

"The Historie of Error, shewn at Hampton Court on New yeres daie at night, enacted by the children of Pawles."

Malone, who first directed attention to this memorandum, also pointed out a passage in the *Gesta Grayorum* — a contemporary record of the festivities at Gray's Inn, published in 1688 — which shows that "a Comedy of Errors, like to Plautus his Menechmus, was played by the players" during the Christmas Revels at that venerable Inn of Court in December, 1594. In 1595 there was published in London a free translation of the *Menæchmi*.* Finally, Meres gives us evidence that Shakespeare's *Comedy of Errors* was written at least as early as 1597. These are all the facts on record from which we can determine the origin of this comedy or the date of its production; but as the old *History of Error* is entirely lost, and as we do not know whether the play at Gray's Inn was Shakespeare's Comedy or the older History, we are unable to decide from these data whether Shake-

* "A pleasant and fine Conceited Comœdie, taken out of the most excellent wittie Poet Plautus: Chosen purposely from out the rest, as least harmefull, and yet most delightfull. Written in English by W. W. — London, Printed by Tho. Creede, and are to be sold by William Barley, at his shop in Gratious streete. 1595." 4to.

This W. W. is supposed by Anthony Wood, in his *Athenæ Oxonienses*, to have been William Warner, the author of *Albion's England*, a sort of chronicle in verse, first published at London in 1586. 4to.

speare's play existed in any form before the publication of the translation from Plautus.

Of internal evidence upon this subject there is very little, and that not of much weight. *Dromio's* reply to *Antipholus*, Act III. Sc. 2, that he found France in the forehead of the globe-like dame who asserted uxorial rights over him, "armed and reverted,* making war against her heir," is, however, so plainly a punning allusion to the war of the League, which was closed by Henry IV.'s apostasy in 1593, that there can hardly be a doubt as to the existence of the passage before that date. For although it is true that 'heire' might be a misprint or loose spelling of 'haire,' to which it is changed in the folio of 1632, the allusion yet exists in as full force, in the otherwise senseless words "armed and reverted, making war," and the pun remains with a different spelling. The likeness between the phraseology of the translated *Menæchmi* and *The Comedy of Errors* is very slight indeed; and all other similarity is due, of course, to the original. *Adriana* says, Act II. Sc. 1, "poor I am but his stale," and the Wife in the translated *Menæchmi* says, "He makes me a stale and a laughing stock": W. W. translates,

> "—— nunc ibo in tabernam: vasa et argentum tibi
> Referam,"

"Ile go strait to the Inne, and deliver up my accounts, and all your stuffe," and *Antipholus* of Syracuse says, "Come to the Centaur; fetch our stuff from thence;" and although 'stuff' and 'stale' were generally used in Shakespeare's time as they are here used, in these speeches they have somewhat the air of reminiscences.

That the author of *The Comedy of Errors* knew the story of the *Menæchmi*, needs, of course, no setting forth; but that he had studied it closely, either in the original or in a translation, is evident from similarity in minor points between the plays. In both the resident brother is married; in both the wife is shrewish; in both she has brought her husband a large dowry; in both the Courtesan appears; and in both the resident brother seeks refuge at her table from the jealous clamors of his wife; the incident of the chain is common to both, and is used by each dramatist, though with a difference, for the same purpose; in

* A misprint, left uncorrected here, will be noticed hereafter.

both the wandering brother gives his purse to his servant to be carried to the inn; in both the wife, on account of the behavior of his double, finally supposes her husband to be lunatic, and in the one case sends and in the other brings a leech to take him in charge, who in both encounters the husband himself. It is also noteworthy that in the first stage directions of the original, one *Antipholus* is called "*Errotis*" and the other "*Sereptus*," — misprints, doubtless, for '*Erraticus*' and '*Surreptus*,' — meaning 'wandering' and 'stolen.' Now, in *The Comedy of Errors* the resident brother is not stolen, but in the *Menæchmi* he is, and is designated as *Surreptus*; and the traveller, who is not called *Erraticus* in Plautus' Dramatis Personæ, but *Sosicles*, is, however, called 'the Traveller' in W. W.'s translation. This translation, although not published until 1595, had then been made and handed about for some time, as we know by the address of "The Printer to the Readers" which introduces it. In this he says, or, without doubt, the author for him, — "The writer hereof (loving Readers) having diverse of this Poettes Comedies Englished, for the use and delight of his private friends, who in Plautus owne words are not able to understand them: I have prevailed so far with him as to let this one go farther abroad," &c.

In the absence of evidence which amounts to proof, we may yet form an opinion; and my own, based upon a consideration of the facts just stated and of the play itself, is, that Shakespeare, at the very beginning of his dramatic career, wishing to supply his theatre with an amusing comedy to take the place of a rude imitation of the *Menæchmi*, already somewhat known to the public, read that play in the original as thoroughly as his "small Latin" (small in the estimation of so complete a scholar as Jonson) enabled him to read it; that he also read W. W.'s translation in manuscript; and that then, using for the more comic parts the doggerel verse in which the elder play was written, for the passages of sentiment the alternate rhymes of which *Venus and Adonis* and *Romeo and Juliet* show his early preference and his mastery, and for the serious Scenes the blank verse which he was the first to bring to perfection, and which appears in great though not yet matured beauty in *The Two Gentlemen of Verona*, he wrote *The Comedy of Errors*: that, in the extravagant Scenes, he deliberately imitated, *populo ut placeret*, the versification of the old play, and perhaps adopted some of it with improvement; that this was done about 1589–90; and that the play thus produced may have been somewhat rewritten by him in its first and last Scenes in the long period during which it remained unprinted in the possession of the theatre.

It is to be observed that although the poetical value of *The Two Gentlemen of Verona* is much greater than that of *The Comedy of Errors*, the dramatic arrangement of the latter is much more skilful, and indicates longer theatrical experience on the part of the author.

The difference between the comedy of the Latin and that of the English dramatist is very wide, both in the way of addition and alteration; the most important addition being that of another pair of twins as attendants upon those who figure in the Latin play. The introduction of these tends greatly to complicate the confusion out of which the fun of this extravaganza arises. Whether the thought was original with Shakespeare or was taken from the old play, we have no means of ascertaining; but in the use made of the bondsmen we recognize the younger hand of him in whose maturer works his perception of the ridiculous and enjoyment of the broadest humor are no less apparent than his delight in all that is grand and beautiful in Man and Nature. Yet the very passages in which the *Dromios* are most prominent are those which seem most unmistakably the production of an inferior and more ancient writer. How difficult is it to believe that the rhyming part of Act III. Sc. 1, for instance, was written, at any time or for any purpose, by the author of the fine blank verse which precedes and follows it! It is more than possible that the two slaves were added in the older play to doubly supply the clown or buffoon, without which, on our ancient stage, a comedy was not a comedy. In the substitution of *Luciana*, the sister of *Adriana*, for the Father of the Latin comedy, we very surely have an indication of Shakespeare's dramatic skill; the expostulations which he puts into the mouth of the young woman are far more convincing and to the purpose than the reproaches which Plautus makes the old man deal out to both husband and wife. The introduction of *Luciana* also enabled the author to establish, in the relations between her and *Antipholus* of Syracuse, a new interest entirely wanting to the Latin play. The Parasite, who figures so largely in the *Menæchmi*, as in all Latin comedies, is omitted, as a character altogether foreign to the taste of an English audience, and needless to the production of that confusion which is the only motive of Shakespeare's play; in which, too, the action is more intricate than in its model, the movement more rapid, and the spirit much more lively, light, and humorous.

Concerning the place and the period of the action of this play, it seems that Shakespeare did not trouble himself to form a very accurate idea. The Ephesus of *The Comedy of Errors* is much like the Bohemia of *The Winter's Tale* — a remote, unknown place, yet with a familiar and imposing name, and therefore well suited to the purposes of one who as poet and dramatist cared much for men and little for things, and to whose perception the accidental was entirely eclipsed by the essential. Anachronisms are scattered through it with a profusion which could only be the result of entire indifference — in fact, of an absolute want of thought upon the subject. The existence of an abbey in Ephesus, however, is not to be considered as among them. For Christianity was established there about the middle of the fourth century; and Ephesus remained a Greek and Christian city till about A. D. 1313. The action of the play may, perhaps, be referred to about the middle of this period.

The choice of costume is in a great measure arbitrary. The twins must of course be attired in pairs alike, else they could not be mistaken for each other; and the improbability, extending to impossibility, that one master and servant should arrive in Ephesus dressed just as their doubles were on the day of their arrival, is a postulate permitted in the construction of a farce like this. Any ancient Natolian costume is admissible for the principal characters; and dramatic propriety will not be violated by giving to *Balthasar* and the friend of *Antipholus* of Syracuse the dress of Italian merchants, and to *Pinch* that of an English schoolmaster, or leech, or conjurer of Shakespeare's day. But an entirely conventional costume may be adopted; the only object being to remove the action out of the present and the actual.

The text, the only source of which is the first folio, exists there in a state approaching purity, the errors being altogether due to the accidents of the printing office, and, generally, easy of correction. Some were, however, left to be for the first time rectified in this edition.

DRAMATIS PERSONÆ.

SOLINUS, *Duke of* Ephesus.
ÆGEON, *a Merchant of* Syracuse.
ANTIPHOLUS *of* Ephesus, } *Twin Brothers, Sons to*
ANTIPHOLUS *of* Syracuse, } Ægeon *and* Æmilia.
DROMIO *of* Ephesus, } *Twin Brothers, Attendants on*
DROMIO *of* Syracuse, } *the two* Antipholuses.
BALTHAZAR, *a Merchant.*
ANGELO, *a Goldsmith.*
A Merchant, *Friend to* Antipholus *of* Syracuse.
A Merchant, *Creditor of* Angelo.
PINCH, *a Schoolmaster.*

ÆMILIA, *Wife to* Ægeon.
ADRIANA, *Wife to* Antipholus *of* Ephesus.
LUCIANA, *her Sister.*
LUCE, *Servant to* Adriana.
A Courtezan.

Gaoler, Officers, *and other* Attendants.

SCENE: Ephesus.

THE COMEDY OF ERRORS

ACT I.

Scene I. — A Hall in the Duke's Palace.

Enter Duke *of* Ephesus, Ægeon, Gaoler, Officers, *and other* Attendants.

Ægeon.

PROCEED, Solinus, to procure my fall,
And, by the doom of death, end woes and all.
Duke. Merchant of Syracusa, plead no more.
I am not partial, to infringe our laws:
The enmity and discord, which of late
Sprung from the rancorous outrage of your Duke
To merchants, our well-dealing countrymen, —
Who, wanting guilders to redeem their lives,
Have seal'd his rigorous statutes with their bloods, —
Excludes all pity from our threat'ning looks.
For, since the mortal and intestine jars
'Twixt thy seditious countrymen and us,
It hath in solemn synods been decreed,
Both by the Syracusians and ourselves,
To admit no traffic to our adverse towns:
Nay, more, if any, born at Ephesus,

Be seen at Syracusian marts and fairs,—
Again, if any Syracusian born
Come to the bay of Ephesus, he dies;
His goods confiscate to the Duke's dispose,
Unless a thousand marks be levied,
To quit the penalty, and to ransom him.
Thy substance, valued at the highest rate,
Cannot amount unto a hundred marks;
Therefore, by law thou art condemn'd to die.

Æge. Yet this my comfort; when your words are done,
My woes end likewise with the evening sun.

Duke. Well, Syracusian; say, in brief, the cause
Why thou departedst from thy native home,
And for what cause thou cam'st to Ephesus.

Æge. A heavier task could not have been impos'd,
Than I to speak my griefs unspeakable;
Yet, that the world may witness, that my end
Was wrought by nature, not by vile offence,
I'll utter what my sorrow gives me leave.
In Syracusa was I born, and wed
Unto a woman, happy but for me,
And by me [too], had not our hap been bad.
With her I liv'd in joy: our wealth increas'd,
By prosperous voyages I often made
To Epidamnum, till my factor's death,
And the great care of goods at random left,
Drew me from kind embracements of my spouse:
From whom my absence was not six months old,
Before herself (almost at fainting under
The pleasing punishment that women bear)
Had made provision for her following me,
And soon, and safe, arrived where I was.
There had she not been long, but she became
A joyful mother of two goodly sons;

And, which was strange, the one so like the other,
As could not be distinguish'd but by names.
That very hour, and in the self-same inn,
A meaner woman was delivered
Of such a burden, male twins, both alike.
Those, for their parents were exceeding poor,
I bought, and brought up to attend my sons.
My wife, not meanly proud of two such boys,
Made daily motions for our home return:
Unwilling, I agreed. Alas, too soon we came aboard!
A league from Epidamnum had we sail'd,
Before the always-wind-obeying deep
Gave any tragic instance of our harm:
But longer did we not retain much hope;
For what obscured light the heavens did grant
Did but convey unto our fearful minds
A doubtful warrant of immediate death;
Which, though myself would gladly have embrac'd,
Yet the incessant weepings of my wife,
Weeping before for what she saw must come,
And piteous plainings of the pretty babes,
That mourn'd for fashion, ignorant what to fear,
Forc'd me to seek delays for them and me.
And this it was, — for other means was none. —
The sailors sought for safety by our boat,
And left the ship, then sinking-ripe, to us.
My wife, more careful for the latter-born,
Had fasten'd him unto a small spare mast,
Such as sea-faring men provide for storms:
To him one of the other twins was bound,
Whilst I had been like heedful of the other.
The children thus dispos'd, my wife and I,
Fixing our eyes on whom our care was fix'd,
Fasten'd ourselves at either end the mast,
And, floating straight, obedient to the stream,

Were carried towards Corinth, as we thought.
At length the sun, gazing upon the earth,
Dispers'd those vapours that offended us,
And by the benefit of his wish'd light
The seas wax'd calm, and we discovered
Two ships, from far making amain to us;
Of Corinth that, of Epidaurus this:
But ere they came, — O, let me say no more!
Gather the sequel by that went before.

Duke. Nay, forward, old man: do not break off so;
For we may pity, though not pardon thee.

Æge. O, had the gods done so, I had not now
Worthily term'd them merciless to us!
For, ere the ships could meet, by twice five leagues,
We were encounter'd by a mighty rock,
Which being violently borne upon,
Our helpful ship was splitted in the midst;
So that, in this unjust divorce of us,
Fortune had left to both of us alike
What to delight in, what to sorrow for.
Her part, poor soul! seeming as burdened
With lesser weight, but not with lesser woe,
Was carried with more speed before the wind;
And in our sight they three were taken up
By fishermen of Corinth, as we thought.
At length another ship had seiz'd on us;
And knowing whom it was their hap to save,
Gave healthful welcome to their shipwrack'd guests,
And would have reft the fishers of their prey,
Had not their bark been very slow of sail;
And therefore homeward did they bend their course. —
Thus have you heard me sever'd from my bliss,
That by misfortunes was my life prolonged,
To tell sad stories of my own mishaps.

Duke. And, for the sake of them thou sorrowest for,

Do me the favour to dilate at full
What hath befall'n of them, and thee, till now.

Æge. My youngest boy, and yet my eldest care,
At eighteen years became inquisitive
After his brother, and importun'd me,
That his attendant (so his case was like,
Reft of his brother, but retain'd his name)
Might bear him company in the quest of him;
Whom whilst I labour'd of a love to see,
I hazarded the loss of whom I lov'd.
Five summers have I spent in farthest Greece,
Roaming clean through the bounds of Asia;
And, coasting homeward, came to Ephesus,
Hopeless to find, yet loath to leave unsought
Or that, or any place that harbours men.
But here must end the story of my life;
And happy were I in my timely death,
Could all my travels warrant me they live.

Duke. Hapless Ægeon, whom the Fates have mark'd
To bear the extremity of dire mishap!
Now, trust me, were it not against our laws,
Against my crown, my oath, my dignity,
Which princes, would they, may not disannul,
My soul should sue as advocate for thee.
But though thou art adjudged to the death,
And passed sentence may not be recall'd
But to our honour's great disparagement,
Yet will I favour thee in what I can:
Therefore, merchant, I'll limit thee this day,
To seek thy [life] by beneficial help.
Try all the friends thou hast in Ephesus;
Beg thou, or borrow, to make up the sum,
And live; if no, then thou art doom'd to die.—
Gaoler, take him to thy custody.

Gaoler. I will, my lord.

Æge. Hopeless, and helpless, doth Ægeon wend,
But to procrastinate his liveless end. [*Exeunt*.

SCENE II.

A public Place.

Enter ANTIPHOLUS *and* DROMIO *of* Syracuse, *and* *a* Merchant.

Merchant. Therefore, give out you are of Epidamnum,
Lest that your goods too soon be confiscate.
This very day, a Syracusian merchant
Is apprehended for arrival here;
And, not being able to buy out his life,
According to the statute of the town,
Dies ere the weary sun set in the west.
There is your money that I had to keep.

Antipholus of Syracuse. Go, bear it to the Centaur, where we host,
And stay there, Dromio, till I come to thee.
Within this hour it will be dinner-time:
Till that, I'll view the manners of the town,
Peruse the traders, gaze upon the buildings,
And then return and sleep within mine inn,
For with long travel I am stiff and weary.
Get thee away.

Dromio of Syracuse. Many a man would take you at your word,
And go indeed, having so good a mean. [*Exit*.

Ant. S. A trusty villain, sir; that very oft,
When I am dull with care and melancholy,
Lightens my humour with his merry jests.

What, will you walk with me about the town,
And then go to my inn, and dine with me?

Mer. I am invited, sir, to certain merchants,
Of whom I hope to make much benefit;
I crave your pardon. Soon at five o'clock,
Please you, I'll meet with you upon the mart,
And afterwards consort you till bed-time:
My present business calls me from you now.

Ant. S. Farewell till then. I will go lose myself,
And wander up and down to view the city.

Mer. Sir, I commend you to your own content. [*Exit.*

Ant. S. He that commends me to mine own content,
Commends me to the thing I cannot get.
I, to the world, am like a drop of water
That, in the ocean, seeks another drop;
Who, falling there to find his fellow forth,
Unseen, inquisitive, confounds himself:
So I, to find a mother and a brother,
In quest of them, unhappy, lose myself.

Enter DROMIO *of* Ephesus.

Here comes the almanack of my true date.—
What now? How chance thou art return'd so soon?

Dromio of Ephesus. Return'd so soon! rather approach'd too late.
The capon burns, the pig falls from the spit,
The clock hath strucken twelve upon the bell;
My mistress made it one upon my cheek:
She is so hot, because the meat is cold;
The meat is cold, because you come not home;
You come not home, because you have no stomach;
You have no stomach, having broke your fast;

But we, that know what 'tis to fast and pray,
Are penitent for your default to-day.

Ant. S. Stop in your wind, sir. Tell me this, I pray;
Where have you left the money that I gave you?

Dro. E. O! sixpence, that I had o' Wednesday last
To pay the saddler for my mistress' crupper.
The saddler had it, sir; I kept it not.

Ant. S. I am not in a sportive humour now.
Tell me, and dally not, where is the money?
We being strangers here, how dar'st thou trust
So great a charge from thine own custody?

Dro. E. I pray you, jest, sir, as you sit at dinner.
I from my mistress come to you in post;
If I return, I shall be post indeed,
For she will score your fault upon my pate.
Methinks, your maw, like mine, should be your clock,
And strike you home without a messenger.

Ant. S. Come, Dromio, come; these jests are out of season:
Reserve them till a merrier hour than this.
Where is the gold I gave in charge to thee?

Dro. E. To me, sir? why, you gave no gold to me.

Ant. S. Come on, sir knave; have done your foolishness,
And tell me how thou hast dispos'd thy charge.

Dro. E. My charge was but to fetch you from the mart
Home to your house, the Phœnix, sir, to dinner.
My mistress, and her sister, stay for you.

Ant. S. Now, as I am a Christian, answer me,
In what safe place you have bestow'd my money,
Or I shall break that merry sconce of yours,

That stands on tricks when I am undispos'd.
Where is the thousand marks thou hadst of me?

Dro. E. I have some marks of yours upon my pate;
Some of my mistress' marks upon my shoulders,
But not a thousand marks between you both.
If I should pay your worship those again,
Perchance, you will not bear them patiently.

Ant. S. Thy mistress' marks! what mistress, slave, hast thou?

Dro. E. Your worship's wife, my mistress at the Phœnix;
She that doth fast till you come home to dinner,
And prays that you will hie you home to dinner.

Ant. S. What, wilt thou flout me thus unto my face,
Being forbid? There, take you that, sir knave. [*Strikes him.*

Dro. E. What mean you, sir? for God's sake, hold your hands.
Nay, an you will not, sir, I'll take my heels. [*Exit.*

Ant. S. Upon my life, by some device or other
The villain is o'er-raught of all my money.
They say, this town is full of cozenage;
As, nimble jugglers that deceive the eye,
Dark-working sorcerers that change the mind,
Soul-killing witches that deform the body,
Disguised cheaters, prating mountebanks,
And many such like liberties of sin:
If it prove so, I will be gone the sooner.
I'll to the Centaur to go seek this slave:
I greatly fear my money is not safe. [*Exit.*

ACT II.

SCENE I. — Court in the House of ANTIPHOLUS.

Enter ADRIANA *and* LUCIANA.

ADRIANA.

NEITHER my husband, nor the slave return'd,
That in such haste I sent to seek his master?
Sure, Luciana, it is two o'clock.

Luciana. Perhaps, some merchant hath invited him,
And from the mart he's somewhere gone to dinner.
Good sister, let us dine, and never fret.
A man is master of his liberty:
Time is their master; and, when they see time,
They'll go, or come: if so, be patient, sister.

Adr. Why should their liberty than ours be more?

Luc. Because their business still lies out o' door.

Adr. Look, when I serve him so, he takes it [ill].

Luc. O! know he is the bridle of your will.

Adr. There's none but asses will be bridled so.

Luc. Why, headstrong liberty is lash'd with woe
There's nothing, situate under Heaven's eye,
But hath his bound, in earth, in sea, in sky:
The beasts, the fishes, and the winged fowls,
Are their males' subjects, and at their controls.
Men, more divine, the masters of all these,
Lords of the wide world and wild wat'ry seas,
Indued with intellectual sense and souls,
Of more pre-eminence than fish and fowls,
Are masters to their females, and their lords:
Then, let your will attend on their accords.

Adr. This servitude makes you to keep unwed.
Luc. Not this, but troubles of the marriage-bed.
Adr. But, were you wedded, you would bear some sway.
Luc. Ere I learn love, I'll practise to obey.
Adr. How if your husband start some other where?
Luc. Till he come home again, I would forbear.
Adr. Patience unmov'd, no marvel though she pause;
They can be meek that have no other cause.
A wretched soul, bruis'd with adversity,
We bid be quiet, when we hear it cry;
But were we burden'd with like weight of pain,
As much, or more, we should ourselves complain;
So thou, that hast no unkind mate to grieve thee,
With urging helpless patience would'st relieve me:
But if thou live to see like right bereft,
This fool-begg'd patience in thee will be left.
Luc. Well, I will marry one day, but to try.—
Here comes your man: now is your husband nigh.

Enter DROMIO *of* Ephesus.

Adr. Say, is your tardy master now at hand?

Dro. E. Nay, he is at two hands with me, and that my two ears can witness.

Adr. Say, didst thou speak with him? Know'st thou his mind?
Dro. E. Ay, ay; he told his mind upon mine ear.
Beshrew his hand, I scarce could understand it.

Luc. Spake he so doubtfully, thou could'st not feel his meaning?

Dro. E. Nay, he struck so plainly, I could too well feel his blows; and withal so doubtfully, that I could scarce understand them.

Adr. But say, I pr'ythee, is he coming home?
It seems, he hath great care to please his wife.

Dro. E. Why, mistress, sure my master is horn-mad.

Adr. Horn-mad, thou villain!

Dro. E. I mean not cuckold-mad;
But, sure, he is stark mad.
When I desir'd him to come home to dinner,
He ask'd me for a thousand marks in gold:
'Tis dinner-time, quoth I; my gold, quoth he:
Your meat doth burn, quoth I; my gold, quoth he:
Will you come [home], quoth I? my gold, quoth he:
Where is the thousand marks I gave thee, villain?
The pig, quoth I, is burn'd; my gold, quoth he:
My mistress, sir, quoth I; hang up thy mistress;
I know not thy mistress; out on thy mistress!

Luc. Quoth who?

Dro. E. Quoth my master:
I know, quoth he, no house, no wife, no mistress.
So that my errand, due unto my tongue,
I thank him, I bear home upon my shoulders;
For, in conclusion, he did beat me there.

Adr. Go back again, thou slave, and fetch him home.

Dro. E. Go back again, and be new beaten home?
For God's sake, send some other messenger.

Adr. Back, slave, or I will break thy pate across.

Dro. E. And he will bless that cross with other beating.
Between you, I shall have a holy head.

Adr. Hence, prating peasant! fetch thy master home.

Dro. E. Am I so round with you, as you with me,
That like a foot-ball you do spurn me thus?
You spurn me hence, and he will spurn me hither:

If I last in this service, you must case me in leather. [*Exit.*

Luc. Fie, how impatience low'reth in your face!

Adr. His company must do his minions grace,
Whilst I at home starve for a merry look.
Hath homely age th' alluring beauty took
From my poor cheek? then he hath wasted it:
Are my discourses dull? barren my wit?
If voluble and sharp discourse be marr'd,
Unkindness blunts it more than marble hard.
Do their gay vestments his affections bait?
That's not my fault; he's master of my state.
What ruins are in me, that can be found
By him not ruin'd? then is he the ground
Of my defeatures. My decayed fair
A sunny look of his would soon repair;
But, too unruly deer, he breaks the pale,
And feeds from home: poor I am but his stale.

Luc. Self-harming jealousy!—fie! beat it hence.

Adr. Unfeeling fools can with such wrongs dispense.
I know his eye doth homage other where,
Or else, what lets it but he would be here?
Sister, you know he promis'd me a chain:
Would that alone, [alone] he would detain,
So he would keep fair quarter with his bed!
I see, the jewel best enamelled
Will lose his beauty: yet though gold 'bides still,
That others touch, an often touching will
Wear gold; and no man that hath a name,
By falsehood and corruption doth it shame.
Since that my beauty cannot please his eye,
I'll weep what's left away, and weeping die.

Luc. How many fond fools serve mad jealousy! [*Exeunt.*

Scene II.

A public Place.

Enter Antipholus *of* Syracuse.

Ant. S. The gold I gave to Dromio is laid up
Safe at the Centaur; and the heedful slave
Is wander'd forth, in care to seek me out.
By computation, and mine host's report,
I could not speak with Dromio, since at first
I sent him from the mart. See, here he comes.

Enter Dromio *of* Syracuse.

How now, sir? is your merry humour alter'd?
As you love strokes, so jest with me again.
You know no Centaur? You receiv'd no gold?
Your mistress sent to have me home to dinner?
My house was at the Phœnix? Wast thou mad,
That thus so madly thou didst answer me?

Dro. S. What answer, sir? when spake I such a word?

Ant. S. Even now, even here, not half an hour since.

Dro. S. I did not see you since you sent me hence,
Home to the Centaur, with the gold you gave me.

Ant. S. Villain, thou didst deny the gold's receipt,
And told'st me of a mistress, and a dinner;
For which, I hope, thou felt'st I was displeas'd.

Dro. S. I am glad to see you in this merry vein.
What means this jest? I pray you, master, tell me.

Ant. S. Yea, dost thou jeer, and flout me in the teeth?
Think'st thou I jest? Hold, take thou that, and that.
[*Beats him.*

Dro. S. Hold, sir, for God's sake! now your jest
is earnest:
Upon what bargain do you give it me?
Ant. S. Because that I familiarly sometimes
Do use you for my fool, and chat with you,
Your sauciness will jest upon my love,
And make a common of my serious hours.
When the sun shines let foolish gnats make sport,
But creep in crannies when he hides his beams.
If you will jest with me, know my aspect,
And fashion your demeanour to my looks,
Or I will beat this method in your sconce.

Dro. S. Sconce, call you it? so you would leave battering, I had rather have it a head: An you use these blows long, I must get a sconce for my head, and insconce it too; or else I shall seek my wit in my shoulders. But, I pray, sir, why am I beaten?

Ant. S. Dost thou not know?

Dro. S. Nothing, sir; but that I am beaten.

Ant. S. Shall I tell you why?

Dro. S. Ay, sir, and wherefore; for, they say, every why hath a wherefore.

Ant. S. Why, first, — for flouting me; and then, wherefore, — for urging it the second time to me.

Dro. S. Was there ever any man thus beaten out
of season,
When in the why and the wherefore is neither
rhyme nor reason? —
Well, sir, I thank you.

Ant. S. Thank me, sir? for what?

Dro. S. Marry, sir, for this something that you gave me for nothing.

Ant. S. I'll make you amends next, to give you nothing for something. But say, sir, is it dinner-time?

Dro. S. No, sir: I think the meat wants that I have.

Ant. S. In good time, sir; what's that?

Dro. S. Basting.

Ant. S. Well, sir, then 'twill be dry.

Dro. S. If it be, sir, I pray you eat none of it.

Ant. S. Your reason?

Dro. S. Lest it make you choleric, and purchase me another dry basting.

Ant. S. Well, sir, learn to jest in good time: there's a time for all things.

Dro. S. I durst have denied that before you were so choleric.

Ant. S. By what rule, sir?

Dro. S. Marry, sir, by a rule as plain as the plain bald pate of Father Time himself.

Ant. S. Let's hear it.

Dro. S. There's no time for a man to recover his hair that grows bald by nature.

Ant. S. May he not do it by fine and recovery?

Dro. S. Yes, to pay a fine for a periwig, and recover the lost hair of another man.

Ant. S. Why is Time such a niggard of hair, being, as it is, so plentiful an excrement?

Dro. S. Because it is a blessing that he bestows on beasts: and what he hath scanted men in hair, he hath given them in wit.

Ant. S. Why, but there's many a man hath more hair than wit.

Dro. S. Not a man of those but he hath the wit to lose his hair.

Ant. S. Why, thou didst conclude hairy men plain dealers, without wit.

Dro. S. The plainer dealer, the sooner lost: yet he loseth it in a kind of jollity.

Ant. S. For what reason?

Dro. S. For two; and sound ones too.

Ant. S. Nay, not sound, I pray you.

Dro. S. Sure ones then.

Ant. S. Nay, not sure, in a thing falling.

Dro. S. Certain ones then.

Ant. S. Name them.

Dro. S. The one, to save the money that he spends in trimming; the other, that at dinner they should not drop in his porridge.

Ant. S. You would all this time have prov'd there is no time for all things.

Dro. S. Marry, and did, sir; namely, is no time to recover hair lost by nature.

Ant. S. But your reason was not substantial why there is no time to recover.

Dro. S. Thus I mend it: Time himself is bald, and therefore, to the world's end, will have bald followers.

Ant. S. I knew 'twould be a bald conclusion.
But soft! who wafts us yonder?

Enter ADRIANA *and* LUCIANA.

Adr. Ay, ay, Antipholus, look strange, and frown:
Some other mistress hath thy sweet aspects:
I am not Adriana, nor thy wife.
The time was once, when thou, unurg'd, would'st vow
That never words were music to thine ear,
That never object pleasing in thine eye,
That never touch well welcome to thy hand,
That never meat sweet-savour'd in thy taste,
Unless I spake, or look'd, or touch'd, or carv'd to thee.
How comes it now, my husband, O! how comes it,
That thou art then estranged from thyself?

Thyself I call it, being strange to me,
That, undividable, incorporate,
Am better than thy dear self's better part.
Ah, do not tear away thyself from me;
For know, my love, as easy may'st thou fall
A drop of water in the breaking gulf,
And take unmingled thence that drop again,
Without addition or diminishing,
As take from me thyself, and not me too.
How dearly would it touch thee to the quick,
Should'st thou but hear I were licentious,
And that this body, consecrate to thee,
By ruffian lust should be contaminate!
Would'st thou not spit at me, and spurn at me,
And hurl the name of husband in my face,
And tear the stain'd skin off my harlot-brow,
And from my false hand cut the wedding-ring,
And break it with a deep divorcing vow?
I know thou canst; and therefore, see thou do it.
I am possess'd with an adulterate blot;
My blood is mingled with the crime of lust:
For, if we two be one, and thou play false,
I do digest the poison of thy flesh,
Being strumpeted by thy contagion.
Keep, then, fair league and truce with thy true bed;
I live distain'd, thou one dishonoured.

Ant. S. Plead you to me, fair dame? I know you not.
In Ephesus I am but two hours old,
As strange unto your town as to your talk;
Who, every word by all my wit being scann'd,
Want wit in all, one word to understand.

Luc. Fie, brother: how the world is chang'd with you!

When were you wont to use my sister thus?
She sent for you by Dromio home to dinner.

Ant. S. By Dromio?

Dro. S. By me?

Adr. By thee; and this thou didst return from him, —
That he did buffet thee, and, in his blows,
Denied my house for his, me for his wife.

Ant. S. Did you converse, sir, with this gentlewoman?
What is the course and drift of your compact?

Dro. S. I, sir? I never saw her till this time.

Ant. S. Villain, thou liest; for even her very words
Didst thou deliver to me on the mart.

Dro. S. I never spake with her in all my life.

Ant. S. How can she thus then call us by our names,
Unless it be by inspiration?

Adr. How ill agrees it with your gravity
To counterfeit thus grossly with your slave,
Abetting him to thwart me in my mood!
Be it my wrong, you are from me exempt,
But wrong not that wrong with a more contempt.
Come, I will fasten on this sleeve of thine;
Thou art an elm, my husband, I a vine,
Whose weakness, married to thy stronger state,
Makes me with thy strength to communicate:
If aught possess thee from me, it is dross,
Usurping ivy, brier, or idle moss;
Who, all for want of pruning, with intrusion
Infect thy sap, and live on thy confusion.

Ant. S. To me she speaks; she moves me for her theme!
What, was I married to her in my dream,

Or sleep I now, and think I hear all this?
What error drives our eyes and ears amiss?
Until I know this sure uncertainty,
I'll entertain the forced fallacy.

Luc. Dromio, go bid the servants spread for dinner.

Dro. S. O, for my beads! I cross me for a sinner.
This is the fairy land: O, spite of spites!
We talk with goblins, owles, [elves,] and sprites.
If we obey them not, this will ensue,
They'll suck our breath, or pinch us black and blue.

Luc. Why prat'st thou to thyself, and answer'st not?
Dromio, thou drone, thou snail, thou slug, thou sot!

Dro. S. I am transformed, master, am I not?

Ant. S. I think thou art, in mind, and so am I.

Dro. S. Nay, master, both in mind and in my shape.

Ant. S. Thou hast thine own form.

Dro. S. No, I am an ape.

Luc. If thou art chang'd to aught, 'tis to an ass.

Dro. S. 'Tis true; she rides me, and I long for grass.
'Tis so, I am an ass; else it could never be,
But I should know her as well as she knows me.

Adr. Come, come; no longer will I be a fool,
To put the finger in the eye and weep,
Whilst man and master laugh my woes to scorn.
Come, sir, to dinner. — Dromio, keep the gate. —
Husband, I'll dine above with you to-day,
And shrive you of a thousand idle pranks. —
Sirrah, if any ask you for your master,
Say he dines forth, and let no creature enter. —
Come, sister. — Dromio, play the porter well.

Ant. S. Am I in Earth, in Heaven, or in Hell?

Sleeping or waking? mad, or well-advis'd?
Known unto these, and to myself disguis'd?
I'll say as they say, and persever so,
And in this mist, at all adventures, go.

Dro. S. Master, shall I be porter at the gate?

Adr. Ay; and let none enter, lest I break your pate.

Luc. Come, come, Antipholus; we dine too late.
[*Exeunt.*

ACT III.

Scene I. — Before the House of Antipholus.

Enter Antipholus *of* Ephesus, Dromio *of* Ephesus, Angelo, *and* Balthazar.

Antipholus of Ephesus.

Good Signior Angelo, you must excuse us all;
My wife is shrewish when I keep not hours.
Say that I linger'd with you at your shop,
To see the making of her carcanet,
And that to-morrow you will bring it home;
But here's a villain that would face me down
He met me on the mart, and that I beat him,
And charg'd him with a thousand marks in gold;
And that I did deny my wife and house. —
Thou drunkard, thou, what didst thou mean by this?

Dro. E. Say what you will, sir, but I know what I know.
That you beat me at the mart, I have your hand to show:

If the skin were parchment, and the blows you gave were ink,
Your own hand-writing would tell you what I think.

Ant. E. I think thou art an ass.

Dro. E. Marry, so it doth appear,
By the wrongs I suffer, and the blows I bear.
I should kick, being kick'd; and being at that pass,
You would keep from my heels, and beware of an ass.

Ant. E. Y' are sad, Signior Balthazar: pray God our cheer
May answer my good-will, and your good welcome here.

Bal. I hold your dainties cheap, sir, and your welcome dear.

Ant. E. O, Signior Balthazar, either at flesh or fish,
A table-full of welcome makes scarce one dainty dish.

Bal. Good meat, sir, is common; that every churl affords.

Ant. E. And welcome more common, for that's nothing but words.

Bal. Small cheer and great welcome makes a merry feast.

Ant. E. Ay, to a niggardly host, and more sparing guest:
But though my cates be mean, take them in good part;
Better cheer may you have, but not with better heart.
But soft! my door is lock'd. Go bid them let us in.

Dro. E. Maud, Bridget, Marian, Cicely, Gillian, Gin'!

Dro. S. [*Within.*] Mome, malt-horse, capon, coxcomb, idiot, patch!
Either get thee from the door, or sit down at the hatch.

Dost thou conjure for wenches, that thou call'st for such store,
When one is one too many? Go, get thee from the door.

Dro. E. What patch is made our porter? — My master stays in the street.

Dro. S. Let him walk from whence he came, lest he catch cold on 's feet.

Ant. E. Who talks within there? hoa! open the door.

Dro. S. Right, sir: I'll tell you when, an you'll tell me wherefore.

Ant. E. Wherefore? for my dinner: I have not din'd to-day.

Dro. S. Nor to-day here you must not, come again when you may.

Ant. E. What art thou, that keep'st me out from the house I owe?

Dro. S. The porter for this time, sir; and my name is Dromio.

Dro. E. O villain! thou hast stolen both mine office and my name:
The one ne'er got me credit, the other mickle blame.
If thou hadst been Dromio to-day in my place,
Thou would'st have chang'd thy face for a name, or thy name for a face.

Luce. [*Within.*] What a coil is there, Dromio: who are those at the gate?

Dro. E. Let my master in, Luce.

Luce. Faith, no; he comes too late;
And so tell your master.

Dro. E. O Lord! I must laugh: —
Have at you with a proverb. — Shall I set in my staff?

Luce. Have at you with another: that's — when? can you tell?

Dro. S. If thy name be called Luce, Luce, thou hast answer'd him well.

Ant. E. Do you hear, you minion? you'll let us in, I hope?

[-]

Luce. I thought to have ask'd you.

Dro. S. And you said, no.

Dro. E. So; come, help! well struck; there was blow for blow.

Ant. E. Thou baggage, let me in.

Luce. Can you tell for whose sake?

Dro. E. Master, knock the door hard.

Luce. Let him knock till it ache.

Ant. E. You'll cry for this, minion, if I beat the door down.

Luce. What needs all that, and a pair of stocks in the town?

Adr. [*Within.*] Who is that at the door, that keeps all this noise?

Dro. S. By my troth, your town is troubled with unruly boys.

Ant. E. Are you there, wife? you might have come before.

Adr. Your wife, sir knave? go, get you from the door.

Dro. E. If you went in pain, master, this knave would go sore.

Ang. Here is neither cheer, sir, nor welcome: we would fain have either.

Bal. In debating which was best, we shall part with neither.

Dro. E. They stand at the door, master: bid them welcome hither.

Ant. E. There is something in the wind, that we cannot get in.

Dro. E. You would say so, master, if your garments were thin.
Your cake here is warm within; you stand here in the cold:
It would make a man mad as a buck to be so bought and sold.

Ant. E. Go, fetch me something: I'll break ope the gate.

Dro. S. Break any breaking here, and I'll break your knave's pate.

Dro. E. A man may break a word with you, sir, and words are but wind;
Ay, and break it in your face, so he break it not behind.

Dro. S. It seems, thou want'st breaking. Out upon thee, hind!

Dro. E. Here's too much out upon thee! I pray thee, let me in.

Dro. S. Ay, when fowls have no feathers, and fish have no fin.

Ant. E. Well, I'll break in. Go, borrow me a crow.

Dro. E. A crow without feather? master, mean you so?
For a fish without a fin, there's a fowl without a feather.
If a crow help us in, sirrah, we'll pluck a crow together.

Ant. E. Go, get thee gone: fetch me an iron crow.

Bal. Have patience, sir; O! let it not be so:
Herein you war against your reputation,
And draw within the compass of suspect
Th' unviolated honour of your wife.
Once this,—Your long experience of her wisdom,

Her sober virtue, years, and modesty,
Plead on her part some cause to you unknown;
And doubt not, sir, but she will well excuse
Why at this time the doors are made against you.
Be rul'd by me: depart in patience,
And let us to the Tiger all to dinner;
And, about evening, come yourself alone
To know the reason of this strange restraint.
If by strong hand you offer to break in,
Now, in the stirring passage of the day,
A vulgar comment will be madė of it;
And that supposed by the common rout,
Against your yet ungalled estimation,
That may with foul intrusion enter in,
And dwell upon your grave when you are dead:
For slander lives upon succession,
For ever housed, where it gets possession.

Ant. E. You have prevail'd: I will depart in quiet,
And, in despite of mirth, mean to be merry.
I know a wench of excellent discourse,
Pretty and witty, wild and yet, too, gentle:
There will we dine. This woman that I mean,
My wife (but, I protest, without desert,)
Hath oftentimes upbraided me withal:
To her will we to dinner.—Get you home,
And fetch the chain; by this, I know, 'tis made:
Bring it, I pray you, to the Porpentine;
For there's the house. That chain will I bestow
(Be it for nothing but to spite my wife)
Upon mine hostess there. Good sir, make haste.
Since mine own doors refuse to entertain me,
I'll knock elsewhere, to see if they'll disdain me.

Ang. I'll meet you at that place, some hour hence.

Ant. E. Do so. This jest shall cost me some expense. [*Exeunt.*

SCENE II.

Court in the House of ANTIPHOLUS.

Enter LUCIANA *and* ANTIPHOLUS *of* Syracuse.

Luc. And may it be that you have quite forgot
A husband's office? Shall, Antipholus,
Even in the spring of love, thy love-springs rot?
Shall love, in building, grow so ruinous?
If you did wed my sister for her wealth,
Then, for her wealth's sake, use her with more kindness;
Or if you like elsewhere, do it by stealth:
Muffle your false love with some show of blindness;
Let not my sister read it in your eye:
Be not thy tongue thy own shame's orator;
Look sweet, speak fair, become disloyalty;
Apparel vice like virtue's harbinger:
Bear a fair presence, though your heart be tainted;
Teach sin the carriage of a holy saint:
Be secret-false; what need she be acquainted?
What simple thief brags of his own attaint?
'Tis double wrong, to truant with your bed,
And let her read it in thy looks at board.
Shame hath a bastard fame, well managed;
Ill deeds are doubled with an evil word.
Alas, poor women! make us but believe,
Being compact of credit, that you love us;
Though others have the arm, show us the sleeve,
We in your motion turn, and you may move us.
Then, gentle brother, get you in again:
Comfort my sister, cheer her, call her wife.
Tis holy sport to be a little vain,
When the sweet breath of flattery conquers strife.

Ant. S. Sweet mistress, (what your name is else, I know not,
Nor by what wonder you do hit of mine,)
Less in your knowledge, and your grace you shew not,
Than our Earth's wonder; more than Earth divine.
Teach me, dear creature, how to think and speak:
Lay open to my earthy gross conceit,
Smother'd in errors, feeble, shallow, weak,
The folded meaning of your words' deceit.
Against my soul's pure truth, why labour you
To make it wander in an unknown field?
Are you a god? would you create me new?
Transform me then, and to your power I'll yield.
But if that I am I, then well I know,
Your weeping sister is no wife of mine,
Nor to her bed no homage do I owe:
Far more, far more, to you do I decline.
O, train me not, sweet mermaid, with thy note,
To drown me in thy sister's flood of tears.
Sing, siren, for thyself, and I will dote:
Spread o'er the silver waves thy golden hairs,
And as a bride I'll take thee, and there lie;
And, in that glorious supposition, think
He gains by death, that hath such means to die:
Let Love, being light, be drowned if she sink!

Luc. What! are you mad, that you do reason so?

Ant. S. Not mad, but mated; how, I do not know.

Luc. It is a fault that springeth from your eye.

Ant. S. For gazing on your beams, fair sun, being by.

Luc. Gaze where you should, and that will clear your sight.

Ant. S. As good to wink, sweet love, as look on night.

Luc. Why call you me love? call my sister so.

Ant. S. Thy sister's sister.

Luc. That's my sister.

Ant. S. No;
It is thyself, mine own self's better part;
Mine eye's clear eye, my dear heart's dearer heart;
My food, my fortune, and my sweet hope's aim,
My sole Earth's-heaven, and my Heaven's claim.

Luc. All this my sister is, or else should be.

Ant. S. Call thyself sister, sweet, for I aim thee.
Thee will I love, and with thee lead my life:
Thou hast no husband yet, nor I no wife.
Give me thy hand.

Luc. O, soft, sir! hold you still:
I'll fetch my sister, to get her good-will. [*Exit.*

Enter DROMIO *of* Syracuse, *hastily.*

Ant. S. Why, how now, Dromio! where run'st thou so fast?

Dro. S. Do you know me, sir? am I Dromio? am I your man? am I myself?

Ant. S. Thou art Dromio, thou art my man, thou art thyself.

Dro. S. I am an ass; I am a woman's man, and besides myself.

Ant. S. What woman's man? and how besides thyself?

Dro. S. Marry, sir, besides myself, I am due to a woman; one that claims me, one that haunts me, one that will have me.

Ant. S. What claim lays she to thee?

Dro. S. Marry, sir, such claim as you would lay to your horse; and she would have me as a beast: not that, I being a beast, she would have me; but that she, being a very beastly creature, lays claim to me.

Ant. S. What is she?

Dro. S. A very reverend body; ay, such a one as a man may not speak of, without he say, sir-reverence. I have but lean luck in the match, and yet she is a wondrous fat marriage.

Ant. S. How dost thou mean, a fat marriage?

Dro. S. Marry, sir, she's the kitchen-wench, and all grease; and I know not what use to put her to, but to make a lamp of her and run from her by her own light. I warrant, her rags and the tallow in them, will burn a Poland winter: if she lives till doomsday, she'll burn a week longer than the whole world.

Ant. S. What complexion is she of?

Dro. S. Swart, like my shoe, but her face nothing like so clean kept: for why? she sweats, a man may go over shoes in the grime of it.

Ant. S. That's a fault that water will mend.

Dro. S. No, sir; 'tis in grain: Noah's flood could not do it.

Ant. S. What's her name?

Dro. S. Nell, sir; but her name and three quarters, that is, an ell and three quarters, will not measure her from hip to hip.

Ant. S. Then she bears some breadth?

Dro. S. No longer from head to foot, than from hip to hip: she is spherical, like a globe; I could find out countries in her.

Ant. S. In what part of her body stands Ireland?

Dro. S. Marry, sir, in her buttocks: I found it out by the bogs.

Ant. S. Where Scotland?

Dro. S. I found it by the barrenness, hard, in the palm of the hand.

Ant. S. Where France?

Dro. S. In her forehead; arm'd and revolted, making war against her heir.

Ant. S. Where England?

Dro. S. I look'd for the chalky cliffs, but I could find no whiteness in them: but I guess, it stood in her chin, by the salt rheum that ran between France and it.

Ant. S. Where Spain?

Dro. S. Faith, I saw it not; but I felt it hot in her breath.

Ant. S. Where America, the Indies?

Dro. S. O! sir, upon her nose, all o'er embellished with rubies, carbuncles, sapphires, declining their rich aspect to the hot breath of Spain, who sent whole armadoes of carracks to be ballast at her nose.

Ant. S. Where stood Belgia, the Netherlands?

Dro. S. O! sir, I did not look so low. To conclude, this drudge, or diviner, laid claim to me; call'd me Dromio; swore I was assur'd to her: told me what privy marks I had about me, as the mark of my shoulder, the mole in my neck, the great wart on my left arm, that I, amaz'd, ran from her as a witch: and, I think, if my breast had not been made of faith, and my heart of steel, she had transform'd me to a curtall-dog, and made me turn i' th' wheel.

Ant. S. Go, hie thee presently post to the road,
And if the wind blow any way from shore,
I will not harbour in this town to-night.
If any bark put forth, come to the mart,
Whore I will walk till thou return to me.
If every one knows us, and we know none,
'Tis time, I think, to trudge, pack, and begone.

Dro. S. As from a bear a man would run for life,
So fly I from her that would be my wife. [*Exit.*

Ant. S. There's none but witches do inhabit here,

And therefore 'tis high time that I were hence.
She that doth call me husband, even my soul
Doth for a wife abhor; but her fair sister,
Possess'd with such a gentle sovereign grace,
Of such enchanting presence and discourse,
Hath almost made me traitor to myself:
But, lest myself be guilty to self-wrong,
I'll stop mine ears against the mermaid's song.

Enter ANGELO.

Ang. Master Antipholus?

Ant. S. Ay, that's my name.

Ang. I know it well, sir. Lo, here is the chain.
I thought to have ta'en you at the Porpentine;
The chain unfinish'd made me stay thus long.

Ant. S. What is your will that I shall do with this?

Ang. What please yourself, sir: I have made it for you.

Ant. S. Made it for me, sir? I bespoke it not.

Ang. Not once, nor twice, but twenty times you have.
Go home with it, and please your wife withal;
And soon at supper-time I'll visit you,
And then receive my money for the chain.

Ant. S. I pray you, sir, receive the money now,
For fear you ne'er see chain, nor money, more.

Ang. You are a merry man, sir. Fare you well. [*Exit.*

Ant. S. What I should think of this, I cannot tell;
But this I think, there's no man is so vain,
That would refuse so fair an offer'd chain.
I see, a man here needs not live by shifts,
When in the streets he meets such golden gifts.
I'll to the mart, and there for Dromio stay:
If any ship put out, then straight away. [*Exit.*

ACT IV.

SCENE I. — A public Place.

Enter a Merchant, ANGELO, *and an* Officer.

MERCHANT.

YOU know, since Pentecost the sum is due,
And, since, I have not much importun'd you;
Nor now I had not, but that I am bound
To Persia, and want guilders for my voyage:
Therefore make present satisfaction,
Or I'll attach you by this officer.

Ang. Even just the sum, that I do owe to you,
Is growing to me by Antipholus;
And, in the instant that I met with you,
He had of me a chain: at five o'clock,
I shall receive the money for the same.
Pleaseth you walk with me down to his house,
I will discharge my bond, and thank you too.

Enter ANTIPHOLUS *of* Ephesus, *and* DROMIO *of* Ephesus, *from the* Courtezan's.

Officer. That labour may you save: see where he comes.

Ant. E. While I go to the goldsmith's house, go thou
And buy a rope's-end; that will I bestow
Among my wife and her confederates,
For locking me out of my doors by day. —
But soft, I see the goldsmith. — Get thee gone;
Buy thou a rope, and bring it home to me.

Dro. E. I buy a thousand pound a-year? I buy a rope? [*Exit.*

Ant. E. A man is well holp up that trusts to you:
I promised your presence, and the chain;
But neither chain nor goldsmith came to me.
Belike, you thought our love would last too long,
If it were chain'd together, and therefore came not.

Ang. Saving your merry humour, here's the note
How much your chain weighs to the utmost caract,
The fineness of the gold, and chargeful fashion,
Which doth amount to three odd ducats more
Than I stand debted to this gentleman:
I pray you, see him presently discharg'd,
For he is bound to sea, and stays but for it.

Ant. E. I am not furnish'd with the present money;
Besides, I have some business in the town.
Good signior, take the stranger to my house,
And with you take the chain, and bid my wife
Disburse the sum on the receipt thereof:
Perchance, I will be there as soon as you.

Ang. Then you will bring the chain to her yourself?

Ant. E. No; bear it with you, lest I come not time enough.

Ang. Well, sir, I will. Have you the chain about you?

Ant. E. An if I have not, sir, I hope you have,
Or else you may return without your money.

Ang. Nay, come, I pray you, sir, give me the chain:
Both wind and tide stays for this gentleman,
And I, to blame, have held him here too long.

Ant. E. Good lord! you use this dalliance, to excuse
Your breach of promise to the Porpentine.

I should have chid you for not bringing it,
But, like a shrew, you first begin to brawl.

Mer. The hour steals on: I pray you, sir, dispatch.

Ang. You hear how he importunes me: — the chain.

Ant. E. Why, give it to my wife, and fetch your money.

Ang. Come, come; you know, I gave it you even now.
Either send the chain, or send me by some token.

Ant. E. Fie! now you run this humour out of breath.
Come, where's the chain? I pray you, let me see it.

Mer. My business cannot brook this dalliance.
Good sir, say whe'r you'll answer me, or no?
If not, I'll leave him to the officer.

Ant. E. I answer you! what should I answer you?

Ang. The money that you owe me for the chain.

Ant. E. I owe you none, till I receive the chain.

Ang. You know, I gave it you half an hour since.

Ant. E. You gave me none: you wrong me much to say so.

Ang. You wrong me more, sir, in denying it:
Consider how it stands upon my credit.

Mer. Well, officer, arrest him at my suit.

Off. I do, and charge you in the Duke's name to obey me.

Ang. This touches me in reputation. —
Either consent to pay this sum for me,
Or I attach you by this officer.

Ant. E. Consent to pay thee that I never had?
Arrest me, foolish fellow, if thou dar'st.

Ang. Here is thy fee: arrest him, officer. —

I would not spare my brother in this case,
If he should scorn me so apparently.

Off. I do arrest you, sir: you hear the suit.

Ant. E. I do obey thee, till I give thee bail. —
But, sirrah, you shall buy this sport as dear,
As all the metal in your shop will answer.

Ang. Sir, sir, I shall have law in Ephesus,
To your notorious shame, I doubt it not.

Enter DROMIO *of* Syracuse.

Dro. S. Master, there is a bark of Epidamnum,
That stays but till her owner comes aboard,
And then, sir, she bears away. Our fraughtage, sir,
I have convey'd aboard, and I have bought
The oil, the balsamum, and aqua-vitæ.
The ship is in her trim: the merry wind
Blows fair from land; they stay for nought at all,
But for their owner, master, and yourself.

Ant. E. How now? a madman? Why, thou peevish sheep,
What ship of Epidamnum stays for me?

Dro. S. A ship you sent me to, to hire waftage.

Ant. E. Thou drunken slave, I sent thee for a rope;
And told thee to what purpose, and what end.

Dro. S. You sent me for a rope's-end as soon.
You sent me to the bay, sir, for a bark.

Ant. E. I will debate this matter at more leisure,
And teach your ears to list me with more heed.
To Adriana, villain, hie thee straight;
Give her this key, and tell her, in the desk
That's cover'd o'er with Turkish tapestry,
There is a purse of ducats: let her send it.
Tell her, I am arrested in the street,
And that shall bail me. Hie thee, slave, be gone.

On, officer, to prison till it come.
[*Exeunt* Merchant, ANGELO, Officer,
and ANT. E.

Dro. S. To Adriana? that is where we din'd,
Where Dowsabel did claim me for her husband:
She is too big, I hope, for me to compass.
Thither I must, although against my will,
For servants must their masters' minds fulfil. [*Exit.*

SCENE II.

Court in the House of ANTIPHOLUS.

Enter ADRIANA *and* LUCIANA.

Adr. Ah! Luciana, did he tempt thee so?
Might'st thou perceive austerely in his eye
That he did plead in earnest? yea or no?
Look'd he or red, or pale? or sad, or merrily?
What observation mad'st thou in this case,
Of his heart's meteors tilting in his face?

Luc. First he deni'd you had in him no right.

Adr. He meant, he did me none: the more my spite.

Luc. Then swore he that he was a stranger here.

Adr. And true he swore, though yet forsworn he were.

Luc. Then pleaded I for you.

Adr. And what said he?

Luc. That love I begg'd for you, he begg'd of me.

Adr. With what persuasion did he tempt thy love?

Luc. With words that in an honest suit might move.
First, he did praise my beauty; then, my speech.

Adr. Didst speak him fair?

Luc. Have patience, I beseech.

Adr. I cannot, nor I will not, hold me still:
My tongue, though not my heart, shall have his will.
He is deformed, crooked, old, and sere,
Ill-fac'd, worse bodied, shapeless every where;
Vicious, ungentle, foolish, blunt, unkind,
Stigmatical in making, worse in mind.

Luc. Who would be jealous, then, of such a one?
No evil lost is wail'd when it is gone.

Adr. Ah! but I think him better than I say,
And yet would herein others' eyes were worse.
Far from her nest the lapwing cries away:
My heart prays for him, though my tongue do curse.

Enter DROMIO *of* Syracuse.

Dro. S. Here, go: the desk! the purse! sweet, now make haste.

Luc. How hast thou lost thy breath?

Dro. S. By running fast.

Adr. Where is thy master, Dromio? is he well?

Dro. S. No, he's in Tartar limbo, worse than Hell:
A devil in an everlasting garment hath him,
One whose hard heart is button'd up with steel;
A fiend, a fairy pitiless and rough;
A wolf, nay, worse, a fellow all in buff;
A back-friend, a shoulder-clapper, one that countermands
The passages of alleys, creeks, and narrow lands:
A hound that runs counter, and yet draws dry-foot well;
One that, before the judgment, carries poor souls to Hell.

Adr. Why, man, what is the matter?

Dro. S. I do not know the matter: he is 'rested on the case.

Adr. What, is he arrested? tell me, at whose suit.

Dro. S. I know not at whose suit he is arrested, well;
But is in a suit of buff which 'rested him, that can I tell.
Will you send him, mistress, redemption? the money in his desk?

Adr. Go fetch it, sister. — This I wonder at;
[*Exit* LUCIANA.
That he, unknown to me, should be in debt: —
Tell me, was he arrested on a band?

Dro. S. Not on a band, but on a stronger thing;
A chain, a chain: do you not hear it ring?

Adr. What, the chain?

Dro. S. No, no, the bell. 'Tis time that I were gone:
It was two ere I left him, and now the clock strikes one.

Adr. The hours come back! that did I never hear.

Dro. S. O, yes; if any hour meet a serjeant, a' turns back for very fear.

Adr. As if Time were in debt! how fondly dost thou reason!

Dro. S. Time is a very bankrupt, and owes more than he's worth to season.
Nay, he's a thief too: have you not heard men say
That Time comes stealing on by night and day?
If he be in debt and theft, and a serjeant in the way,
Hath he not reason to turn back an hour in a day?

Enter LUCIANA.

Adr. Go, Dromio: there's the money, bear it straight,
And bring thy master home immediately. —
Come, sister; I am press'd down with conceit,
Conceit, my comfort, and my injury. [*Exeunt.*

SCENE III.

A public Place.

Enter ANTIPHOLUS *of* Syracuse.

Ant. S. There's not a man I meet but doth salute me,
As if I were their well acquainted friend;
And every one doth call me by my name.
Some tender money to me, some invite me:
Some other give me thanks for kindnesses:
Some offer me commodities to buy:
Even now a tailor call'd me in his shop,
And show'd me silks that he had bought for me,
And, therewithal, took measure of my body.
Sure, these are but imaginary wiles,
And Lapland sorcerers inhabit here.

Enter DROMIO *of* Syracuse.

Dro. S. Master, here's the gold you sent me for. What have you got the picture of old Adam new apparell'd?

Ant. S. What gold is this? What Adam dost thou mean?

Dro. S. Not that Adam that kept the Paradise, but that Adam that keeps the prison: he that goes in the calf's-skin that was kill'd for the prodigal: he that came behind you, sir, like an evil angel, and bid you forsake your liberty.

Ant. S. I understand thee not.

Dro. S. No? why, 'tis a plain case: he that went, like a base-viol, in a case of leather: the man, sir, that, when gentlemen are tired, gives them a stop, and 'rests them: he, sir, that takes pity on decayed men, and gives them suits of durance; he that sets up his rest to do more exploits with his mace than a morris-pike.

Ant. S. What, thou mean'st an officer?

Dro. S. Ay, sir, the Serjeant of the Band; he that brings any man to answer it that breaks his band; one that thinks a man always going to bed, and says, 'God give you good rest!'

Ant. S. Well, sir, there rest in your foolery. Is there any ship puts forth to-night? may we be gone?

Dro. S. Why, sir, I brought you word an hour since that the bark Expedition put forth to-night; and then were you hindered by the Serjeant to tarry for the hoy Delay. Here are the angels that you sent for to deliver you.

Ant. S. The fellow is distract, and so am I;
And here we wander in illusions.
Some blessed power deliver us from hence!

Enter Courtezan.

Courtezan. Well met, well met, Master Antipholus.
I see, sir, you have found the goldsmith now:
Is that the chain you promis'd me to-day?

Ant. S. Satan, avoid! I charge thee, tempt me not!

Dro. S. Master, is this Mistress Satan?

Ant. S. It is the Devil.

Dro. S. Nay, she is worse; she is the Devil's dam; and here she comes in the habit of a light wench: and thereof comes that the wenches say, "God damn me," that's as much as to say, 'God make me a light wench.' It is written, they appear to men like angels of light: light is an effect of fire, and fire will burn; *ergo*, light wenches will burn. Come not near her.

Cour. Your man and you are marvellous merry, sir.
Will you go with me? we'll mend our dinner here.

Dro. S. Master, if you do, expect spoon-meat, and bespeak a long spoon.

Ant. S. Why, Dromio?

Dro. S. Marry, he must have a long spoon that must eat with the Devil.

Ant. S. Avoid, thou fiend! what tell'st thou me of supping?
Thou art, as you are all, a sorceress:
I conjure thee to leave me, and be gone.

Cour. Give me the ring of mine you had at dinner,
Or for my diamond the chain you promis'd,
And I'll be gone, sir, and not trouble you.

Dro. S. Some devils ask but the parings of one's nail,
A rush, a hair, a drop of blood, a pin,
A nut, a cherry-stone;
But she, more covetous, would have a chain.
Master, be wise: an if you give it her,
The Devil will shake her chain, and fright us with it.

Cour. I pray you, sir, my ring, or else the chain.
I hope you do not mean to cheat me so.

Ant. S. Avaunt, thou witch! Come, Dromio, let us go.

Dro. S. 'Fly pride,' says the peacock: Mistress, that you know. [*Exeunt* ANT. *and* DRO.

Cour. Now, out of doubt, Antipholus is mad,
Else would he never so demean himself.
A ring he hath of mine worth forty ducats;
And for the same he promis'd me a chain:
Both one and other he denies me now.
The reason that I gather he is mad,

Besides this present instance of his rage,
Is a mad tale he told to-day at dinner
Of his own doors being shut against his entrance.
Belike, his wife, acquainted with his fits,
On purpose shut the doors against his way.
My way is now, to hie home to his house,
And tell his wife, that, being lunatic,
He rush'd into my house, and took perforce
My ring away. This course I fittest choose,
For forty ducats is too much to lose. [*Exit.*

Scene IV.

The Same.

Enter Antipholus *of* Ephesus, *and an* Officer.

Ant. E. Fear me not, man; I will not break away:
I'll give thee, ere I leave thee, so much money,
To warrant thee, as I am 'rested for.
My wife is in a wayward mood to-day,
And will not lightly trust the messenger:
That I should be attach'd in Ephesus,
I tell you, 'twill sound harshly in her ears.

Enter Dromio *of* Ephesus *with a rope's-end.*

Here comes my man: I think he brings the money.—
How now, sir? have you that I sent you for?

Dro. E. Here's that, I warrant you, will pay them all.

Ant. E. But where's the money?

Dro. E. Why, sir, I gave the money for the rope.

Ant. E. Five hundred ducats, villain, for a rope?

Dro. E. I'll serve you, sir, five hundred at the rate.

Ant. E. To what end did I bid thee hie thee home?

Dro. E. To a rope's-end, sir; and to that end am I return'd.

Ant. E. And to that end, sir, I will welcome you. [*Beats him.*

Off. Good sir, be patient.

Dro. E. Nay, 'tis for me to be patient; I am in adversity.

Off. Good now, hold thy tongue.

Dro. E. Nay, rather persuade him to hold his hands.

Ant. E. Thou whoreson, senseless villain!

Dro. E. I would I were senseless, sir; that I might not feel your blows.

Ant. E. Thou art sensible in nothing but blows, and so is an ass.

Dro. E. I am an ass, indeed: you may prove it by my long ears. I have serv'd him from the hour of my nativity to this instant, and have nothing at his hands for my service, but blows. When I am cold, he heats me with beating; when I am warm, he cools me with beating: I am wak'd with it when I sleep, rais'd with it when I sit, driven out of doors with it when I go from home, welcom'd home with it when I return: nay, I bear it on my shoulders, as a beggar wont her brat; and, I think, when he hath lam'd me, I shall beg with it from door to door.

Ant. E. Come, go along: my wife is coming yonder.

Enter ADRIANA, LUCIANA, *the* Courtezan, PINCH, *and others.*

Dro. E. Mistress, *respice finem*, respect your end; or rather the prophecy, like the parrot, 'Beware the rope's-end.'

Ant. E. Wilt thou still talk? [*Beats him.*

Cour. How say you now? is not your husband mad?

Adr. His incivility confirms no less. —
Good Doctor Pinch, you are a conjurer;
Establish him in his true sense again,
And I will please you what you will demand.

Luc. Alas, how fiery and how sharp he looks!

Cour. Mark, how he trembles in his ecstasy!

Pinch. Give me your hand, and let me feel your pulse.

Ant. E. There is my hand, and let it feel your ear.

Pinch. I charge thee, Satan, hous'd within this man,
To yield possession to my holy prayers,
And to thy state of darkness hie thee straight:
I conjure thee by all the saints in Heaven.

Ant. E. Peace, doting wizard, peace! I am not mad.

Adr. O, that thou wert not, poor distressed soul!

Ant. E. You minion, you; are these your customers?
Did this companion with the saffron face
Revel and feast it at my house to-day,
Whilst upon me the guilty doors were shut,
And I denied to enter in my house?

Adr. O, husband, God doth know, you din'd at home;
Where 'would you had remain'd until this time,
Free from these slanders and this open shame!

Ant. E. Din'd at home! Thou, villain, what say'st thou?

Dro. E. Sir, sooth to say, you did not dine at home.

Ant. E. Were not my doors lock'd up, and I shut out?

Dro. E. Perdy, your doors were lock'd, and you shut out.

Ant. E. And did not she herself revile me there?

Dro. E. Sans fable, she herself revil'd you there.

Ant. E. Did not her kitchen-maid rail, taunt, and scorn me?

Dro. E. Certes, she did; the kitchen-vestal scorn'd you.

Ant. E. And did not I in rage depart from thence?

Dro. E. In verity, you did: — my bones bear witness,
That since have felt the vigour of his rage.

Adr. Is't good to soothe him in these contraries?

Pinch. It is no shame: the fellow finds his vein,
And, yielding to him, humours well his frenzy.

Ant. E. Thou hast suborn'd the goldsmith to arrest me.

Adr. Alas, I sent you money to redeem you,
By Dromio here, who came in haste for it.

Dro. E. Money by me! heart and good-will you might;
But, surely, master, not a rag of money.

Ant. E. Went'st not thou to her for a purse of ducats?

Adr. He came to me, and I deliver'd it.

Luc. And I am witness with her that she did.

Dro. E. God and the rope-maker bear me witness,
That I was sent for nothing but a rope!

Pinch. Mistress, both man and master is possess'd:
I know it by their pale and deadly looks.
They must be bound, and laid in some dark room.

Ant. E. Say, wherefore didst thou lock me forth to-day,
And why dost thou deny the bag of gold?

Adr. I did not, gentle husband, lock thee forth.

Dro. E. And, gentle master, I receiv'd no gold;
But I confess, sir, that we were lock'd out.

Adr. Dissembling villain! thou speak'st false in both.

Ant. E. Dissembling harlot! thou art false in all,
And art confederate with a damned pack
To make a loathsome, abject scorn of me;
But with these nails I'll pluck out these false eyes,
That would behold in me this shameful sport.

Enter three or four, and offer to bind ANTIPHOLUS *and* DROMIO.

Adr. O bind him, bind him! let him not come near me.
Pinch. More company! — the fiend is strong within him.
Luc. Ah me! poor man, how pale and wan he looks!
Ant. E. What, will you murther me? Thou gaoler, thou,
I am thy prisoner: wilt thou suffer them
To make a rescue?
Off. Masters, let him go:
He is my prisoner, and you shall not have him.
Pinch. Go, bind this man, for he is frantic too.
Adr. What wilt thou do, thou peevish officer?
Hast thou delight to see a wretched man
Do outrage and displeasure to himself?
Off. He is my prisoner: if I let him go,
The debt he owes will be requir'd of me.
Adr. I will discharge thee, ere I go from thee.
Bear me forthwith unto his creditor,
And, knowing how the debt grows, I will pay it.
Good Master Doctor, see him safe convey'd
Home to my house. — O, most unhappy day!
Ant. E. O, most unhappy strumpet!
Dro. E. Master, I am here enter'd in bond for you.
Ant. E. Out on thee, villain! wherefore dost thou mad me?

Dro. E. Will you be bound for nothing? be mad, good master;
Cry, The Devil! —

Luc. God help, poor souls! how idlely do they talk.

Adr. Go bear him hence. — Sister, go you with me. —

[*Exeunt* PINCH *and assistants with* ANTIPHOLUS *and* DROMIO.

Say now, whose suit is he arrested at?

Off. One Angelo, a goldsmith; do you know him?

Adr. I know the man. What is the sum he owes?

Off. Two hundred ducats.

Adr. Say, how grows it due?

Off. Due for a chain your husband had of him.

Adr. He did bespeak a chain for me, but had it not.

Cour. When as your husband, all in rage, to-day
Came to my house and took away my ring,
(The ring I saw upon his finger now)
Straight after did I meet him with a chain.

Adr. It may be so, but I did never see it. —
Come, gaoler, bring me where the goldsmith is:
I long to know the truth hereof at large.

Enter ANTIPHOLUS *of* Syracuse, *with his rapier drawn, and* DROMIO *of* Syracuse.

Luc. God, for thy mercy! they are loose again.

Adr. And come with naked swords. Let's call more help,
To have them bound again.

Off. Away! they'll kill us.

[*Exeunt* ADRIANA, LUCIANA, *and* Officer.

Ant. S. I see, these witches are afraid of swords.

Dro. S. She that would be your wife now ran from you.

Ant. S. Come to the Centaur; fetch our stuff from thence:
I long that we were safe and sound aboard.

Dro. S. Faith, stay here this night; they will surely do us no harm: you saw they speak us fair, give us gold. Methinks they are such a gentle nation, that, but for the mountain of mad flesh that claims marriage of me, I could find in my heart to stay here still, and turn witch.

Ant. S. I will not stay to-night for all the town;
Therefore away, to get our stuff aboard. [*Exeunt.*

ACT V.

SCENE I. — The Same. Before an Abbey.

Enter Merchant *and* ANGELO.

ANGELO.

I AM sorry, sir, that I have hinder'd you;
But, I protest, he had the chain of me,
Though most dishonestly he doth deny it.

Mer. How is the man esteem'd here in the city?

Ang. Of very reverend reputation, sir,
Of credit infinite, highly belov'd,
Second to none that lives here in the city:
His word might bear my wealth at any time.

Mer. Speak softly: yonder, as I think, he walks.

Enter ANTIPHOLUS *and* DROMIO *of* Syracuse.

Ang. 'Tis so; and that self chain about his neck,

Which he forswore, most monstrously, to have.
Good sir, draw near to me; I'll speak to him. —
Signior Antipholus, I wonder much
That you would put me to this shame and trouble;
And not without some scandal to yourself,
With circumstance and oaths so to deny
This chain which now you wear so openly:
Beside the charge, the shame, imprisonment,
You have done wrong to this my honest friend;
Who, but for staying on our controversy,
Had hoisted sail and put to sea to-day.
This chain you had of me: can you deny it?

Ant. S. I think I had: I never did deny it.

Mer. Yes, that you did, sir; and forswore it too.

Ant. S. Who heard me to deny it, or forswear it?

Mer. These ears of mine, thou know'st, did hear thee.
Fie on thee, wretch! 'tis pity that thou liv'st
To walk where any honest men resort.

Ant. S. Thou art a villain to impeach me thus.
I'll prove mine honour and mine honesty
Against thee presently, if thou dar'st stand.

Mer. I dare, and do defy thee for a villain.
[*They draw.*

Enter ADRIANA, LUCIANA, Courtezan, *and others.*

Adr. Hold! hurt him not, for God's sake! he is mad. —
Some get within him; take his sword away.
Bind Dromio too, and bear them to my house.

Dro. S. Run, master, run; for God's sake take a house!
This is some priory: — in, or we are spoil'd.
[*Exeunt* ANTIPHOLUS *and* DROMIO *to the Abbey.*

Enter the Lady Abbess.

Abbess. Be quiet, people. Wherefore throng you hither?

Adr. To fetch my poor distracted husband hence.
Let us come in, that we may bind him fast
And bear him home for his recovery.

Ang. I knew he was not in his perfect wits.

Mer. I am sorry, now, that I did draw on him.

Abb. How long hath this possession held the man?

Adr. This week he hath been heavy, sour, sad:
And much different from the man he was;
But, till this afternoon, his passion
Ne'er brake into extremity of rage.

Abb. Hath he not lost much wealth by wrack of sea?
Buried some dear friend? Hath not else his eye
Stray'd his affection in unlawful love?
A sin prevailing much in youthful men
Who give their eyes the liberty of gazing.
Which of these sorrows is he subject to?

Adr. To none of these, except it be the last;
Namely, some love, that drew him oft from home.

Abb. You should for that have reprehended him.

Adr. Why, so I did.

Abb. Ay, but not rough enough.

Adr. As roughly as my modesty would let me.

Abb. Haply, in private.

Adr. And in assemblies too

Abb. Ay, but not enough.

Adr. It was the copy of our conference.
In bed, he slept not for my urging it;
At board, he fed not for my urging it;
Alone, it was the subject of my theme;
In company, I often glanc'd [at] it:
Still did I tell him it was vile and bad.

Abb. And thereof came it that the man was mad:
The venom clamours of a jealous woman
Poison more deadly than a mad dog's tooth.
It seems his sleeps were hinder'd by thy railing,
And thereof comes it that his head is light.
Thou say'st his meat was sauc'd with thy upbraidings:
Unquiet meals make ill digestions;
Thereof the raging fire of fever bred:
And what's a fever but a fit of madness?
Thou say'st his sports were hinder'd by thy brawls:
Sweet recreation barr'd, what doth ensue
But moody and dull melancholy,
Kinsman to grim and comfortless despair,
And at her heels a huge infectious troop
Of pale distemperatures and foes to life?
In food, in sport, and life-preserving rest
To be disturb'd, would mad or man or beast.
The consequence is, then, thy jealous fits
Have scar'd thy husband from the use of wits.
Luc. She never reprehended him but mildly,
When he demean'd himself rough, rude, and wildly. —
Why bear you these rebukes, and answer not?
Adr. She did betray me to my own reproof. —
Good people, enter, and lay hold on him.
Abb. No; not a creature enters in my house.
Adr. Then, let your servants bring my husband forth.
Abb. Neither: he took this place for sanctuary,
And it shall privilege him from your hands,
Till I have brought him to his wits again,
Or lose my labour in essaying it.
Adr. I will attend my husband, be his nurse,
Diet his sickness; for it is my office,
And will have no attorney but myself;
And therefore let me have him home with me.

Abb. Be patient; for I will not let him stir,
Till I have us'd the approved means I have,
With wholesome syrups, drugs, and holy prayers,
To make of him a formal man again.
It is a branch and parcel of mine oath,
A charitable duty of my order;
Therefore depart, and leave him here with me.

Adr. I will not hence, and leave my husband here;
And ill it doth beseem your holiness
To separate the husband and the wife.

Abb. Be quiet, and depart: thou shalt not have him. [*Exit* Abbess.

Luc. Complain unto the Duke of this indignity.

Adr. Come, go: I will fall prostrate at his feet,
And never rise until my tears and prayers
Have won his Grace to come in person hither,
And take perforce my husband from the Abbess.

Mer. By this, I think, the dial points at five:
Anon, I'm sure, the Duke himself in person
Comes this way to the melancholy vale,
The place of death and sorry execution,
Behind the ditches of the Abbey here.

Ang. Upon what cause?

Mer. To see a reverènd Syracusian merchant,
Who put unluckily into this bay
Against the laws and statutes of this town,
Beheaded publicly for his offence.

Ang. See, where they come: we will behold his death.

Luc. Kneel to the Duke before he pass the Abbey.

Enter DUKE *attended:* ÆGEON *bare-headed; with the* Headsman *and other* Officers.

Duke. Yet once again proclaim it publicly,

If any friend will pay the sum for him,
He shall not die: so much we tender him.

Adr. Justice, most sacred Duke, against the Abbess!

Duke. She is a virtuous and a reverend lady:
It cannot be, that she hath done thee wrong.

Adr. May it please your Grace, Antipholus, my husband,
Who I made lord of me, and all I had,
At your important letters, this ill day
A most outrageous fit of madness took him,
That desp'rately he hurried through the street,
(With him his bondman, all as mad as he)
Doing displeasure to the citizens
By rushing in their houses, bearing thence
Rings, jewels, any thing his rage did like.
Once did I get him bound, and sent him home,
Whilst to take order for the wrongs I went,
That here and there his fury had committed.
Anon, I wot not by what strong escape,
He broke from those that had the guard of him,
And with his mad attendant and himself,
Each one with ireful passion, with drawn swords,
Met us again, and, madly bent on us,
Chas'd us away: till, raising of more aid,
We came again to bind them. Then they fled
Into this Abbey, whither we pursu'd them;
And here the Abbess shuts the gates on us,
And will not suffer us to fetch him out,
Nor send him forth, that we may bear him hence.
Therefore, most gracious Duke, with thy command,
Let him be brought forth, and borne hence for help.

Duke. Long since thy husband serv'd me in my wars,
And I to thee engag'd a prince's word,

When thou didst make him master of thy bed,
To do him all the grace and good I could. —
Go, some of you, knock at the Abbey gate,
And bid the Lady Abbess come to me.
I will determine this before I stir.

Enter a Servant.

Serv. O mistress, mistress! shift and save yourself.
My master and his man are both broke loose,
Beaten the maids a-row, and bound the doctor,
Whose beard they have sing'd off with brands of fire;
And ever, as it blaz'd, they threw on him
Great pails of puddled mire to quench the hair.
My master preaches patience to him; and, the while,
His man with scissors nicks him like a fool;
And, sure, unless you send some present help,
Between them they will kill the conjurer.

Adr. Peace, fool! thy master and his man are here:
And that is false thou dost report to us.

Serv. Mistress, upon my life, I tell you true;
I have not breath'd, almost, since I did see it.
He cries for you, and vows, if he can take you,
To scorch your face, and to disfigure you.
[*Cry within*
Hark, hark, I hear him, mistress: fly, be gone.

Duke. Come, stand by me; fear nothing. Guard with halberds!

Adr. Ah me, it is my husband! Witness you,
That he is borne about invisible:
Even now we hous'd him in the Abbey here,
And now he's there, past thought of human reason.

Enter ANTIPHOLUS *and* DROMIO *of* Ephesus.

Ant. E. Justice, most gracious Duke! O! grant me justice,
Even for the service that long since I did thee,
When I bestrid thee in the wars, and took
Deep scars to save thy life; even for the blood
That then I lost for thee, now grant me justice.

Æge. Unless the fear of death doth make me dote,
I see my son Antipholus, and Dromio!

Ant. E. Justice, sweet Prince, against that woman there!
She whom thou gav'st to me to be my wife,
That hath abused and dishonour'd me,
Even in the strength and height of injury.
Beyond imagination is the wrong
That she this day hath shameless thrown on me.

Duke. Discover how, and thou shalt find me just.

Ant. E. This day, great Duke, she shut the doors upon me,
While she with harlots feasted in my house.

Duke. A grievous fault. Say, woman, didst thou so?

Adr. No, my good lord: myself, he, and my sister,
To-day did dine together. So befall my soul,
As this is false he burthens me withal.

Luc. Ne'er may I look on day, nor sleep on night,
But she tells to your highness simple truth.

Ang. O, perjur'd woman! They are both forsworn:
In this the madman justly chargeth them.

Ant. E. My liege, I am advised what I say;
Neither disturb'd with the effect of wine,
Nor heady-rash provok'd with raging ire,

Albeit my wrongs might make one wiser mad.
This woman lock'd me out this day from dinner:
That goldsmith there, were he not pack'd with her,
Could witness it, for he was with me then;
Who parted with me to go fetch a chain,
Promising to bring it to the Porpentine,
Where Balthazar and I did dine together.
Our dinner done, and he not coming thither,
I went to seek him: in the street I met him,
And in his company, that gentleman.
There did this perjur'd goldsmith swear me down,
That I this day of him receiv'd the chain,
Which, God he knows, I saw not; for the which
He did arrest me with an officer.
I did obey, and sent my peasant home
For certain ducats: he with none return'd.
Then fairly I bespoke the officer,
To go in person with me to my house.
B' th' way we met my wife, her sister, and a rabble
more
Of vile confederates: along with them
They brought one Pinch, a hungry lean-fac'd villain,
A mere anatomy, a mountebank,
A thread-bare juggler, and a fortune-teller,
A needy, hollow-ey'd, sharp-looking wretch,
A living dead man. This pernicious slave,
Forsooth, took on him as a conjurer,
And, gazing in mine eyes, feeling my pulse,
And with no face, as 'twere, out-facing me,
Cries out, I was possess'd. Then, altogether
They fell upon me, bound me, bore me thence,
And in a dark and dankish vault at home
There left me and my man, both bound together;
Till, gnawing with my teeth my bonds in sunder,
I gain'd my freedom, and immediately

Ran hither to your Grace, whom I beseech
To give me ample satisfaction
For these deep shames and great indignities.

Ang. My lord, in truth, thus far I witness with him,
That he din'd not at home, but was lock'd out.

Duke. But had he such a chain of thee, or no?

Ang. He had, my lord; and when he ran in here,
These people saw the chain about his neck.

Mer. Besides, I will be sworn, these ears of mine
Heard you confess you had the chain of him,
After you first forswore it on the mart,
And, thereupon, I drew my sword on you;
And then you fled into this Abbey here,
From whence, I think, you are come by miracle.

Ant. E. I never came within these Abbey walls,
Nor ever didst thou draw thy sword on me.
I never saw the chain, so help me Heaven!
And this is false you burthen me withal.

Duke. Why, what an intricate impeach is this!
I think you all have drunk of Circe's cup.
If here you hous'd him, here he would have been;
If he were mad, he would not plead so coldly: —
You say he din'd at home; the goldsmith here
Denies that saying. — Sirrah, what say you?

Dro. E. Sir, he din'd with her, there, at the Porpentine.

Cour. He did, and from my finger snatch'd that ring.

Ant. E. 'Tis true, my liege; this ring I had of her.

Duke. Saw'st thou him enter at the Abbey here?

Cour. As sure, my liege, as I do see your Grace.

Duke. Why, this is strange. — Go call the Abbess hither. —

I think you are all mated, or stark mad.
[*Exit an* Attendant.

Æge. Most mighty Duke, vouchsafe me speak a word.
Haply, I see a friend will save my life,
And pay the sum that may deliver me.

Duke. Speak freely, Syracusian, what thou wilt.

Æge. Is not your name, sir, call'd Antipholus,
And is not that your bondman Dromio?

Dro. E. Within this hour I was his bondman, sir;
But he, I thank him, gnaw'd in two my cords:
Now am I Dromio, and his man, unbound.

Æge. I am sure you both of you remember me.

Dro. E. Ourselves we do remember, sir, by you;
For lately we were bound, as you are now.
You are not Pinch's patient, are you, sir?

Æge. Why look you strange on me? you know me well.

Ant. E. I never saw you in my life till now.

Æge. O! grief hath chang'd me since you saw me last;
And careful hours, with Time's deformed hand,
Have written strange defeatures in my face:
But tell me yet, dost thou not know my voice?

Ant. E. Neither.

Æge. Dromio, nor thou?

Dro. E. No, trust me, sir, nor I.

Æge. I am sure thou dost.

Dro. E. Ay, sir; but I am sure I do not; and whatsoever a man denies, you are now bound to believe him.

Æge. Not know my voice? O, time's extremity!
Hast thou so crack'd and splitted my poor tongue
In seven short years that here my only son

Knows not my feeble key of untun'd cares?
Though now this grained face of mine be hid
In sap-consuming winter's drizzled snow,
And all the conduits of my blood froze up,
Yet hath my night of life some memory,
My wasting lamps some fading glimmer left,
My dull, deaf ears a little use to hear:
All these old witnesses (I cannot err)
Tell me thou art my son Antipholus.

Ant. E. I never saw my father in my life.

Æge. But seven years since, in Syracusa, boy,
Thou know'st we parted. But, perhaps, my son,
Thou sham'st to acknowledge me in misery.

Ant. E. The Duke, and all that know me in the city,
Can witness with me that it is not so.
I ne'er saw Syracusa in my life.

Duke. I tell thee, Syracusian, twenty years
Have I been patron to Antipholus,
During which time he ne'er saw Syracusa.
I see, thy age and dangers make thee dote.

Enter Abbess, *with* Antipholus *of* Syracuse *and* Dromio *of* Syracuse.

Abb. Most mighty Duke, behold a man much wrong'd. [*All gather to see them.*

Adr. I see two husbands, or mine eyes deceive me!

Duke. One of these men is Genius to the other;
And so of these: which is the natural man,
And which the spirit? Who deciphers them?

Dro. S. I, sir, am Dromio: command him away.

Dro. E. I, sir, am Dromio: pray let me stay.

Ant. S. Ægeon, art thou not? — or else his ghost.

Dro. S. O, my old master! Who hath bound him here?

Abb. Whoever bound him, I will loose his bonds,
And gain a husband by his liberty.—
Speak, old Ægeon, if thou be'st the man
That hadst a wife once call'd Æmilia,
That bore thee at a burden two fair sons.
O! if thou be'st the same Ægeon, speak,
And speak unto the same Æmilia!

Æge. If I dream not, thou art Æmilia.
If thou art she, tell me, where is that son
That floated with thee on the fatal raft?

Abb. By men of Epidamnum, he, and I,
And the twin Dromio, all were taken up;
But, by and by, rude fishermen of Corinth
By force took Dromio and my son from them,
And me they left with those of Epidamnum.
What then became of them, I cannot tell;
I, to this fortune that you see me in.

Duke. Why, here begins his morning story right.
These two Antipholus', these two so like,
And these two Dromios, one in semblance,—
Besides her urging of her wrack at sea;—
These are the parents to these children,
Which accidentally are met together.
Antipholus, thou cam'st from Corinth first.

Ant. S. No, sir, not I: I came from Syracuse.

Duke. Stay, stand apart: I know not which is which.

Ant. E. I came from Corinth, my most gracious lord.

Dro. E. And I with him.

Ant. E. Brought to this town by that most famous warrior,
Duke Menaphon, your most renowned uncle.

Adr. Which of you two did dine with me to-day?

Ant. S. I, gentle mistress.

Adr. And are not you my husband?
Ant. E. No; I say nay to that.
Ant. S. And so do I, yet did she call me so;
And this fair gentlewoman, her sister here,
Did call me brother. — What I told you then,
I hope I shall have leisure to make good,
If this be not a dream I see and hear.
Ang. That is the chain, sir, which you had of me.
Ant. S. I think it be, sir: I deny it not.
Ant. E. And you, sir, for this chain arrested me.
Ang. I think I did, sir: I deny it not.
Adr. I sent you money, sir, to be your bail,
By Dromio; but I think, he brought it not.
Dro. E. No, none by me.
Ant. S. This purse of ducats I receiv'd from you,
And Dromio, my man, did bring them me.
I see, we still did meet each other's man,
And I was ta'en for him, and he for me,
And thereupon these errors all arose.
Ant. E. These ducats pawn I for my father here.
Duke. It shall not need: thy father hath his life.
Cour. Sir, I must have that diamond from you.
Ant. E. There, take it; and much thanks for my good cheer.
Abb. Renowned Duke, vouchsafe to take the pains
To go with us into the Abbey here,
And hear at large discoursed all our fortunes;
And all that are assembled in this place,
That by this sympathized one day's error
Have suffer'd wrong, go, keep us company,
And we shall make full satisfaction.
Twenty-five years have I but gone in travail
Of you, my sons; and till this present hour
My heavy burthen here delivered. —
The Duke, my husband, and my children both,

And you the calendars of their nativity,
Go to a gossips' feast, and joy with me:
After so long grief, such nativity!

Duke. With all my heart: I'll gossip at this feast.

[*Exeunt* Duke, Abbess, ÆGEON, Courtezan, Merchant, ANGELO, *and* Attendants.

Dro. S. Master, shall I fetch your stuff from shipboard?

Ant. E. Dromio, what stuff of mine hast thou embark'd?

Dro. S. Your goods, that lay at host, sir, in the Centaur.

Ant. S. He speaks to me.—I am your master, Dromio:
Come, go with us; we'll look to that anon.
Embrace thy brother there; rejoice with him.

[*Exeunt* ANT. S. *and* E., ADR., *and* LUC.

Dro. S. There is a fat friend at your master's house,
That kitchen'd me for you to-day at dinner:
She now shall be my sister, not my wife.

Dro. E. Methinks, you are my glass, and not my brother:
I see by you I am a sweet-fac'd youth.
Will you walk in to see their gossiping?

Dro. S. Not I, sir: you are my elder.

Dro. E. That's a question: how shall we try it?

Dro. S. We'll draw cuts for the senior: till then, lead thou first.

Dro. E. Nay, then thus:
We came into the world like brother and brother;
And now, let's go hand in hand, not one before another.

[*Exeunt.*

NOTES ON THE COMEDY OF ERRORS.

ACT FIRST.

Scene I.

p. 141. "—— wanting *guilders*" :— The guilder is both a Flemish and a German coin; the former being about thirty-eight cents in value, the latter about eighty-seven.

" "Both by the *Syracusians*" :— This is the uniform orthography of the folio, showing plainly that the presence of the *i* is not accidental, and indicating the pronunciation of the word. Therefore, and not because Bentley approved of it, it is retained. Bentley was at the needless trouble of deriving Syracusians from Συρακούσιοι; but a similar introduction of *i* is a very common error in classic neology.

p. 142. "And by me [*too*]" :— 'Too,' omitted in the first, was added in the second folio.

" "—— voyages I often *made*" :— A merchant was said to make a voyage when he sent a ship on one. It is evident, from the context, that *Ægeon* did not go to Epidamnum until after the death of his factor there.

" "To *Epidamnum*" :— This word is uniformly spelled "Epidamium" in the first folio; but being a proper name, it is corrected, although an English adjective formed from it, like "Syracusian," above, should not be. The case differs, too, from that of 'Argier' in *The Tempest*; that being a different word from 'Algiers,' not an improper spelling of it. Epidamnum is the town at which the travelling brother in the *Menæchmi* arrives.

" "A mean*er* woman," &c. :— The folio has "A *meane* woman," — the *r* having dropped out. This slight error not having been perceived, the interpolation of 'poor,' — "A *poor* mean woman," — made in the second folio, has, of necessity, been hitherto retained, in spite of the disagreeable repetition of the word in the next line but one. That the use of the comparative implied no positive meanness of condition in *Ægeon's* wife, the whole literature of Shakespeare's day, and these two instances out of several in his own plays, may be brought to prove.

"*Pros.* Thou and thy meaner fellows your last service
Did worthily perform." *Tempest*, Act IV. Sc. 1.

"*Qu. Eliz.* And meaner than myself have had like
fortune." *3 Henry VI.*, Act IV. Sc. 1.

p. 144. "*Were* carried towards Corinth": — The original has "*Was* carried," a disagreement which is of very frequent occurrence in the original text of this comedy. It may possibly be the result of carelessness, but seems rather to be indicative of the early period at which parts of the play were written. See the *Preface*, Vol. I. Perhaps this antique rudeness should not be polished away; but the text has been for so many years regulated according to established usage, and an adherence to the original would so deform the language and annoy the general reader, that previous custom has been conformed to. In all editions hitherto the change has been made silently.

"—— violently borne *upon*": — The original has "*up*," the second folio "up *upon*." The correction required is obvious.

" "Gave *healthful* welcome": — The second folio needlessly substituted "*helpful*," which many editors adopted.

p. 145. "What *hath* befall'n of them, and *thee*": — The original has "*have*" and "*they*." The correction was made in the second folio.

" "Roaming *clean* through," &c.: — This word, in its sense of 'entirely,' 'perfectly,' is so commonly used in America, that Steevens' remark, made seventy-five years ago, that it is "still used in the northern parts of England," is valuable on this side the water only because it is one of the many evidences that the English of the Bible and of Shakespeare exists in greater purity here than there.

" "To seek thy [*life*]": — The original has, "To seek thy *help* by beneficial help." This part of the play was surely written by Shakespeare, and although Mr. Dyce says, in the words of Malone, that the jingle is quite in Shakespeare's manner, let who will believe that he wrote, at any time, such tautological nonsense. Shakespeare often repeats a word, or uses one which sounds much like another which has just preceded it, in a manner seeming to indicate that he sought the 'jingle,' or, rather, I think, that the similarity of sound suggested the second word; but he never sacrifices sense to sound, as he would have done by saying that a man sought help by help. Mr. Singer proposed to read 'fine;' Mr. Collier suggested 'hope,' which was afterward found in his folio of 1632; but it was Ægeon's *life* that he was to seek by beneficial help. The *Duke* says, "though thou art adjudged to the *death*, yet will I favour thee; . . . therefore I'll limit thee this day to seek thy" —— what? With what other word than 'life' could he fitly close his sentence? The error did not result from a mistake of one word for the other, but almost surely from a confusion of memory in the mind of the compositor, who set the whole line at once. Pope read 'life.'

p. 146. "—— doth Ægeon *wend*": — Steevens and others, writing for our great grandfathers, and Halliwell, writing for us, call this word obsolete. In America it is not as commonly used as 'come' or 'go,' only because there is less frequent occasion for it.

" "—— his *live*less end": — So the first folio: not by a typographical error or careless writing, or from unsettled orthography, but because that was a form of the word in use when the line was written.

SCENE II.

" "*Enter* ANTIPHOLUS": — The old stage direction here is, "*Enter* ANTIPHOLUS *Erotes*," afterward ANTIPHOLUS *Errotis*, — corruptions of *Erraticus*. See *Introduction*.

" "A trusty *villain*": — a faithful bondsman: the original signification of the word. So *Iago* speaks of "honest knaves," — 'knave' meaning 'servant.' See Notes on *Othello*, Act I. Sc. 1.

p. 147. "And afterwards consort you," &c.: — It is more than probable that 'with' has dropped, or was omitted, between "consort" and "you;" but 'consort' was used without the preposition; and the rhythm of the line may be preserved by making "bed time" a spondee.

p. 148. "I shall be *post* indeed": — Scores were kept on posts.

"Kate she keeps the schore, syr,
And schores yt on the post."

See the third of *Three Curious Ballads*, published by the Shakespeare Society. But the post thus scored was probably the door-post.

" "—— should be your *clock*": — The folio has "*cook*:" — a manifest error, corrected by Pope.

p. 149. "The villain is *o'er-raught*": — over-reached.

ACT SECOND.

Scene I.

p. 150. "Court in the House of Antipholus": — The original is without stage directions, or division into Scenes. Modern editors, from and including Malone, have most unaccountably made the interviews between *Adriana* and her sister and *Dromio* and others, occur in "A public Place." Setting aside the absurdity of making two women walk out into a street or square on either of the occasions in question, on this, *Adriana* says that neither husband nor slave has *returned;* and when *Dromio* appears, she tells him twice to go *back* to his master and fetch him *home*, and he replies, "Go *back* again, and be new beaten *home?*" It is almost needless to say that the place of the Scene is the house of *Antipholus*. I have placed it in the court; because in Eastern houses, and those of all tropical countries, there is an inner court open to the street, in which the females of the household pass much time: into this court the *Dromios* would run with their messages, and in a part of such a court, covered with an arched roof, *Adriana* would most probably sit at dinner in the first Scene of the next Act.

" "—— he takes it [ill]": — The folio has "he takes it *thus*." That the text, which is that of the second folio, is correct, appears not only from the rhyme, but the sense. 'Thus' refers to nothing.

p. 151. "Spake he so *doubtfully*": — Both here and in *Dromio's* reply, Mr. Collier's folio of 1632 has "*doubly*."

p. 152. "He ask'd me for a *thousand* marks": — The original has "a *hundred;*" an error which was corrected in the second folio.

" "Will you come [*home*], quoth I": — Theobald supplied the word in brackets, which is not in the folio, but which the rhythm requires, and which was probably passed over in MS. on account of its similarity to the word immediately before it.

p. 153. "—— his *stale*": — Steevens takes this to mean 'his pretended wife,' the sportsman's stalking horse having been called a stale; but is not the more obvious signification of the word the more appropriate?

" "Would that alone, *alone*," &c.: — The original has "*a love*" for the second 'alone:' an obvious error, corrected in the second folio.

p. 153. "I see tne jewel," &c.: — This passage stands thus corrupted in the folio: —

"I see the Iewell best enameled
Will loose his beautie: yet *the* gold bides still
That others touch, *and* often touching will,
Where gold and no man that hath a name,
By falshood and corruption doth it shame."

The restoration is the resultant of the labors of Theobald, (or Warburton,) Steevens, and Collier. The corruption was produced by mistaking 'tho'' for 'the,' 'an' for 'and,' and 'wear' (by the ear) for 'where.' Theobald read,

"and *so* no man that hath a name
But falsehood," &c.:

Heath, more plausibly,

"and *so a* man that hath a name
By falsehood and corruption doth it shame."

Scene II.

p. 155. "Hold, *sir* — Pray, *sir* — Ay, *sir* — Nothing, *sir*": — This use of 'sir,' — a word which is scattered in just this way through the dramatic literature of the golden age of English letters and of the English language "as thick as leaves in Vallombrosa," — the Great Britons of to-day sneer at as an Americanism! It occurs here, in a short dialogue, at least twenty times, and in Act V. Sc. 1, p. 202, five times in five consecutive lines.

p. 156. "—— *fine* and *recovery*": — This is a law term for a now obsolete mode of transferring a title to real estate. The frequent occurrence of such phrases in Shakespeare's works and his very accurate use of them, have been justly considered as evidence that he had studied law before he went to London. See *Life*, Vol. I.

" "—— what he hath scanted *men* in hair": — The original has "*them*." Theobald made the necessary correction.

p. 157. "—— in a thing *falling*": — The folio has "*falsing*," with a long *s*, of course, — a very easy mistake for the word in the text, which was suggested by Heath, though on very insufficient ground. That it is the word, however, is shown by *Antipholus*' expression, "not *sure*," (for 'sure' was of old opposed not to 'false,' but to 'uncertain,' 'insecure,') and *Dromio's*, "they should not *drop*;" and besides, in what possible sense is the hair *falsing*? Yet that word has hitherto been retained.

" "—— to save the money that he spends in *trimming*": — The folio has "*trying*," quite plainly an error for 'tryming,' — the loss of a man's hair saving him, of course, all expense in getting it cut. Pope read "'*tiring*,'" which is less conformable to the sense and the old word. The proper word appears in both Mr. Collier's and Mr. Singer's corrected copies of the folio of 1632.

p. 157. "—— namely, *is* no time to recover hair": — An elision for 'there is,' quite suitable to *Dromio*. We have had the same just before in *Measure for Measure*, Act I. Sc. 5, twice.

> "The Duke is very strangely gone from hence;
> — Bore many gentlemen," &c.,

for '*He* bore,' &c.:

> "Doth he so seek his life?
> Has censur'd him," &c.,

for '*He* has censured,' &c.; and we have the same just after in this play, Act IV. Sc. 2, "But is in a suit of buff," &c., for "But *he* is in," &c. The first folio has "*in* no time," — easily misprinted for "*is*," &c. But the error has hitherto remained undetected; Malone and all his successors reading "*e'en*," a forced correction and a strange expression in this place, and the second folio, which Mr. Dyce would follow, cutting the knot by dropping the word altogether.

p. 158. "I live distain'd, thou *one dishonoured*": — The folio has "*undishonoured*," a very easy typographical error for 'one dishonoured,' — 'one' being spelled '*o n*': see Notes on this word, *Two Gentlemen of Verona*, Act II. Sc. 1, and *Merry Wives of Windsor*, Act II. Sc. 1. The error, however, has hitherto remained uncorrected, and has caused much trouble, and a perversion of the author's meaning. It has been even attempted to make "distain'd" mean 'unstained,' that is, exactly the reverse of what it does and ever did mean; which is absurd, as Mr. Dyce perceived; and he, therefore, (Theobald having made the suggestion,) would have it a *misprint* for '*un*stained,' which is not probable, especially if it were succeeded by '*un*-dishonoured.' Besides, this gives a meaning directly opposed to the tenor of *Adriana's* speech. She believes *Antipholus* guilty; and says to him, "I *am* possessed with an adulterate blot," "I *do* digest the poison of thy flesh," &c., "Keep, then, fair league," &c., for now "I live distain'd, thou one dishonoured."

" "Want wit in all, one word," &c.: — Never was point more needed, even in the prologue to *Pyramus and Thisbe*, to prevent plain sense from becoming absolute nonsense; and yet this comma, which appears in the original folio, has, strangely enough, been omitted in every modern edition until the present.

p 160. "—— the *forced* fallacy": — The original has "*free'd*," which, being manifestly an error, Pope read '*favoured*,' Steevens '*offered*,' and Mr. Collier's folio of 1632 '*proffered*.' The second word has been hitherto justly preferred to a place in the text, as it conforms most nearly both to the sense of the passage and to the trace of the word in the original, although remote enough from the latter. *Adriana's* persistence, and *Antipholus*' phrase, "*sure* uncertainty," in the previous line, show that there was an easily made misprint of 'free'd' for 'forced.'

"—— goblins, *owles*, [*elves*,] and sprites": — The original has "goblins, owles, and sprights," thus leaving the line imperfect. The second folio has "goblins, owles, and *elves* sprights," upon which the hitherto accepted reading, "goblins, owls, and *elvish* sprites," is founded. But as Shakespeare never elsewhere designates sprites or fairies as elvish, although he had so often occasion for doing so, had he deemed the epithet a fit or a proper one, and as elves always figure in his fairy land, we are warranted in believing that he did not make this one instance doubly exceptional. "Owl*es*" is retained because its old dissyllabic pronunciation of the plural seems evidently intended here. For these reasons the editor had thus regulated the line before the discovery of Mr. Collier's folio of 1632, in which the same reading was found.

"Dromio, thou *drone*": — The original has "Dromio, thou *Dromio*," which, if it stood alone, and *Luciana* were calling out to *Dromio* at a distance, to attract his attention, would be correct, as such repetition was the habit of the time: but she is evidently relieving her vexation by heaping abusive epithets upon him, and he stands close by, attending to her. The second '*Dromio*,' too, crushes a line already overloaded by the first. The habit alluded to probably produced the misprint, which Theobald pointed out.

ACT THIRD.

Scene I.

p. 161. "Before the house of Antipholus": — Since Malone's time the locality of this Scene has been, in all editions hitherto, A Public Place. But it plainly passes before the house of *Antipholus*; and though that was a public place, so was any other part of the city. See the corresponding Note, Act II. Sc. 1.

p. 162. "*Mome* . . . idiot, *patch*": — 'Mome,' a word of uncertain etymology, meant 'a stupid fool': 'patch,' applied at first to a professed fool, from his party-colored costume, (instances of which use of the word are frequent in these plays,) was also used as a term of contempt and reproach; as, for instance, in the old rhyme, preserved by that eminent *littératrice* to whom we owe more than to any, or perhaps all, of her successors, *Mother Goose*: —

> "Cross patch, draw the latch,
> Sit by the fire and spin."

p. 163. "—— thy name for *a face*": — The folio has "*an asse*," with two long *s*'s. What *Dromio* could mean by changing a name for an ass, would pose the Sphinx and Œdipus. Both the sense and the rhyme justify the reading in the text, which appeared in Mr. Collier's folio of 1632.

p. 164. "If thy name be called *Luce*,
Luce, thou hast answered him well."

To understand *Dromio* of Syracuse's commendation of the girl's retort to his brother's proverb, it is necessary to remember that a pike was called a luce.

" "Do you hear, you minion," &c.: — Malone's conjecture, that a line had been lost here, which he rested only upon the lack of a rhyme for "hope" at the end of this one, is supported by the subsequent context. As the text stands now, *Luce's* reply to *Antipholus*, *Dromio* of Syracuse's reply to her, and his brother's remark upon the retort, are not only without point, but actually without a subject. Theobald tried to help the matter by reading 'I *trow*,' which supplies the rhyme by making a triplet; and the same reading was found in Mr. Collier's folio of 1632; but the missing rhyme is the least of the trouble. Should the *Historie of Error* ever come to light, what is lost may possibly be found.

" "Let him knock till it *ache*": — The original spells this word *ake*. Although the noun was pronounced 'aitch,' the verb, whether singular or plural, seems to have had the *ch* hard.

p. 165. "It *seems* thou want'st breaking": — In the original we have "It seem*es*;" and although this was the common orthography of the time, it would appear from the rhythm that the ancient dissyllabic pronunciation was intended; else why was 'wantest' contracted? So, in the next line but one, we have "I when fowl*es*" in the original; a second syllable being equally desirable for the rhythm. The aspect of the rhyming part of this Scene is in all respects consistent with the supposition that it was written before Shakespeare's day.

p. 165. "—— of *her* wisdom" :—The folio has "*your* wisdom," by a mistake so palpable as hardly to require notice, and which occurs more than once in this play; in even the printed text of which, the use of the old abbreviations, 'y^e' for 'the,' and 'y^r' for 'your,' and 'y^t' for 'that,' is remarkably common. Hence the easy mistake of 'her,' the *h* having a bow below the line, for 'y^r.'

p. 166. "—— to the *Porpentine*" :—This orthography uniformly occurs in the folio in this and all the other plays in which the name of the animal is mentioned. It is not a different way of spelling 'porcupine,' but a different word, or at least a different form of the word, and therefore must not be disturbed. This decision is also that of Mr. Dyce, who gives it, by quotation and argument, a support almost superfluous.

Scene II.

p. 167. "—— grow so *ruinous*" :—The folio has "*ruinate*," which the rhyme shows to be wrong. The correction is Malone's. The folio has also "building*s*" for "building."

" "—— make us *but* believe" :—The folio has "*not*."

p. 168. "—— to you I do *decline*" :—lean: used of old in the sense of 'incline.'

" "—— as a *bride* I'll take thee" :—The folio reads "as a *bud*," &c.; a palpable misprint, this correction of which is due to the happy conjecture of Mr. Howard Stanton. It is fully sustained, and indeed required, by the last line of the speech.

" "Not mad, but *mated*" :—crazed, bewildered.

" "Gaze *where* you should" :—The folio misprints, "*when*."

p. 169. "—— for I *aim* thee" :—I seek thee: a common use of 'aim' in Shakespeare's day. The folio has "*am*." The correction is by Steevens. Rowe read 'mean.'

"—— and *besides* myself" :—The unwarrantable custom of the day having made two words of 'beside' and 'besides,' which are one and the same in all respects, except a slight terminal corruption in the latter, it is proper to point out that *Dromio* says he is 'beside himself,' i. e., 'distracted;' the idea that he is another man than himself being conveyed by way of pun. There is no more difference between 'beside' and 'besides' than between 'a little way' and its corruption, 'a little way*s*;' and the text should be changed to 'beside,' were it not that so doing would seem to recognize a distinction which does not exist, and destroy one of the best and most accessible proofs that there is but one word, i. e., 'beside;' — the *s* having been indifferently used or omitted in the orthography of the day when Shakespeare's plays were written, and of that when the Bible was translated. So, "he . . . is horne-mad, and talketh like a man besides himself." Holland's *Translation of Livy*. "Paul, thou art besides thyself." *Acts* xxvi. 24, editions of 1535, 1599, and 1607.

p. 170. "—— without he say *sir reverence*": — Malone first quoted Blount's Glossography, 1682, to show that 'sir reverence' was a vulgar corruption of '*salva reverentia!*' It was; but that sense is not to the purpose, except in the way of pun. *Dromio* alludes to the filthy condition of the "beastly creature," and makes use of the dirtiest possible comparison: "for he hath wares that are not worth a save reverence — *nam merces habet quæ non* merdâ *valent*." *Janua Linguarum*. 1640. Sig. B 3. And see Grose's *Vulgar Tongue*.

" "—— for why? she sweats, a man may go," &c.: — That is, 'she sweats *so* that a man may go,' &c. Mr. Dyce would remove the interrogation mark and take "for why she sweats" to mean 'because she sweats.' But this is entirely unnecessary.

" "—— her name *and* three quarters": — The folio has "*is*," — a palpable misprint.

p. 171. "—— arm'd and *revolted*, making war against her *heir*": — An allusion to the war of the League against Henry of Navarre, who became heir to the throne of France in 1589. See *Introduction*. In the Variorum edition are two pages of annotation upon the last word of the passage, by Theobald, Johnson, and Malone. Johnson contends that *Dromio* alludes only to a certain stage of that French disease, ("*nomenque a gente recepit*,") gibes upon which seem to have been the standing joke of the stage in Shakespeare's day. The folio has "arm'd and *reverted*;" but although the latter word has been silently retained in the text hitherto, it is plainly a misprint, and the easiest possible, for 'revolted.' The former word was very rarely used in Shakespeare's day, and then exclusively in its radical sense, 'to return.' Minsheu does not even define it; but merely refers to 'return.' It could not be intended as a synonyme for 'revolt;' and any other sense is inadmissible, whether we read 'heir' or 'hair.' Cotgrave, Florio, Cooper, Phillips, and Littleton, as well as Minsheu, all completely sustain this emendation by their definitions.

ACT FOURTH.

Scene I.

p. 173. "—— and *her* confederates": — The folio has "*their*."

p. 174. "—— to the utmost *caract*": — now spelled 'carat:' a weight of twelve grains.

"Perchance I *will* be there": — 'I will,' instead of 'I shall,' is a Scotticism, says English Douce: it is an Irishism, says Scotch Reed: and an ancient Anglicism, says Irish Malone.

p. 175. "—— or send *me by* some token": — This is the original text, and means 'send some word by me which will be a token to your wife that I come from you:' as, for instance, in Marston's *Dutch Courtesan*, Act III. Sc. 1.: —

"*Mrs. Mulligrub*. By what token are you sent? — by no token? Nay, I have wit.

"*Cocledemoy*. He sent me by the same token that he was dry shaved this morning."

Yet I cannot but think that there has been a transposition, and that we should read, 'send *by me* some token.' A moment before *Antipholus* had said to *Angelo*, —

"— with you *take the chain*, and bid my wife
Disburse the sum *on the receipt* thereof."

It is natural that the goldsmith should want the chain or a voucher for it.

"—— say *whe'r* you'll answer": — for 'whether you'll answer.'

p. 176. "*Enter* Dromio *of* Syracuse": — "*from the bay*," adds the first folio.

" "—— thou *peevish* sheep": — thou silly sheep.

" "—— to *hire* waftage": — Here 'hire' is a dissyllable: it is spelled "hier" in the folio.

Scene II.

p. 177. "*Of* his heart's meteors": — The original has "*Oh*."

" "—— he *deni'd* you had in him *no* right": — This is a pure Greek construction. See Note on "nor Nature never lends," *Measure for Measure*, Act I. Sc. 1.

p. 178. "—— *sweet*, now make haste": — Mr. Collier's folio has "*swift*."

" "—— in an *everlasting garment*": — That is, as *Dromio* says soon after, "all in buff," the uniform of serjeants, which was very durable.

p. 178. "A fiend, a *fairy*":—So the original, which was changed by Theobald and in Mr. Collier's folio of 1632 to '*fury*.' It is not improbable that 'fury' was the author's word; but in Shakespeare's early days all fairies were not necessarily supposed to be like *Oberon* and *Titania* or their attendants; there were fairies pitiless and rough; and therefore the text must stand.

" "—— *runs counter* and yet *draws dry foot*":—Hunting cant. To 'run counter' is to run the wrong way; to 'draw dry foot,' to hunt by the scent of the foot.

" "—— carries poor souls to *Hell*":—'Hell' was a cant word for 'prison.'

" "—— he's 'rested *on the case*":—The 'action on the case' was so called because it was brought upon the case as described, for a wrong done without force, for the redress of which there was no particular form of procedure provided by law. It is now, *ipso nomine*, obsolete.

p. 179. "But *is* in a suit of buff":—For '*he* is':—an elliptical mode of expression not uncommon of old. See Note on "namely, is no time," Act II. Sc. 2.

" "*That* he, unknown," &c.:—The folio has "*Thus*," which the second folio corrected.

" "—— if any *hour* meet a sergeant":—To understand *Dromio's* joke, it is necessary to remember that 'hour' and 'whore' were both of old pronounced *hoor*,—the word originally having been *hure*, Anglo-Saxon.

" "If *he* be in debt":—The folio has "If *I*," which Malone corrected. Rowe read, 'If *Time*,' and is followed by Mr. Dyce, who supposes 'I' to be a misprint for 'T.,' used as an abbreviation for 'Time.'

Scene III.

p. 180. "Some *other* give me thanks":—This is not a misprint for 'Some others.' The plural form 'others' is of comparatively recent introduction. The more common expression in Shakespeare's day was 'other some.'

" "What have you got the picture of old Adam new apparell'd":—The old Adam new apparelled was the serjeant in buff leather, whom *Dromio* compares to Adam in his dress of skins, or, perhaps, in his own buff; and Mr. Collier says that 'what have you got' is still a vulgar phrase for 'what have you done with.' The passage, however, still seems awkward, and is perhaps corrupt. Theobald read, 'What, have you *got rid* of,' &c.

" "—— gives them a *stop*":—The original has "*sob*,"

a manifest misprint for the word in the text. In all modern editions hitherto, except Mr. Collier's, who retains 'sob,' it has been changed to '*fob*'! a word equally devoid of any shade of meaning here. For how does an officer give men a *fob*? and could giving a man a *fob* rest or arrest him? giving him a *stop* would do both.

p. 181. "—— a morris-pike": — a Moorish pike; an ancient weapon.

p. 182. "—— expect spoonmeat *and* bespeak a long spoon": — The folio misprints "*or* bespeak."

"Avoid, *thou* fiend": — The folio has "Avoid *then*," the easiest of all misprints from the similarity of *o* and *e* in old MS., and of *n* and *u* in all MS. 'Then' has no relation. The correction was made in Mr. Collier's folio of 1632. Mr. Dyce proposes 'Avoid *thee*;' but while *e* and *o* were almost identical in appearance, *e* and *u* were very unlike. Just below *Antipholus* says, "Avaunt, thou witch."

SCENE IV.

p. 184. "—— like the parrot," &c.: — It was the custom to teach parrots to prophesy ill luck. Warburton makes the following apt quotation from *Hudibras*, which refers to *Ralpho's* skill in augury: —

"Could tell what subtlest parrots mean,
That speak and think contrary clean;
What member 'tis of whom they talk,
When they cry *Rope*, and *Walk, knave, walk*."

p. 185. "—— your *customers*": — those to whose company you are accustomed: of old, a common use of the word.

" "Perdy": — a corruption of '*par Dieu*.'

p. 186. "—— my bones *bear* witness": — The folio has "*bears*." See Note on "Were carried towards Corinth," Act I. Sc. 1. These disagreements are so common in the old text of this play that further notice of them is needless.

p. 187. "*Enter three or four*," &c.: — This is the stage direction of the folio. The attempt is successful, as we see by the text.

p. 188. "*Exeunt* ADRIANA," &c.: — The folio has, "*Run all out*," after *Adriana's* speech, and after the Officer's, "*Exeunt omnes, as fast as may be, frighted*."

p. 189. "—— fetch our *stuff*": — luggage, baggage. "In that day, he which shall be upon the house top, and his stuff in the house, let him not come down to take it away." *Luke* xvii. 31.

ACT FIFTH.

Scene I.

p. 190. "—— thou know'st did hear thee": — Capell read, to complete the rhythm, 'did hear thee, *sir;*' but if a word be lost, which is not improbable, we should rather read, "These ears of mine, thou know'st, did hear thee *swear.*" Editors generally make the line lamely out by reading, "thou know*est.*"

" "Some get within *him*": — his guard.

" "[*Exeunt . . . to the* Abbey": — The folio has "*Priory.*"

p. 191. "—— heavy, *sour,* sad": — Here and elsewhere 'sour' is a dissyllable. This use of it is a remnant of the more ancient spelling and pronunciation *sower,* that being the orthography in the original text.

" "—— the *copy* of our conference": — that which was constantly before us, the subject of our conference. Some editors would have the word to be 'co-pie,' from the Latin *copia,* and used as Cooper uses it in his translation of Cicero's phrase "*copiose et abundanter loqui,*" — 'to use his words with great copie and abundance of eloquence.' But this is needlessly going very far for very little.

" "I often glanced [at] it" — 'At,' wanting in the original, is supplied in Mr. Collier's folio of 1632.

p. 192. "And at *her* heels": — Thus the folio. Heath suggested and Malone read "*their* heels," because of the disagreement in gender between "her" and "kinsman;" but this is entirely inadmissible; for it is melancholy alone at whose heels follows the infectious troop. Ritson justly remarked that "*kinsman* means no more than *near relation;*" and Mr. Verplanck clearly solves whatever difficulty there may be in the passage, by quoting the following lines from *The Merchant of Venice,* (Act III. Sc. 2,) in which *Portia* calls herself—

> "—— the *lord*
> Of this fair manor, *master* o'er my servants,
> Queen o'er myself."

Heath reads "moody *moping* and dull," &c.: Singer, "moody *sadness* and dull," &c.

p. 193. "—— a *formal* man": — a reasonable man. See Note on "these poor, informal women," *Measure for Measure,* Act V. Sc. 1.

" "The place of *death*": — The folio has "*depth,*" which Rowe corrected. Mr. Hunter would retain the original word as meaning "the *Barathrum*, or deep pit into which offenders were cast"!

p. 194. "*Who* I made lord of me": — Thus the original, in opposition, as Shakespeare and his contemporaries constantly were, to modern usage.

" "—— your *important* letters": — for 'importunate letters.' The word is so used elsewhere in these plays.

p. 195. "—— nicks him like a fool": — Malone quotes the following illustrative passage from Gent's *Choice of Change*, 1598. "Three things used by monks which provoke other men to laugh at their follies: They are shaven and notched on the head, like fooles," &c.

p. 196. "While she with *harlots* feasted": — 'Harlot' at first meant only a person hired. Thus Chaucer uses it in the *Sompnoures Tale*, 7336: —

"A stourdy harlot ay went hem byhynde
That was hir hostis man," &c.

But, like 'villain,' which originally meant 'a bondsman,' it came to be used as a term of reproach, and, at first, to men as well as women. Its peculiar reproach, when applied to women, is strictly derived from the venality which its radical sense implies. Every wanton is not necessarily a harlot in the original signification of the word. See Note on 'villain,' Act I. Sc. 2, and on 'knave,' *Othello*, Act I. Sc. 1.

p. 198. "And this is false," &c.: — Mr. Dyce would read, quite needlessly,

"I never saw the chain. So help me Heaven,
As this is false," &c.

p. 201. "If I dream not," &c.: — In the original this speech, and the next by the *Abbess*, are preceded by the first six lines of the *Duke's* next speech: an error strangely left to be corrected by Capell.

" "These are the parents," &c.: — Malone supposed that the preceding line had been lost. But *Ægeon's* morning story and the consequent conviction flash on the *Duke's* mind at once.

" "—— to these *children*": — 'Children' is here in effect a trisyllable. The plural form was of old, and still is in some places and among certain classes, 'childer:' — who has not heard it in the mouths of Irish emigrants? See, also, in an account dated 1564, published in Halliwell's *Life of Shakespeare*, p. 47. — "Item, payd to Alen for techyng the chylder, iiij *li*." To this succeeded 'childeren,' *en* being the fine old Saxon plural form which we are continually hissing ourselves for having laid aside, except in a few honest, homely words like 'oxen,' 'brethren,' &c. The trisyllabic use of the word is a relic of this old plural.

p. 202. "—— these errors *all* arose": — The folio has "*are* arose;" but can there be a doubt that the reading of the text, which, being of the obvious kind, occurred to several editors and was found in Mr. Collier's folio of 1632, is correct?

" "*Twenty-five* years," &c.: — The original has "*Thirty-three*," which, as *Ægeon* says that he had parted from his boy seven years before, when the latter was eighteen must be wrong.

" "My heavy burthen *here* delivered": — That is, 'I have gone in travail until this present hour delivered me here of my heavy burthen.' The folio has "*are* delivered," with manifest error. Theobald and Mr. Knight read,

"*nor* till this present hour
My heavy burthen*s* are delivered:"

Mr. Collier,

"My heavy burden *un*delivered:"

Mr. Singer and Mr. Dyce,

"My heavy burden *ne'er* delivered:"

a writer in *Blackwood's Magazine*, August, 1853,

"My heavy burden *has* delivered:"

but the reading of the text does less violence to the original than either of these, and gives what appears to me a better, more natural expression of *Emilia's* idea.

p. 203. "and *joy* with me:
After so long grief such *nativity*."

The original has "and *go* with me," which Heath happily corrected by the substitution of the word in the text. Mr. Singer reads "such festivity," which is a plausible suggestion on account of the occurrence of 'nativity' just before. But a long travail and a happy birth is plainly the dominant thought of *Emilia's* speech, and "a gossip's feast" was a feast of those who assisted at a birth or came in immediately after it.

" "[*Exeunt* ANT. S. *and* E.," &c.: — The old stage direction is "*Exeunt omnes. Mane[n]t the two Dromios and two brothers.*" But from the last speech of *Antipholus* of Syracuse, it is plain that he and his brother go out with the other gentlefolk, and that the two bondsmen remain behind.

MUCH ADO ABOUT NOTHING.

"Much adoe about Nothing. *As it hath been sundrie times publikely* acted by the right honourable, the Lord Chamberlaine his seruants. *Written by William Shakespeare.* — LONDON Printed by V. S. for Andrew Wise, and William Aspley. 1600." 4to. 36 leaves.

Much Ado about Nothing occupies twenty-one pages in the folio of 1623, viz., from p. 101 to p. 121 inclusive, in the division of Comedies. It is there divided into Acts, but not into Scenes, and is without a list of Dramatis Personæ. In the quarto there is no division into Acts.

MUCH ADO ABOUT NOTHING.

INTRODUCTION.

BANDELLO, an Italian novelist who died three years before Shakespeare was born, furnished him with the incident upon which this play hinges — the trick by which *Borachio* slanders *Hero* to her lover. It is found also in Ariosto's *Orlando Furioso*, Book V., and in Spenser's *Faerie Queene*, Book II. Can. 4, an English translation of the former of which, by Sir John Harington, was published in 1591. No translation of Bandello's novel is known; but if any reader of Shakespeare finds it difficult to believe that such a man, at the age of thirty-five years, — fifteen of which he had passed in literary pursuits, at a time when Italian was more commonly known to educated Englishmen than French is now, — had mastered enough of that language to be able to read a short tale in it, I must confess myself but ill disposed to help him out of the further perplexity in which he will be involved by the knowledge, that, while in neither Ariosto's nor Spenser's version of the story is there the slightest coincidence with *Much Ado about Nothing* in name of person or place, in Bandello's, the friend and patron of the lover is *Don Pedro of Arragon*, the father of the lady, *Lionato*, and the scene, Messina, and that in Bandello alone are found the incidents of the entrance of the repudiated lady's window by a servant of her calumniator, her swooning and pretended death, the promise to her father to marry at his bidding, and her subsequent restoration to her repentant lover. The Italian's contribution to the play is limited to these few bare names and almost barren incidents; for *Benedick* and *Beatrice*, *Dogberry* and *Verges*, *John* the Bastard, and even *Conrade*, *Borachio* and *Margaret*, and all that they do and say else, are Shakespeare's own. Not only so, but the four first-named characters, being purely English, and giving the tone to the composition, make *Much Ado about Nothing* a comedy of contemporary English manners.

We are able to determine the date of the production of this play with accuracy quite sufficient to all the purposes for which exactness in such matters is valuable. It was published in 1600; *England's Parnassus*, which appeared also in that year, contains no quotation from it; and Meres, who could not have passed it unnoticed, when he did notice *The Comedy of Errors* and *The Two Gentlemen of Verona*, does not mention it in his citation, so often referred to, which was published in 1598. We may therefore conclude that *Much Ado about Nothing* was written in 1598 or 1599. There is no internal evidence upon this point; for Chalmers' conjecture, that when *Beatrice* says, "you had musty victual, and he hath holp to eat it," an allusion is meant to an infirmity in the English commissariat of that day, which, from recent Crimean experience, seems chronic, rests on a foundation entirely too slender and fanciful.

The text of the folio is printed with comparatively few and trifling errors, most of which are easy of correction, either by conjecture or by the aid of the quarto, which is also remarkably well printed for a dramatic publication of the period. Each copy contains a few words and brief sentences omitted from the other. It is plain from the repetition of certain somewhat striking errors of the press, which are particularly indicated in the Notes, that the folio was printed from a copy of the quarto edition; and this fact has caused most editors to adhere to the text of the latter, as "the more ancient authority," Mr. Collier giving, as an additional reason, his opinion that "the changes from the 4to in the folio are nearly all for the worse." As to its being the earlier printed edition, this fact has, evidently, no weight in deciding between the authority of an edition which is authenticated and that of one which is not; and not only is this truth applicable in the present instance, but we know that the copy of the quarto from which the authenticated folio was printed had been used in Shakespeare's theatre as the prompter's book, and there subjected to several alterations and corrections; and thus its essential differences from the quarto have a special and peculiar demand upon our deference. The important errors (to a reader) of the quarto which the folio leaves uncorrected are of such a nature that they might remain without inconvenience upon a prompter's book; — such are the printing of verse as prose and the use of the names of actors, instead of those of characters, as prefixes. The various differences of text bearing upon this point are all considered in the Notes.

As to preference between the readings of the two editions, that is mere matter of opinion; and fortunately the cases in which such preference may be exercised — not by any means admitting that it should be — are of comparatively little moment. But I am surprised that any reader of Shakespeare should consider, for instance, the change of "any man that knows the *statutes*," in the quarto, to "any man that knows the *statues*," in the folio, for the worse, or think the same of the change from "*beat*" in the quarto to "*bear*," in the lines,

> "—— a thousand innocent shames
> In angel whiteness bear away those blushes,"

in the folio: — the difference between a vision of angelic white-winged innocence bearing away, all shameful, the blushes of the shrinking girl, and a vision of the same impersonated virtue violently beating them off, being one about the propriety or the beauty of which there would seem to be no room for discussion. The significant change in *Dogberry's* speech, Act III. Sc. 5, from "exam*ination*," in the quarto, to "exam*ine*," in the folio, is remarked upon at length in the Notes: its character admits no doubt that it was made 'by authority.'

The readings of the folio, in all important variations, seem to me much preferable to those of the quarto; but the former is followed in this edition, with assistance from the latter in cases of apparent misprint only, not for that reason, but because the folio was printed, — and carefully printed for the day, even as to punctuation, contracted syllables, and capital letters, — from a copy which had evidently had the benefit of at least a partial correction, and because it has the authority of Heminge and Condell, Shakespeare's fellow-actors.

As to the period of the action and the costume of *Much Ado about Nothing*, the former is not determinable within narrow bounds; and it is of no consequence that it should be; for the list of dramatis personæ is of the composite sort, and the exteriors which the characters present must of necessity be those of different times and nations. A Sicilian costume of any period anterior to the writing of the comedy, and during which the island was under the dominion of Spain and involved in war, is appropriate to the personages of higher rank; and we must look to the England of Shakespeare's day to furnish dresses for *Dogberry* the Constable, *Verges* the Headborough, the Sexton, and the Watch. Vecelli is authority for the former, and a wood-cut on the title page of Dekker's *O per se O*, 1612, for the Watch among the latter.

We call this play *Much Ado about Nothing;* but it seems clear to me that Shakespeare and his contemporaries called it *Much Ado about Noting;* a pun being intended between 'nothing' and 'noting,' which were then pronounced alike, and upon which pun depends by far the more important significance of the title. This is not the place for minute orthoepical discussion; but that accented vowels had their pure and simple sound in a very much greater degree in Shakespeare's time than now, and that this was preserved in compound words, no sufficiently observant person, familiar with the literature of that time, can have failed to notice. Upon this fact depends, for instance, the *Host's* joke in *The Merry Wives of Windsor*, Act III. Sc. 1, "he gives me the proverbs and the no-verbs;" — and I remark here that the pronunciation '*pro*-verb' still lingers in New England. Shakespeare's contemporary John Florio tells us, in his Rules for the Italian Tongue appended to his Dictionary, that the "round or firm" Italian *o* "is ever pronounced as our *o* in these wordes: Bone, *Dog*, Flow, *God*, *Rod*, Stone, Tone;" by which we see that three words of the seven have lost the pure sound of *o*. This is rather less than the proportion of those which have undergone a similar change throughout the language. But a joke of *Touchstone's* is quite decisive upon the point that the combination *o t h* was sometimes, at least, pronounced *ote*. He says, (*As You Like It*, Act III. Sc. 3,) "I am here with thee and thy *goats*, as the most capricious poet, honest Ovid, was among the *Goths;*" and if the pronunciation of '*Goths*' was not '*gotes*,' he might as well have said 'among the Vandals.' To this add another example, even more conclusive — the spelling, in the original, of 'mote' in the following line, (*Love's Labour's Lost*, Act IV. Sc. 3,) and in every other instance in which the word is used in that volume, although it was pronounced *mote*, and had been so spelled in earlier days: —

"You found his *Moth*, the King your *Moth* did see."

In this very play, too, is another passage especially in point, — that in which (Act II. Sc. 3) *Balthazar* uses the words 'note,' 'notes,' and '*noting*,' and *Don Pedro* replies, "Note, notes, forsooth, and *nothing*." Here, if 'nothing' were pronounced *nothing*, the Prince might as well have said 'any thing;' but both quarto and folio give him his pun as well as his jeer. Theobald, failing to perceive this, changed 'nothing' to 'noting;' and so the passage remained until the present day. In the great Roman tragedy, too, of the Triumvir and the Egyptian Queen, the original has either *Anthonie*, *Anthony*, or even *Anthonius*, although the man was called then, as now, *Mark Antony*. So *Antonio* of *The Tempest* is *Anthonio* in the original, and *Armado* in *Love's Labour's Lost* is generally *Armatho;* and a common word which occurs in this play, 'lantern,' (so written originally and always so pronounced,) was in Shakespeare's day, and until recently, spelled *lanthorn;* and the last syllable of 'murder,' then written *murther*, seems to have been pronounced somewhat like the same syllable of the French *meurtre*.

But as to the significance of the title. The play is *Much Ado about Nothing* only in a very vague and general sense, but *Much Ado about Noting* in one especially apt and descriptive; for the much ado is produced entirely by noting. It begins with the noting of the Prince and *Claudio*, first by *Antonio's* man, and then by *Borachio*, who reveals their conference to *John;* it goes on with *Benedick* noting the Prince, *Leonato*, and *Claudio* in the garden, and again with *Beatrice* noting *Margaret* and *Ursula* in the same place; the incident upon which its action turns is the noting of *Borachio's* interview with *Margaret* by the Prince and *Claudio;* and finally, the incident which unravels the plot is the noting of *Borachio* and *Conrade* by the Watch. That this sense, 'to observe,' 'to watch,' was one in which 'note' was commonly used, it is quite needless to show by reference to the literature and the lexicographers of Shakespeare's day; it is hardly obsolete; and even of the many instances in Shakespeare's works, I will quote only one, from *As You Like It*, Act III. Sc. 2, which happens to be in all points correspondent. "*Enter* ORLANDO *and* JAQUES.] *Celia*. You bring me out:— Soft! comes he not here? *Ros*. 'Tis he! Slink by and note him." Upon the other point let these lines of Shakespeare's speak:—

"Till Nature, as she wrought thee, fell a-*doting*,
And by addition me of thee defeated,
By adding one thing to my purpose *nothing*."

Sonnet XX.

DRAMATIS PERSONÆ.

DON PEDRO, *Prince of* Arragon.
JOHN, *his bastard Brother.*
CLAUDIO, *a young Lord of* Florence.
BENEDICK, *a young Lord of* Padua.
LEONATO, *Governor of* Messina.
ANTONIO, *his Brother.*
BALTHAZAR, *Servant to* Don Pedro.
BORACHIO, } *followers of* John.
CONRADE, }
DOGBERRY, } *two Officers.*
VERGES, }
Friar FRANCIS.
A Sexton.
A Boy.

HERO, *Daughter to* Leonato.
BEATRICE, *Niece to* Leonato.
MARGARET, } *Gentlewomen attending on* Hero.
URSULA, }

Messengers, Watchmen, *and* Attendants.

SCENE: Messina.

MUCH ADO ABOUT NOTHING.

ACT I.

SCENE I.—Before LEONATO'S House.

Enter LEONATO, HERO, BEATRICE, *and others, with a* Messenger.

LEONATO.

I LEARN in this letter, that Don Pedro of Arragon comes this night to Messina.

Messenger. He is very near by this: he was not three leagues off when I left him.

Leon. How many gentlemen have you lost in this action?

Mess. But few of any sort, and none of name.

Leon. A victory is twice itself, when the achiever brings home full numbers. I find here, that Don Pedro hath bestowed much honour on a young Florentine, called Claudio.

Mess. Much deserv'd on his part, and equally remembered by Don Pedro: he hath borne himself beyond the promise of his age, doing in the figure of a lamb the feats of a lion: he hath, indeed, better better'd expectation than you must expect of me to tell you how.

Leon. He hath an uncle here in Messina will be very much glad of it.

Mess. I have already delivered him letters, and there appears much joy in him; even so much, that joy could not show itself modest enough without a badge of bitterness.

Leon. Did he break out into tears?

Mess. In great measure.

Leon. A kind overflow of kindness. There are no faces truer than those that are so wash'd: how much better is it to weep at joy than to joy at weeping?

Beatrice. I pray you, is Signior Montanto return'd from the wars, or no?

Mess. I know none of that name, lady: there was none such in the army of any sort.

Leon. What is he that you ask for, niece?

Hero. My cousin means Signior Benedick of Padua.

Mess. O! he's return'd, and as pleasant as ever he was.

Beat. He set up his bills here in Messina, and challeng'd Cupid at the flight; and my uncle's Fool, reading the challenge, subscrib'd for Cupid, and challeng'd him at the bird-bolt. — I pray you, how many hath he kill'd and eaten in these wars? But how many hath he kill'd? for, indeed, I promis'd to eat all of his killing.

Leon. 'Faith, niece, you tax Signior Benedick too much; but he'll be meet with you, I doubt it not.

Mess. He hath done good service, lady, in these wars.

Beat. You had musty victual, and he hath holp

to eat it: he is a very valiant trencher-man; he hath an excellent stomach.

Mess. And a good soldier too, lady.

Beat. And a good soldier to a lady; but what is he to a lord?

Mess. A lord to a lord, a man to a man; stuff'd with all honourable virtues.

Beat. It is so, indeed: he is no less than a stuff'd man; but for the stuffing,—Well, we are all mortal.

Leon. You must not, sir, mistake my niece. There is a kind of merry war betwixt Signior Benedick and her: they never meet, but there's a skirmish of wit between them.

Beat. Alas! he gets nothing by that. In our last conflict four of his five wits went halting off, and now is the whole man govern'd with one; so that if he have wit enough to keep himself warm, let him bear it for a difference between himself and his horse; for it is all the wealth that he hath left, to be known a reasonable creature.—Who is his companion now? He hath every month a new sworn brother.

Mess. Is't possible?

Beat. Very easily possible: he wears his faith but as the fashion of his hat; it ever changes with the next block.

Mess. I see, lady, the gentleman is not in your books.

Beat. No; an he were, I would burn my study. But, I pray you, who is his companion? Is there no young squarer now, that will make a voyage with him to the Devil?

Mess. He is most in the company of the right noble Claudio.

Beat. O Lord! he will hang upon him like a disease: he is sooner caught than the pestilence, and the taker runs presently mad. God help the noble Claudio! if he have caught the Benedick, it will cost him a thousand pound ere he be cur'd.

Mess. I will hold friends with you, lady.

Beat. Do, good friend.

Leon. You'll ne'er run mad, niece.

Beat. No, not till a hot January.

Mess. Don Pedro is approach'd.

Enter Don PEDRO, JOHN the Bastard, CLAUDIO, BENEDICK, BALTHAZAR, *and others.*

Don Pedro. Good Signior Leonato, you are come to meet your trouble: the fashion of the world is to avoid cost, and you encounter it.

Leon. Never came trouble to my house in the likeness of your Grace; for trouble being gone, comfort should remain; but when you depart from me, sorrow abides, and happiness takes his leave.

D. Pedro. You embrace your charge too willingly. I think this is your daughter.

Leon. Her mother hath many times told me so.

Benedick. Were you in doubt, that you ask'd her?

Leon. Signior Benedick, no; for then were you a child.

D. Pedro. You have it full, Benedick; we may guess by this what you are, being a man. — Truly, the lady fathers herself. — Be happy, lady, for you are like an honourable father.

Bene. If Signior Leonato be her father, she would not have his head on her shoulders for all Messina, as like him as she is.

Beat. I wonder that you will still be talking, Signior Benedick: no body marks you.

Bene. What, my dear Lady Disdain! are you yet living?

Beat. Is it possible disdain should die, while she hath such meet food to feed it as Signior Benedick? Courtesy itself must convert to disdain, if you come in her presence.

Bene. Then is courtesy a turn-coat. But it is certain I am loved of all ladies, only you excepted; and I would I could find in my heart that I had not a hard heart, for, truly, I love none.

Beat. A dear happiness to women: they would else have been troubled with a pernicious suitor. I thank God, and my cold blood, I am of your humour for that: I had rather hear my dog bark at a crow than a man swear he loves me.

Bene. God keep your ladyship still in that mind; so some gentleman or other shall 'scape a predestinate scratch'd face.

Beat. Scratching could not make it worse, an 'twere such a face as yours were.

Bene. Well, you are a rare parrot-teacher.

Beat. A bird of my tongue is better than a beast of yours.

Bene. I would my horse had the speed of your tongue, and so good a continuer. But keep your way o' God's name; I have done.

Beat. You always end with a jade's trick; I know you of old.

D. Pedro. This is the sum of all. — Leonato, — Signior Claudio, and Signior Benedick — my dear friend Leonato hath invited you all. I tell him we shall stay here at the least a month, and he heartily prays some occasion may detain us longer: I dare swear he is no hypocrite, but prays from his heart.

Leon. If you swear, my lord, you shall not be forsworn. — Let me bid you welcome, my lord: being reconciled to the Prince, your brother, I owe you all duty.

John. I thank you: I am not of many words, but I thank you.

Leon. Please it your Grace lead on?

D. Pedro. Your hand, Leonato: we will go together. [*Exeunt all but* BENEDICK *and* CLAUDIO.

Claudio. Benedick, didst thou note the daughter of Signior Leonato?

Bene. I noted her not; but I look'd on her.

Claud. Is she not a modest young lady?

Bene. Do you question me, as an honest man should do, for my simple true judgment; or would you have me speak after my custom, as being a professed tyrant to their sex?

Claud. No; I pray thee speak in sober judgment.

Bene. Why, i'faith, methinks she's too low for a high praise, too brown for a fair praise, and too little for a great praise: only this commendation I can afford her; that were she other than she is, she were unhandsome; and being no other but as she is, I do not like her.

Claud. Thou think'st I am in sport: I pray thee, tell me truly how thou lik'st her.

Bene. Would you buy her, that you inquire after her?

Claud. Can the world buy such a jewel?

Bene. Yea, and a case to put it into. But speak you this with a sad brow? or do you play the flouting Jack, to tell us Cupid is a good hare-finder, and Vulcan a rare carpenter? Come, in what key shall a man take you, to go in the song?

Claud. In mine eye she is the sweetest lady that ever I look'd on.

Bene. I can see yet without spectacles, and I see

no such matter: there's her cousin, an she were not possess'd with a fury, exceeds her as much in beauty as the first of May doth the last of December. But I hope you have no intent to turn husband, have you?

Claud. I would scarce trust myself, though I had sworn the contrary, if Hero would be my wife.

Bene. Is't come to this, i' faith? Hath not the world one man, but he will wear his cap with suspicion? Shall I never see a bachelor of threescore again? Go to, i' faith; an thou wilt needs thrust thy neck into a yoke, wear the print of it, and sigh away Sundays. Look; Don Pedro is returned to seek you.

Enter Don PEDRO.

D. Pedro. What secret hath held you here, that you followed not to Leonato's?

Bene. I would your Grace would constrain me to tell.

D. Pedro. I charge thee on thy allegiance.

Bene. You hear, Count Claudio: I can be secret as a dumb man, I would have you think so; but on my allegiance, — mark you this, on my allegiance. — He is in love. With who? — now that is your Grace's part. — Mark, how short his answer is: — with Hero, Leonato's short daughter.

Claud. If this were so, so were it utter'd.

Bene. Like the old tale, my lord: "It is not so, nor 'twas not so: but, indeed, God forbid it should be so."

Claud. If my passion change not shortly, God forbid it should be otherwise.

D. Pedro. Amen, if you love her; for the lady is very well worthy.

Claud. You speak this to fetch me in, my lord.

D. Pedro. By my troth, I speak my thought.

Claud. And in faith, my lord, I spoke mine.

Bene. And by my two faiths and troths, my lord, I speak mine.

Claud. That I love her, I feel.

D. Pedro. That she is worthy, I know.

Bene. That I neither feel how she should be loved, nor know how she should be worthy, is the opinion that fire cannot melt out of me: I will die in it at the stake.

D. Pedro. Thou wast ever an obstinate heretic in the despite of beauty.

Claud. And never could maintain his part, but in the force of his will.

Bene. That a woman conceived me, I thank her; that she brought me up, I likewise give her most humble thanks; but that I will have a recheat winded in my forehead, or hang my bugle in an invisible baldrick, all women shall pardon me. Because I will not do them the wrong to mistrust any, I will do myself the right to trust none; and the fine is, (for the which I may go the finer,) I will live a bachelor.

D. Pedro. I shall see thee, ere I die, look pale with love.

Bene. With anger, with sickness, or with hunger, my lord; not with love: prove that ever I lose more blood with love than I will get again with drinking, pick out mine eyes with a ballad-maker's pen and hang me up at the door of a brothel-house for the sign of blind Cupid.

D. Pedro. Well, if ever thou dost fall from this faith, thou wilt prove a notable argument.

Bene. If I do, hang me in a bottle, like a cat, and shoot at me; and he that hits me, let him be clapp'd on the shoulder and call'd Adam.

D. Pedro. Well, as time shall try:
"In time the savage bull doth bear the yoke."

Bene. The savage bull may, but if ever the sensible Benedick bear it, pluck off the bull's horns and set them in my forehead; and let me be vilely painted, and in such great letters as they write, 'Here is good horse to hire,' let them signify under my sign, 'Here you may see Benedick the married man.'

Claud. If this should ever happen, thou would'st be horn-mad.

D. Pedro. Nay, if Cupid have not spent all his quiver in Venice, thou wilt quake for this shortly.

Bene. I look for an earthquake too, then.

D. Pedro. Well, you will temporize with the hours. In the mean time, good Signior Benedick, repair to Leonato's: commend me to him, and tell him I will not fail him at supper; for, indeed, he hath made great preparation.

Bene. I have almost matter enough in me for such an embassage; and so I commit you —

Claud. To the tuition of God: from my house (if I had it) —

D. Pedro. The sixth of July: your loving friend, Benedick.

Bene. Nay, mock not, mock not. The body of your discourse is sometime guarded with fragments, and the guards are but slightly basted on, neither: ere you flout old ends any farther, examine your conscience; and so I leave you. [*Exit* BENEDICK.

Claud. My liege, your Highness now may do me good.

D. Pedro. My love is thine to teach: teach it but how,
And thou shalt see how apt it is to learn
Any hard lesson that may do thee good.

Claud. Hath Leonato any son, my lord?
D. Pedro. No child but Hero; she's his only heir.
Dost thou affect her, Claudio?
Claud. O! my lord,
When you went onward on this ended action,
I look'd upon her with a soldier's eye,
That lik'd, but had a rougher task in hand
Than to drive liking to the name of love;
But now I am return'd, and that war-thoughts
Have left their places vacant, in their rooms
Come thronging soft and delicate desires,
All prompting me how fair young Hero is,
Saying, I lik'd her ere I went to wars —
D. Pedro. Thou wilt be like a lover presently,
And tire the hearer with a book of words.
If thou dost love fair Hero, cherish it,
And I will break with her, [and with her father,
And thou shalt have her.] Was't not to this end,
That thou began'st to twist so fine a story?
Claud. How sweetly do you minister to love,
That know love's grief by his complexion!
But lest my liking might too sudden seem,
I would have salv'd it with a longer treatise.
D. Pedro. What need the bridge much broader than the flood?
The fairest grant is the necessity.
Look, what will serve is fit: 'tis once, thou lovest;
And I will fit thee with the remedy.
I know we shall have revelling to-night:
I will assume thy part in some disguise,
And tell fair Hero I am Claudio;
And in her bosom I'll unclasp my heart,
And take her hearing prisoner with the force
And strong encounter of my amorous tale:
Then, after, to her father will I break;

And, the conclusion is, she shall be thine.
In practice let us put it presently. [*Exeunt.*

Scene II.

A Room in Leonato's House.

Enter Leonato *and* Antonio.

Leon. How now, brother? Where is my cousin, your son? Hath he provided this music?

Antonio. He is very busy about it. But, brother, I can tell you news that you yet dreamt not of.

Leon. Are they good?

Ant. As the event stamps them; but they have a good cover; they show well outward. The Prince and Count Claudio, walking in a thick-pleached alley in my orchard, were thus overheard by a man of mine: the Prince discovered to Claudio that he loved my niece, your daughter, and meant to acknowledge it this night in a dance; and, if he found her accordant, he meant to take the present time by the top, and instantly break with you of it.

Leon. Hath the fellow any wit, that told you this?

Ant. A good sharp fellow: I will send for him, and question him yourself.

Leon. No, no: we will hold it as a dream, till it appear itself; but I will acquaint my daughter withal, that she may be the better prepared for an answer, if peradventure this be true. Go you, and tell her of it. [*Several persons cross the stage.*] Cousins, you know what you have to do. — O, I cry you mercy, friend; go you with me, and I will use your skill. — Good cousin, have a care this busy time. [*Exeunt.*

Scene III.

Another Room in Leonato's House.

Enter John the Bastard *and* Conrade.

Conrade. What the good year, my lord! why are you thus out of measure sad?

John. There is no measure in the occasion that breeds [it], therefore the sadness is without limit.

Con. You should hear reason.

John. And when I have heard it, what blessing brings it?

Con. If not a present remedy, yet a patient sufferance.

John. I wonder, that thou being (as thou say'st thou art) born under Saturn, goest about to apply a moral medicine to a mortifying mischief. I cannot hide what I am: I must be sad when I have cause, and smile at no man's jests; eat when I have stomach, and wait for no man's leisure; sleep when I am drowsy, and tend on no man's business; laugh when I am merry, and claw no man in his humour.

Con. Yea; but you must not make the full show of this till you may do it without controlment. You have of late stood out against your brother, and he hath ta'en you newly into his grace, where it is impossible you should take root but by the fair weather that you make yourself: it is needful that you frame the season for your own harvest.

John. I had rather be a canker in a hedge than a rose in his grace; and it better fits my blood to be disdain'd of all than to fashion a carriage to rob love from any: in this, though I cannot be said to be a flattering honest man, it must not be denied but I am a plain-dealing villain. I am trusted with a muzzle, and enfranchis'd with a clog; therefore I have decreed not to sing in my cage. If I had my mouth, I would bite; if I had my liberty, I would do my liking: in the mean time, let me be that I am, and seek not to alter me.

Con. Can you make no use of your discontent?

John. I will make all use of it, for I use it only. Who comes here? What news, Borachio?

Enter BORACHIO.

Borachio. I came yonder from a great supper: the Prince, your brother, is royally entertained by Leonato, and I can give you intelligence of an intended marriage.

John. Will it serve for any model to build mischief on? What is he, for a fool, that betroths himself to unquietness?

Bora. Marry, it is your brother's right hand.

John. Who? the most exquisite Claudio?

Bora. Even he.

John. A proper squire! And who, [and who]? which way looks he?

Bora. Marry, on Hero, the daughter and heir of Leonato.

John. A very forward March-chick! How came you to this?

Bora. Being entertain'd for a perfumer, as I was smoking a musty room, comes me the Prince and Claudio, hand in hand, in sad conference: I whipp'd behind the arras, and there heard it agreed upon, that the Prince should woo Hero for himself, and having obtain'd her, give her to Count Claudio.

John. Come, come; let us thither: this may prove food to my displeasure. That young start-up hath all the glory of my overthrow: if I can cross him any way, I bless myself every way. You are both sure, and will assist me?

Con. To the death, my lord.

John. Let us to the great supper: their cheer is the greater, that I am subdued. 'Would the cook were of my mind!—Shall we go prove what's to be done?

Bora. We'll wait upon your lordship. [*Exeunt.*

ACT II.

SCENE I.—A Hall in LEONATO'S House.

Enter LEONATO, ANTONIO, HERO, BEATRICE, *and others.*

LEONATO.

WAS not Count John here at supper?

Ant. I saw him not.

Beat. How tartly that gentleman looks! I never can see him, but I am heart-burn'd an hour after.

Hero. He is of a very melancholy disposition.

Beat. He were an excellent man, that were made just in the mid-way between him and Benedick: the one is too like an image, and says nothing; and the other too like my lady's eldest son, evermore tattling.

Leon. Then, half Signior Benedick's tongue in Count John's mouth, and half Count John's melancholy in Signior Benedick's face,—

Beat. With a good leg and a good foot, uncle,

and money enough in his purse, such a man would win any woman in the world, — if he could get her good will.

Leon. By my troth, niece, thou wilt never get thee a husband, if thou be so shrewd of thy tongue.

Ant. In faith, she's too curst.

Beat. Too curst is more than curst: I shall lessen God's sending that way, for it is said, 'God sends a curst cow short horns;' but to a cow too curst he sends none.

Leon. So, by being too curst, God will send you no horns?

Beat. Just, if he send me no husband; for the which blessing, I am at him upon my knees every morning and evening. Lord! I could not endure a husband with a beard on his face: I had rather lie in the woollen.

Leon. You may light on a husband that hath no beard.

Beat. What should I do with him? dress him in my apparel, and make him my waiting gentlewoman? He that hath a beard is more than a youth, and he that hath no beard is less than a man; and he that is more than a youth is not for me; and he that is less than a man I am not for him; therefore I will even take sixpence in earnest of the be'r-'ard, and lead his apes into Hell.

Leon. Well then, go you into Hell?

Beat. No; but to the gate; and there will the Devil meet me, like an old cuckold, with horns on his head, and say, 'Get you to Heaven, Beatrice, get you to Heaven; here's no place for you maids:' so, deliver I up my apes, and away to St. Peter for the Heavens: he shows me where the bachelors sit; and there live we as merry as the day is long.

Ant. Well, niece, [*to* HERO,] I trust, you will be rul'd by your father.

Beat. Yes, 'faith; it is my cousin's duty to make courtesy, and say, 'Father, as it please you:' but yet for all that, cousin, let him be a handsome fellow, or else make another courtesy, and say, 'Father, as it please me.'

Leon. Well, niece, I hope to see you one day fitted with a husband.

Beat. Not till God make men of some other metal than earth. Would it not grieve a woman to be over-master'd with a piece of valiant dust? to make an account of her life to a clod of wayward marl? No, uncle, I'll none: Adam's sons are my brethren; and truly, I hold it a sin to match in my kindred.

Leon. Daughter, remember what I told you: if the Prince do solicit you in that kind, you know your answer.

Beat. The fault will be in the music, cousin, if you be not woo'd in good time: if the Prince be too important, tell him, there is measure in every thing, and so dance out the answer: for, hear me, Hero; wooing, wedding, and repenting, is as a Scotch jig, a measure, and a cinque-pace: the first suit is hot and hasty, like a Scotch jig, and full as fantastical; the wedding, mannerly, modest, as a measure full of state and ancientry; and then comes repentance, and with his bad legs falls into the cinque-pace faster and faster, till he sink into his grave.

Leon. Cousin, you apprehend passing shrewdly.

Beat. I have a good eye, uncle: I can see a church by day-light.

Leon. The revellers are entering, brother. Make good room!

Enter DON PEDRO, CLAUDIO, BENEDICK, BALTHAZAR; JOHN, BORACHIO, MARGARET, URSULA, *and* Maskers.

D. Pedro. Lady, will you walk about with your friend?

Hero. So you walk softly and look sweetly and say nothing, I am yours for the walk; and, especially, when I walk away.

D. Pedro. With me in your company?

Hero. I may say so, when I please.

D. Pedro. And when please you to say so?

Hero. When I like your favour; for God defend, the lute should be like the case!

D. Pedro. My visor is Philemon's roof; within
the house is Jove.

Hero. Why, then your visor should be thatch'd.

D. Pedro. Speak low, if you speak love.
[*Takes her aside.*

Balthazar. Well, I would you did like me.

Margaret. So would not I, for your own sake; for I have many ill qualities.

Balth. Which is one?

Marg. I say my prayers aloud.

Balth. I love you the better; the hearers may cry Amen.

Marg. God match me with a good dancer!

Balth. Amen.

Marg. And God keep him out of my sight, when the dance is done! — Answer, clerk.

Balth. No more words: the clerk is answered.
[*They part.*

Ursula. I know you well enough: you are Signior Antonio.

Ant. At a word, I am not.

Urs. I know you by the waggling of your head.

Ant. To tell you true, I counterfeit him.

Urs. You could never do him so ill-well, unless you were the very man. Here's his dry hand up and down: you are he, you are he.

Ant. At a word, I am not.

Urs. Come, come: do you think I do not know you by your excellent wit? Can virtue hide itself? Go to, mum, you are he: graces will appear, and there's an end. [*They pass on.*

Beat. Will you not tell me who told you so?

Bene. No, you shall pardon me.

Beat. Nor will you not tell me who you are?

Bene. Not now.

Beat. That I was disdainful, and that I had my good wit out of the *Hundred Merry Tales.* — Well, this was Signior Benedick that said so.

Bene. What's he?

Beat. I am sure, you know him well enough.

Bene. Not I, believe me.

Beat. Did he never make you laugh?

Bene. I pray you, what is he?

Beat. Why, he is the Prince's Jester: a very dull fool; only his gift is in devising impossible slanders: none but libertines delight in him; and the commendation is not in his wit, but in his villainy; for he both pleases men and angers them, and then they laugh at him and beat him. I am sure he is in the fleet; I would he had boarded me!

Bene. When I know the gentleman, I'll tell him what you say.

Beat. Do, do: he'll but break a comparison or two on me; which, peradventure, not mark'd, or not laugh'd at, strikes him into melancholy; and then there's a partridge' wing saved, for the fool will eat no supper that night. [*Music within.*] We must follow the leaders.

Bene. In every good thing.

Beat. Nay, if they lead to any ill, I will leave them at the next turning.

[*Dance. Then, exeunt all but* JOHN, BORACHIO, *and* CLAUDIO.

John. Sure, my brother is amorous on Hero, and hath withdrawn her father to break with him about it. The ladies follow her, and but one visor remains.

Bora. And that is Claudio: I know him by his bearing.

John. Are not you Signior Benedick?

Claud. You know me well: I am he.

John. Signior, you are very near my brother in his love: he is enamour'd on Hero. I pray you, dissuade him from her; she is no equal for his birth: you may do the part of an honest man in it.

Claud. How know you he loves her?

John. I heard him swear his affection.

Bora. So did I too; and he swore he would marry her to-night.

John. Come, let us to the banquet.

[*Exeunt* JOHN *and* BORACHIO.

Claud. Thus answer I in name of Benedick,
But hear these ill news with the ears of Claudio.
'Tis certain so: — the Prince woos for himself.
Friendship is constant in all other things,
Save in the office and affairs of love:
Therefore, all hearts in love use their own tongues:
Let every eye negotiate for itself,
And trust no agent; for beauty is a witch
Against whose charms faith melteth into blood.
This is an accident of hourly proof,
Which I mistrusted not. Farewell, therefore, Hero!

Enter BENEDICK.

Bene. Count Claudio?

Claud. Yea, the same.

Bene. Come, will you go with me?

Claud. Whither?

Bene. Even to the next willow, about your own business, Count. What fashion will you wear the garland of? About your neck, like an usurer's chain, or under your arm, like a lieutenant's scarf? You must wear it one way, for the Prince hath got your Hero.

Claud. I wish him joy of her.

Bene. Why, that's spoken like an honest drover: so they sell bullocks. But did you think, the Prince would have served you thus?

Claud. I pray you, leave me.

Bene. Ho! now you strike like the blind man: 'twas the boy that stole your meat, and you'll beat the post.

Claud. If it will not be, I'll leave you. [*Exit.*

Bene. Alas, poor hurt fowl! Now will he creep into sedges. — But, that my Lady Beatrice should know me, and not know me! The Prince's Fool! — Ha! it may be, I go under that title, because I am merry. — Yea; but so I am apt to do myself wrong: I am not so reputed: it is the base, though bitter, disposition of Beatrice, that puts the world into her person, and so gives me out. Well, I'll be revenged as I may.

Enter Don PEDRO, HERO, *and* LEONATO.

D. Pedro. Now, Signior, where's the Count? Did you see him?

Bene. Troth, my lord, I have played the part of

Lady Fame. I found him here as melancholy as a lodge in a warren: I told him, and, I think, [I] told him true, that your Grace had got the [good] will of this young lady; and I offered him my company to a willow tree, either to make him a garland, as being forsaken, or to bind him [up] a rod, as being worthy to be whipp'd.

D. Pedro. To be whipp'd! What's his fault?

Bene. The flat transgression of a school-boy; who, being overjoy'd with finding a bird's nest, shows it his companion, and he steals it.

D. Pedro. Wilt thou make a trust a transgression? The transgression is in the stealer.

Bene. Yet it had not been amiss, the rod had been made, and the garland too; for the garland he might have worn himself, and the rod he might have bestow'd on you, who, as I take it, have stol'n his bird's nest.

D. Pedro. I will but teach them to sing, and restore them to the owner.

Bene. If their singing answer your saying, by my faith, you say honestly.

D. Pedro. The Lady Beatrice hath a quarrel to you: the gentleman, that danc'd with her, told her she is much wrong'd by you.

Bene. O! she misus'd me past the endurance of a block: an oak, but with one green leaf on it, would have answered her: my very visor began to assume life and scold with her. She told me, not thinking I had been myself, that I was the Prince's Jester, and that I was duller than a great thaw; huddling jest upon jest, with such impossible conveyance, upon me, that I stood like a man at a mark, with a whole army shooting at me. She speaks poiniards, and every word stabs: if her breath were as terrible as her terminations, there were no living near her; she would infect to the North Star. I would not marry her, though she were endowed with all that Adam had left him before he transgress'd: she would have made Hercules have turn'd spit, yea, and have cleft his club to make the fire, too. Come, talk not of her; you shall find her the infernal Até in good apparel. I would to God, some scholar would conjure her; for, certainly, while she is here, a man may live as quiet in Hell, as in a sanctuary; and people sin upon purpose, because they would go thither: so, indeed, all disquiet, horror, and perturbation follow her.

Enter CLAUDIO *and* BEATRICE.

D. Pedro. Look, here she comes.

Bene. Will your Grace command me any service to the world's end? I will go on the slightest errand now to the Antipodes, that you can devise to send me on: I will fetch you a toothpicker now from the farthest inch of Asia; bring you the length of Prester John's foot; fetch you a hair off the great Cham's beard; do you any embassage to the Pigmies, rather than hold three words' conference with this harpy. You have no employment for me?

D. Pedro. None, but to desire your good company.

Bene. O God, sir, here's a dish I love not: I cannot endure this Lady Tongue. [*Exit.*

D. Pedro. Come, lady, come; you have lost the heart of Signior Benedick.

Beat. Indeed, my lord, he lent it me a while; and I gave him use for it — a double heart for his single one: marry, once before he won it of me with false dice; therefore your Grace may well say I have lost it.

D. Pedro. You have put him down, lady; you have put him down.

Beat. So I would not he should do me, my lord, lest I should prove the mother of fools. I have brought Count Claudio, whom you sent me to seek.

D. Pedro. Why, how now, Count? wherefore are you sad?

Claud. Not sad, my lord.

D. Pedro. How then? Sick?

Claud. Neither, my lord.

Beat. The Count is neither sad, nor sick, nor merry, nor well; but civil, Count, civil as an orange, and something of a jealous complexion.

D. Pedro. I' faith, lady, I think your blazon to be true; though, I'll be sworn, if he be so, his conceit is false. Here, Claudio, I have wooed in thy name, and fair Hero is won; I have broke with her father, and his good will obtained: name the day of marriage, and God give thee joy!

Leon. Count, take of me my daughter, and, with her, my fortunes: his Grace hath made the match, and all grace say Amen to it!

Beat. Speak, Count, 'tis your cue.

Claud. Silence is the perfectest herald of joy: I were but little happy, if I could say how much.—Lady, as you are mine, I am yours: I give away myself for you, and dote upon the exchange.

Beat. Speak, cousin; or, if you cannot, stop his mouth with a kiss, and let him not speak neither.

D. Pedro. In faith, lady, you have a merry heart.

Beat. Yea, my lord; I thank it, poor fool, it keeps on the windy side of care.—My cousin tells him in his ear, that he is in her heart.

Claud. And so she doth, cousin.

Beat. Good Lord, for alliance!—thus goes every

one to the world but I; and I am sun-burn'd: I may sit in a corner, and cry, heigh ho! for a husband.

D. Pedro. Lady Beatrice, I will get you one.

Beat. I would rather have one of your father's getting. Hath your Grace ne'er a brother like you? Your father got excellent husbands, if a maid could come by them.

D. Pedro. Will you have me, lady?

Beat. No, my lord, unless I might have another for working-days: your Grace is too costly to wear every day. — But, I beseech your Grace, pardon me; I was born to speak all mirth and no matter.

D. Pedro. Your silence most offends me, and to be merry best becomes you; for, out of question, you were born in a merry hour.

Beat. No, sure, my lord, my mother cried; but then there was a star danc'd, and under that was I born. — Cousins, God give you joy!

Leon. Niece, will you look to those things I told you of?

Beat. I cry you mercy, uncle. — By your Grace's pardon. [*Exit* BEATRICE.

D. Pedro. By my troth, a pleasant-spirited lady.

Leon. There's little of the melancholy element in her, my lord: she is never sad, but when she sleeps; and not ever sad then; for I have heard my daughter say, she hath often dream'd of unhappiness, and wak'd herself with laughing.

D. Pedro. She cannot endure to hear tell of a husband.

Leon. O! by no means, she mocks all her wooers out of suit.

D. Pedro. She were an excellent wife for Benedick.

Leon. O Lord! my lord, if they were but a week married, they would talk themselves mad.

D. Pedro. Count Claudio, when mean you to go to church?

Claud. To-morrow, my lord. Time goes on crutches, till Love have all his rites.

Leon. Not till Monday, my dear son, which is hence a just seven-night; and a time too brief, too, to have all things answer [my] mind.

D. Pedro. Come, you shake the head at so long a breathing; but, I warrant thee, Claudio, the time shall not go dully by us. I will, in the interim, undertake one of Hercules' labours, which is, to bring Signior Benedick and the Lady Beatrice into a mountain of affection, th' one with th' other. I would fain have it a match; and I doubt not but to fashion it, if you three will but minister such assistance as I shall give you direction.

Leon. My lord, I am for you, though it cost me ten nights' watchings.

Claud. And I, my lord.

D. Pedro. And you too, gentle Hero?

Hero. I will do any modest office, my lord, to help my cousin to a good husband.

D. Pedro. And Benedick is not the unhopefullest husband that I know. Thus far can I praise him: he is of a noble strain, of approved valour, and confirm'd honesty. I will teach you how to humour your cousin, that she shall fall in love with Benedick; — and I, with your two helps, will so practise on Benedick, that, in despite of his quick wit and his queasy stomach, he shall fall in love with Beatrice. If we can do this, Cupid is no longer an archer: his glory shall be ours, for we are the only love-gods. Go in with me, and I will tell you my drift. [*Exeunt.*

Scene II.

Another Room in Leonato's House.

Enter John the Bastard, *and* Borachio.

John. It is so: the Count Claudio shall marry the daughter of Leonato.

Bora. Yea, my lord; but I can cross it.

John. Any bar, any cross, any impediment will be medicinable to me: I am sick in displeasure to him, and whatsoever comes athwart his affection ranges evenly with mine. How canst thou cross this marriage?

Bora. Not honestly, my lord; but so covertly that no dishonesty shall appear in me.

John. Show me, briefly, how.

Bora. I think I told your lordship, a year since, how much I am in the favour of Margaret, the waiting-gentlewoman to Hero.

John. I remember.

Bora. I can, at any unseasonable instant of the night, appoint her to look out at her lady's chamber-window.

John. What life is in that to be the death of this marriage?

Bora. The poison of that lies in you to temper. Go you to the Prince, your brother: spare not to tell him that he hath wronged his honour in marrying the renowned Claudio (whose estimation do you mightily hold up) to a contaminated stale, such a one as Hero.

John. What proof shall I make of that?

Bora. Proof enough to misuse the Prince, to vex Claudio, to undo Hero, and kill Leonato. Look you for any other issue?

John. Only to despite them I will endeavour any thing.

Bora. Go, then; find me a meet hour to draw Don Pedro and the Count Claudio alone: tell them that you know that Hero loves me; intend a kind of zeal both to the Prince and Claudio, (as in love of your brother's honour, who hath made this match, and his friend's reputation, who is thus like to be cozen'd with the semblance of a maid,) that you have discover'd thus. They will scarcely believe this without trial: offer them instances, which shall bear no less likelihood than to see me at her chamber-window, hear me call Margaret, Hero; hear Margaret term me Claudio; and bring them to see this the very night before the intended wedding: for in the mean time I will so fashion the matter, that Hero shall be absent, and there shall appear such seeming truth of her disloyalty, that jealousy shall be call'd assurance, and all the preparation overthrown.

John. Grow this to what adverse issue it can, I will put it in practice. Be cunning in the working this, and thy fee is a thousand ducats.

Bora. Be you constant in the accusation, and my cunning shall not shame me.

John. I will presently go learn their day of marriage. [*Exeunt.*

SCENE III.

LEONATO'S Garden.

Enter BENEDICK, *a* Boy *following.*

Bene. Boy!

Boy. Signior.

Bene. In my chamber-window lies a book; bring it hither to me in the orchard.

Boy. I am here already, sir.

Bene. I know that; [*Exit* Boy.] but I would have thee hence, and here again. I do much wonder, that one man, seeing how much another man is a fool when he dedicates his behaviours to love, will, after he hath laugh'd at such shallow follies in others, become the argument of his own scorn, by falling in love; and such a man is Claudio. I have known when there was no music with him but the drum and the fife; and now had he rather hear the tabor and the pipe: I have known when he would have walk'd ten mile afoot to see a good armour; and now will he lie ten nights awake, carving the fashion of a new doublet. He was wont to speak plain and to the purpose, like an honest man and a soldier; and now is he turn'd orthographer: his words are a very fantastical banquet—just so many strange dishes. May I be so converted, and see with these eyes? I cannot tell; I think not: I will not be sworn but Love may transform me to an oyster; but I'll take my oath on it, till he have made an oyster of me, he shall never make me such a fool. One woman is fair, yet I am well: another is wise, yet I am well: another virtuous, yet I am well; but till all graces be in one woman, one woman shall not come in my grace. Rich she shall be, that's certain; wise, or I'll none; virtuous, or I'll never cheapen her; fair, or I'll never look on her; mild, or come not near me; noble, or not I, for an angel; of good discourse, an excellent musician, and her hair shall be of what colour it please God. Ha! the Prince and Monsieur Love! I will hide me in the arbour. [*Withdraws.*

Enter Don Pedro, Leonato, Claudio, *and* Balthazar.

D. Pedro. Come, shall we hear this music?

Claud. Yea, my good lord. How still the evening is!
As hush'd on purpose to grace harmony.

D. Pedro. See you where Benedick hath hid himself?

Claud. O, very well, my lord: the music ended
We'll fit the kid-fox with a penny-worth.

D. Pedro. Come, Balthazar, we'll hear that song again.

Balth. O! good my lord, tax not so bad a voice
To slander music any more than once.

D. Pedro. It is the witness still of excellency,
To put a strange face on his own perfection.—
I pray thee, sing, and let me woo no more.

Balth. Because you talk of wooing, I will sing;
Since many a wooer doth commence his suit
To her he thinks not worthy; yet he woos;
Yet will he swear he loves.

D. Pedro. Nay, pray thee, come:
Or, if thou wilt hold longer argument,
Do it in notes.

Balth. Note this before my notes;
There's not a note of mine that's worth the noting.

D. Pedro. Why, these are very crotchets that he speaks;
Note notes, forsooth, and nothing! [*Music.*

Bene. [*In the arbour.*] Now, divine air! now is his soul ravish'd!—Is it not strange, that sheep's guts should hale souls out of men's bodies?—Well, a horn for my money, when all's done.

BALTHAZAR'S Song.

Sigh no more, ladies, sigh no more,
Men were deceivers ever;
One foot in sea and one on shore;
To one thing constant never.

Then sigh not so, but let them go,
And be you blithe and bonny,
Converting all your sounds of woe
Into, Hey nonny, nonny.

Sing no more ditties, sing no mo
Of dumps so dull and heavy;
The frauds of men were ever so,
Since Summer first was leavy.
Then sigh not so, &c.

D. Pedro. By my troth, a good song.

Balth. And an ill singer, my lord.

D. Pedro. Ha? no, no, 'faith; thou singest well enough for a shift.

Bene. An he had been a dog that should have howl'd thus, they would have hang'd him; and I pray God, his bad voice bode no mischief! I had as lief have heard the night-raven, come what plague could have come after it.

D. Pedro. Yea, marry; dost thou hear, Balthazar? I pray thee, get us some excellent music; for to-morrow night we would have it at the Lady Hero's chamber-window.

Balth. The best I can, my lord.

D. Pedro. Do so; farewell. [*Exit* BALTHAZAR.] Come hither, Leonato: what was it you told me of to-day? that your niece Beatrice was in love with Signior Benedick?

Claud. [*Aside to* PEDRO.] O, ay:—stalk on, stalk on; the fowl sits. [*Aloud.*] I did never think that lady would have loved any man.

Leon. No, nor I neither; but most wonderful that she should so dote on Signior Benedick, whom she hath in all outward behaviours seemed ever to abhor

Bene. Is't possible? Sits the wind in that corner?

Leon. By my troth, my lord, I cannot tell what to think of it, but that she loves him with an enraged affection: it is past the infinite of thought.

D. Pedro. May be, she doth but counterfeit.

Claud. 'Faith, like enough.

Leon. O God! counterfeit! There was never counterfeit of passion came so near the life of passion, as she discovers it.

D. Pedro. Why, what effects of passion shows she?

Claud. [*Aside.*] Bait the hook well: this fish will bite.

Leon. What effects, my lord? She will sit you, — you heard my daughter tell you how.

Claud. She did, indeed.

D. Pedro. How, how, I pray you? You amaze me: I would have thought her spirit had been invincible against all assaults of affection.

Leon. I would have sworn it had, my lord; especially against Benedick.

Bene. I should think this a gull, but that the white-bearded fellow speaks it: knavery cannot, sure, hide himself in such reverence.

Claud. [*Aside.*] He hath ta'en th' infection: hold it up.

D. Pedro. Hath she made her affection known to Benedick?

Leon. No, and swears she never will: that's her torment.

Claud. 'Tis true, indeed; so your daughter says: "Shall I," says she, "that have so oft encounter'd him with scorn, write to him that I love him?"

Leon. This says she, now, when she is beginning to write to him; for she'll be up twenty times a night, and there will she sit in her smock, till she have writ a sheet of paper. — My daughter tells us all.

Claud. Now you talk of a sheet of paper, I remember a pretty jest your daughter told us of.

Leon. O! — when she had writ it, and was reading it over, she found Benedick and Beatrice between the sheet?

Claud. That.

Leon. O! she tore the letter into a thousand half pence; rail'd at herself, that she should be so immodest to write to one that she knew would flout her: — "I measure him," says she, "by my own spirit; for I should flout him, if he writ to me; yea, though I love him, I should."

Claud. Then down upon her knees she falls, weeps, sobs, beats her heart, tears her hair, prays; — cries, "O sweet Benedick! God give me patience!"

Leon. She doth indeed: my daughter says so; and the ecstasy hath so much overborne her, that my daughter is sometimes afeard she will do a desperate outrage to herself. It is very true.

D. Pedro. It were good, that Benedick knew of it by some other, if she will not discover it.

Claud. To what end? He would but make a sport of it, and torment the poor lady worse.

D. Pedro. An he should, it were an alms[-deed] to hang him. She's an excellent sweet lady; and, out of all suspicion, she is virtuous.

Claud. And she is exceeding wise.

D. Pedro. In every thing, but in loving Benedick.

Leon. O! my lord, wisdom and blood combating in so tender a body, we have ten proofs to one, that blood hath the victory. I am sorry for her, as I have just cause, being her uncle and her guardian.

D. Pedro. I would she had bestowed this dotage on me; I would have daff'd all other respects, and made her half myself. I pray you, tell Benedick of it, and hear what he will say.

Leon. Were it good, think you?

Claud. Hero thinks surely, she will die; for she says she will die if he love her not, and she will die ere she make her love known, and she will die if he woo her, rather than she will 'bate one breath of her accustomed crossness.

D. Pedro. She doth well: if she should make tender of her love, 'tis very possible he'll scorn it; for the man, as you know all, hath a contemptible spirit.

Claud. He is a very proper man.

D. Pedro. He hath, indeed, a good outward happiness.

Claud. 'Fore God, and in my mind, very wise.

D. Pedro. He doth, indeed, show some sparks that are like wit.

Leon. And I take him to be valiant.

D. Pedro. As Hector, I assure you: and in the managing of quarrels you may see he is wise; for either he avoids them with great discretion, or undertakes them with a christian-like fear.

Leon. If he do fear God, he must necessarily keep peace: if he break the peace, he ought to enter into a quarrel with fear and trembling.

D. Pedro. And so will he do; for the man doth fear God, howsoever it seems not in him by some large jests he will make. Well, I am sorry for your niece. Shall we go seek Benedick, and tell him of her love?

Claud. Never tell him, my lord: let her wear it out with good counsel.

Leon. Nay, that's impossible; she may wear her heart out first.

D. Pedro. Well, we will hear farther of it by your daughter: let it cool the while. I love Benedick well, and I could wish he would modestly examine himself, to see how much he is unworthy to have so good a lady.

Leon. My lord, will you walk? dinner is ready.

Claud. [*Aside.*] If he do not dote on her upon this, I will never trust my expectation.

D. Pedro. [*Aside.*] Let there be the same net spread for her; and that must your daughter and her gentlewoman carry. The sport will be, when they hold one an opinion of another's dotage, and no such matter: that's the scene that I would see, which will be merely a dumb show. Let us send her to call him in to dinner.

[*Exeunt* Don Pedro, Claudio, *and* Leonato.

Benedick *advances from the arbour.*

Bene. This can be no trick: the conference was sadly borne. — They have the truth of this from Hero. They seem to pity the lady. It seems, her affections have their full bent. Love me! why, it must be requited. I hear how I am censur'd. They say, I will bear myself proudly, if I perceive the love come from her: they say, too, that she will rather die than give any sign of affection. — I did never think to marry. — I must not seem proud. — Happy are they that hear their detractions, and can put them to mending. They say, the lady is fair; 'tis a truth, I can bear them witness: and virtuous; 'tis so, I cannot reprove it: and wise, but for loving me; by my troth, it is no addition to her wit, nor no great argument of her folly, for I will be horribly in love with her. I may chance have some odd quirks and remnants of wit broken on me, because I have rail'd so long against marriage; but doth not the appetite alter? A man loves the meat in his youth, that he cannot endure in his age. Shall quips, and sentences, and these paper bullets of the brain, awe a man from the career of his humour? No; the world must be peopled. When I said I would die a bachelor, I did not think I should live till I were married. — Here comes Beatrice. By this day, she's a fair lady: I do spy some marks of love in her.

Enter BEATRICE.

Beat. Against my will, I am sent to bid you come in to dinner.

Bene. Fair Beatrice, I thank you for your pains.

Beat. I took no more pains for those thanks, than you take pains to thank me: if it had been painful, I would not have come.

Bene. You take pleasure, then, in the message?

Beat. Yea, just so much as you may take upon a knife's point, and choke a daw withal. — You have no stomach, signior: fare you well. [*Exit*

Bene. Ha! "Against my will I am sent to bid you come in to dinner" — there's a double meaning in that. "I took no more pains for those thanks, than you took pains to thank me" — that's as much as to say, any pains that I take for you is as easy as thanks. — If I do not take pity of her, I am a villain: if I do not love her, I am a Jew. I will go get her picture. [*Exit.*

ACT III.

Scene I. — Leonato's Garden.

Enter Hero, Margaret, *and* Ursula.

Hero.

GOOD Margaret, run thee to the parlour;
There shalt thou find my cousin Beatrice
Proposing with the Prince and Claudio:
Whisper her ear, and tell her, I and Ursula
Walk in the orchard, and our whole discourse
Is all of her: say, that thou overheard'st us;
And bid her steal into the pleached bower,
Where honey-suckles, ripen'd by the sun,
Forbid the sun to enter, like favourites,
Made proud by princes, that advance their pride
Against that power that bred it. — There will she hide her,
To listen our propose. This is thy office;
Bear thee well in it, and leave us alone.

Marg. I'll make her come, I warrant you, presently. [*Exit.*

Hero. Now, Ursula, when Beatrice doth come,
As we do trace this alley up and down,
Our talk must only be of Benedick:
When I do name him, let it be thy part
To praise him more than ever man did merit.
My talk to thee must be, how Benedick
Is sick in love with Beatrice: of this matter
Is little Cupid's crafty arrow made,
That only wounds by hearsay.

Enter BEATRICE, *behind.*

Now begin;
For look where Beatrice, like a lapwing, runs
Close by the ground, to hear our conference.
Urs. The pleasant'st angling is to see the fish
Cut with her golden oars the silver stream,
And greedily devour the treacherous bait:
So angle we for Beatrice; who even now
Is couched in the woodbine coverture.
Fear you not my part of the dialogue.
Hero. Then go we near her, that her ear lose nothing
Of the false sweet bait that we lay for it.—
No, truly, Ursula, she is too disdainful;
I know her spirits are as coy and wild
As haggards of the rock.
Urs. But are you sure
That Benedick loves Beatrice so entirely?
Hero. So says the Prince, and my new-trothed lord.
Urs. And did they bid you tell her of it, Madam?
Hero. They did intreat me to acquaint her of it;
But I persuaded them, if they lov'd Benedick,
To wish him wrestle with affection,
And never to let Beatrice know of it.
Urs. Why did you so? Doth not the gentleman
Deserve as full, as fortunate a bed,
As ever Beatrice shall couch upon?
Hero. O god of love! I know he doth deserve
As much as may be yielded to a man;
But Nature never fram'd a woman's heart
Of prouder stuff than that of Beatrice:
Disdain and scorn ride sparkling in her eyes,
Misprising what they look on; and her wit

Values itself so highly, that to her
All matter else seems weak. She cannot love,
Nor take no shape nor project of affection,
She is so self-endeared.

Urs. Sure, I think so;
And therefore, certainly, it were not good
She knew his love, lest she make sport at it.

Hero. Why, you speak truth. I never yet saw man,
How wise, how noble, young, how rarely featur'd,
But she would spell him backward: if fair-fac'd,
She would swear the gentleman should be her sister:
If black, why, Nature, drawing of an antic,
Made a foul blot: if tall, a lance ill-headed:
If low, an agate very vilely cut:
If speaking, why, a vane blown with all winds:
If silent, why, a block moved with none.
So turns she every man the wrong side out,
And never gives to truth and virtue that
Which simpleness and merit purchaseth.

Urs. Sure, sure, such carping is not commendable.

Hero. No; not to be so odd, and from all fashions
As Beatrice is, cannot be commendable.
But who dare tell her so? If I should speak,
She would mock me into air: O! she would laugh me
Out of myself, press me to death with wit.
Therefore let Benedick, like cover'd fire,
Consume away in sighs, waste inwardly:
It were a bitter death to die with mocks,
Which is as bad as die with tickling.

Urs. Yet tell her of it: hear what she will say.

Hero. No; rather I will go to Benedick,

And counsel him to fight against his passion:
And, truly, I'll devise some honest slanders
To stain my cousin with. One doth not know
How much an ill word may empoison liking.

Urs. O! do not do your cousin such a wrong.
She cannot be so much without true judgment
(Having so swift and excellent a wit,
As she is priz'd to have) as to refuse
So rare a gentleman as Signior Benedick.

Hero. He is the only man of Italy,
Always excepted my dear Claudio.

Urs. I pray you, be not angry with me, Madam;
Speaking my fancy, Signior Benedick,
For shape, for bearing, argument, and valour,
Goes foremost in report through Italy.

Hero. Indeed, he hath an excellent good name.

Urs. His excellence did earn it, ere he had it.—
When are you married, Madam?

Hero. Why, every day;—to-morrow. Come, go in:
I'll show thee some attires, and have thy counsel,
Which is the best to furnish me to-morrow.

Urs. [*Aside.*] She's ta'en, I warrant you: we have caught her, Madam.

Hero. [*Aside.*] If it prove so, then loving goes by haps:
Some Cupid kills with arrows, some with traps.

[*Exeunt* HERO *and* URSULA; BEATRICE *comes forward.*

Beat. What fire is in mine ears? Can this be true?
Stand I condemn'd for pride and scorn so much?
Contempt, farewell! and maiden pride, adieu!
No glory lives behind the back of such.

And, Benedick, love on: I will requite thee,
  Taming my wild heart to thy loving hand.
If thou dost love, my kindness shall incite thee
  To bind our loves up in a holy band;
For others say thou dost deserve, and I
Believe it better than reportingly. [*Exit.*

SCENE II.

A Room in LEONATO's House.

Enter DON PEDRO, CLAUDIO, BENEDICK, *and* LEONATO.

D. Pedro. I do but stay till your marriage be consummate, and then go I toward Arragon.

Claud. I'll bring you thither, my Lord, if you'll vouchsafe me.

D. Pedro. Nay; that would be as great a soil in the new gloss of your marriage as to show a child his new coat, and forbid him to wear it. I will only be bold with Benedick for his company; for from the crown of his head to the sole of his foot, he is all mirth: he hath twice or thrice cut Cupid's bow-string, and the little hangman dare not shoot at him. He hath a heart as sound as a bell, and his tongue is the clapper; for what his heart thinks, his tongue speaks.

Bene. Gallants, I am not as I have been.

Leon. So say I: methinks you are sadder.

Claud. I hope he be in love.

D. Pedro. Hang him, truant! there's no true drop of blood in him, to be truly touch'd with love. If he be sad, he wants money.

Bene. I have the tooth-ache.

D. Pedro. Draw it.

Bene. Hang it!

Claud. You must hang it first, and draw it afterwards.

D. Pedro. What! sigh for the tooth-ache?

Leon. Where is but a humour, or a worm?

Bene. Well, every one can master a grief, but he that has it.

Claud. Yet say I, he is in love.

D. Pedro. There is no appearance of fancy in him, unless it be a fancy that he hath to strange disguises; as to be a Dutchman to-day, a Frenchman to-morrow, [or in the shape of two countries at once; as a German from the waist downward, all slops, and a Spaniard from the hip upward, no doublet.] Unless he have a fancy to this foolery, as it appears he hath, he is no fool for fancy, as you would have it appear he is.

Claud. If he be not in love with some woman, there is no believing old signs: he brushes his hat o' mornings; what should that bode?

D. Pedro. Hath any man seen him at the barber's?

Claud. No; but the barber's man hath been seen with him; and the old ornament of his cheek hath already stuff'd tennis-balls.

Leon. Indeed, he looks younger than he did, by the loss of a beard.

D. Pedro. Nay, he rubs himself with civet: can you smell him out by that?

Claud. That's as much as to say, the sweet youth's in love.

D. Pedro. The greatest note of it is his melancholy.

Claud. And when was he wont to wash his face?

D. Pedro. Yea, or to paint himself? for the which, I hear what they say of him.

Claud. Nay, but his jesting spirit, which is now crept into a lutestring, and now govern'd by stops.

D. Pedro. Indeed, that tells a heavy tale for him. Conclude he is in love.

Claud. Nay, but I know who loves him.

D. Pedro. That would I know too: I warrant, one that knows him not.

Claud. Yes, and his ill conditions; and, in despite of all, dies for him.

D. Pedro. She shall be buried — with her face upwards.

Bene. Yet is this no charm for the toothache. — Old signior, walk aside with me: I have studied eight or nine wise words to speak to you, which these hobby-horses must not hear.

[*Exeunt* BENEDICK *and* LEONATO.

D. Pedro. For my life, to break with him about Beatrice.

Claud. 'Tis even so. Hero and Margaret have by this played their parts with Beatrice, and then the two bears will not bite one another when they meet.

Enter JOHN the Bastard.

John. My lord and brother, God save you.

D. Pedro. Good den, brother.

John. If your leisure serv'd, I would speak with you.

D. Pedro. In private?

John. If it please you; yet Count Claudio may hear; for what I would speak of concerns him.

D. Pedro. What's the matter?

John. [*To* CLAUDIO.] Means your lordship to be married to-morrow?

D. Pedro. You know, he does.

John. I know not that, when he knows what I know.

Claud. If there be any impediment, I pray you, discover it.

John. You may think, I love you not: let that appear hereafter, and aim better at me by that I now will manifest. For my brother, I think, he holds you well, and in dearness of heart hath holp to effect your ensuing marriage; surely, suit ill spent, and labour ill bestowed!

D. Pedro. Why, what's the matter?

John. I came hither to tell you; and, circumstances shorten'd, (for she has been too long a talking of,) the lady is disloyal.

Claud. Who? Hero?

John. Even she: Leonato's Hero, your Hero, every man's Hero.

Claud. Disloyal?

John. The word is too good to paint out her wickedness: I could say, she were worse: think you of a worse title, and I will fit her to it. Wonder not till farther warrant: go but with me to-night, you shall see her chamber-window enter'd, even the night before her wedding-day: if you love her then, to-morrow wed her; but it would better fit your honour to change your mind.

Claud. May this be so?

D. Pedro. I will not think it.

John. If you dare not trust that you see, confess not that you know. If you will follow me, I will show you enough; and when you have seen more, and heard more, proceed accordingly.

Claud. If I see any thing to-night, why I should

not marry her to-morrow, in the congregation, where I should wed, there will I shame her.

D. Pedro. And, as I wooed for thee to obtain her, I will join with thee to disgrace her.

John. I will disparage her no farther, till you are my witnesses: bear it coldly but till night, and let the issue show itself.

D. Pedro. O day untowardly turned!

Claud. O mischief strangely thwarting!

John. O plague right well prevented! So will you say, when you have seen the sequel. [*Exeunt.*

Scene III.

A Street.

Enter Dogberry *and* Verges, *with the* Watch.

Dogberry. Are you good men and true?

Verges. Yea, or else it were pity but they should suffer salvation, body and soul.

Dogb. Nay, that were a punishment too good for them, if they should have any allegiance in them, being chosen for the Prince's Watch.

Verg. Well, give them their charge, neighbour Dogberry.

Dogb. First, who think you the most desartless man to be Constable?

1 *Watch.* Hugh Oatcake, sir, or George Seacoal, for they can write and read.

Dogb. Come hither, neighbour Seacoal. God hath bless'd you with a good name: to be a well-favoured man is the gift of fortune, but to write and read comes by nature.

2 *Watch.* Both which, Master Constable,—

Dogb. You have: I knew it would be your answer. Well, for your favour, sir, why, give God thanks, and make no boast of it; and for your writing and reading, let that appear when there is no need of such vanity. You are thought here to be the most senseless and fit man for the Constable of the Watch; therefore bear you the lanthorn. This is your charge. You shall comprehend all vagrom men: you are to bid any man stand, in the Prince's name.

2 *Watch.* How, if 'a will not stand?

Dogb. Why then, take no note of him, but let him go; and presently call the rest of the Watch together, and thank God you are rid of a knave.

Verg. If he will not stand when he is bidden, he is none of the Prince's subjects.

Dogb. True, and they are to meddle with none but the Prince's subjects. — You shall also make no noise in the streets; for for the Watch to babble and talk is most tolerable, and not to be endured.

2 *Watch.* We will rather sleep than talk: we know what belongs to a Watch.

Dogb. Why, you speak like an ancient and most quiet watchman; for I cannot see how sleeping should offend; only, have a care that your bills be not stol'n. Well, you are to call at all the ale-houses, and bid those that are drunk get them to bed.

2 *Watch.* How, if they will not?

Dogb. Why then, let them alone till they are sober: if they make you not then the better answer, you may say, they are not the men you took them for.

2 *Watch.* Well, sir.

Dogb. If you meet a thief, you may suspect him, by virtue of your office, to be no true man; and, for such kind of men, the less you meddle or make with them, why, the more is for your honesty.

2 *Watch*. If we know him to be a thief, shall we not lay hands on him?

Dogb. Truly, by your office you may; but, I think, they that touch pitch will be defil'd. The most peaceable way for you, if you do take a thief, is, to let him show himself what he is, and steal out of your company.

Verg. You have been always call'd a merciful man, partner.

Dogb. Truly, I would not hang a dog by my will; much more a man who hath any honesty in him.

Verg. If you hear a child cry in the night, you must call to the nurse, and bid her still it.

2 *Watch*. How, if the nurse be asleep, and will not hear us?

Dogb. Why then, depart in peace, and let the child wake her with crying; for the ewe that will not hear her lamb when it baes, will never answer a calf when he bleats.

Verg. 'Tis very true.

Dogb. This is the end of the charge. You, Constable, are to present the Prince's own person: if you meet the Prince in the night, you may stay him.

Verg. Nay, by'r lady, that, I think, 'a cannot.

Dogb. Five shillings to one on't, with any man that knows the statues, he may stay him: marry, not without the Prince be willing; for, indeed, the watch ought to offend no man, and it is an offence to stay a man against his will.

Verg. By'r lady, I think, it be so.

Dogb. Ha, ha, ha! Well, masters, good night: an' there be any matter of weight chances, call up me. Keep your fellows' counsels and your own, and good night. Come, neighbour.

2 *Watch*. Well, Masters, we hear our charge: let

us go sit here upon the church-bench till two, and then all to bed.

Dogb. One word more, honest neighbours. I pray you watch about Signior Leonato's door; for the wedding being there to-morrow, there is a great coil to-night. Adieu, be vigitant, I beseech you.

[*Exeunt* DOGBERRY *and* VERGES.

Enter BORACHIO *and* CONRADE.

Bora. What! Conrade!

Watch. [*Aside.*] Peace! stir not!

Bora. Conrade, I say!

Con. Here, man; I am at thy elbow.

Bora. Mass! and my elbow itch'd; I thought, there would a scab follow.

Con. I will owe thee an answer for that; and now forward with thy tale.

Bora. Stand thee close, then, under this penthouse; for it drizzles rain, and I will, like a true drunkard, utter all to thee.

Watch. [*Aside.*] Some treason, Masters; yet stand close.

Bora. Therefore know, I have earned of Don John a thousand ducats.

Con. Is it possible that any villainy should be so dear?

Bora. Thou should'st rather ask, if it were possible any villainy should be so rich; for when rich villains have need of poor ones, poor ones may make what price they will.

Con. I wonder at it.

Bora. That shows thou art unconfirm'd. Thou knowest, that the fashion of a doublet, or a hat, or a cloak, is nothing to a man.

Con. Yes, it is apparel.

Bora. I mean, the fashion.

Con. Yes, the fashion is the fashion.

Bora. Tush! I may as well say, the fool's the fool. But seest thou not what a deformed thief this fashion is?

Watch. [*Aside.*] I know that Deformed; 'a has been a vile thief this seven year: 'a goes up and down like a gentleman. I remember his name.

Bora. Didst thou not hear somebody?

Con. No: 'twas the vane on the house.

Bora. Seest thou not, I say, what a deformed thief this fashion is? how giddily 'a turns about all the hot bloods between fourteen and five and thirty? sometime, fashioning them like Pharaoh's soldiers in the reechy painting; sometime, like god Bel's priests in the old church window; sometime, like the shaven Hercules in the smirch'd worm-eaten tapestry, where his cod-piece seems as massy as his club?

Con. All this I see, and I see that the fashion wears out more apparel than the man. But art not thou thyself giddy with the fashion too, that thou hast shifted out of thy tale into telling me of the fashion?

Bora. Not so, neither; but know, that I have to-night wooed Margaret, the Lady Hero's gentlewoman, by the name of Hero: she leans me out at her mistress' chamber-window, bids me a thousand times good night. — I tell this tale vilely: — I should first tell thee, how the Prince, Claudio, and my master, planted, and placed, and possessed by my master, Don John, saw afar off in the orchard this amiable encounter.

Con. And thought thy Margaret was Hero?

Bora. Two of them did, the Prince and Claudio; but the devil, my master, knew she was Margaret;

and partly by his oaths, which first possess'd them, partly by the dark night, which did deceive them, but chiefly by my villainy, which did confirm any slander that Don John had made, away went Claudio enraged; — swore he would meet her, as he was appointed, next morning at the temple, and there, before the whole congregation, shame her with what he saw o'er-night, and send her home again without a husband.

1 *Watch.* We charge you in the Prince's name, stand.

2 *Watch.* Call up the right Master Constable. We have here recovered the most dangerous piece of lechery that ever was known in the commonwealth.

1 *Watch.* And one Deformed is one of them: I know him; 'a wears a lock.

Con. Masters, Masters!

2 *Watch.* You'll be made bring Deformed forth, I warrant you.

Con. Masters, —

1 *Watch.* Never speak: we charge you, let us obey you to go with us.

Bora. We are like to prove a goodly commodity, being taken up of these men's bills.

Con. A commodity in question, I warrant you. Come, we'll obey you. [*Exeunt.*

SCENE IV.

A Room in LEONATO'S House.

Enter HERO, MARGARET, *and* URSULA.

Hero. Good Ursula, wake my cousin Beatrice, and desire her to rise.

Urs. I will, lady.

Hero. And bid her come hither.

Urs. Well. [*Exit* URSULA.

Marg. Troth, I think your other rabato were better.

Hero. No, pray thee, good Meg, I'll wear this.

Marg. By my troth, 's not so good; and, I warrant, your cousin will say so.

Hero. My cousin's a fool, and thou art another. I'll wear none but this.

Marg. I like the new tire within excellently, if the hair were a thought browner; and your gown's a most rare fashion, i' faith. I saw the Duchess of Milan's gown, that they praise so.

Hero. O, that exceeds, they say.

Marg. By my troth, 's but a night-gown in respect of yours: cloth o' gold, and cuts, and lac'd with silver, set with pearls, down sleeves, side sleeves, and skirts round, under-borne with a bluish tinsel; but for a fine, quaint, graceful, and excellent fashion, yours is worth ten on 't.

Hero. God give me joy to wear it, for my heart is exceeding heavy!

Marg. 'Twill be heavier soon by the weight of a man.

Hero. Fie upon thee! art not asham'd?

Marg. Of what, lady? of speaking honourably? Is not marriage honourable in a beggar? Is not your lord honourable without marriage? I think you would have me say, saving your reverence, 'a husband:' an bad thinking do not wrest true speaking, I'll offend nobody. Is there any harm in 'the heavier for a husband'? None, I think, an it be the right husband and the right wife; otherwise 'tis light, and not heavy: ask my Lady Beatrice else; here she comes.

Enter BEATRICE.

Hero. Good morrow, coz.

Beat. Good morrow, sweet Hero.

Hero. Why, how now? do you speak in the sick tune?

Beat. I am out of all other tune, methinks.

Marg. Clap 's into *Light o' love;* that goes without a burthen: do you sing it, and I'll dance it.

Beat. Yea, Light o' love, with your heels! — then, if your husband have stables enough, you'll look he shall lack no barns.

Marg. O, illegitimate construction! I scorn that with my heels.

Beat. 'Tis almost five o'clock, cousin: 'tis time you were ready. By my troth, I am exceeding ill. — Heigh ho!

Marg. For a hawk, a horse, or a husband?

Beat. For the letter that begins them all, H.

Marg. Well, an you be not turn'd Turk, there's no more sailing by the Star.

Beat. What means the fool, 'trow?

Marg. Nothing I; but God send every one their heart's desire!

Hero. These gloves the Count sent me, they are an excellent perfume.

Beat. I am stuff'd, cousin, I cannot smell.

Marg. A maid, and stuff'd! there's goodly catching of cold.

Beat. O, God help me! God help me! how long have you profess'd apprehension?

Marg. Ever since you left it. Doth not my wit become me rarely?

Beat. It is not seen enough; you should wear it in your cap. — By my troth, I am sick.

Marg. Get you some of this distill'd *carduus benedictus*, and lay it to your heart: it is the only thing for a qualm.

Hero. There thou prick'st her with a thistle.

Beat. *Benedictus!* why *benedictus?* you have some moral in this *benedictus*.

Marg. Moral? no, by my troth, I have no moral meaning; I meant, plain holy-thistle. You may think, perchance, that I think you are in love: nay, by'r lady, I am not such a fool to think what I list; nor I list not to think what I can; nor, indeed, I cannot think, if I would think my heart out of thinking, that you are in love, or that you will be in love, or that you can be in love. Yet Benedick was such another, and now is he become a man: he swore he would never marry; and yet now, in despite of his heart, he eats his meat without grudging: and how you may be converted, I know not, but, methinks, you look with your eyes as other women do.

Beat. What pace is this that thy tongue keeps?

Marg. Not a false gallop.

Enter URSULA.

Urs. Madam, withdraw: the Prince, the Count, Signior Benedick, Don John, and all the gallants of the town are come to fetch you to church.

Hero. Help to dress me, good coz, good Meg, good Ursula. [*Exeunt.*

SCENE V.

Another Room in LEONATO'S House.

Enter LEONATO, *with* DOGBERRY *and* VERGES.

Leon. What would you with me, honest neighbour?

Dogb. Marry, sir, I would have some confidence with you, that decerns you nearly.

Leon. Brief, I pray you; for, you see, it is a busy time with me.

Dogb. Marry, this it is, sir.

Verg. Yes, in truth it is, sir.

Leon. What is it, my good friends?

Dogb. Goodman Verges, sir, speaks a little off the matter: an old man, sir, and his wits are not so blunt, as, God help, I would desire they were; but, in faith, honest as the skin between his brows.

Verg. Yes, I thank God, I am as honest as any man living, that is an old man, and no honester than I.

Dogb. Comparisons are odorous: *palabras*, neighbour Verges.

Leon. Neighbours, you are tedious.

Dogb. It pleases your worship to say so, but we are the poor Duke's officers; but, truly, for mine own part, if I were as tedious as a King, I could find in my heart to bestow it all of your worship.

Leon. All thy tediousness on me, ah?

Dogb. Yea, an 'twere a thousand times more than 'tis; for I hear as good exclamation on your worship as of any man in the city, and though I be but a poor man, I am glad to hear it.

Verg. And so am I.

Leon. I would fain know what you have to say.

Verg. Marry, sir, our watch to-night, excepting your worship's presence, have ta'en a couple of as arrant knaves as any in Messina.

Dogb. A good old man, sir; he will be talking: as they say, when the age is in, the wit is out. God help us! it is a world to see!—Well said, i' faith, neighbour Verges:—well, God's a good man: an two men ride of a horse, one must ride behind. — An honest soul, i' faith, sir: by my troth he is, as ever broke bread; but, God is to be worshipp'd: all men are not alike; alas, good neighbour!

Leon. Indeed, neighbour, he comes too short of you.

Dogb. Gifts, that God gives.

Leon. I must leave you.

Dogb. One word, sir. Our watch, sir, have, indeed, comprehended two aspicious persons, and we would have them this morning examined before your worship.

Leon. Take their examination yourself, and bring it me: I am now in great haste, as may appear unto you.

Dogb. It shall be suffigance.

Leon. Drink some wine ere you go. Fare you well.

Enter a Messenger.

Mess. My lord, they stay for you to give your daughter to her husband.

Leon. I'll wait upon them: I am ready.

[*Exeunt* LEONATO *and* Messenger.

Dogb. Go, good partner, go; get you to Francis Seacoal; bid him bring his pen and inkhorn to the gaol: we are now to examine those men.

Verg. And we must do it wisely.

Dogb. We will spare for no wit, I warrant you; here's that shall drive some of them to a 'non-come': only get the learned writer to set down our excommunication, and meet me at the gaol. [*Exeunt.*

ACT IV.

SCENE I. — The Inside of a Church.

Enter Don PEDRO, JOHN the Bastard, LEONATO, Friar, CLAUDIO, BENEDICK, HERO, BEATRICE, Guests, *and* Attendants.

LEONATO.

COME, Friar Francis, be brief: only to the plain form of marriage, and you shall recount their particular duties afterwards.

Friar. You come hither, my lord, to marry this lady?

Claud. No.

Leon. To be married to her; Friar, you come to marry her.

Friar. Lady, you come hither to be married to this Count?

Hero. I do.

Friar. If either of you know any inward impediment, why you should not be conjoined, I charge you on your souls to utter it.

Claud. Know you any, Hero?

Hero. None, my lord.

Friar. Know you any, Count?

Leon. I dare make his answer; none.

Claud. O, what men dare do! what men may do! what men daily do, [not knowing what they do!]

Bene. How now! Interjections? Why then, "some be of laughing, as, ha! ha! he!"

Claud. Stand thee by, Friar. — Father, by your
leave:

Will you with free and unconstrained soul
Give me this maid, your daughter?

Leon. As freely, son, as God did give her me.

Claud. And what have I to give you back, whose worth
May counterpoise this rich and precious gift?

D. Pedro. Nothing, unless you render her again.

Claud. Sweet Prince, you learn me noble thankfulness. —
There, Leonato; take her back again:
Give not this rotten orange to your friend;
She's but the sign and semblance of her honour. —
Behold, how like a maid she blushes here:
O, what authority and show of truth
Can cunning sin cover itself withal!
Comes not that blood, as modest evidence,
To witness simple virtue? Would you not swear,
All you that see her, that she were a maid,
By these exterior shows? But she is none:
She knows the heat of a luxurious bed;
Her blush is guiltiness, not modesty.

Leon. What do you mean, my lord?

Claud. Not to be married,
Not to knit my soul to an approved wanton.

Leon. Dear my lord, if you, in your own proof,
Have vanquish'd the resistance of her youth,
And made defeat of her virginity, —

Claud. I know what you would say: if I have known her,
You'll say, she did embrace me as a husband,
And so extenuate the 'forehand sin:
No, Leonato,
I never tempted her with word too large:
But, as a brother to his sister, shewed
Bashful sincerity and comely love.

Hero. And seem'd I ever otherwise to you?
Claud. Out on thee! Seeming! I will write against it:
You seem to me as Dian in her orb,
As chaste as is the bud ere it be blown;
But you are more intemperate in your blood
Than Venus, or those pamper'd animals
That rage in savage sensuality.
Hero. Is my lord well, that he doth speak so wide?
Leon. Sweet Prince, why speak not you?
D. Pedro. What should I speak?
I stand dishonour'd, that have gone about
To link my dear friend to a common stale.
Leon. Are these things spoken, or do I but dream?
John. Sir, they are spoken, and these things are true.
Bene. This looks not like a nuptial.
Hero. True? O God!
Claud. Leonato, stand I here?
Is this the Prince? Is this the Prince's brother?
Is this face Hero's? Are our eyes our own?
Leon. All this is so; but what of this, my lord?
Claud. Let me but move one question to your daughter,
And, by that fatherly and kindly power
That you have in her, bid her answer truly.
Leon. I charge thee do [so], as thou art my child.
Hero. O God, defend me! how am I beset!—
What kind of catechising call you this?
Claud. To make you answer truly to your name.
Hero. Is it not Hero? Who can blot that name
With any just reproach?
Claud. Marry, that can Hero:
Hero itself can blot out Hero's virtue.
What man was he talk'd with you yesternight

Out at your window, betwixt twelve and one?
Now, if you are a maid, answer to this.

Hero. I talk'd with no man at that hour, my lord.

D. Pedro. Why, then are you no maiden. — Leonato,
I am sorry you must hear: upon mine honour,
Myself, my brother, and this grieved Count,
Did see her, hear her, at that hour last night,
Talk with a ruffian at her chamber window;
Who hath, indeed, most like a liberal villain,
Confess'd the vile encounters they have had
A thousand times in secret.

John. Fie, fie! they are not to be nam'd, my lord,
Not to be spoken of;
There is not chastity enough in language,
Without offence to utter them. Thus, pretty lady,
I am sorry for thy much misgovernment.

Claud. O Hero! what a Hero hadst thou been,
If half thy outward graces had been placed
About thy thoughts, and counsels of thy heart!
But, fare thee well, most foul, most fair! farewell,
Thou pure impiety, and impious purity!
For thee I'll lock up all the gates of love,
And on my eye-lids shall conjecture hang,
To turn all beauty into thoughts of harm,
And never shall it more be gracious.

Leon. Hath no man's dagger here a point for me?
[HERO *swoons.*

Beat. Why, how now, cousin! wherefore sink you down?

John. Come, let us go. These things, come thus to light,
Smother her spirits up.
[*Exeunt* DON PEDRO, JOHN, *and* CLAUDIO

Bene. How doth the lady?

Beat. Dead, I think: — help, uncle! —
Hero! why, Hero! — Uncle! — Signior Benedick! —
Friar!

Leon. O Fate! take not away thy heavy hand:
Death is the fairest cover for her shame,
That may be wish'd for.

Beat. How now, cousin Hero?

Friar. Have comfort, lady.

Leon. Dost thou look up?

Friar. Yea; wherefore should she not?

Leon. Wherefore? Why, doth not every earthly thing
Cry shame upon her? Could she here deny
The story that is printed in her blood? —
Do not live, Hero; do not ope thine eyes;
For did I think thou would'st not quickly die,
Thought I thy spirits were stronger than thy shames,
Myself would, on the rearward of reproaches,
Strike at thy life. Griev'd I, I had but one?
Chid I, for that, at frugal Nature's frame?
O, one too much by thee! Why had I one?
Why ever wast thou lovely in my eyes?
Why had I not, with charitable hand,
Took up a beggar's issue at my gates;
Who smeared thus, and mir'd with infamy,
I might have said, 'No part of it is mine;
This shame derives itself from unknown loins'?
But mine, and mine I lov'd, and mine I prais'd,
And mine that I was proud on; mine so much,
That I myself was to myself not mine,
Valuing of her; why, she — O! she is fallen
Into a pit of ink, that the wide sea
Hath drops too few to wash her clean again,
And salt too little, which may season give
To her foul tainted flesh!

Bene. Sir, sir, be patient.
For my part, I am so attir'd in wonder,
I know not what to say.

Beat. O, on my soul, my cousin is belied!

Bene. Lady, were you her bedfellow last night?

Beat. No, truly not; although, until last night,
I have this twelvemonth been her bedfellow.

Leon. Confirm'd, confirm'd! O, that is stronger made,
Which was before barr'd up with ribs of iron!
Would the two Princes lie? and Claudio lie,
Who lov'd her so, that, speaking of her foulness,
Wash'd it with tears? Hence! from her; let her die.

Friar. Hear me a little;
For I have only silent been so long,
And given way unto this course of fortune,
By noting of the lady: I have mark'd
A thousand blushing apparitions
To start into her face; a thousand innocent shames,
In angel whiteness, bear away those blushes;
And in her eye there hath appear'd a fire,
To burn the errors that these Princes hold
Against her maiden truth. — Call me a fool;
Trust not my reading, nor my observations,
Which with experimental seal doth warrant
The tenor of my book; trust not my age,
My reverence, calling, nor divinity,
If this sweet lady lie not guiltless here
Under some biting error.

Leon. Friar, it cannot be.
Thou seest, that all the grace that she hath left,
Is, that she will not add to her damnation
A sin of perjury: she not denies it.
Why seek'st thou, then, to cover with excuse
That which appears in proper nakedness?

Friar. Lady, what man is he you are accus'd of?
Hero. They know, that do accuse me: I know none.
If I know more of any man alive
Than that which maiden modesty doth warrant,
Let all my sins lack mercy! — O, my father!
Prove you that any man with me convers'd
At hours unmeet, or that I yesternight
Maintain'd the change of words with any creature,
Refuse me, hate me, torture me to death.
Friar. There is some strange misprision in the Princes.
Bene. Two of them have the very bent of honour;
And if their wisdoms be misled in this,
The practice of it lives in John the Bastard,
Whose spirits toil in frame of villainies.
Leon. I know not. If they speak but truth of her,
These hands shall tear her: if they wrong her honour,
The proudest of them shall well hear of it.
Time hath not yet so dried this blood of mine,
Nor age so eat up my invention,
Nor fortune made such havoc of my means,
Nor my bad life reft me so much of friends,
But they shall find, awak'd in such a kind,
Both strength of limb, and policy of mind,
Ability in means, and choice of friends,
To quit me of them throughly.
Friar. Pause a while,
And let my counsel sway you in this case.
Your daughter, here, the Princes left for dead;
Let her a while be secretly kept in,
And publish it, that she is dead indeed:
Maintain a mourning ostentation;

And on your family's old monument
Hang mournful epitaphs, and do all rites
That appertain unto a burial.

Leon. What shall become of this? What will this do?

Friar. Marry, this, well carried, shall on her behalf
Change slander to remorse; that is some good:
But not for that dream I on this strange course,
But on this travail look for greater birth.
She dying, as it must be so maintain'd,
Upon the instant that she was accus'd,
Shall be lamented, pitied, and excus'd
Of every hearer; for it so falls out,
That what we have we prize not to the worth,
Whiles we enjoy it, but being lack'd and lost,
Why, then we rack the value; then we find
The virtue, that possession would not show us,
Whiles it was ours. — So will it fare with Claudio:
When he shall hear she died upon his words,
Th' idea of her life shall sweetly creep
Into his study of imagination,
And every lovely organ of her life
Shall come apparell'd in more precious habit,
More moving, delicate, and full of life,
Into the eye and prospect of his soul,
Than when she liv'd indeed: — then shall he mourn,
(If ever love had interest in his liver,)
And wish he had not so accused her;
No, though he thought his accusation true.
Let this be so, and doubt not but success
Will fashion the event in better shape
Than I can lay it down in likelihood.
But if all aim but this be levell'd false,
The supposition of the lady's death

Will quench the wonder of her infamy;
And, if it sort not well, you may conceal her,
As best befits her wounded reputation,
In some reclusive and religious life,
Out of all eyes, tongues, minds, and injuries.

Bene. Signior Leonato, let the Friar advise you:
And though you know my inwardness and love
Is very much unto the Prince and Claudio,
Yet, by mine honour, I will deal in this
As secretly and justly as your soul
Should with your body.

Leon. Being that I flow in grief,
The smallest twine may lead me.

Friar. 'Tis well consented; presently away,
For to strange sores strangely they strain the cure. —
Come, lady, die to live: this wedding day,
Perhaps, is but prolong'd: have patience, and endure.

[*Exeunt* Friar, HERO, *and* LEONATO.

Bene. Lady Beatrice, have you wept all this while?

Beat. Yea, and I will weep a while longer.

Bene. I will not desire that.

Beat. You have no reason; I do it freely.

Bene. Surely, I do believe your fair cousin is wrong'd.

Beat. Ah, how much might the man deserve of me that would right her!

Bene. Is there any way to show such friendship?

Beat. A very even way, but no such friend.

Bene. May a man do it?

Beat. It is a man's office, but not yours.

Bene. I do love nothing in the world so well as you. Is not that strange?

Beat. As strange as the thing I know not. It

were as possible for me to say, I loved nothing so well as you; but believe me not, and yet I lie not: I confess nothing, nor I deny nothing. — I am sorry for my cousin.

Bene. By my sword, Beatrice, thou lov'st me.

Beat. Do not swear by it, and eat it.

Bene. I will swear by it that you love me; and I will make him eat it, that says I love not you.

Beat. Will you not eat your word?

Bene. With no sauce that can be devised to it. I protest I love thee.

Beat. Why then, God forgive me!

Bene. What offence, sweet Beatrice?

Beat. You have stayed me in a happy hour: I was about to protest I loved you.

Bene. And do it with all thy heart.

Beat. I love you with so much of my heart, that none is left to protest.

Bene. Come, bid me do any thing for thee.

Beat. Kill Claudio.

Bene. Ha! not for the wide world.

Beat. You kill me to deny. Farewell.

Bene. Tarry, sweet Beatrice.

Beat. I am gone, though I am here: — there is no love in you. — Nay, I pray you, let me go.

Bene. Beatrice, —

Beat. In faith, I will go.

Bene. We'll be friends first.

Beat. You dare easier be friends with me than fight with mine enemy.

Bene. Is Claudio thine enemy?

Beat. Is he not approved in the height a villain, that hath slandered, scorned, dishonoured my kinswoman? — O, that I were a man! — What! bear her in hand until they come to take hands, and then with public accusation, uncovered slander, unmitigated rancour, — O God, that I were a man! I would eat his heart in the market-place.

Bene. Hear me, Beatrice —

Beat. Talk with a man out at a window! — a proper saying.

Bene. Nay, but Beatrice —

Beat. Sweet Hero! — she is wrong'd, she is slandered, she is undone.

Bene. Beat—

Beat. Princes and Counties! Surely, a princely testimony, a goodly count — confect; a sweet gallant, surely! O, that I were a man for his sake! or that I had any friend would be a man for my sake! But manhood is melted into court'sies, valour into compliment, and men are only turned into tongue, and trim ones too: he is now as valiant as Hercules that only tells a lie and swears it. — I cannot be a man with wishing, therefore I will die a woman with grieving.

Bene. Tarry, good Beatrice. By this hand, I love thee.

Beat. Use it for my love some other way than swearing by it.

Bene. Think you in your soul the Count Claudio hath wrong'd Hero?

Beat. Yea, as sure as I have a thought, or a soul.

Bene. Enough! I am engag'd, I will challenge him. I will kiss your hand, and so I leave you. By this hand, Claudio shall render me a dear account. As you hear of me, so think of me. Go, comfort your cousin: I must say she is dead; and so, farewell. [*Exeunt.*

Scene II.

A Prison.

Enter Dogberry, Verges, *and* Sexton, *in gowns; and the* Watch, *with* Conrade *and* Borachio.

Dogb. Is our whole dissembly appear'd?

Verg. O! a stool and a cushion for the Sexton.

Sexton. Which be the malefactors?

Dogb. Marry, that am I and my partner.

Verg. Nay, that's certain: we have the exhibition to examine.

Sexton. But which are the offenders that are to be examined? let them come before Master Constable.

Dogb. Yea, marry, let them come before me.— What is your name, friend?

Bora. Borachio.

Dogb. Pray write down 'Borachio.'—Yours, sirrah?

Con. I am a gentleman, sir, and my name is Conrade.

Dogb. Write down 'Master gentleman Conrade.'— Masters, do you serve God?

[*Con. Bora.* Yea, sir, we hope.

Dogb. Write down that 'they hope they serve God': —and write 'God' first; for God defend but God should go before such villains!]—Masters, it is proved already that you are little better than false knaves, and it will go near to be thought so shortly. How answer you for yourselves?

Con. Marry, sir, we say we are none.

Dogb. A marvellous witty fellow, I assure you; but I will go about with him.—Come you hither, sirrah; a word in your ear, sir: I say to you, it is thought you are false knaves.

Bora. Sir, I say to you, we are none.

Dogb. Well, stand aside. — 'Fore God, they are both in a tale. Have you writ down, that they are none?

Sexton. Master Constable, you go not the way to examine: you must call forth the Watch that are their accusers.

Dogb. Yea, marry, that's the eftest way: — Let the Watch come forth. — Masters, I charge you, in the Prince's name, accuse these men.

1 *Watch.* This man said, sir, that Don John, the Prince's brother, was a villain.

Dogb. Write down 'Prince John a villain.' Why, this is flat perjury, to call a prince's brother, villain.

Bora. Master Constable —

Dogb. Pray thee, fellow, peace: I do not like thy look, I promise thee.

Sexton. What heard you him say else?

2 *Watch.* Marry, that he had received a thousand ducats of Don John, for accusing the lady Hero wrongfully.

Dogb. Flat burglary as ever was committed.

Verg. Yea, by th' mass, that it is.

Sexton. What else, fellow?

1 *Watch.* And that Count Claudio did mean, upon his words, to disgrace Hero before the whole assembly, and not marry her.

Dogb. O villain! thou wilt be condemn'd into everlasting redemption for this.

Sexton. What else?

2 *Watch.* This is all.

Sexton. And this is more, Masters, than you can

deny. Prince John is this morning secretly stol'n away: Hero was in this manner accus'd, in this very manner refus'd, and, upon the grief of this, suddenly died. Master Constable, let these men be bound, and brought to Leonato: I will go before, and show him their examination. [*Exit.*

Dogb. Come, let them be opinion'd.

Con. Let them be, in the hands of coxcomb.

Dogb. God's my life! where's the Sexton? let him write down the Prince's officer, coxcomb.—Come, bind them.—Thou naughty varlet!

Con. Away! you are an ass; you are an ass.

Dogb. Dost thou not suspect my place? Dost thou not suspect my years?—O, that he were here to write me down, an ass!—But, masters, remember, that I am an ass; though it be not written down, yet forget not that I am an ass.—No, thou villain, thou art full of piety, as shall be prov'd upon thee by good witness. I am a wise fellow; and, which is more, an officer; and, which is more, a householder; and, which is more, as pretty a piece of flesh as any in Messina; and one that knows the law, go to; and a rich fellow enough, go to; and a fellow that hath had losses; and one that hath two gowns, and every thing handsome about him. Bring him away. O, that I had been writ down, an ass!

[*Exeunt.*

ACT V.

SCENE I. — Before LEONATO'S House.

Enter LEONATO *and* ANTONIO.

ANTONIO.

IF you go on thus, you will kill yourself;
And 'tis not wisdom thus to second grief
Against yourself.

Leon. I pray thee, cease thy counsel,
Which falls into mine ears as profitless
As water in a sieve. Give not me counsel;
Nor let no comforter delight mine ear,
But such a one whose wrongs do suit with mine:
Bring me a father that so lov'd his child,
Whose joy of her is overwhelm'd like mine,
And bid him speak of patience;
Measure his woe the length and breadth of mine,
And let it answer every strain for strain;
As thus for thus, and such a grief for such,
In every lineament, branch, shape, and form:
If such a one will smile, and stroke his beard,
And, sorrow's wag, cry hem, when he should groan,
Patch grief with proverbs, make misfortune drunk
With candle-wasters; bring him yet to me,
And I of him will gather patience.
But there is no such man; for, brother, men
Can counsel, and speak comfort to that grief
Which they themselves not feel; but, tasting it,
Their counsel turns to passion, which before
Would give preceptial medicine to rage,
Fetter strong madness in a silken thread,

Charm ache with air, and agony with words.
No, no; 'tis all men's office to speak patience
To those that wring under the load of sorrow,
But no man's virtue, nor sufficiency,
To be so moral when he shall endure
The like himself. Therefore give me no counsel:
My griefs cry louder than advertisement.

Ant. Therein do men from children nothing differ.

Leon. I pray thee, peace! I will be flesh and blood;
For there was never yet philosopher
That could endure the tooth-ache patiently,
However they have writ the style of gods,
And made a push at chance and sufferance.

Ant. Yet bend not all the harm upon yourself;
Make those that do offend you suffer too.

Leon. There thou speak'st reason: nay, I will do so.
My soul doth tell me Hero is belied,
And that shall Claudio know; so shall the Prince,
And all of them that thus dishonour her.

Enter Don Pedro *and* Claudio.

Ant. Here comes the Prince and Claudio, hastily.

D. Pedro. Good den, good den.

Claud. Good day to both of you.

Leon. Hear you, my lords,—

D. Pedro. We have some haste, Leonato.

Leon. Some haste, my lord!—well, fare you well, my lord:—
Are you so hasty now?—well, all is one.

D. Pedro. Nay, do not quarrel with us, good old man.

Ant. If he could right himself with quarrelling,
Some of us would lie low.

Claud. Who wrongs him?
Leon. Marry, thou dost wrong me; thou, dissembler, thou. —
Nay, never lay thy hand upon thy sword;
I fear thee not.
Claud. Marry, beshrew my hand,
If it should give your age such cause of fear.
In faith, my hand meant nothing to my sword.
Leon. Tush, tush, man! never fleer and jest at me;
I speak not like a dotard, nor a fool;
As, under privilege of age, to brag
What I have done being young, or what would do,
Were I not old. Know, Claudio, to thy head,
Thou hast so wrong'd mine innocent child and me,
That I am forc'd to lay my reverence by,
And with gray hairs and bruise of many days,
Do challenge thee to trial of a man.
I say, thou hast belied mine innocent child:
Thy slander hath gone through and through her heart,
And she lies buried with her ancestors,
O! in a tomb where never scandal slept,
Save this of hers, fram'd by thy villainy.
Claud. My villainy?
Leon. Thine, Claudio; thine, I say.
D. Pedro. You say not right, old man.
Leon. My lord, my lord,
I'll prove it on his body, if he dare,
Despite his nice fence, and his active practice,
His May of youth, and bloom of lustihood.
Claud. Away! I will not have to do with you.
Leon. Canst thou so daff me? Thou hast kill'd my child:
If thou kill'st me, boy, thou shalt kill a man.

Ant. He shall kill two of us, and men indeed:
But that's no matter; let him kill one first:—
Win me and wear me;—let him answer me.—
Come, follow me, boy! come, sir boy, come, follow me.
Sir boy, I'll whip you from your foining fence;
Nay, as I am a gentleman, I will.

Leon. Brother—

Ant. Content yourself. God knows I lov'd my niece;
And she is dead; slander'd to death by villains,
That dare as well answer a man, indeed,
As I dare take a serpent by the tongue.
Boys, apes, braggarts, Jacks, milksops!

Leon. Brother Antony—

Ant. Hold you content. What, man! I know them, yea,
And what they weigh, even to the utmost scruple:
Scambling, out-facing, fashion-mong'ring boys,
That lie, and cog, and flout, deprave and slander,
Go anticly, and show outward hideousness,
And speak off half a dozen dang'rous words,
How they might hurt their enemies—if they durst;
And this is all!

Leon. But, brother Antony—

Ant. Come, 'tis no matter:
Do not you meddle; let me deal in this.

D. Pedro. Gentlemen both, we will not wake your patience.
My heart is sorry for your daughter's death;
But, on mine honour, she was charg'd with nothing
But what was true, and very full of proof.

Leon. My lord, my lord!—

D. Pedro. I will not hear you.

Enter BENEDICK.

Leon. No?
Come, brother, away.—I will be heard.—

Ant. And shall, or some of us will smart for it.
[*Exeunt* LEONATO *and* ANTONIO.

D. Pedro. See, see: here comes the man we went to seek.

Claud. Now, Signior, what news?

Bene. Good day, my lord.

D. Pedro. Welcome, Signior: you are almost come to part almost a fray.

Claud. We had like to have had our two noses snapp'd off with two old men without teeth.

D. Pedro. Leonato and his brother. What think'st thou? Had we fought, I doubt, we should have been too young for them.

Bene. In a false quarrel there is no true valour. I came to seek you both.

Claud. We have been up and down to seek thee; for we are high-proof melancholy, and would fain have it beaten away. Wilt thou use thy wit?

Bene. It is in my scabbard: shall I draw it?

D. Pedro. Dost thou wear thy wit by thy side?

Claud. Never any did so, though very many have been beside their wit.—I will bid thee draw, as we do the minstrels; draw to pleasure us.

D. Pedro. As I am an honest man, he looks pale.—Art thou sick, or angry?

Claud. What! courage, man! What though care kill'd a cat, thou hast mettle enough in thee to kill care.

Bene. Sir, I shall meet your wit in the career, an you charge it against me.—I pray you, choose another subject.

Claud. Nay then, give him another staff: this last was broke cross.

D. Pedro. By this light, he changes more and more. I think he be angry indeed.

Claud. If he be, he knows how to turn his girdle.

Bene. Shall I speak a word in your ear?

Claud. God bless me from a challenge!

Bene. You are a villain. — I jest not: — I will make it good how you dare, with what you dare, and when you dare. — Do me right, or I will protest your cowardice. You have kill'd a sweet lady, and her death shall fall heavy on you. Let me hear from you.

Claud. Well, I will meet you, so I may have good cheer.

D. Pedro. What, a feast? a feast?

Claud. I' faith, I thank him; he hath bid me to a calf's-head and a capon, the which if I do not carve most curiously, say my knife's naught. — Shall I not find a woodcock too?

Bene. Sir, your wit ambles well: it goes easily.

D. Pedro. I'll tell thee how Beatrice prais'd thy wit the other day. I said, thou hadst a fine wit: "True," said she, "a fine little one:" "No," said I, "a great wit:" "Right," says she, "a great gross one:" "Nay," said I, "a good wit:" "Just," said she, "it hurts nobody:" "Nay," said I, "the gentleman is wise:" "Certain," said she, "a wise gentleman:" "Nay," said I, "he hath the tongues:" "That I believe," said she, "for he swore a thing to me on Monday night, which he forswore on Tuesday morning: there's a double tongue; there's two tongues." Thus did she, an hour together, transshape thy particular virtues; yet at last she concluded with a sigh, thou wast the prop'rest man in Italy.

Claud. For the which she wept heartily, and said she car'd not.

D. Pedro. Yea, that she did; but yet, for all that, an if she did not hate him deadly, she would love him dearly. The old man's daughter told us all.

Claud. All, all; and moreover, God saw him when he was hid in the garden.

D. Pedro. But when shall we set the savage bull's horns on the sensible Benedick's head?

Claud. Yea, and text underneath, "Here dwells Benedick the married man!"

Bene. Fare you well, boy: you know my mind. I will leave you now to your gossip-like humour: you break jests as braggarts do their blades, which, God be thanked, hurt not.—My lord, for your many courtesies I thank you: I must discontinue your company. Your brother, the Bastard, is fled from Messina: you have, among you, kill'd a sweet and innocent lady. For my Lord Lack-beard, there, he and I shall meet; and till then, peace be with him. [*Exit* BENEDICK.

D. Pedro. He is in earnest.

Claud. In most profound earnest; and, I'll warrant you, for the love of Beatrice.

D. Pedro. And hath challeng'd thee?

Claud. Most sincerely.

D. Pedro. What a pretty thing man is when he goes in his doublet and hose, and leaves off his wit!

Enter DOGBERRY, VERGES, *and the* Watch, *with* CONRADE *and* BORACHIO.

Claud. He is then a giant to an ape: but then is an ape a doctor to such a man.

D. Pedro. But, soft you; let me be: pluck up, my heart, and be sad! Did he not say my brother was fled?

Dogb. Come, you, sir: if Justice cannot tame you, she shall ne'er weigh more reasons in her balance. Nay, an you be a cursing hypocrite once, you must be look'd to.

D. Pedro. How now! two of my brother's men bound? Borachio one?

Claud. Hearken after their offence, my lord.

D. Pedro. Officers, what offence have these men done?

Dogb. Marry, sir, they have committed false report; moreover, they have spoken untruths; secondarily, they are slanders; sixth and lastly, they have belied a lady; thirdly, they have verified unjust things; and, to conclude, they are lying knaves.

D. Pedro. First, I ask thee what they have done? thirdly, I ask thee what's their offence? sixth and lastly, why they are committed? and, to conclude, what you lay to their charge?

Claud. Rightly reasoned, and in his own division; and, by my troth, there's one meaning well suited.

D. Pedro. Whom have you offended, masters, that you are thus bound to your answer? this learned constable is too cunning to be understood. What's your offence?

Bora. Sweet Prince, let me go no farther to mine answer: do you hear me, and let this Count kill me. I have deceived even your very eyes: what your wisdoms could not discover, these shallow fools have brought to light, who, in the night, overheard me confessing to this man how Don John, your brother, incensed me to slander the Lady Hero; how you were brought into the orchard, and saw me court Margaret in Hero's garments; how you disgrac'd her, when you should marry her. My villainy they have upon record, which I had rather seal with my death than repeat over to my shame. The lady is dead upon mine and my master's false accusation; and, briefly, I desire nothing but the reward of a villain.

D. Pedro. Runs not this speech like iron through your blood?

Claud. I have drunk poison whiles he utter'd it.

D. Pedro. But did my brother set thee on to this?

Bora. Yea; and paid me richly for the practice of it.

D. Pedro. He is compos'd and fram'd of treachery.—
And fled he is upon this villainy.

Claud. Sweet Hero! now thy image doth appear
In the rare semblance that I lov'd it first.

Dogb. Come; bring away the plaintiffs: by this time our Sexton hath reformed Signior Leonato of the matter. And, Masters, do not forget to specify, when time and place shall serve, that I am an ass.

Verg. Here, here comes Master Signior Leonato, and the Sexton too.

Enter LEONATO, ANTONIO, *and the* Sexton.

Leon. Which is the villain? Let me see his eyes,
That when I note another man like him,
I may avoid him. Which of these is he?

Bora. If you would know your wronger, look on me.

Leon. Art thou the slave that with thy breath hast kill'd
Mine innocent child?

Bora. Yea, even I alone.

Leon. No, not so, villain; thou beliest thyself:
Here stand a pair of honourable men,
A third is fled, that had a hand in it.—
I thank you, Princes, for my daughter's death:

Record it with your high and worthy deeds.
'Twas bravely done, if you bethink you of it.

Claud. I know not how to pray your patience,
Yet I must speak. Choose your revenge yourself;
Impose me to what penance your invention
Can lay upon my sin: yet sinn'd I not,
But in mistaking.

D. Pedro. By my soul, nor I;
And yet, to satisfy this good old man,
I would bend under any heavy weight
That he'll enjoin me to.

Leon. I cannot bid you bid my daughter live;
That were impossible; but, I pray you both,
Possess the people in Messina, here,
How innocent she died: and, if your love
Can labour aught in sad invention,
Hang her an epitaph upon her tomb,
And sing it to her bones: sing it to-night.—
To-morrow morning come you to my house,
And since you could not be my son-in-law,
Be yet my nephew. My brother hath a daughter,
Almost the copy of my child that's dead,
And she alone is heir to both of us:
Give her the right you should have giv'n her cousin,
And so dies my revenge.

Claud. O! noble sir,
Your over-kindness doth wring tears from me.
I do embrace your offer;—and dispose
For henceforth of poor Claudio.

Leon. To-morrow, then, I will expect your coming:
To-night I take my leave.—This naughty man
Shall face to face be brought to Margaret,
Who, I believe, was pack'd in all this wrong,
Hir'd to it by your brother.

Bora. No, by my soul, she was not;

Nor knew not what she did when she spoke to
me;
But always hath been just and virtuous,
In any thing that I do know by her.

Dogb. Moreover, sir, which, indeed, is not under white and black, this plaintiff here, the offender, did call me ass: I beseech you, let it be remember'd in his punishment. And also, the Watch heard them talk of one Deformed: they say he wears a key in his ear, and a lock hanging by it, and borrows money in God's name; the which he hath us'd so long, and never paid, that now men grow hard-hearted, and will lend nothing for God's sake. Pray you examine him upon that point.

Leon. I thank thee for thy care and honest pains.

Dogb. Your worship speaks like a most thankful and reverend youth; and I praise God for you.

Leon. There's for thy pains.

Dogb. God save the foundation!

Leon. Go: I discharge thee of thy prisoner, and I thank thee.

Dogb. I leave an arrant knave with your worship; which I beseech your worship to correct yourself, for the example of others. God keep your worship; I wish your worship well: God restore you to health. I humbly give you leave to depart, and if a merry meeting may be wish'd, God prohibit it. — Come, neighbour.

[*Exeunt* DOGBERRY, VERGES, *and* Watch.

Leon. Until to-morrow morning, lords, farewell.

Ant. Farewell, my lords: we look for you to-
morrow.

D. Pedro. We will not fail.

Claud. To-night I'll mourn with Hero.

[*Exeunt* DON PEDRO *and* CLAUDIO.

Leon. Bring you these fellows on; we'll talk with Margaret,
How her acquaintance grew with this lewd fellow. [*Exeunt.*

SCENE II.

LEONATO'S Garden.

Enter BENEDICK *and* MARGARET, *meeting.*

Bene. Pray thee, sweet Mistress Margaret, deserve well at my hands by helping me to the speech of Beatrice.

Marg. Will you, then, write me a sonnet in praise of my beauty?

Bene. In so high a style, Margaret, that no man living shall come over it; for, in most comely truth, thou deservest it.

Marg. To have no man come over me? why, shall I always keep below stairs?

Bene. Thy wit is as quick as the greyhound's mouth; it catches.

Marg. And yours as blunt as the fencer's foils, which hit, but hurt not.

Bene. A most manly wit, Margaret; it will not hurt a woman: and so, I pray thee, call Beatrice. I give thee the bucklers.

Marg. Give us the swords, we have bucklers of our own.

Bene. If you use them, Margaret, you must put in the pikes with a vice; and they are dangerous weapons for maids.

Marg. Well, I will call Beatrice to you, who, I think, hath legs. [*Exit* MARGARET.

Bene. And therefore will come.

The god of love, [Singing.]
That sits above,
And knows me, and knows me,
How pitiful I deserve, —

I mean in singing; but in loving, Leander the good swimmer, Troilus the first employer of panders, and a whole book full of these quondam carpet-mongers, whose names yet run smoothly in the even road of a blank verse, why, they were never so truly turned over and over as my poor self, in love. Marry, I cannot show it in rhyme; I have tried: I can find out no rhyme to 'lady' but 'baby,' an innocent rhyme; for 'scorn,' 'horn,' a hard rhyme; for 'school,' 'fool,' a babbling rhyme — very ominous endings. No, I was not born under a rhyming planet, for I cannot woo in festival terms. —

Enter BEATRICE.

Sweet Beatrice, would'st thou come when I call'd thee?

Beat. Yea, Signior; and depart when you bid me.

Bene. O, stay but till then!

Beat. 'Then' is spoken; fare you well now: — and yet, ere I go, let me go with that I came [for]; which is, with knowing what hath pass'd between you and Claudio.

Bene. Only foul words; and thereupon I will kiss thee.

Beat. Foul words is but foul wind, and foul wind is but foul breath, and foul breath is noisome; therefore I will depart unkiss'd.

Bene. Thou hast frighted the word out of his right sense, so forcible is thy wit. But, I must tell thee plainly, Claudio undergoes my challenge; and either

I must shortly hear from him, or I will subscribe him a coward. And, I pray thee now, tell me for which of my bad parts didst thou first fall in love with me?

Beat. For them altogether; which maintain'd so politic a state of evil that they will not admit any good part to intermingle with them. But for which of my good parts did you first suffer love for me?

Bene. "Suffer love"! a good epithet. I do suffer love, indeed; for I love thee against my will.

Beat. In spite of your heart, I think. Alas, poor heart! If you spite it for my sake, I will spite it for yours; for I will never love that which my friend hates.

Bene. Thou and I are too wise to woo peaceably.

Beat. It appears not in this confession; there's not one wise man among twenty that will praise himself.

Bene. An old, an old instance, Beatrice, that liv'd in the time of good neighbours. If a man do not erect, in this age, his own tomb ere he dies, he shall live no longer in monument than the bell rings and the widow weeps.

Beat. And how long is that, think you?

Bene. Question: — why, an hour in clamour, and a quarter in rheum: therefore is it most expedient for the wise (if Don Worm, his conscience, find no impediment to the contrary) to be the trumpet of his own virtues, as I am to myself. So much for praising myself, who, I myself will bear witness, is praiseworthy. And now tell me, how doth your cousin?

Beat. Very ill.

Bene. And how do you?

Beat. Very ill too.

Bene. Serve God, love me, and mend. There will I leave you too, for here comes one in haste.

Enter URSULA.

Urs. Madam, you must come to your uncle. Yonder's old coil at home: it is proved, my Lady Hero hath been falsely accus'd, the Prince and Claudio mightily abus'd; and Don John is the author of all, who is fled and gone. Will you come presently?

Beat. Will you go hear this news, Signior?

Bene. I will live in thy heart, die in thy lap, and be buried in thy eyes; and, moreover, I will go with thee to thy uncle's. [*Exeunt.*

SCENE III.

The Inside of a Church.

Enter Don PEDRO, CLAUDIO, *and* Attendants, *with music and tapers.*

Claud. Is this the monument of Leonato?

Atten. It is, my lord.

Claud. [*Reads.*]

Epitaph.

Done to death by slanderous tongues
Was the Hero that here lies:
Death, in guerdon of her wrongs,
Gives her fame which never dies.
So the life, that died with shame,
Lives in death with glorious fame.

Hang thou there upon the tomb,
Praising her when I am dumb.—

Now, music, sound, and sing your solemn hymn.

Song.

Pardon, goddess of the night,
Those that slew thy virgin knight;
For the which, with songs of woe,
Round about her tomb they go.
Midnight, assist our moan;
Help us to sigh and groan,
Heavily, heavily:
Graves, yawn, and yield your dead,
Till death be uttered,
Heavenly, heavenly.

Claud. Now, unto thy bones good night!
Yearly will I do this rite.

D. Pedro. Good morrow, Masters: put your torches out.
The wolves have prey'd; and look, the gentle day,
Before the wheels of Phœbus, round about
Dapples the drowsy East with spots of gray.
Thanks to you all, and leave us: fare you well.

Claud. Good morrow, Masters: each his several way.

D. Pedro. Come, let us hence, and put on other weeds;
And then to Leonato's we will go.

Claud. And Hymen now with luckier issue speeds
Than this, for whom we render'd up this woe!

[*Exeunt.*

Scene IV.

A Room in Leonato's House.

Enter Leonato, Antonio, Benedick, Beatrice, Margaret, Ursula, Friar, *and* Hero.

Friar. Did I not tell you she was innocent?

Leon. So are the Prince and Claudio, who accus'd her

Upon the error that you heard debated:
But Margaret was in some fault for this,
Although against her will, as it appears
In the true course of all the question.

Ant. Well, I am glad that all things sort so well.

Bene. And so am I, being else by faith enforc'd
To call young Claudio to a reckoning for it.

Leon. Well, daughter, and you gentlewomen all,
Withdraw into a chamber by yourselves,
And, when I send for you, come hither mask'd:
The Prince and Claudio promis'd by this hour
To visit me. — You know your office, brother;
You must be father to your brother's daughter,
And give her to young Claudio. [*Exeunt* Ladies.

Ant. Which I will do with confirm'd countenance.

Bene. Friar, I must entreat your pains, I think.

Friar. To do what, Signior?

Bene. To bind me, or undo me; one of them. —
Signior Leonato, truth it is, good Signior,
Your niece regards me with an eye of favour.

Leon. That eye my daughter lent her: 'tis most true.

Bene. And I do with an eye of love requite her.

Leon. The sight whereof, I think, you had from me,
From Claudio, and the Prince. But what's your will?

Bene. Your answer, sir, is enigmatical:
But, for my will, my will is, your good will
May stand with ours, this day to be conjoin'd
In the state of honourable marriage: —
In which, good Friar, I shall desire your help.

Leon. My heart is with your liking.

Friar. And my help.

[Here comes the Prince, and Claudio.]

Enter Don PEDRO *and* CLAUDIO, *with* Attendants.

D. Pedro. Good morrow to this fair assembly.

Leon. Good morrow, Prince; good morrow, Claudio:
We here attend you. Are you yet determin'd
To-day to marry with my brother's daughter?

Claud. I'll hold my mind were she an Ethiop.

Leon. Call her forth, brother: here's the Friar ready. [*Exit* ANTONIO.

D. Pedro. Good morrow, Benedick. Why, what's the matter,
That you have such a February face,
So full of frost, of storm, and cloudiness?

Claud. I think he thinks upon the savage bull.—
Tush! fear not, man, we'll tip thy horns with gold,
And all Europa shall rejoice at thee,
As once Europa did at lusty Jove,
When he would play the noble beast in love.

Bene. Bull Jove, sir, had an amiable low;
And some such strange bull leap'd your father's cow,
And got a calf in that same noble feat
Much like to you, for you have just his bleat.

Enter ANTONIO, *with the* Ladies, *masked.*

Claud. For this I owe you: here come other reckonings.
Which is the lady I must seize upon?

Leon. This same is she, and I do give you her.

Claud. Why, then she's mine.—Sweet, let me see your face.

Leon. No, that you shall not, till you take her hand
Before this Friar, and swear to marry her.

Claud. Give me your hand before this holy Friar:
I am your husband if you like of me.

Hero. And when I liv'd, I was your other wife:
[*Unmasking.*
And when you lov'd, you were my other husband.

Claud. Another Hero?

Hero. Nothing certainer.
One Hero died [defil'd]; but I do live,
And, surely as I live, I am a maid.

D. Pedro. The former Hero! Hero that is dead!

Leon. She died, my lord, but whiles her slander liv'd.

Friar. All this amazement can I qualify;
When after that the holy rites are ended,
I'll tell you largely of fair Hero's death:
Mean time, let wonder seem familiar,
And to the chapel let us presently.

Bene. Soft and fair, Friar.—Which is Beatrice?

Beat. I answer to that name. [*Unmasking.*] What is your will?

Bene. Do not you love me?

Beat. Why, no; no more than reason.

Bene. Why, then, your uncle, and the Prince, and Claudio,
Have been deceived: [for] they swore you did.

Beat. Do not you love me?

Bene. Troth, no; no more than reason.

Beat. Why, then, my cousin, Margaret, and Ursula,
Are much deceiv'd; for they did swear you did.

Bene. They swore that you were almost sick for me.

Beat. They swore that you were well-nigh dead for me.

Bene. 'Tis no such matter.—Then, you do not love me?

Beat. No, truly, but in friendly recompense.

Leon. Come, cousin, I am sure you love the gentleman.

Claud. And I'll be sworn upon't that he loves her;
For here's a paper, written in his hand,
A halting sonnet of his own pure brain,
Fashion'd to Beatrice.

Hero. And here's another,
Writ in my cousin's hand, stol'n from her pocket,
Containing her affection unto Benedick.

Bene. A miracle! here's our own hands against our hearts. — Come, I will have thee; but, by this light, I take thee for pity.

Beat. I would not deny you; — but, by this good day, I yield upon great persuasion, and, partly, to save your life, for I was told you were in a consumption.

Bene. Peace! I will stop your mouth.

D. Pedro. How dost thou, Benedick, the married man?

Bene. I'll tell thee what, Prince; a college of wit-crackers cannot flout me out of my humour. Dost thou think I care for a satire, or an epigram? No: if a man will be beaten with brains, he shall wear nothing handsome about him. In brief, since I do purpose to marry, I will think nothing to any purpose that the world can say against it; and therefore never flout at me for [what] I have said against it; for man is a giddy thing, and this is my conclusion. — For thy part, Claudio, I did think to have beaten thee; but, in that thou art like to be my kinsman, live unbruis'd, and love my cousin.

Claud. I had well hop'd thou would'st have denied Beatrice, that I might have cudgell'd thee out of thy single life, to make thee a double dealer; which, out of question, thou wilt be, if my cousin do not look exceeding narrowly to thee.

Bene. Come, come, we are friends. — Let's have a dance ere we are married, that we may lighten our own hearts, and our wives' heels.

Leon. We'll have dancing afterward.

Bene. First, of my word; therefore, play, music! — Prince, thou art sad; get thee a wife, get thee a wife: there is no staff more reverend than one tipp'd with horn.

Enter a Messenger.

Mess. My lord, your brother John is ta'en in flight,
And brought with armed men back to Messina.

Bene. Think not on him till to-morrow: I'll devise thee brave punishments for him. — Strike up, pipers.

[*Dance. — Exeunt.*

NOTES ON MUCH ADO ABOUT NOTHING.

ACT FIRST.

Scene I.

p. 229. "*Enter* Leonato": — Here the stage direction in folio and quarto is, "Enter Leonato Gouernour of Messina, *Innogen his wife,*" &c.; and at the commencement of the next Act, "Enter Leonato, his brother, *his wife,*" &c.; but as *Imogen* neither speaks nor is spoken to, and, (as Mr. Dyce has well observed,) could not remain upon the stage dumb at the interrupted nuptial of her daughter, and as she is not in any way alluded to, it is plain that she has no place among the Dramatis Personæ. The name is probably a transcript from the first draft of the play, in making which the author had a plan which he afterward abandoned.

" "—— Don *Pedro* of Arragon": — "Don *Peter*" in both folio and quarto, here and immediately after; but in the next stage direction, and afterward, "Don *Pedro.*"

p. 230. "—— Signior *Montanto*": — *Beatrice* speaks of the soldier who dwells so much in her thoughts, by a term of the fencing school.

" "—— of any *sort*": — Plainly, none 'of any kind;' but Warburton and Mr. Dyce would have it, 'of any quality,' 'of any rank' — meaning 'high quality,' 'high rank.' But 'sort,' unless used absolutely, without qualification of degree or merit, as we sometimes use 'character' to mean 'good character,' cannot be thus arbitrarily raised from its inferior and general sense to one higher and particular; and no instance of such a use has been quoted. Throughout Shakespeare's works and those of his contemporaries it is used to mean class and condition, of all sorts; for instance, "The other sorts be even

Seruingmen." *A briefe Conceipte of English Pollicy.* 4to. 1598. fol. 336. See *Shakespeare's Scholar*, p. 166.

p. 230. "He *set up his bills* here": — Posting small placards, was, in Shakespeare's day, the only mode of making matters public, except proclaiming them by a crier.

" "—— at the *flight* . . . at the *bird-bolt*": — The flight arrow was long, and was used for long shots: the bolt was short and thick, and suited only to short distances.

" "—— he hath holp to *eat* it": — The folio has "*ease*," with a long *s*, the quarto "*eate*," — a difference hardly worth notice.

p. 231. "Is there no young *squarer*": — So long as quarrelsome boys 'square off' at each other, explanation of this word is superfluous.

p. 232. "*Enter* Don PEDRO, JOHN *the Bastard*," &c.: — Thus the direction of the folio, in which *John* is generally so styled; but sometimes *John* and *Sir John*.

" "—— Leonato, *you are* come": — The quarto reads, "*are you* come."

" "Were you in doubt": — The quarto adds "Sir."

p. 233. "*This* is the sum," &c.: — The quarto has "*That* is," &c.

p. 234. "—— to tell us Cupid is a good *hare-finder*," &c.: — So much confusing comment has been made on this plain passage, that it is pardonable to point out that *Benedick* asks 'do you mean to tell us that the blind boy has the eyes of a greyhound, and that Vulcan's forge and anvil are used to work wood?'

p. 235. "*Enter* Don PEDRO": — Both folio and quarto add, "JOHN *the Bastard;*" but with evident error; for *John* afterward learns from *Borachio* what passes at this interview.

" "—— it is not so, nor 'twas not so," &c. — This is the burden of a fearful old story, as bloody as *Blue Beard*, without its whimsicality, which will be found in the Variorum Edition, related upon the authority of Blakeway. In the story is a motto, "Be bold, be bold, but not too bold," found also in *The Faerie Queene*, B. III. C. xi. 54.

p. 236. "I *speak* mine": — The quarto, "*spoke*."

" "—— in the force of his will": — Warburton's professional eye first detected the allusion here to heresy, as defined in scholastic divinity; according to which it was not merely heterodox opinion, but a wilful adherence to such opinion. The subject was a familiar one in Shakespeare's day.

p. 236. "—— a *recheat* winded in my forehead": — The recall which the hunter blew upon his horn was called the 're-cheat.' *Benedick's* meaning is sufficiently obvious.

" "—— hang me *in a bottle, like a cat*": — It was a cruel sport of the day to shoot at a cat in a bottle.

" "—— and called *Adam*": — An allusion to one of the three celebrated archers, Adam Bell, Clym of the Clough, and William of Cloudesley. See the *Outlaw's Ballad* in Percy's *Reliques of English Poetry*.

p. 237. "In time the savage bull," &c.: — This line is quoted, with a slight error, from Kyd's *Spanish Tragedy*, Act II.

" "—— if Cupid have not spent all his quiver *in Venice*": — The courtezans and intriguing ladies of Venice were famous, the world over.

" "—— ere you flout *old ends*," &c.: — alluding to the old formal phrases for closing letters, such as Don *Pedro* and *Claudio* have just been quoting.

p. 238. "—— [and with her father," &c.]: — These words are not in the folio: making just one line, and in the multiplicity of 'ands,' they were evidently skipped.

SCENE II.

p. 239. "*Enter* LEONATO *and* ANTONIO": — In the stage direction here, both in folio and quarto, *Antonio* is called "an old man, brother to Leonato;" and in succeeding directions and prefixes, "Old man," or "Brother."

" "—— I can tell you news": — The quarto has "*strange* news;" and in *Antonio's* next speech, "thus *much* overheard."

" "—— thick-*pleached*": — thickly interwoven.

SCENE III.

p. 240. "—— in the occasion that breeds [it]": — Both folio and quarto lack 'it,' which is from Mr. Collier's folio of 1632. In *Conrade's* next speech but one the quarto has, "*at least* a patient sufferance;" and in his next after, "you should take *true* root."

" "—— a *canker* in a hedge": — a dog-rose.

p. 241. "I *will* make all use," &c.: — The quarto reads, "I make."

" "And who, [*and who*]": — This iteration, tame in

itself, and out of place after the Bastard has, with deliberation, called *Claudio* "a proper squire," is entirely unsuited to the taciturn phlegm of *John;* and I have not a doubt that the second 'and who' is an accidental repetition, and that we should read, "And who? which way looks he?"

p. 241. "I whipp'd behind": — The quarto has, "I whipp'd *me* behind," &c.

ACT SECOND.

Scene I.

p. 243. "—— if *he* could get her good will": — The quarto and folio have here, "if *a* could," &c. — 'a' being, in Shakespeare's day, and still, in some parts of England, a vulgar colloquialism for 'he.' Throughout the quarto impression of this play 'a' is constantly put for the pronoun; but in the folio, with comparative rarity. That this is the result of the corrections made at the theatre in the quarto copy from which the folio was printed, (See *Introduction*,) is plain, from the appearance of this change only in speeches of those of the higher ranks among the dramatis personæ. In a few instances, however, the change is not made in those; and that this is the result of inadvertence is shown by the appearance in the original of 'I' and 'a' in the same speech. In such cases the evident design of the authentic text is perfected in the present edition; while the characteristic vulgarism is allowed, as in that text, to remain in the mouths which it becomes: — a course which has not hitherto been taken.

" "—— earnest of the *be'r-'ard*": — i. e., the bear-ward, — spelled, in both folio and quarto, "*berrord*," which shows the pronunciation of the term, and indicates the proper manner of printing it.

" "—— and away to St. Peter *for the Heavens*": — Gifford shows that "for the Heavens" was a pretty oath in Shakespeare's day, and Mr. Dyce would place the colon after 'Peter,' and read, "for the Heavens, he shows," &c. But from the context it appears that here the obvious meaning of the phrase is the proper one.

p. 244. "—— *Father*, as it please you": — 'Father' is omitted in the folio; evidently by accident. It appears in the quarto.

" "—— too *important*": — i. e., importunate. See Note on "important letters," *Com. of Err.*, Act V. Sc. 1.

p. 244. "—— modest, as a *measure*": — a stately dance. Mr. Collier's folio of 1632 reads, a line or two below, "till he sink *apace* into his grave." The pun is a tolerable one for the old dabbler; but out of place; and Shakespeare would not write "*till* he sink *apace*." It occurs in Marston's *Insatiate Countess*, Act II., where Mr. Collier's corrector may have found it; and it was suggested by Capell.

p. 245. "*Enter* Don PEDRO . . . BALTHAZAR; JOHN": — The folio and quarto have "Balthazar *or dumb* John" — evidently a misprint for '*and don* John.' That *Balthazar* was in no sense dumb, we have already had ample evidence. The old copies have "*Maskers with a drum*."

"—— within the house is *Jove*": — The folio has "*love*," which, of course, is a misprint for 'Jove,' the word in the quarto. The story of *Baucis* and *Philemon* is related in Ovid's *Metamorphoses*, Book 8.

" "Well, I would you did like me": — This and the two following speeches are assigned in both folio and quarto to *Benedick*. Theobald first saw that the whole of the dialogue with *Margaret* belongs to *Balthazar*; which is so plain when attention is directed to the matter, that it seems strange it had not been discovered before. *Benedick* is at this time engaged with *Beatrice*; as we see by their entrance, almost immediately after, in the midst of a conversation, of which we hear only the close. The mistake is one of a kind which is common, for the reason assigned by Mr. Dyce, that "two prefixes, each beginning with the same letter, are frequently confounded by transcribers and printers." See Note on "Let them be in the hands," &c. Act IV. Sc. 2.

p. 246. "—— the *Hundred Merry Tales*": — "A C Mery Tales" is the title of an old jest book printed first by Rastell, and therefore between 1517 and 1533. Only one copy is known to exist; and that is imperfect. It was discovered in 1815 by the Rev. Professor Conybeare, of Oxford. A few copies were reprinted by that prince of modern printers, Whittingham, under the superintendence of Mr. Singer; — and a very pretty sort of book it was for a young lady to have her good wit out of.

" "—— *only his* gift is in devising," &c.: — i. e., *his only* gift, &c., for which it is more than possible that the text is an accidental transposition.

p. 248. "—— 'twas the boy that stole your meat": — The story to which this speech refers appears to be entirely lost on both sides of the water. I have never heard of or met with any other allusion to it.

p. 248. "*Enter* Don PEDRO, HERO, and LEONATO": — The direction in the folio is, "*Enter the Prince,*" and afterward, "*Enter Claudio and Beatrice, Leonato, Hero;*" but in the quarto we have, "*Enter the* Prince, Hero, Leonato, John *and* Borachio, *and* Conrade," and afterward, "*Enter* Claudio and *Beatrice.*" In both we have specimens of the carelessness with which entries were marked in early impressions of old plays. But although *John* and *Borachio* do not appear until the next Scene, and *Conrade* not at all, the quarto is plainly correct in making *Hero* and *Leonato* enter with Don *Pedro,* leaving *Beatrice* and *Claudio* to follow some time after. For not only does *Benedick* say, "I told him true, that your Grace had got the good will of *this young lady,*" — i. e., *Hero;* but *Beatrice,* soon after she comes in, says to the Prince, "I have brought Count Claudio, *whom you sent me to seek.*" These two speeches seem to group the characters as they appear in the text.

p. 249. "—— the [good] will of this young lady": — The folio has "the will," and just before, "I think told him true," the words in brackets, in the text, which are found in the quarto, having, quite surely, been omitted by accident.

" "—— terrible as *her* terminations": — The folio omits 'her,' accidentally without a doubt.

p. 250. "—— the *infernal Até* in good apparel": — Although *Até* was not a Fury, but the Goddess of Discord, Warburton's opinion that this is "a pleasant allusion to the custom of ancient poets and painters, who represent the furies in raggs," is most probably correct.

" "—— Prester John's foot": — Prester John was the fabulous ruler of an unknown country supposed to be in the far East. No one of course knew any thing of him, yet almost every one believed in his existence, and believed with wonder. See Sir John Mandeville's account of his travels, written in the fourteenth century.

" "—— a hair *off* the great Cham's beard": — The first folio and the quarto have "off;" and so have all the ancient copies. Therefore, and because the word has a very appropriate signification, it should stand; although all modern editions, hitherto, have '*of,*' because old printers and old writers did not always distinguish between 'off' and 'of.' When in doubt, take the authentic text.

" "—— *this* Lady Tongue" — Thus the folio. The second folio has "this lady'*s* Tongue," which, on account of the allusion to 'a dish,' is possibly the correct reading. The quarto has "*my* lady Tongue."

p. 251. "—— something of *a* jealous complexion" : — The quarto has "*that* jealous complexion." The Spanish orange was called the Civil orange — the name being so spelled and pronounced.

" "—— that he is in *her* heart" : — So the quarto : the folio has "*my* heart" — a manifest error.

" "—— thus goes every one *to the world* but I" : — For a woman to 'go to the world' was for her to be married; the phrase signifying either to go the way of the world, or to take a place in the world.

p. 252. "—— never *sad*, but when she sleeps" — never serious.

"—— to *hear tell* of a husband" : — This form of speech, which Shakespeare constantly puts into the mouth of personages of the highest rank, but which is now never heard in Old England, except, perhaps, in the remotest rural districts, is in common use in New England. The idiom is pure English. "And yet I sawe in that little time, in one Citie, more libertie to sinne, then euer I heard tell of in our noble Citie of London in ix yeare." Ascham's *Schoolemaster*, 4to., 1589, fol. 27 a.

p. 253. "—— answer [my] mind" : — The folio omits "my," which is found in the quarto.

" "—— *th'* one with *th'* other" : — Thus both folio and quarto, and yet all modern editions have '*the*' in both instances. The pronunciation, as could be shown by numberless instances, was *t' one* and *t' other* — the latter of which survives to us. The number of similar cases in which the text of Shakespeare is faithfully given in this alone of all modern editions — that is, since 1685 — is countless: they have been necessarily passed without notice, with very rare exceptions. Editors will misrepresent the text in a characteristic though trivial point, like this, and yet affront the common sense of mankind by a labored explanation of what Shakespeare meant by "a mountain of affection."

" "—— of a noble *strain*" : — descent, line-age, — from the Anglo-Saxon *strynd*; the common word 'strain' having a different root.

Scene II.

p. 255. "—— hear Margaret term me *Claudio*" : — Thus both folio and quarto. Theobald read, "term me *Borachio*;" — plausibly; as to those who were deceived, *Hero's* error would have seemed of a very different kind if they had had reason to suppose she thought her visitant really *Claudio*, and as *Claudio* himself was to be a spectator of the scene. He has been generally followed till of recent years: and Mr. Collier agrees with him, although he gives the old text! That text is right; for, plainly, *Borachio* wheedled *Margaret* into playing with him at a scene between the other lovers. He himself declares, Act V. Sc. 1, that she was innocent of any attempt to injure her mistress; and as for *Claudio*, it was enough for him to know (as he thought) that he heard *Hero* "term" another than he *Claudio*.

p. 255. "—— such seeming truth of *her* disloyalty": — The old copies have for 'her' the very needless and unpleasant repetition, "*Heroes;*" which, there can hardly be a doubt, was the result of a mistaking of 'her,' in the MS., for a customary abbreviation of the proper name. Thus, in the quarto, 'Margaret' is printed "*Marg.*" just before.

Scene III.

" "*Enter* Benedick," &c.: — Folio and quarto have "Enter Benedick *alone*," the Boy's entrance not being noticed.

" "—— in the *orchard*": — 'Orchard' (originally 'hort-yard') and 'garden' were synonymous in Shakespeare's day.

p. 256. "—— now is he turn'd *orthographer*": — Folio and quarto have orthography.

" "—— her hair shall be *of what colour it please God*": — See Act III. Sc. 4. "I like the new tire within excellently, if the hair were a thought browner." Mr. Verplanck reasonably supposes that Shakespeare "had an especial and somewhat whimsical [though, why whimsical?] dislike to all disguises of the head by art." They were but too common in his day.

' "*Enter* Don Pedro . . . *and* Balthazar": — The quarto has, "*Enter* Prince, Leonato, Claudio, *musicke*," and afterward, "*Enter* Balthaser *with musicke;*" but the folio has only, and in the first place, "*Enter Prince, Leonato, Claudio,* and *Jacke Wilson*," giving us plainly in this Scene, as in another of this play, a transcript from the very prompt book used at Shakespeare's theatre. Jack Wilson not being "nominated" in the quarto, it is plain that the copy from which the folio was printed has other authority than that which pertains to the older edition; and besides, if he were the distinguished Dr. John Wilson, of Oxford, which is more than probable, (See Rimbault's *Who was Jack Wilson?* and *Shakespeare's Scholar*, p. 166) he was not the "music" which entered when that edition was printed; for he was then only about six years old, but about twenty-nine, of course, when the folio was published. The context shows plainly that *Balthazar* enters in company with the Prince and the others, after having sung a solo to them just before.

p. 257. "We'll fit the *kid*-fox": — 'Kid,' as meaning 'young,' is still in use among the lower classes in England. It is more than probable, however, that we should read '*hid*-fox.'

" "Note notes, forsooth, and *nothing*": — This is one of many evidences that *th* used to be pronounced as *t*, and 'nothing' as 'no-ting.' But the orthoepical point not having been noticed hitherto, Theobald read '*noting*,' and was invariably followed, until Mr. Collier restored the original word, merely, however, on the principle of adherence to "the oldest authority." See *Introduction*.

p. 258. "*Then sigh not so*," &c.: — In most modern editions, and in all of the present century, this line has hitherto been improperly printed as two. The occurrence of a rhyme in the middle of an octosyllabic line which itself is rhymed with by another only at the close, is common in our early ballad poetry.

" "*The* frauds *of men* were ever so": — Thus the folio; the quarto has "The fraud of men *was*," &c.

" "—— *stalk* on, the fowl sits": — An allusion to the use of the stalking horse behind which the ancient fowler hid himself from the birds.

p. 260. "—— prays; — *cries*, 'O sweet Benedick!'" &c.: — Folio and quarto have "prayes, *curses*, O sweet Benedick," &c. In Mr. Collier's folio of 1632 'curses' was changed to 'cries,' for which it might easily be misprinted, and which, there can be no doubt, is the correct word; for why should *Beatrice* curse? Mr. Singer adopts the change. But the needful correction was thus but partly made; for *Claudio* having already said that *Beatrice* "weeps, sobs," it is plain that "cries" means that she *cries out*, "O sweet Benedick!" Hitherto the text has predicated nothing of her exclamation.

" "—— an alms[-*deed*] to hang him": — Folio and quarto have "an *alms* to hang him;" but there can scarcely be a doubt that Mr. Collier's folio of 1632 is correct in reading 'alms-*deed*.' 'An alms' meant only a charitable gift; but 'an alms-deed' was a recognized phrase, almost a word, signifying not only such an act, but any equally worthy. Thus *Queen Margaret* says to *Gloster* in *Henry VI., Part* 3, Act V. Sc. 5, "murther is thy alms-deed."

p. 261. "—— I would have *daff'd*," &c.: — i. e., doffed.

p. 261. "—— a *contemptible* spirit" : — i. e., contemptuous — a frequent use of the word in Shakespeare's day.

" "—— you may *see* he is wise" : — The quarto has "*say*" and afterward, "*most* christian-like."

" "Shall we go *seek* Benedick" : — The folio has "*see*," which, from the situation of the parties, seems to be a misprint for 'seek,' which is found in the quarto.

p. 262. "—— unworthy *to have* so good a lady" : — The quarto omits 'to have.'

" "—— and her gentlewo*man* carry" : — The quarto has "gentlewo*men*."

ACT THIRD.

Scene I.

p. 264. "*Proposing* with the Prince" : — conversing — from the French *propos*, 'discourse.'

" "To listen our *propose*" : — The folio has "*purpose*;" but although instances of the use of that word in the sense of 'conversation' occur, there can be no doubt that it is in this case a misprint for the word found in the quarto. See the previous Note.

p. 265. "—— *haggards* of the rock" : — wild hawks of the mountains.

p. 266. "If *black*" : — Dark-complexioned men were called black. "Black men are pearls in beauteous ladies' eyes." *Two Gentlemen of Verona*, Act V. Sc. 2.

" "—— an *agate* very vilely cut" : — This comparison to the diminutive figures sculptured upon agate seal rings, was not uncommon in Shakespeare's day.

" "—— *press me to death* with wit" : — The *peine forte et dure*, used of old as the last resort to compel accused persons to plead, was inflicted by stretching them on their backs upon their dungeon floor, and gradually heaping heavy weights upon the chest and abdomen until a plea was extorted or death ensued. During the process, the sufferer was allowed only water from the pool nearest the prison.

" "It were a *bitter* death to die with mocks."

The original has "*better*," an obvious and easy misprint for the word in the text, to which it is corrected in the second folio. The quarto has the same error and another, "a *better* death *than* die," &c., which reading has most strangely been given in all modern editions hitherto, to the entire disregard of the context as well as of the authentic copy. For, "It were a *better* death *than* die with mocks" can only refer to *Benedick's* consuming away in sighs; whereas it is herself that *Hero* represents as being in danger of being pressed to death with wit, if she reveal *Benedick's* passion, and "*therefore*," she says, "let Benedick consume." *He* is threatened with no other danger from *Beatrice* than that in which he is already represented to be from her charms. Mr. Collier incorrectly quotes the text of the folio as "a better death *than* to die," &c. 'Tickling' is here a trisyllable.

p. 267. "Why, *every day;* — to-morrow": — Mr. Collier's folio of 1632 has "*in a* day" — a plausible emendation; but the original text is correct. *Hero* uses a form of expression which has survived in America, although it is not in common use. It appears, for instance, in business announcements, sometimes seen in the newspapers, that certain goods will be ready 'in all next month.'

" "She's *ta'en*": — The quarto has, "She's *lim'd*."

SCENE II.

p. 269. "—— or a *worm*": — the tooth-ache was formerly supposed to be caused by a worm at the root of the tooth.

" "—— every one *can* master a grief," &c.: — The original has "cannot" — an obvious error.

" "—— all *slops*": — loose trousers or breeches. We still have 'slop-shops.' That part of the allusion to the aping of foreign fashions that time out of mind has been characteristic of the English race, which is enclosed in brackets, is found only in the quarto. It seems not to have been stricken out by the author; for without it, *Benedick's* "foolery" would be somewhat incomplete.

" "And when was he wont to *wash his face?*" — That the benign effect of the tender passion upon *Benedick* in this regard should be so particularly noticed, requires, perhaps, the remark, that in Shakespeare's time our race had not abandoned itself to that reckless use of water, either for ablution or potation, which has more recently become one of its characteristic traits.

p. 270. "—— with her *face upwards*": — Theobald read, "with her *heels* upwards" — a needless change, which Heath well opposed by pointing out that the author "prepares the reader to expect somewhat uncommon or extraordinary; and the humor consists in the disappointment of that expectation." It is plain, too, that the Prince alludes to that burial mentioned by *Perdita* in the *The Winter's Tale*, Act IV. Sc. 3: —

> "Not like a corse; but if—not to be buried,
> But quick, and in mine arms."

p. 270. "Good *den*, brother": — 'Good den' was a colloquial abbreviation of 'Good even.'

p. 272. "—— till *night*": — The quarto has "till *mid*night."

Scene III.

" "*Enter* Dogberry *and* Verges," &c.: — In the original stage-direction *Verges* is simply designated as the "compartner" of *Dogberry*.

p. 273. "—— that your *bills* be not stol'n": — The 'bill' was a long-handled weapon like a halberd, uniting the spear and the axe. The entire costume of these watchman Scenes is that of Shakespeare's own time and country. In the original stage-direction for Sc. 3 of this Act, "Goodman *Verges*" is called the "*Headborough*." The Watch was chosen and regulated much after *Dogberry's* fashion in *Stratford on Avon*. Among the papers published by Mr. Halliwell in his *Life of Shakespeare* is an Inventory of the goods of Henry Field, a townsman of Shakespeare's, dated 1592. In it we find, "*In the yeord these*: — One bucket with cocke, lyncks, cord and wyandlesse, one old heare, fowr half quarters bagges good and badde, one watching byll." Watchmen carried the bill in Litchfield, England, till Dr. Johnson's time, as he assures us.

p. 274. "If you hear a child cry," &c.: — This is not much of a caricature; for in the *Statutes of the Streets*, printed in 1598, it is ordered that "no man . . . shall whistle after the houre of nyne of the clock in the night," or "keep any rule whereby any such suddaine outcry be made in the still of the night, as making an affray or beating his wife or servant," &c.

" "—— that knows the *statues*": — So the original. The quarto has "stat*utes*;" the change from which, in the folio, will hardly be admitted to be among those which, according to Mr. Collier, are for the worse. See *Introduction*.

"Keep your fellows' counsels and your own": — This is a part of the oath of a grand jury man, and is reasonably considered by Malone as among the indications that Shakespeare was at some period of his life very familiar with legal forms.

p. 274. "—— and I will, *like a true drunkard,* utter all to thee": — *Borachio* was not drunk, nor did he mean to represent himself as drunk at that time. This part of his reply is an allusion to his name, which was the Italian term for a gross, gluttonous, bibulous liver. "*Boraccia,* a boracho or bottle made of goates skin, such as they use in Spaine. *Boracchiare,* to gluttonize." Florio's *Ital. Dic.* The unlettered, uncultured Shakespeare must surely have acquired such knowledge as this by witchcraft.

p. 275. "—— thou art *unconfirm'd*": — Though 'unconfirmed' may mean 'not fixed in the ways of the world,' it seems to me more than probable that Shakespeare wrote 'unconformed' — to the world, of course.

p. 276. "—— in the *reechy* painting": — 'Reechy' is discolored by smoke. It is the adjective of 'reek,' from the A. S. *recan.*

" "And thought *thy* Margaret was Hero?"

This reading of the authentic copy has been hitherto most strangely set aside in favor of the less appropriate and significant text of the quarto: — "And thought *they* Margaret," &c.

p. 277. "—— 'a wears *a lock*": — Love locks were very commonly worn by the young men of Shakespeare's day.

" "Never speak": — In both folio and quarto these words are given to *Conrade,* by an evident error which Theobald corrected.

Scene IV.

p. 278. "—— your other *rabato*": — a kind of ruff, called by Dekker, "your stiff-necked rebatoes."

" "—— down sleeves, side sleeves": — The dress was made after a fashion which is illustrated in many old portraits. Beside a sleeve which fitted more or less closely to the arm and extended to the wrist, there was another, for ornament, which hung from the shoulder, wide and open. 'Side' was used of old to mean 'long,' from the A. S. *sid,* 'ample.' Occleve thus ridicules the sumptuous and senseless side sleeve: —

"Now hath this land little neede of broomes
 To sweepe away the filth out of the street,
Sen side-sleeves of pennilesse groomes
 Will it up-licke, be it drie or weete."

— A function now transferred to ladies' skirts.

p. 279. "*Light o' Love*": — This was a dance tune, popular of old. It is mentioned in the *Two Gentlemen of Verona*, Act I. Sc. 2. The notes of the air are printed in the Variorum Shakespeare and in Chappel's *Ancient English Airs.*

p. 279. "—— you'll *look* he shall lack no *barns*" :—The quarto has, "you'll *see*." They will lose the point of *Beatrice's* retort who do not know that the Scottish 'bairns' was 'barns' in English, and was very commonly used of old.

" "For the letter that begins them all, H."

The word 'ache' used to be pronounced like the letter H. See "Fill all thy bones with aches." *The Tempest*, Act I. Sc. 2.

p. 280. "—— *carduus benedictus*" :—The *carduus benedictus*, or blessed thistle, was thought of old to possess sovereign healing virtues, and to be particularly efficacious in affections of the heart. It is the *Atractylis Hirsuta* of Botany.

Scene V.

" "*Enter* . . . Verges" :—It has before been stated in these notes that the folio in this Scene designates *Dogberry's* partner as the *Headborough*, both in the stage-directions and in most of the prefixes.

p. 281. "—— *palabras*" :—Spanish for 'words.' It was in quite common use, even among the *Dogberrys* and the *Slys* of Shakespeare's day: 'palaver' is a corruption of it.

" "All thy tediousness on me, *ah?*"—Thus folio and quarto. It is a small matter, but all modern editions before this have "All thy tediousness on me? *ha!*"—a different sentence and another word.

" "—— an 'twere a thousand *times* more" :—The quarto has "*pounds.*"

" "—— God's a good man" :—This is a very ancient saying, and is found in various old authors.

p. 282. "It shall be suffigance" :—Here both folio and quarto have "*Exit*,"—the only direction of the sort in those copies for this part of the Scene. The error is patent.

" "—— we are now to *examine those* men" :—Thus the folio: the quarto, which is followed for the blunder's sake, in almost all modern editions, has "examin*ation these* men." That the former words are found in the authentic copy, and, being there, have a clear and appropriate sense, is sufficient reason for giving them in the text; but there is another for believing them to be the correct reading. — The blunder in the quarto is entirely out of place in *Dogberry's* mouth: it is not of the sort which Shakespeare has made characteristic of his mind. *Dogberry* mistakes the significance of words, but never errs in the forms of speech: he is not able to discriminate between sounds that are like without being the same; but he is never at fault in grammar: and this putting of a substantive into his mouth for a verb is entirely at variance with his habit of thought, and confounds his cacology with that which is of quite another sort. Shakespeare made him blunder in almost every speech he utters; but his blunders are those of pretending ignorance and conceited folly. If he would but use a vocabulary suited to his capacity, and talk only about what he understands, his speech might be without ideas, but it would also be without faults. Often as there was occasion for him to utter a falsely constructed sentence or misuse the parts of speech, Shakespeare never makes him do so; unless we are to believe the evidence of the unauthentic against that of the authentic copy, that this is a solitary instance of such incongruity.

p. 282. "—— to a *non come*": — Thus both folio and quarto. By printing it *non com.*, more like the abbreviation of the Latin *non compos*, modern editors have lost a part of *Dogberry's* mystification.

ACT FOURTH.

Scene I.

p. 283. "—— [not knowing what they do!]": — These words are found only in the quarto. The sentence is so filled with repetitions that this clause might easily escape the eye or the memory of a compositor; and therefore to exclude it entirely would hardly be justifiable. This consideration rather than its intrinsic value, or the certainty that it was not struck out, or that it was ever written by Shakespeare, secures it a place in the present text.

" "—— 'some be of laughing, as, ha! ha! he!'" — *Benedick* quotes from the old accidences.

p. 285. "Out on thee! Seeming!" — The punctuation of the folio is, "Out on thee, seeming, I will write against it," &c. Pope read, "Out on *thy* seeming," and has been followed by all editors, except Mr. Collier, (who retains the original punctuation and supposes *Claudio* to call

Hero 'seeming,') and Mr. Knight and Mr. Verplanck, who read, "Out on *the* seeming!"

p. 285. "I charge thee do [so]": — The folio omits 'so,' which is found in the quarto.

" "Hero *itself*": — Some read, "Hero *herself*," which is plausible; but *Claudio*, in reply to *Hero's* question, speaks of the name, not directly of her who bears it.

p. 286. "Fie, fie!" &c.: — This is the arrangement of the original, which Capell, who has been generally followed, did not mend by reading,

"Fie, fie! they are
Not to be nam'd, my lord; not to be spoke of."

The folio has 'spoken;' the quarto, '*spoke*.'

p. 287. "—— on the *rearward* of reproaches": — The folio has "*reward*," evidently a typographical error for "rereward" of the quarto.

" "—— frugal Nature's *frame*": — i. e., at the disposition, the design of Providence. It is, however, not impossible that Mr. Collier's folio of 1632 is correct in reading "Nature's *frown*." The misprint would be very easy, and the word is highly appropriate.

" "Who *smeared* thus": — The quarto has "*smirched*."

p. 288. "For I have only *silent been*," &c.: — All editions hitherto have this line,

"For I have only *been silent* so long;"

which is just such sort of verse as,

"Lay your knife and your fork across your plate."

The reason of the corruption is that in quarto and folio the first four lines of this speech are printed as prose, thus: —

"*Fri.* Heare me a little, for I haue onely bene silent so long, and giuen way unto this course of fortune, by noting of the Ladie, I haue markt.
A thousand blushing apparitions," &c.

Can there be a doubt, that after the passage was put in type in the quarto it broke down? and that, not being easily divided, on account of the hemistich, it was arranged as well as possible in the form of prose, the transposition in question being then accidentally made? The quarto having been used as a stage copy (See *Historical Sketch of the Text*, Vol. I.,) and the folio printed from it, (See *Introduction*,) this arrangement of the passage was perpetuated; for the error was not of a sort which demanded correction in a prompter's book.

p. 288. "—— *bear* away those blushes": — The quarto has "*beat*," which Mr. Collier gives. See *Introduction*.

" "My *reverence*, calling," &c.: — Mr. Collier's folio of 1632 has "My *reverend* calling," &c., the correctness of which is so probable, and the misprint which it involves, so easy, that, were it not for the great danger it would involve to the whole text, thus to set aside an intelligible authentic reading, there could be no hesitation in accepting it; and this is almost equally true with regard to the substitution, in the same volume, of '*bliting*' (i. e., blighting) for "biting" in the last line of the same speech. But as to 'reverence,' see Act V. Sc. 1.

"Know, Claudio, to thy head,
Thou hast so wrong'd mine innocent child and me,
That I am forc'd to lay my reverence by," &c.

p. 289. "—— the *Princes* left for dead": — Folio and quarto have,

"Your daughter, here the Princesse (left for dead.)"

But *Hero* was not a Princess; nor is it intimated that she was of a rank even approaching the princely. The Princes had just left her for dead. The same error occurred and has been corrected in *The Tempest*, Act I. Sc. 2.

p. 290. "—— we *rack* the value": — i. e., 'we violently increase the value.' The use of 'rack' in this sense — preserved in 'rack-rent' — is certainly three hundred years old, if not more. It frequently occurs in the *Conceipt of English Pollicie*, published in 1589, which is referred to on several occasions in these Notes.

" "—— in his *liver*": — The liver was supposed to be the seat of amorous passion.

"*Ford.* Love my wife?
Pistol. With liver burning hot."
Merry Wives of Windsor, Act II. Sc. 1.

" "—— and doubt not but *success*": — i. e., what follows, what succeeds. A signification similar to that which 'succeed' has in "Owe and succeed thy weakness." See Note on *Measure for Measure*, Act II. Sc. 4.

p. 292. "You kill me to deny": — The quarto has, "deny *it*," which Mr. Collier gives, although, as he well remarks, "Shakespeare and other writers of his time, and afterwards, not unfrequently employ 'deny' in the sense of *refuse*; and so it may be taken in the folio."

p. 293. "Princes and *Counties!*" — 'County' was the orthography of Shakespeare's day for *Comte*, the French title corresponding to 'Earl' in English. It occurs several times in Shakespeare's works, though much less frequently than 'Count.' This is the only instance of the plural. In the quarto of this play the orthography is always *county* or *counte*, which is in the folio altered to *Count* in every instance but this. See the next Note.

p. 293. "—— a goodly *count* — *confect*; a sweet gallant surely": — Thus the folio, with a comma, of course, instead of our dash, between 'count' and 'confect.' *Beatrice* here is "huddling jest upon jest with impossible conveyance." Her wit and her anger working together, she at once calls *Claudio's* accusation "a goodly *conte* confect," i. e., a story made up, and him a "*count* confect," i. e., a nobleman of sugar candy; for he was plainly a pretty fellow and a dandy; and then she clenches the nail that she has driven home, by adding "a sweet gallant, surely!" This sense of the passage (which seems to have escaped all apprehension hitherto, the consequence being an almost universal corruption of the text) is further evident from the inter-dependence of the whole exclamation, "Surely a princely *testimony*, a goodly *count*," — the first part of which would be strangely out of place, if there were no pun in the second. In Shakespeare's time the French title 'Count' was pronounced like 'conte' or 'compte,' meaning 'a fictitious story,' a word which was then in common use. For instance: "to let you heare Prouerbes which very Artificers haue in their mouth, and comptes which are used to be told by the fireside." Guazzo's *Civile Conversation*, 4to. 1586. fol. 6 b. "— pleasant Jests, Fables, Allegories, Similitudes, Prouerbes, Comptes, and other delightfull speach." *Ib.*, fol. 62 b. 'Conteur,' another word then in vogue, meant, as Shakespeare's contemporary, Cotgrave, tells us, "an idle talker, vaine speaker, ordinarie teller of old wives tales." Comfects, confects, comfets, or comfits (for the four orthographies were indifferently used) were so called because they were made up, as the etymology shows; and see Cotgrave, *in v. confection*. 'Conte' suggested not only 'count' but 'confect,' the first vowel sound being the same in all. The quarto has "a goodly *counte*, counte confect," which has been generally adopted with the explanation that "*Beatrice* first calls *Claudio* 'count,' and then gives him his title, 'count confect!'" But surely this acceptation, which has been hitherto universal, loses the point of *Beatrice's* innuendo, deprives what is left of its proper connection, and is inconsistent with the quickness and concentration of her wit and the state of mind in which she is. We can easily imagine the bitter sneer with which *Beatrice* flings out 'Count — confect,' lingering a perceptible moment on the first syllable of the latter word; but that her stopping, "in the tempest and whirlwind of her passion," to repeat 'a goodly Count, Count confect,' would be unnatural in any one, and particularly unlike her, we do not need the evidence of the authentic edition to tell us. It has taken many lines, as it almost always must, to describe and explain what would flash instantaneously upon the mind of an auditor in Shakespeare's day, or of a reader prepared to receive it in this. The text should be 'a goodly *conte* — confect,' were it not that 'conte,' 'compte,' and 'count' were used interchangeably when this play was written.

p. 293. "—— manhood is melted into *court'sies*":— Both folio and quarto (though they differ much in mere orthography) have "*cursies*." It is possible that we should read 'curses,' — *Beatrice* meaning that there was nothing left of men but words — curses and compliments.

Scene II.

p. 294. "*Enter* . . . Sexton":— In the stage-direction of the folio he is called "the *Town Clerk*." There is great confusion in the prefixes of this Scene. Those to *Dogberry's* speeches have generally *Kempe*, (once misprinted *Keeper*,) — the name of the actor who performed the part, — sometimes *Const*[*able*], and once *Andrew*; though Kempe's name was William, and no actor named Andrew is known to have been in Shakespeare's company. The speeches of *Verges* are prefixed, *Cowley*, the name of the actor who bore that part; and the *Towne Clerke* of the stage-direction becomes *Sexton* in the prefixes. The folio follows the quarto, though with the variations of orthography common at the time, some abbreviations, and one substitution in an important passage noticed below.

"Marry, that am I," &c.:— This is the speech assigned to *Andrew* in the old copies.

"Yea, sir, we hope":— The words of this speech and the next between brackets are found only in the quarto; — perhaps, as Blackstone suggested, in consequence of the statute, 3 Jac. I. *c.* 21, against the profane employment of the name of the Creator. Mr. Collier suggests that the passage might have been omitted because it was "an interpolation of the actors." It probably *was* inserted by an actor of the company — one William Shakespeare: there were hardly two in one theatre who could do that. He did it that *Dogberry* might have an answer to the question he asks.

p. 295. "—— and brought to *Leonato*" :— The quarto has "*Leonatoes*."

p. 296. "Let them be, in the hands of coxcomb" : — Thus both folio and quarto — the speech, however, being erroneously assigned in the quarto to "*Couley*," (i. e., *Verges*,) and in the folio to the "*Sex*" [*ton*]. The error in the first case was caused by a manifest and very natural mistake of the printer, and in the second by an unavailing attempt to rectify that mistake. The prefixes in this case are important; for it is only to a neglect to examine them with the care which becomes an editor of these works, that Theobald's ingenious disturbance of the text, (by breaking this speech in two to give part of it to *Verges* and part to *Conrade*,) and the hitherto universal acquiescence in this violence for a century and a quarter, can be attributed. The folio is plainly incorrect in attributing the speech to the *Sexton*; for it is one that he would not make; and *Dogberry's* exclamation at it shows that the *Sexton* leaves immediately after his preceding speech. It is equally plain that it does not belong to *Verges*; for he would not wish to make it, and would not dare, if he wished. But must it therefore be given in fragments to *Verges* and *Conrade*? No: because, as a whole, it is entirely suited to the jeering *Conrade*; and in the MS. from which the quarto was printed, it was, without a doubt, assigned to him by the abbreviated prefix *Con.*, which being mistaken for *Cou.*, the name was printed *Couley*. Mr. Dyce's observation that "two prefixes, each beginning with the same letter, are frequently confounded by transcribers and printers" is particularly in point here. The great probability thus shown is made certainty by the facts, that the names of characters were abbreviated or printed at length indifferently, even in the text, as we have already seen, Act II. Sc. 2, — that *Conrade's* name is generally, if not always, abbreviated *Con.*, — that Cowley's is, in every other case but the present, except one, printed, both in quarto and folio, *Cowley*, — and that the one other exceptional case is in the very next speech but one, "Away! you're an ass," &c., which, — too plainly *Conrade's* to need a word in support of the assignment of it to him that has been made silently, or with mere mention, by all editors, — has yet, in both quarto and folio, the prefix *Couley*. It is strange, that, as in the latter instance every one who has thought of the matter has been certain, and justly certain, that *Couley* had been printed for *Conrade*, in the former no one has hitherto suspected the same mistake; which, except for the unaccountable and bewildering attempt in the folio to help the matter by assigning the speech to the *Sexton*, is just as patent. Theobald read, —

"*Verg.* Let them be in the hands —
Con. *Off*, Coxcomb!"

Mr. Collier's folio of 1632, —

"*Sex.* Let them be *bound*.
Borach. *Off* coxcomb!"

Capell, —

"*Verg.* Let them be in *bands*.
Con. *Off*, coxcomb!"

ACT FIFTH.

Scene I.

p. 297. "Nor let no comfort*er*": — Thus the quarto: the folio misprints, "comf*ort*."

" "And, *sorrow's wag*": — Folio and quarto have, "And *sorrow, wagge*," from which sense cannot be extracted, and for which the text is an easy misprint. Mr. Collier would have "sorrow, wag!" mean 'sorrow, away!' which it might; but what a line of disconnected thoughts does it give us! —

"And, sorrow, away! cry hem, when he should groan."

Mr. Knight reads, —

"And, sorrow wag, cry, — hem when he should groan."

But beside the awkwardness of the first part of the sentence, 'cry hem' was a phrase of itself, and the words must not be separated. Dr. Johnson, by a bold transposition, obtained a good sense and the reading which has been current hitherto: —

"*Cry* sorrow, wag! *and* hem when he should groan."

But although articles, prepositions, and pronouns may be supposed to have been accidentally transposed, it will not do thus to shift the important words of a sentence from beginning to middle; or we could make any passage mean any thing. Heath proposed, "And sorrow*ing*." Capell read, "*Bid* sorrow wag," &c. All the attempts at emendation have rested on the assumption that 'wag' is a verb, or represents one, except Steevens', who read, "And, *sorry* wag;" but is it not plain that *Leonato* calls the man who in his affliction smiles and strokes his beard, hems, patches grief with proverbs, and drowns it in midnight revelry, 'sorrow's wag'?

p. 298. "And made a *push*": — an old form of 'pish.'

p. 298. "—— drunk with *candle-wasters*" : — A term applied to those who sat up late at night; and here plainly meaning midnight roisterers.

p. 299. "—— than *advertisement*" : — instruction.

p. 300. "—— fashion-*mong'ring* boys" : — Folio and 4to. have "*monging*," which may be an old form of the word.

p. 301. "*Enter* BENEDICK" : — *Benedick* enters here in the old copies, and not just after the brothers go out, as he is usually made to do. It is the more natural and unconstrained arrangement.

" "—— *draw*, as we do the minstrels" : — i. e., draw their bows "to pleasure us."

p. 302. "—— this last was *broke cross*" : — Shakespeare himself has furnished the best explanation of this tilting phrase in *As You Like It*, Act II. Sc. 4: "— swears brave oaths, and breaks them bravely, quite traverse, athwart the heart of his lover; as a puny tilter, that spurs his horse but on one side, breaks his staff like a noble goose."

" "—— how to *turn his girdle*" : — i. e., how get at his sword-hilt.

p. 303. "*Enter* DOGBERRY," &c. : — Here, as on the previous entrance of *Benedick*, the more natural arrangement of the folio has been set aside: in this case, to make *Dogberry* enter and speak at once.

p. 304. "—— ne'er weigh more *reasons*," &c. : — It must be remembered, as in reading *Falstaff's* "If reasons were as plenty as blackberries," that 'raisin' used to be pronounced as we now pronounce 'reason.' The custom has not entirely passed away.

" "—— your brother *incensed* me," &c. : — inflamed, instigated — so used in *Richard III.*, Act III. Sc. 1, and in *Henry VIII.*, Act I. Sc. 2.

p. 305. "Art thou the slave" : — The folio repeats 'thou' — obviously by accident.

p. 306. "—— was *pack'd*" : — i. e., compact, combined in all this wrong. So in *Comedy of Errors*, Act V. Sc. 1: —

> "The goldsmith there, were he not pack'd with her,
> Could witness it; for he was with me then."

p. 307. "God save the foundation!" — This phrase was used by those who received assistance from benevolent institutions or foundations.

p. 308. "— with this *lewd* fellow" : — As there is some disagreement with regard to the meaning of 'lewd' here, it is proper to remark that the word first appears in our language meaning merely 'ignorant,' of which numberless instances might be given from Robert of Gloucester, Piers Ploughman, Wiclif, and Chaucer. It then became, very naturally, a synonyme for the lay people as opposed to the clergy — clerks; and of course the sense of 'wicked,' 'depraved,' as opposed to 'holy,' was inevitably soon attached to it. This appears to be its signification here, and also in the passage (*Acts* xvii. 5,) "certain lewd fellows of the baser sort." The limitation of the word to the sense of 'lascivious' is arbitrary, unwarranted, and quite modern.

p. 308. "—— shall I always keep below stairs?" — Mr. Singer plausibly suggests that we should read, "keep *them* below stairs." Under the circumstances, however, *Margaret's* wit may limit the purposes for which she would go above stairs.

" "I give thee *the bucklers*": — i. e., I give thee the victory, — my shield as well as yours.

p. 309. "*The god of love*": — Steevens says that this is the beginning of an old ballad by William Elderton. It is printed as prose in folio and quarto.

" "—— *for* I cannot woo," &c.: — The quarto has "*nor*."

" "—— with that I came [for]": — Both the old editions omit 'for,' which was supplied by Rowe.

p. 311. "Yonder's *old coil* at home": — We have seen before (*Merry Wives*, Act I. Sc. 4) that 'old' was an augmentative: 'coil' meant 'confusion.'

Scene III.

" "It is, my lord": — This reply is assigned to an attendant "*Lord*" in folio and quarto. The heading, "*Epitaph*," is upon the same line; but there can be no doubt that *Claudio* reads the verses which he has brought to hang upon the tomb of his mistress. The lines, "Now unto thy bones," &c., which can belong to none but him, have the prefix "*Lo.*"

p. 312. "*Heavenly, heavenly.*"

The quarto has, by a misprint which may almost be called obvious, "*heavily, heavily;*" the mistake being caused by a supposition that this line was meant for a repetition of the third above. This reading, however, although destructive of the fine sense that death is to be uttered (i. e., expelled, outer-ed) by the power of Heaven, and indeed of all sense whatever, has yet been adopted by most modern editors; and it is advocated by Mr. Dyce, because "it goes so *heavily* with my disposition," (*Hamlet*, Act II. Sc. 2,) is misprinted, "it goes so *heavenly*," &c., in the folio!

Scene IV.

p. 313. "[Here comes," &c.]: — The folio omits this line.

p. 314. "This same is she," &c.: — Theobald, who has been followed by almost all editors, gave this speech to *Antonio*. Folio and quarto assign it to *Leonato;* and as he had already, in the first Scene of this Act, offered and promised the hand of his pretended niece to *Claudio*, there can be surely nothing more improper in his giving it to her.

p. 315. "One Hero died [defil'd]": — The folio omits 'defil'd.' Mr. Collier's folio of 1632 reads '*belied*,' — a specious suggestion; but the correctness of the old word is established by the remainder of *Hero's* speech:

"but I do live,
And surely as I live, *I am a maid.*"

″ "—— [for] they swore you did": — The old copies omit 'for.' Hanmer inserted it, and it was found in Mr. Collier's folio of 1632. There can hardly be a doubt that this was proper, especially as 'deceived,' which is contracted in the corresponding line below, is not contracted in this, thereby rendering one syllable necessary to the rhythm. In the folio this speech is printed as prose.

″ "They swore *that* you," &c.: — The folio omits 'that' in this and in the next line, and 'such' in the third.

p. 316. "Peace! I will stop your mouth": — In folio and quarto this speech has the prefix *Leon.*; but the error is too plain to permit us to defer, with Mr. Collier, to their authority. How was *Leonato* to stop *Beatrice's* mouth? and why, if *Leonato* stopped it, does the Prince immediately cry, "How dost thou, *Benedick, the married man?*"

″ "—— for [what] I have said against it": — The folio omits 'what.'

LOVE'S LABOUR'S LOST.

"*A* PLEASANT Conceited Comedie CALLED, Loues labors lost. As it was presented before her Highnes this last Christmas. Newly corrected and augmented *By W. Shakespere.* Imprinted at London by *W. W.* for *Cutbert Burby.*" 1598. 4to. 38 leaves.

Love's Labour's Lost occupies twenty-three pages in the folio of 1623, viz., from p. 122 to p. 144, inclusive, in the division of Comedies. It is there divided into Acts, but not into Scenes, and is without a list of Dramatis Personæ, which was first supplied by Rowe.

LOVE'S LABOUR'S LOST.

INTRODUCTION.

COLERIDGE'S opinion in favor of the very early production of *Love's Labour's Lost* has been quoted by most recent editors; but surely no intelligent and observant reader can need the aid of so eminent a critic to establish in him the belief that this play is among the first that Shakespeare wrote. No other seems to present so many claims to be considered the very first that he composed entirely. The earliest known edition is the quarto of 1598; but as the copy from which this professes to be printed was "newly corrected and augmented," in order to its presentation at Court, that date is but the limit before which it must have been originally written, successfully performed, and partly rewritten; so that the mention of it by Meres, in the same year, is of no consequence. This correction and augmentation, too, diminished the amount of internal evidence as to the early writing of the play in its original form; for it cannot be doubted that Shakespeare applied the knife to those parts which bore most unmistakable marks of youth and inexperience, and that what he added was, in style at least, worthy of him in his thirty-fifth year. These latter passages hardly any intelligent reader can fail to detect when told that they exist. The end of the fifth Act, after the announcement of the death of the King of France, is one of them; and there accident left trace of the alteration to which the play had been subjected, in the printing of a passage which was, or which should have been erased, because it was superseded by an augmentation of the identical thought in another and a more appropriate place. But had there been an edition previous to the correction, its date would hardly reach back to that of the production of the comedy, which was probably not later than 1588.

The reasons for believing it to be the earliest of its author's entirely original plays are, — the unfitness of the subject for dramatic treatment, and the want of experience shown in the conduct of the plot and the arrangement of stage effect; in both which points it is much inferior to either *The Two Gentlemen of Verona* or *The Comedy of Errors*, one of which must be its rival for the honor of being Shakespeare's maiden effort as a dramatic author : — the purely external and verbal character of the faults and foibles at which its satire is aimed, even in its very title; which are just such as would excite the spleen of a very young man who to genius added common sense, and who had just commenced a literary career : — the fact that when Shakespeare was from twenty to twenty-five years old, the affectation in speech known as Euphuism was at its height; *Euphues his England* having been published in 1580 : — the inferiority of all the characters in strong original traits, even to those of *The Two Gentlemen of Verona* or *The Comedy of Errors*; *Armado* alone having a clear and well defined individuality, and his figure, though deftly drawn, being somewhat common-place in kind for Shakespeare, while *Birone*, *Rosaline*, and *Dull* are rather germs of character than characters : — the use of couplets, alternate rhymes, and even doggerel in the more dignified parts of the work : — the fact that Monarcho, who is alluded to in Act IV. Sc. 1, died before 1580; as we know by Churchyard's epitaph upon him, bearing that date : — and, last not least, as it appears to me, in the innovating omission of a professed Fool's or Jester's part from the list of dramatis personæ; for it is ever the ambitious way of youthful genius to aim at novelty of form in its first essays, while yet in treatment it falls unconsciously into a vein of reminiscence; afterward it is apt to return to established forms, and to show originality in treatment. So Shakespeare, on the rebound, (for *Love's Labour's Lost*, it is safe to say, was never popular,) put two Fools into both *The Two Gentlemen of Verona* and *The Comedy of Errors;* and afterward, in nearly all his comedies, and even in some of his grandest tragedies, he introduced this character, so essential to the enjoyment of a large part of the audience for which he wrote; asserting his plastic power over his own genius by moulding his wit, his humor, his pathos, and his wisdom into forms which find fit utterance beneath the Jester's cap and chime with the tinkle of his bells.

No source of the plot of *Love's Labour's Lost* has been discovered; but that the play is founded upon some older work, its undramatic character, its needless fulness of detail, its air of artificial romance, and the attribution of particular personal traits — such as black eyes and a dark complexion to one, great size to another, and a face pitted with the small-pox to another of the ladies, and the merely incidental hints that one of the king's friends is an officer in the army and extremely youthful — seem unmistakable evidence; and that the story is of French origin, is as clearly shown by the nationality of the titles, the Gallicism of calling a love-letter a *capon*, the appearance of the strong French negative, *point*, twice, and the use of *seigneur* instead of 'signior.' Mr. Collier supposes, with some reason, that the appearance of *Armado* and *Holofernes* in the dramatis personæ is indicative of an acquaintance with the early Italian drama, in which the Spanish braggart and the pedant were stereotyped characters; but Warburton's declaration, that the latter was a satire on John Florio, rests upon assumptions not worthy of serious attention.

As there never was a Ferdinand, King of Navarre, and history records no mortgage of any part of France to Navarre for war expenses, the period of the action is quite indeterminable.* The costume may therefore be the French dress of any period before the end of the sixteenth century, for all the characters except *Armado* (whose plumage should show some Spanish feathers) and *Sir Nathaniel*, *Holofernes*, and *Dull*, who are plainly an English curate, an English schoolmaster, and an English thirdborough of Shakespeare's time.

The text of this play is but slightly corrupted, and that in unimportant passages, in either the folio or the quarto edition. A repetition of certain errors shows that the former was printed from a copy of the latter. Mr. Collier remarks truly that the folio adds some errors of its own; but he does not remark — perhaps because he failed to observe — that it corrects a great many more than it makes. There are also variations which came from another source than the quarto; and thus it is plain that although the folio itself was not exempt from accidents, these do not invalidate its authenticity, or exempt us from the obligation to accept its deliberate changes as authoritative, and to regard the quarto only as auxiliary to the formation of the text.

* The Rev. Joseph Hunter has, however, pointed out a passage in Monstrelet's Chronicles, which mentions a negotiation between the King of France and a Charles of Navarre, that resulted in the obligation of the former to pay the latter two hundred thousand crowns. *New Illustrations*, &c., Vol. I. p. 256.

DRAMATIS PERSONÆ.

FERDINAND, *King of* Navarre.

BIRONE, LONGAVILLE, DUMAINE, } *Lords, attending on the King.*

BOYET, MERCADE, } *Lords, attending on the Princess of* France.

DON ADRIANO DE ARMADO, *a Spaniard.*

SIR NATHANIEL, *a Curate.*

HOLOFERNES, *a Schoolmaster.*

DULL, *a Constable.*

COSTARD, *a Clown.*

MOTH, [*or* MOTE,] *Page to* Armado.

A Forester.

PRINCESS *of* France.

ROSALINE, MARIA, KATHARINE, } *Ladies, attending on the Princess.*

JAQUENETTA, *a country Wench.*

Officers *and* others, *attendants on the King and Princess.*

SCENE: Navarre.

LOVE'S LABOUR'S LOST.

ACT I.

Scene I.—Navarre. A Park, near a Palace.

Enter the King, Birone, Longaville, *and* Dumaine.

King.

LET fame, that all hunt after in their lives,
Live register'd upon our brazen tombs,
And then grace us in the disgrace of death;
When, spite of cormorant devouring Time,
Th' endeavour of this present breath may buy
That honour which shall bate his scythe's keen edge,
And make us heirs of all eternity.
Therefore, brave conquerors!—for so you are,
That war against your own affections,
And the huge army of the world's desires,—
Our late edict shall strongly stand in force.
Navarre shall be the wonder of the world:
Our Court shall be a little Academe,
Still and contemplative in living art.
You three, Birone, Dumaine, and Longaville,

Have sworn for three years' term to live with me,
My fellow-scholars, and to keep those statutes
That are recorded in this schedule here:
Your oaths are past, and now subscribe your names,
That his own hand may strike his honour down
That violates the smallest branch herein.
If you are arm'd to do, as sworn to do,
Subscribe to your deep oaths, and keep it too.

Longaville. I am resolv'd: 'tis but a three years' fast:
The mind shall banquet, though the body pine.
Fat paunches have lean pates; and dainty bits
Make rich the ribs, but bankerout the wits.

Dumaine. My loving lord, Dumaine is mortified.
The grosser manner of these world's delights
He throws upon the gross world's baser slaves:
To love, to wealth, to pomp, I pine and die,
With all these living in philosophy.

Birone. I can but say their protestation over;
So much, dear liege, I have already sworn, —
That is, To live and study here three years.
But there are other strict observances;
As, not to see a woman in that term,
Which, I hope well, is not enrolled there:
And one day in a week to touch no food,
And but one meal on every day beside,
The which, I hope, is not enrolled there:
And then, to sleep but three hours in the night,
And not be seen to wink of all the day,
(When I was wont to think no harm all night,
And make a dark night, too, of half the day,)
Which, I hope well, is not enrolled there.
O! these are barren tasks, too hard to keep,
Not to see ladies, study, fast, not sleep.

King. Your oath is pass'd to pass away from these.

Bir. Let me say no, my liege, an if you please.
I only swore to study with your Grace,
And stay here in your Court for three years' space.
Long. You swore to that, Birone, and to the rest.
Bir. By yea, and nay, sir, then I swore in jest.
What is the end of study, let me know?
King. Why, that to know which else we should not know.
Bir. Things hid and barr'd, you mean, from common sense?
King. Ay, that is study's god-like recompense.
Bir. Come on, then: I will swear to study so,
To know the thing I am forbid to know;
As thus, — to study where I well may dine,
When I to feast expressly am forbid;
Or study where to meet some mistress fine,
When mistresses from common sense are hid;
Or, having sworn too hard-a-keeping oath,
Study to break it, and not break my troth.
If study's gain be thus, and this be so,
Study knows that which yet it doth not know.
Swear me to this, and I will ne'er say no.
King. These be the stops that hinder study quite,
And train our intellects to vain delight.
Bir. Why, all delights are vain; and that most vain,
Which, with pain purchas'd, doth inherit pain:
As, painfully to pore upon a book,
To seek the light of truth; while truth, the while,
Doth falsely blind the eyesight of his look.
Light, seeking light, doth light of light beguile:
So, ere you find where light in darkness lies,
Your light grows dark by losing of your eyes.
Study me how to please the eye indeed,
By fixing it upon a fairer eye;

Who dazzling so, that eye shall be his heed,
  And give him light that it was blinded by.
Study is like the heaven's glorious sun,
  That will not be deep-search'd with saucy looks:
Small have continual plodders ever won,
  Save base authority from others' books.
These earthly godfathers of heaven's lights,
  That give a name to every fixed star,
Have no more profit of their shining nights
  Than those that walk, and wot not what they are.
Too much to know is to know naught but fame;
And every godfather can give a name.

King. How well he's read, to reason against reading!

Dum. Proceeded well, to stop all good proceeding!

Long. He weeds the corn, and still lets grow the weeding.

Bir. The Spring is near when green geese are a breeding.

Dum. How follows that?

Bir. Fit in his place and time.

Dum. In reason nothing.

Bir. Something, then, in rhyme.

King. Birone is like an envious sneaping frost,
  That bites the first-born infants of the Spring.

Bir. Well, say I am: why should proud Summer boast,
  Before the birds have any cause to sing?
Why should I joy in an abortive birth?
At Christmas I no more desire a rose
Than wish a snow in May's new-fangled shews,
But like of each thing that in season grows.
So you to study now; — it is too late:
That were to climb the house o'er to unlock the gate.

King. Well, sit you out: go home, Birone: adieu!

Bir. No, my good lord; I have sworn to stay with you:

And, though I have for barbarism spoke more
  Than for that angel knowledge you can say,
Yet confident I'll keep what I have swore,
  And bide the penance of each three years' day.
Give me the paper: let me read the same;
And to the strict'st decrees I'll write my name.

King. How well this yielding rescues thee from shame!

Bir. [Reads.] "*Item: That no woman shall come within a mile of my Court.*" Hath this been proclaimed?

Long. Four days ago.

Bir. Let's see the penalty. [*Reads.*] "*On pain of losing her tongue.*"—Who devis'd this penalty?

Long. Marry, that did I.

Bir. Sweet lord, and why?

Long. To fright them hence with that dread penalty.

Bir. A dangerous law against gentility! [*Reads.*] "*Item: If any man be seen to talk with a woman within the term of three years, he shall endure such public shame as the rest of the Court shall possibly devise.*"

This article, my liege, yourself must break;
  For, well you know, here comes in embassy
The French King's daughter with yourself to speak,—
  A maid of grace, and complete majesty,—
About surrender up of Aquitain
  To her decrepit, sick, and bed-rid father:
Therefore, this article is made in vain,
  Or vainly comes th' admired Princess hither.

King. What say you, lords? why, this was quite
forgot.
Bir. So study evermore is overshot:
While it doth study to have what it would,
It doth forget to do the thing it should;
And when it hath the thing it hunteth most,
'Tis won, as towns with fire; so won, so lost.
King. We must of force dispense with this decree:
She must lie here, on mere necessity.
Bir. Necessity will make us all forsworn
Three thousand times within this three years' space;
For every man with his affects is born;
Not by might master'd, but by special grace.
If I break faith, this word shall speak for me,
I am forsworn on mere necessity.—
So to the laws at large I write my name; [*Subscribes.*
And he that breaks them in the least degree,
Stands in attainder of eternal shame.
Suggestions are to others as to me;
But, I believe, although I seem so loath,
I am the last that will last keep his oath.
But is there no quick recreation granted?
King. Ay, that there is. Our Court, you know,
is haunted
With a refined traveller of Spain;
A man in all the world's new fashion planted,
That hath a mint of phrases in his brain:
One, who the music of his own vain tongue
Doth ravish like enchanting harmony;
A man of complements, whom right and wrong
Have chose as umpire of their mutiny:
This child of fancy, that Armado hight,
For interim to our studies shall relate
In high-born words the worth of many a knight
From tawny Spain, lost in the world's debate.

How you delight, my lords, I know not, I,
But, I protest, I love to hear him lie,
And I will use him for my minstrelsy.

Bir. Armado is a most illustrious wight,
A man of fire-new words, fashion's own knight.

Long. Costard, the swain, and he shall be our sport;
And so to study; — three years is but short.

Enter DULL, *with a letter, and* COSTARD.

Dull. Which is the Duke's own person?

Bir. This, fellow. What would'st?

Dull. I myself reprehend his own person, for I am his Grace's tharborough: but I would see his own person in flesh and blood.

Bir. This is he.

Dull. Signior Arme — Arme — commends you. There's villainy abroad: this letter will tell you more.

Costard. Sir, the contempts thereof are as touching me.

King. A letter from the magnificent Armado.

Bir. How low soever the matter, I hope in God for high words.

Long. A high hope for a low having: God grant us patience!

Bir. To hear, or forbear laughing?

Long. To hear meekly, sir, and to laugh moderately, or to forbear both.

Bir. Well, sir, be it as the style shall give us cause to climb in the merriness.

Cost. The matter is to me, sir, as concerning Jaquenetta. The manner of it is, I was taken with the manner.

Bir. In what manner?

Cost. In manner and form following, sir; all those three: I was seen with her in the manor house, sitting with her upon the form, and taken following her into the Park; which, put together, is in manner and form following. Now, sir, for the manner, — it is the manner of a man to speak to a woman; for the form, — in some form.

Bir. For the following, sir?

Cost. As it shall follow in my correction; and God defend the right!

King. Will you hear this letter with attention?

Bir. As we would hear an oracle.

Cost. Such is the simplicity of man to hearken after the flesh.

King. [Reads.] "*Great Deputy, the welkin's vicegerent, and sole dominator of Navarre, my soul's earth's God, and body's fostering patron,* —"

Cost. Not a word of Costard yet.

King. "*So it is,* —"

Cost. It may be so; but if he say it is so, he is, in telling true, but so.

King. Peace!

Cost. — be to me, and every man that dares not fight.

King. No words.

Cost. — of other men's secrets, I beseech you.

King. "*So it is, besieged with sable-coloured melancholy, I did commend the black-oppressing humour to the most wholesome physic of thy health-giving air; and, as I am a gentleman, betook myself to walk. The time when? About the sixth hour; when beasts most graze, birds best peck, and men sit down to that nourishment which is called supper. So much for the time when. Now for the ground which; which, I mean, I walk'd upon: it is ycleped thy Park. Then for the place where; where, I mean, I did encounter that obscene and most preposterous event, that draweth from my snow-white pen the ebon-coloured ink, which here thou viewest, beholdest, surveyest, or seest. But to the place, where:—it standeth north-north-east and by east from the west corner of thy curious-knotted garden: there did I see that low-spirited swain, that base minnow of thy mirth,—"*

Cost. Me.

King. "*—that unletter'd small-knowing soul,—*"

Cost. Me.

King. "*—that shallow vassal,—*"

Cost. Still me.

King. "*—which, as I remember, hight Costard,—*"

Cost. O! me.

King. "*—sorted and consorted, contrary to thy established proclaimed edict and continent canon, with—with,—O! with—but with this I passion to say wherewith,—*"

Cost. With a wench.

King. "*—with a child of our grandmother Eve, a female; or, for thy more sweet understanding, a woman. Him I (as my ever-esteemed duty pricks me on) have sent to thee, to receive the meed of punishment, by thy sweet Grace's officer, Anthony Dull, a man of good repute, carriage, bearing, and estimation.*"

Dull. Me, an't shall please you: I am Anthony Dull.

King. "*For Jaquenetta, (so is the weaker vessel called,) which I apprehended with the aforesaid swain, I keep her as a vessel of thy law's fury; and shall, at the least of thy sweet notice, bring her to trial. Thine, in all complements of devoted and heart-burning heat of duty.* DON ADRIANO DE ARMADO."

Bir. This is not so well as I looked for, but the best that ever I heard.

King. Ay, the best for the worst. — But, sirrah, what say you to this?

Cost. Sir, I confess the wench.

King. Did you hear the proclamation?

Cost. I do confess much of the hearing it, but little of the marking of it.

King. It was proclaimed a year's imprisonment to be taken with a wench.

Cost. I was taken with none, sir: I was taken with a damosel.

King. Well, it was proclaimed damosel.

Cost. This was no damosel neither, sir: she was a virgin.

King. It is so varied, too, for it was proclaimed virgin.

Cost. If it were, I deny her virginity: I was taken with a maid.

King. This maid will not serve your turn, sir.

Cost. This maid will serve my turn, sir.

King. Sir, I will pronounce your sentence: you shall fast a week with bran and water.

Cost. I had rather pray a moneth with mutton and porridge.

King. And Don Armado shall be your keeper. —
My lord Birone, see him deliver'd o'er:
And go we, lords, to put in practice that
Which each to other hath so strongly sworn.

[*Exeunt* KING, LONGAVILLE, *and* DUMAINE.

Bir. I'll lay my head to any good man's hat,
These oaths and laws will prove an idle scorn. —
Sirrah, come on.

Cost. I suffer for the truth, sir; for true it is, I was taken with Jaquenetta, and Jaquenetta is a true girl; and, therefore, welcome the sour cup of prosperity! Affliction may one day smile again; and until then, Sit down, Sorrow! [*Exeunt.*

SCENE II.

The Park, near ARMADO'S House.

Enter ARMADO *and* MOTH.

Armado. Boy, what sign is it, when a man of great spirit grows melancholy?

Moth. A great sign, sir, that he will look sad.

Arm. Why? sadness is one and the self-same thing, dear imp.

Moth. No, no; O lord! sir, no.

Arm. How canst thou part sadness and melancholy, my tender juvenal?

Moth. By a familiar demonstration of the working, my tough seigneur.

Arm. Why tough seigneur? why tough seigneur?

Moth. Why tender juvenal? why tender juvenal?

Arm. I spoke it, tender juvenal, as a congruent epitheton appertaining to thy young days, which we may nominate tender.

Moth. And I, tough seigneur, as an appertinent title to your old time, which we may name tough.

Arm. Pretty, and apt.

Moth. How mean you, sir? I pretty, and my saying apt; or I apt, and my saying pretty?

Arm. Thou pretty, because little.

Moth. Little pretty, because little. Wherefore apt?

Arm. And therefore apt, because quick.

Moth. Speak you this in my praise, master?

Arm. In thy condign praise.

Moth. I will praise an eel with the same praise.

Arm. What, that an eel is ingenious?

Moth. That an eel is quick.

Arm. I do say, thou art quick in answers. Thou heat'st my blood.

Moth. I am answer'd, sir.

Arm. I love not to be cross'd.

Moth. [*Aside.*] He speaks the mere contrary: crosses love not him?

Arm. I have promis'd to study three years with the Duke.

Moth. You may do it in an hour, sir.

Arm. Impossible.

Moth. How many is one thrice told?

Arm. I am ill at reck'ning: it fitteth the spirit of a tapster.

Moth. You are a gentleman, and a gamester, sir.

Arm. I confess both: they are both the varnish of a complete man.

Moth. Then, I am sure, you know how much the gross sum of deuce-ace amounts to.

Arm. It doth amount to one more than two.

Moth. Which the base vulgar [do] call three.

Arm. True.

Moth. Why, sir, is this such a piece of study? Now here's three studied ere you'll thrice wink; and how easy it is to put years to the word three, and study three years in two words, the dancing horse will tell you.

Arm. A most fine figure!

Moth. [*Aside.*] To prove you a cipher.

Arm. I will hereupon confess I am in love; and, as it is base for a soldier to love, so am I in love with a base wench. If drawing my sword against the humour of affection would deliver me from the reprobate thought of it, I would take desire prisoner, and ransom him to any French courtier for a new devis'd court'sy. I think scorn to sigh: methinks, I should out-swear Cupid. Comfort me, boy. What great men have been in love?

Moth. Hercules, master.

Arm. Most sweet Hercules! — More authority, dear boy, name more; and, sweet my child, let them be men of good repute and carriage.

Moth. Samson, master: he was a man of good carriage, great carriage; for he carried the town-gates on his back, like a porter; and he was in love.

Arm. O well-knit Samson! strong-jointed Samson! I do excel thee in my rapier, as much as thou didst me in carrying gates. I am in love, too. Who was Samson's love, my dear Moth?

Moth. A woman, master.

Arm. Of what complexion?

Moth. Of all the four, or the three, or the two, or one of the four.

Arm. Tell me precisely of what complexion.

Moth. Of the sea-water green, sir.

Arm. Is that one of the four complexions?

Moth. As I have read, sir; and the best of them too.

Arm. Green, indeed, is the colour of lovers; but to have a love of that colour, methinks, Samson had small reason for it. He, surely, affected her for her wit.

Moth. It was so, sir, for she had a green wit.

Arm. My love is most immaculate white and red.

Moth. Most maculate thoughts, master, are mask'd under such colours.

Arm. Define, define, well-educated infant.

Moth. My father's wit, and my mother's tongue, assist me!

Arm. Sweet invocation of a child; most pretty, and pathetical!

Moth. If she be made of white and red,
Her faults will ne'er be known;
For blushing cheeks by faults are bred,
And fears by pale-white shown:
Then, if she fear, or be to blame,
By this you shall not know;
For still her cheeks possess the same,
Which native she doth owe.

A dangerous rhyme, master, against the reason of white and red.

Arm. Is there not a ballad, boy, of the King and the Beggar?

Moth. The world was very guilty of such a ballad some three ages since, but, I think, now 'tis not to be found; or, if it were, it would neither serve for the writing, nor the tune.

Arm. I will have that subject newly writ o'er, that I may example my digression by some mighty precedent. Boy, I do love that country girl, that I took in the Park with the rational hind Costard: she deserves well.

Moth. [*Aside.*] To be whipp'd; and yet a better love than my master.

Arm. Sing, boy: my spirit grows heavy in love.

Moth. And that's great marvel, loving a light wench.

Arm. I say, sing.

Moth. Forbear till this company be past.

Enter Dull, Costard, *and* Jaquenetta.

Dull. Sir, the Duke's pleasure is, that you keep Costard safe: and you must let him take no delight, nor no penance; but 'a must fast three days a week.

For this damsel, I must keep her at the Park; she is allow'd for the day-woman. Fare you well.

Arm. I do betray myself with blushing. — Maid.

Jaquenetta. Man.

Arm. I will visit thee at the Lodge.

Jaq. That's hereby.

Arm. I know where it is situate.

Jaq. Lord, how wise you are!

Arm. I will tell thee wonders.

Jaq. With that face?

Arm. I love thee.

Jaq. So I heard you say.

Arm. And so farewell.

Jaq. Fair weather after you!

Dull. Come, Jaquenetta, away.

[*Exeunt* DULL *and* JAQUENETTA.

Arm. Villain, thou shalt fast for thy offences, ere thou be pardoned.

Cost. Well, sir, I hope, when I do it, I shall do it on a full stomach.

Arm. Thou shalt be heavily punished.

Cost. I am more bound to you than your followers; for they are but lightly rewarded.

Arm. Take away this villain: shut him up.

Moth. Come, you transgressing slave: away!

Cost. Let me not be pent up, sir: I will fast, being loose.

Moth. No, sir; that were fast and loose: thou shalt to prison.

Cost. Well, if ever I do see the merry days of desolation that I have seen, some shall see —

Moth. What shall some see?

Cost. Nay, nothing, Master Moth, but what they look upon. It is not for prisoners to be [too] silent in their words; and therefore I will say nothing: I thank God I have as little patience as another man, and therefore I can be quiet.

[*Exeunt* MOTH *and* COSTARD.

Arm. I do affect the very ground, (which is base,) where her shoe, (which is baser,) guided by her foot, (which is basest,) doth tread. I shall be forsworn, (which is a great argument of falsehood,) if I love; and how can that be true love which is falsely attempted? Love is a familiar; Love is a devil: there is no evil angel but Love. Yet was Samson so tempted; and he had an excellent strength: yet was Solomon so seduced; and he had a very good wit. Cupid's butt-shaft is too hard for Hercules' club, and therefore too much odds for a Spaniard's rapier. The first and second cause will not serve my turn: the passado he respects not, the duello he regards not: his disgrace is to be called boy; but his glory is to subdue men. Adieu, valour! rust, rapier! be still, drum! for your manager is in love; yea, he loveth. Assist me, some extemporal god of rhyme! for, I am sure, I shall turn sonnets. Devise, wit! write, pen! for I am for whole volumes in folio. [*Exit.*

ACT II.

SCENE I. — Another Part of the Park. A Pavilion and Tents at a distance.

Enter the PRINCESS *of* France, ROSALINE, MARIA, KATHARINE, BOYET, Lords, *and* Attendants.

Boyet.

NOW, Madam, summon up your dearest spirits.
Consider whom the King your father sends,
To whom he sends, and what's his embassy:
Yourself, held precious in the world's esteem,
To parley with the sole inheritor
Of all perfections that a man may owe,
Matchless Navarre; the plea of no less weight
Than Aquitain, a dowry for a Queen.
Be now as prodigal of all dear grace
As nature was in making graces dear,
When she did starve the general world beside,
And prodigally gave them all to you.

Princess. Good Lord Boyet, my beauty, though but mean,
Needs not the painted flourish of your praise:
Beauty is bought by judgment of the eye,
Not utter'd by base sale of chapmen's tongues.
I am less proud to hear you tell my worth
Than you much willing to be counted wise
In spending your wit in the praise of mine.
But now to task the tasker. — Good Boyet,
You are not ignorant, all-telling fame
Doth noise abroad, Navarre hath made a vow,
Till painful study shall out-wear three years,

No woman may approach his silent Court:
Therefore to 's seemeth it a needful course,
Before we enter his forbidden gates,
To know his pleasure; and in that behalf,
Bold of your worthiness, we single you
As our best moving fair solicitor.
Tell him the daughter of the King of France,
On serious business, craving quick despatch,
Importunes personal conference with his Grace.
Haste, signify so much; while we attend,
Like humble-visag'd suitors, his high will.

Boyet. Proud of employment, willingly I go. [*Exit.*

Prin. All pride is willing pride, and yours is so.—
Who are the votaries, my loving lords,
That are vow-fellows with this virtuous Duke?

1 *Lord.* Longaville is one.

Prin. Know you the man?

Maria. I know him, Madam: at a marriage feast,
Between Lord Perigort and the beauteous heir
Of Jaques Falconbridge, solemnized
In Normandy, saw I this Longaville.
A man of sovereign parts he is esteem'd;
Well fitted in arts, glorious in arms:
Nothing becomes him ill that he would well.
The only soil of his fair virtue's gloss,
If virtue's gloss will stain with any soil,
Is a sharp wit match'd with too blunt a will;
Whose edge hath power to cut, whose will still wills
It should none spare that come within his power.

Prin. Some merry mocking lord, belike; is't so?

Mar. They say so most that most his humours know.

Prin. Such short-liv'd wits do wither as they grow.
Who are the rest?

Katharine. The young Dumaine, a well-accomplish'd youth,
Of all that virtue love, for virtue lov'd:
Most power to do most harm, least knowing ill,
For he hath wit to make an ill shape good,
And shape to win grace though he had no wit.
I saw him at the Duke Alençon's once;
And much too little of that good I saw
Is my report to his great worthiness.

Rosaline. Another of these students at that time
Was there with him, if I have heard a truth.
Birone they call him; but a merrier man,
Within the limit of becoming mirth,
I never spent an hour's talk withal.
His eye begets occasion for his wit;
For every object that the one doth catch,
The other turns to a mirth-moving jest,
Which his fair tongue (conceit's expositor)
Delivers in such apt and gracious words,
That aged ears play truant at his tales,
And younger hearings are quite ravished,
So sweet and voluble is his discourse.

Prin. God bless my ladies! are they all in love,
That every one her own hath garnished
With such bedecking ornaments of praise?

Mar. Here comes Boyet.

Enter BOYET.

Prin. Now, what admittance, lord?

Boyet. Navarre had notice of your fair approach;
And he and his competitors in oath
Were all address'd to meet you, gentle lady,

Before I came. Marry, thus much I have learn'd,
He rather means to lodge you in the field,
Like one that comes here to besiege his Court,
Than seek a dispensation for his oath,
To let you enter his unpeopled house.
Here comes Navarre. [*The ladies mask.*

Enter KING, LONGAVILLE, DUMAINE, BIRONE, *and* Attendants.

King. Fair Princess, welcome to the Court of Navarre.

Prin. Fair, I give you back again; and welcome I have not yet: the roof of this court is too high to be yours, and welcome to the wide fields too base to be mine.

King. You shall be welcome, Madam, to my Court.

Prin. I will be welcome then. Conduct me thither.

King. Hear me, dear lady: I have sworn an oath.

Prin. Our Lady help my lord! he'll be forsworn.

King. Not for the world, fair Madam, by my will.

Prin. Why, will shall break it; will, and nothing else.

King. Your ladyship is ignorant what it is.

Prin. Were my lord so, his ignorance were wise,
Where now his knowledge must prove ignorance.
I hear your Grace hath sworn out house-keeping:
'Tis deadly sin to keep that oath, my lord,
And sin to break it.
But pardon me; I am too sudden-bold:
To teach a teacher ill beseemeth me.
Vouchsafe to read the purpose of my coming,
And suddenly resolve me in my suit. [*Gives a paper.*

King. Madam, I will, if suddenly I may.

Prin. You will the sooner that I were away,
For you'll prove perjur'd if you make me stay.
Bir. Did not I dance with you in Brabant once?
Ros. Did not I dance with you in Brabant once?
Bir. I know you did.
Ros. How needless was it then,
To ask the question!
Bir. You must not be so quick.
Ros. 'Tis 'long of you, that spur me with such questions.
Bir. Your wit's too hot; it speeds too fast; 'twill tire.
Ros. Not till it leave the rider in the mire.
Bir. What time o' day?
Ros. The hour that fools should ask.
Bir. Now fair befall your mask!
Ros. Fair fall the face it covers!
Bir. And send you many lovers!
Ros. Amen, so you be none.
Bir. Nay, then will I begone.
King. Madam, your father here doth intimate
The payment of a hundred thousand crowns;
Being but th' one half of an entire sum,
Disbursed by my father in his wars.
But say that he, or we, (as neither have,)
Receiv'd that sum, yet there remains unpaid
A hundred thousand more; in surety of the which,
One part of Aquitain is bound to us,
Although not valued to the money's worth.
If, then, the King your father will restore
But that one half which is unsatisfied,
We will give up our right in Aquitain,
And hold fair friendship with his Majesty.
But that, it seems, he little purposeth,
For here he doth demand to have repaid

An hundred thousand crowns; and not demands,
On payment of a hundred thousand crowns,
To have his title live in Aquitain;
Which we much rather had depart withal,
And have the money by our father lent,
Than Aquitain, so gelded as it is.
Dear Princess, were not his requests so far
From reason's yielding, your fair self should make
A yielding, 'gainst some reason in my breast,
And go well satisfied to France again.

Prin. You do the King my father too much wrong,
And wrong the reputation of your name,
In so unseeming to confess receipt
Of that which hath so faithfully been paid.

King. I do protest, I never heard of it;
And, if you prove it, I'll repay it back,
Or yield up Aquitain.

Prin. We arrest your word.
Boyet, you can produce acquittances
For such a sum, from special officers
Of Charles, his father.

King. Satisfy me so.

Boyet. So please your Grace, the packet is not come,
Where that and other specialties are bound:
To-morrow you shall have a sight of them.

King. It shall suffice me: at which interview,
All liberal reason would I yield unto.
Mean time, receive such welcome at my hand,
As honour, without breach of honour, may
Make tender of to thy true worthiness.
You may not come, fair Princess, in my gates;
But here without you shall be so receiv'd,
As you shall deem yourself lodg'd in my heart,
Though so deni'd fair harbour in my house.

Your own good thoughts excuse me, and farewell:
To-morrow we shall visit you again.

Prin. Sweet health and fair desires consort your Grace!

King. Thy own wish wish I thee in every place!
[*Exeunt* KING *and his train.*

Bir. Lady, I will commend you to mine own heart.

Ros. Pray you, do my commendations; I would be glad to see it.

Bir. I would, you heard it groan.

Ros. Is the fool sick?

Bir. Sick at the heart.

Ros. Alack! let it blood.

Bir. Would that do it good?

Ros. My physic says, ay.

Bir. Will you prick't with your eye?

Ros. No *point*, with my knife.

Bir. Now, God save thy life!

Ros. And yours from long living!

Bir. I cannot stay thanksgiving. [*They retire.*

Dum. Sir, I pray you, a word. What lady is that same?

Boyet. The heir of Alençon, Katharine her name.

Dum. A gallant lady. Monsieur, fare you well.
[*Exit.*

Long. I beseech you a word. What is she in the white?

Boyet. A woman sometimes, if you saw her in the light.

Long. Perchance, light in the light. I desire her name.

Boyet. She hath but one for herself; to desire that, were a shame.

Long. Pray you, sir, whose daughter?

Boyet. Her mother's, I have heard.

Long. God's blessing on your beard!

Boyet. Good sir, be not offended.
She is an heir of Falconbridge.

Long. Nay, my choler is ended.
She is a most sweet lady.

Boyet. Not unlike, sir: that may be. [*Exit* LONG.

Bir. What's her name, in the cap?

Boyet. Rosaline, by good hap.

Bir. Is she wedded, or no?

Boyet. To her will, sir, or so.

Bir. O! you are welcome, sir. Adieu.

Boyet. Farewell to me, sir, and welcome to you.
[*Exit* BIRONE. — *Ladies unmask.*

Mar. That last is Birone, the merry mad-cap lord:
Not a word with him but a jest.

Boyet. And every jest but a word.

Prin. It was well done of you to take him at his word.

Boyet. I was as willing to grapple, as he was to board.

Mar. Two hot sheeps, marry!

Boyet. And wherefore not ships?
No sheep, sweet lamb, unless we feed on your lips.

Mar. You sheep, and I pasture: shall that finish the jest?

Boyet. So you grant pasture for me.
[*Offering to kiss her.*

Mar. Not so, gentle beast.
My lips are no common, though several they be.

Boyet. Belonging to whom?

Mar. To my fortunes and me.

Prin. Good wits will be jangling; but, gentles, agree.
This civil war of wits were much better us'd
On Navarre and his book-men, for here 'tis abus'd.

Boyet. If my observation, (which very seldom lies,)
By the heart's still rhetoric, disclosed with eyes,
Deceive me not now, Navarre is infected.

Prin. With what?

Boyet. With that which we lovers entitle affected.

Prin. Your reason?

Boyet. Why, all his behaviours did make their retire
To the court of his eye, peeping thorough desire:
His heart, like an agate, with your print impressed,
Proud with his form, in his eye pride expressed:
His tongue, all impatient to speak and not see,
Did stumble with haste in his eye-sight to be;
All senses to that sense did make their repair,
To feel only looking on fairest of fair.
Methought, all his senses were lock'd in his eye,
As jewels in crystal for some prince to buy;
Who, tend'ring their own worth, from whence they were glass'd,
Did point you to buy them, along as you pass'd.
His face's own margent did quote such amazes,
That all eyes saw his eyes enchanted with gazes.
I'll give you Aquitain, and all that is his,
An you give him, for my sake, but one loving kiss.

Prin. Come to our pavilion: Boyet is dispos'd.

Boyet. But to speak that in words which his eye hath disclos'd.
I only have made a mouth of his eye,
By adding a tongue, which I know will not lie.

Ros. Thou art an old love-monger, and speakest skilfully.

Mar. He is Cupid's grandfather, and learns news of him.

Ros. Then was Venus like her mother, for her father is but grim.

Boyet. Do you hear, my mad wenches?
Mar. No.
Boyet. What then, do you see?
Ros. Ay, our way to be gone.
Boyet. You are too hard for me.
[*Exeunt.*

ACT III.

SCENE I. — Another Part of the Same.

Enter ARMADO *and* MOTH.

ARMADO.

WARBLE, child: make passionate my sense of hearing.

MOTH *sings.* — *Concolinel.*

Arm. Sweet air! — Go, tenderness of years: take this key, give enlargement to the swain, bring him festinately hither; I must employ him in a letter to my love.

Moth. Will you win your love with a French brawl?

Arm. How meanest thou? brawling in French?

Moth. No, my complete master; but to jig off a tune at the tongue's end, canary to it with the feet; humour it with turning up your eye; sigh a note, and sing a note, sometime through the throat, as if you swallowed love with singing love, sometime through the nose, as if you snuff'd up love by smelling love; with your hat penthouse-like, o'er the shop of your eyes; with your arms cross'd on your thin belly doublet, like a rabbit on a spit; or your hands in your pocket, like a man after the old painting; and keep not too long in one tune, but a snip and away. These are complements, these are humours; these betray nice wenches, that would be betrayed without these, and make them men of note, (do you note, men?) that most are affected to these.

Arm. How hast thou purchased this experience?

Moth. By my penny of observation.

Arm. But O, — but O, —

Moth. — the hobby-horse is forgot.

Arm. Call'st thou my love hobby-horse?

Moth. No, master; the hobby-horse is but a colt, and your love, perhaps, a hackney. But have you forgot your love?

Arm. Almost I had.

Moth. Negligent student! learn her by heart.

Arm. By heart, and in heart, boy.

Moth. And out of heart, master; all those three I will prove.

Arm. What wilt thou prove?

Moth. A man, if I live: and this, by, in, and without, upon the instant: by heart you love her, because your heart cannot come by her; in heart you love her, because your heart is in love with her; and out of heart you love her, being out of heart that you cannot enjoy her.

Arm. I am all these three.

Moth. And three times as much more, and yet nothing at all.

Arm. Fetch hither the swain: he must carry me a letter.

Moth. A message well sympathiz'd: a horse to be ambassador for an ass.

Arm. Ha, ha! what sayest thou?

Moth. Marry, sir, you must send the ass upon the horse, for he is very slow-gaited: but I go.

Arm. The way is but short. Away!

Moth. As swift as lead, sir.

Arm. Thy meaning, pretty ingenious?
Is not lead a metal heavy, dull, and slow?

Moth. *Minime*, honest master; or rather, master, no.

Arm. I say, lead is slow.

Moth. You are too swift, sir, to say so:
Is that lead slow which is fir'd from a gun?

Arm. Sweet smoke of rhetoric!
He reputes me a cannon; and the bullet, that's he:—
I shoot thee at the swain.

Moth. Thump, then, and I flee. [*Exit.*

Arm. A most acute juvenal; voluble and free of grace!
By thy favour, sweet welkin, I must sigh in thy face:
Most rude melancholy, valour gives thee place.
My herald is return'd.

Enter MOTH *with* COSTARD.

Moth. A wonder, master! here's a Costard broken in a shin.

Arm. Some enigma, some riddle: come,—thy *l'envoy*;—begin.

Cost. No egma, no riddle, no *l'envoy!* no salve in them all, sir: O, sir, plantain, a plain plantain! no *l'envoy*, no *l'envoy:* no salve, sir, but a plantain.

Arm. By virtue, thou enforcest laughter; thy silly thought, my spleen; the heaving of my lungs provokes me to ridiculous smiling. O, pardon me, my stars! Doth the inconsiderate take salve for *l'envoy*, and the word *l'envoy* for a salve?

Moth. Do the wise think them other? is not *l'envoy* a salve?

Arm. No, page: it is an epilogue, or discourse, to make plain
Some obscure precedence that hath tofore been sain.
I will example it:
The fox, the ape, and the humble-bee,
Were still at odds, being but three.
There's the moral: now the *l'envoy.*

Moth. I will add the *l'envoy.* Say the moral again.

Arm. The fox, the ape, and the humble-bee,
Were still at odds, being but three.

Moth. Until the goose came out of door,
And stay'd the odds by [mak]ing four.
Now will I begin your moral, and do you follow with my *l'envoy.*
The fox, the ape, and the humble-bee,
Were still at odds, being but three.

Arm. Until the goose came out of door,
Staying the odds by [mak]ing four.

Moth. A good *l'envoy,* ending in the goose. Would you desire more?

Cost. The boy hath sold him a bargain, a goose, that's flat.—
Sir, your penny-worth is good, an your goose be fat.—
To sell a bargain well is as cunning as 'fast and loose':
Let me see, a fat *l'envoy;* ay, that's a fat goose.

Arm. Come hither, come hither. How did this argument begin?

Moth. By saying that a costard was broken in a shin.
Then call'd you for the *l'envoy.*

Cost. True, and I for a plantain; thus came your argument in;

Then the boy's fat *l'envoy*, the goose that you bought,
And he ended the market.

Arm. But tell me; how was there a costard broken in a shin?

Moth. I will tell you sensibly.

Cost. Thou hast no feeling of it, Moth: I will speak that *l'envoy*.

I, Costard, running out, that was safely within,
Fell over the threshold, and broke my shin.

Arm. We will talk no more of this matter.

Cost. Till there be more matter in the shin.

Arm. Sirrah Costard, I will enfranchise thee.

Cost. O! marry me to one Frances? — I smell some *l'envoy*, some goose, in this.

Arm. By my sweet soul, I mean, setting thee at liberty, enfreedoming thy person: thou wert immured, restrained, captivated, bound.

Cost. True, true; and now you will be my purgation, and let me loose.

Arm. I give thee thy liberty, set thee [free] from durance; and, in lieu thereof, impose on thee nothing but this: bear this significant to the country maid Jaquenetta. There is remuneration; for the best ward of mine honour is rewarding my dependants. Moth, follow. [*Exit.*

Moth. Like the sequel, I. — Seigneur Costard, adieu.

Cost. My sweet ounce of man's flesh! my incony Jew! — [*Exit* MOTH.

Now will I look to his remuneration. Remuneration! O! that's the Latin word for three farthings: three farthings, remuneration. — 'What's the price of this inkle? a penny: — No, I'll give you a remuneration:' why, it carries it. — Remuneration! — why, it is a fairer name than French crown. I will never buy and sell out of this word.

Enter BIRONE.

Bir. O, my good knave Costard! exceedingly well met.

Cost. Pray you, sir, how much carnation ribbon may a man buy for a remuneration?

Bir. What is a remuneration?

Cost. Marry, sir, half-penny farthing.

Bir. O! why then, three-farthing-worth of silk.

Cost. I thank your worship. God be wi' you.

Bir. O, stay, slave! I must employ thee:
As thou wilt win my favour, good my knave,
Do one thing for me that I shall entreat.

Cost. When would you have it done, sir?

Bir. O! this afternoon.

Cost. Well, I will do it, sir. Fare you well.

Bir. O! thou knowest not what it is.

Cost. I shall know, sir, when I have done it.

Bir. Why, villain, thou must know first.

Cost. I will come to your worship to-morrow morning.

Bir. It must be done this afternoon. Hark, slave!
It is but this: —
The Princess comes to hunt here in the Park,
And in her train there is a gentle lady;
When tongues speak sweetly, then they name her name,
And Rosaline they call her: ask for her,
And to her white hand see thou do commend
This seal'd-up counsel. There's thy guerdon: go.

Cost. Gardon. — O! sweet gardon! better than remuneration; eleven-pence farthing better. Most sweet gardon! — I will do it, sir, in print. — Gardon — remuneration! [*Exit.*

Bir. O!—And I, forsooth, in love! I, that have been Love's whip;
A very beadle to a humorous sigh;
A critic, nay, a night-watch constable,
A domineering pedant o'er the boy,
Than whom no mortal so magnificent!
This wimpled, whining, purblind, wayward boy;
This senior-junior, giant-dwarf, Don Cupid;
Regent of love-rhymes, lord of folded arms,
Th' anointed sovereign of sighs and groans,
Liege of all loiterers and malcontents,
Dread prince of plackets, king of cod-pieces,
Sole imperator, and great general
Of trotting paritors, (O, my little heart!)
And I to be a corporal of his field,
And wear his colours, like a tumbler's hoop!
What? I love! I sue! I seek a wife!
A woman, that is like a German clock,
Still a repairing, ever out of frame,
And never going aright; being a watch,
But being watch'd, that it may still go right?
Nay, to be perjur'd, which is worst of all;
And, among three, to love the worst of all;
A witty wanton with a velvet brow,
With two pitch balls stuck in her face for eyes;
Ay, and, by Heaven, one that will do the deed,
Though Argus were her eunuch and her guard:
And I to sigh for her! to watch for her!
To pray for her! Go to; it is a plague
That Cupid will impose for my neglect
Of his almighty dreadful little might.
Well, I will love, write, sigh, pray, sue, groan:
Some men must love my lady, and some Joan.

[*Exit.*

ACT IV.

SCENE I. — Another Part of the Same.

Enter the PRINCESS, ROSALINE, MARIA, KATHARINE, BOYET, Lords, Attendants, *and a* FORESTER.

PRINCESS.

WAS that the King, that spurr'd his horse so hard
Against the steep uprising of the hill?

Boyet. I know not; but, I think, it was not he.

Prin. Whoe'er he was, he show'd a mounting mind.
Well, lords, to-day we shall have our dispatch:
On Saturday we will return to France. —
Then, Forester, my friend, where is the bush
That we must stand and play the murtherer in?

For. Hereby, upon the edge of yonder coppice;
A stand where you may make the fairest shoot.

Prin. I thank my beauty, I am fair that shoot,
And thereupon thou speak'st the fairest shoot.

For. Pardon me, madam, for I meant not so.

Prin. What, what? first praise me, and then again say, no?
O, short-liv'd pride! Not fair? alack for woe!

For. Yes, madam, fair.

Prin. Nay, never paint me now:
Where fair is not, praise cannot mend the brow.
Here, good my glass, take this for telling true.
[*Giving him money.*
Fair payment for foul words is more than due.

For. Nothing but fair is that which you inherit.

Prin. See, see! my beauty will be sav'd by merit.
O heresy in fair, fit for these days!
A giving hand, though foul, shall have fair praise.—
But come, the bow: —now mercy goes to kill,
And shooting well is then accounted ill.
Thus will I save my credit in the shoot:
Not wounding, pity would not let me do't;
If wounding, then it was to show my skill,
That more for praise than purpose meant to kill.
And, out of question, so it is sometimes:
Glory grows guilty of detested crimes,
When, for fame's sake, for praise, an outward part,
We bend to that the working of the heart;
As I for praise alone now seek to spill
The poor deer's blood, that my heart means no ill.

Boyet. Do not curst wives hold that self-sovereignty
Only for praise' sake, when they strive to be
Lords o'er their lords?

Prin. Only for praise; and praise we may afford
To any lady that subdues a lord.

Enter Costard.

Here comes a member of the commonwealth.

Cost. God dig-you-den all. Pray you, which is the head lady?

Prin. Thou shalt know her, fellow, by the rest that have no heads.

Cost. Which is the greatest lady, the highest?

Prin. The thickest, and the tallest.

Cost. The thickest, and the tallest? it is so; truth is truth.
An your waist, mistress, were as slender as my wit,
One o' these maids' girdles for your waist should be fit.
Are not you the chief woman? you are the thickest here.

Prin. What's your will, sir? what's your will?
Cost. I have a letter, from Monseer Biron to one Lady Rosaline.
Prin. O, thy letter, thy letter! he's a good friend of mine.
Stand aside, good bearer. — Boyet, you can carve;
Break up this capon.
Boyet. I am bound to serve. —
This letter is mistook; it importeth none here:
It is writ to Jaquenetta.
Prin. We will read it, I swear.
Break the neck of the wax, and every one give ear.

Boyet. [Reads.] "*By Heaven, that thou art fair, is most infallible; true, that thou art beauteous; truth itself, that thou art lovely. More fairer than fair, beautiful than beauteous, truer than truth itself, have commiseration on thy heroical vassal! The magnanimous and most illustrate King* Cophetua *set eye upon the pernicious and indubitate beggar* Penelophon; *and he it was that might rightly say,* Veni, vidi, vici; *which to annotanize in the vulgar, (O base and obscure vulgar!)* videlicet, *He came, saw, and overcame: he came, one; saw, two; overcame, three. Who came? the King; Why did he come? to see; Why did he see? to overcome: To whom came he? to the beggar; What saw he? the beggar; Who overcame he? the beggar. The conclusion is victory: on whose side? the King's: the captive is enrich'd: on whose side? the beggar's. The catastrophe is a nuptial: on whose side? the King's? — no, on both in one, or one in both. I am the King; for so stands the comparison: thou the beggar; for so witnesseth thy lowliness. Shall I command thy love? I may. Shall I enforce thy love? I could. Shall I entreat thy love? I will. What shalt thou exchange for rags? robes; for tittles? titles, for thyself? me. Thus, expecting thy reply, I profane my lips on thy foot, my eyes on thy picture, and my heart on thy every part.*

Thine, in the dearest design of industry,
Don Adriano de Armado."

" Thus dost thou hear the Nemean lion roar
'Gainst thee, thou lamb, that standest as his prey;
Submissive fall his princely feet before,
And he from forage will incline to play:
But if thou strive, poor soul, what art thou then?
Food for his rage, repasture for his den."

Prin. What plume of feathers is he that indited this letter?
What vane? what weather-cock? did you ever hear better?

Boyet. I am much deceiv'd, but I remember the style.

Prin. Else your memory is bad, going o'er it erewhile.

Boyet. This Armado is a Spaniard, that keeps here in Court;
A phantasm, a Monarcho, and one that makes sport
To the Prince, and his book-mates.

Prin. Thou, fellow, a word.
Who gave thee this letter?

Cost. I told you; my lord.

Prin. To whom shouldst thou give it?

Cost. From my lord to my lady.

Prin. From which lord to which lady?

Cost. From my lord Birone, a good master of mine,
To a lady of France, that he call'd Rosaline.

Prin. Thou hast mistaken his letter. — Come, lords, away. —

Here, sweet, put up this: 'twill be thine another day.
[*Exeunt* PRINCESS *and Train.*

Boyet. Who is the suitor? who is the suitor?

Ros. Shall I teach you to know?

Boyet. Ay, my continent of beauty.

Ros Why, she that bears the bow.
Finely put off!

Boyet. My lady goes to kill horns; but if thou marry,
Hang me by the neck, if horns that year miscarry.
Finely put on!

Ros. Well then, I am the shooter.

Boyet. And who is your deer?

Ros. If we choose by the horns, yourself: come not near.
Finely put on, indeed!—

Mar. You still wrangle with her, Boyet, and she strikes at the brow.

Boyet. But she herself is hit lower. Have I hit her now?

Ros. Shall I come upon thee with an old saying, that was a man when King Pepin of France was a little boy, as touching the hit it?

Boyet. So I may answer thee with one as old, that was a woman when Queen Guinever of Britain was a little wench, as touching the hit it.

Ros. "*Thou canst not hit it, hit it, hit it,*
Thou canst not hit it, my good man."

Boyet. "*An I cannot, cannot, cannot,*
An I cannot, another can."
[*Exeunt* Ros. *and* KATH.

Cost. By my troth, most pleasant: how both did fit it!

Mar. A mark marvellous well shot; for they both did hit [it].

Boyet. A mark! O! mark but that mark: a mark, says my lady.
Let the mark have a prick in't, to mete at, if it may be.

Mar. Wide o' th' bow hand: i'faith your hand is out.

Cost. Indeed, 'a must shoot nearer, or he'll ne'er hit the clout.

Boyet. An if my hand be out, then belike your hand is in.

Cost. Then will she get the upshot by cleaving the pin.

Mar. Come, come, you talk greasily; your lips grow foul.

Cost. She's too hard for you at pricks, sir: challenge her to bowl.

Boyet. I fear too much rubbing. Good night, my good owl. [*Exeunt* BOYET *and* MARIA.

Cost. By my soul, a swain! a most simple clown!
Lord, Lord! how the ladies and I have put him down!
O' my troth, most sweet jests! most incony vulgar wit!
When it comes so smoothly off, so obscenely, as it were, so fit.
Armado o' the to side, — O, a most dainty man!
To see him walk before a lady, and to bear her fan!
To see him kiss his hand! and how most sweetly 'a will swear! —
And his page o' t' other side, that handful of wit!
Ah, Heavens, it is a most pathetical nit!
[*Noise of shooting within.*
Sola, sola! [*Exit* COSTARD.

SCENE II.

The Same.

Enter HOLOFERNES, Sir NATHANIEL, *and* DULL.

Nathaniel. Very reverend sport, truly; and done in the testimony of a good conscience.

Holofernes. The deer was, as you know, *sanguis*, — in blood; ripe as a pomewater, who now hangeth like a jewel in the ear of *cælo*, — the sky, the welkin, the heaven; and anon falleth, like a crab, on the face of *terra*, — the soil, the land, the earth.

Nath. Truly, Master Holofernes, the epithets are sweetly varied, like a scholar at the least: but, sir, I assure ye, it was a buck of the first head.

Hol. Sir Nathaniel, *haud credo.*

Dull. 'Twas not a *haud credo*, 'twas a pricket.

Hol. Most barbarous intimation! yet a kind of insinuation, as it were, *in via*, in way of explication, *facère*, as it were, replication, or, rather, *ostentare*, to show, as it were, his inclination, — after his undressed, unpolished, uneducated, unpruned, untrained, or rather unlettered, or, ratherest, unconfirmed fashion, — to insert again my *haud credo* for a deer.

Dull. I said the deer was not a *haud credo:* 'twas a pricket.

Hol. Twice sod simplicity, *bis coctus!* — O, thou monster Ignorance, how deformed dost thou look!

Nath. Sir, he hath never fed of the dainties that are bred in a book; he hath not eat paper, as it were; he hath not drunk ink: his intellect is not replenished; he is only an animal, only sensible in the duller parts;

And such barren plants are set before us, that we thankful should be
(Which we of taste and feeling are) for those parts that do fructify in us more than he:
For as it would ill become me to be vain, indiscreet, or a fool,
So were there a patch set on learning, to see him in a school:
But, *omne bene*, say I; being of an old father's mind,
'Many can brook the weather, that love not the wind.'

Dull. You two are book men: can you tell by your wit,
What was a month old at Cain's birth, that's not five weeks old as yet?

Hol. Dictynna, good-man Dull; Dictynna, good-man Dull.

Dull. What is Dictynna?

Nath. A title to Phœbe, to Luna, to the moon.

Hol. The moon was a month old when Adam was no more;
And raught not to five weeks, when he came to five-score.
Th' allusion holds in the exchange.

Dull. 'Tis true indeed: the collusion holds in the exchange.

Hol. God comfort thy capacity! I say, th' allusion holds in the exchange.

Dull. And I say the pollusion holds in the exchange; for the moon is never but a month old; and I say beside, that 'twas a pricket that the Princess kill'd.

Hol. Sir Nathaniel, will you hear an extemporal epitaph on the death of the deer? and, to humour the ignorant, call the deer the Princess kill'd, a pricket?

Nath. *Perge*, good Master Holofernes, *perge;* so it shall please you to abrogate scurrility.

Hol. I will something affect the letter, for it argues facility.

The preyful Princess pierc'd and prick'd a pretty pleasing pricket;
Some say a sore; but not a sore, till now made sore with shooting.
The dogs did yell; put L *to sore, then sorel jumps from thicket;*
Or pricket sore, or else sorel; the people fall a hooting.
If sore be sore, then L *to sore makes fifty sores; O sore* L!
Of one sore I an hundred make, by adding but one more L.

Nath. A rare talent!

Dull. If a talent be a claw, look how he claws him with a talent.

Hol. This is a gift that I have, simple; simply a foolish extravagant spirit, full of forms, figures, shapes, objects, ideas, apprehensions, motions, revolutions: these are begot in the ventricle of memory, nourish'd in the womb of *pia mater*, and delivered upon the mellowing of occasion. But the gift is good in those in whom it is acute, and I am thankful for it.

Nath. Sir, I praise the Lord for you, and so may my parishioners; for their sons are well tutor'd by you, and their daughters profit very greatly under you: you are a good member of the commonwealth.

Hol. *Mehercle!* if their sons be ingenuous, they shall want no instruction; if their daughters be capable, I will put it to them; but, *vir sapit, qui pauca loquitur.* A soul feminine saluteth us.

Enter JAQUENETTA *and* COSTARD.

Jaq. God give you good morrow, Master Person.

Hol. Master Person, — *quasi* pers-on. And if one should be pierc'd, which is the one?

Cost. Marry, Master Schoolmaster, he that is likest to a hogshead.

Hol. Of piercing a hogshead! a good lustre of conceit in a turf of earth; fire enough for a flint, pearl enough for a swine: 'tis pretty; it is well.

Jaq. Good Master Parson, be so good as read me this letter: it was given me by Costard, and sent me from Don Armado: I beseech you, read it.

Hol. "*Fauste, precor gelidâ quando pecus omne sub umbrâ*
Ruminat," — and so forth. Ah, good old Mantuan! I may speak of thee as the traveller doth of Venice:

— "*Venegia, Venegia,*
Chi non te vede, non te pregia."

Old Mantuan! old Mantuan! Who understandeth thee not, loves thee not. — *Ut, re, sol, la, mi, fa.* — Under pardon, sir, what are the contents? or, rather, as Horace says in his — What, my soul, verses?

Nath. Ay, sir, and very learned.

Hol. Let me hear a staff, a stanza, a verse: *lege, domine.*

Nath. [Reads.] "*If love make me forsworn, how shall I swear to love?*
Ah, never faith could hold, if not to beauty vowed!
Though to myself forsworn, to thee I'll faithful prove;
Those thoughts to me were oaks, to thee like osiers bowed.
Study his bias leaves, and makes his book thine eyes,
Where all those pleasures live, that art would comprehend:

If knowledge be the mark, to know thee shall suffice.
Well learned is that tongue, that well can thee commend;
All ignorant that soul, that sees thee without wonder;
Which is to me some praise, that I thy parts admire.
Thy eye Jove's lightning bears, thy voice his dreadful thunder,
Which, not to anger bent, is music, and sweet fire.
Celestial, as thou art, O! pardon, love, this wrong,
That sings Heaven's praise with such an earthly tongue!

Hol. You find not the apostrophes, and so miss the accent: let me supervise the canzonet. Here are only numbers ratified; but, for the elegancy, facility, and golden cadence of poesy, *caret.* Ovidius Naso was the man: and why, indeed, Naso, but for smelling out the odoriferous flowers of fancy, the jerks of invention? *Imitari* is nothing: so doth the hound his master, the ape his keeper, the 'tired horse his rider. But, damosella, virgin, was this directed to you?

Jaq. Ay, sir, from one Mounsier Birone, one of the strange Queen's lords.

Hol. I will overglance the superscript. "*To the snow-white hand of the most beauteous Lady Rosaline.*" I will look again on the intellect of the letter, for the nomination of the party writing to the person written unto: "*Your ladyship's, in all desired employment, Birone.*" Sir Nathaniel, this Birone is one of the votaries with the King; and here he hath framed a letter to a sequent of the stranger Queen's, which, accidentally, or by the way of progression, hath miscarried. — Trip and go, my sweet: deliver this paper into the royal hand of the King; it may concern much. Stay not thy compliment; I forgive thy duty: adieu.

Jaq. Good Costard, go with me.—Sir, God save your life!

Cost. Have with thee, my girl.

[*Exeunt* COST. *and* JAQ.

Nath. Sir, you have done this in the fear of God, very religiously; and, as a certain Father saith—

Hol. Sir, tell not me of the Father; I do fear colourable colours. But, to return to the verses: did they please you, Sir Nathaniel?

Nath. Marvellous well, for the pen.

Hol. I do dine to-day at the father's of a certain pupil of mine; where if before repast it shall please you to gratify the table with a grace, I will, on my privilege I have with the parents of the foresaid child or pupil, undertake your *ben venuto;* where I will prove those verses to be very unlearned, neither savouring of poetry, wit, nor invention. I beseech your society.

Nath. And thank you too; "for society," saith the text, "is the happiness of life."

Hol. And, certes, the text most infallibly concludes it.—Sir, [*to* DULL,] I do invite you too: you shall not say me nay: *pauca verba.* Away! the gentles are at their game, and we will to our recreation. [*Exeunt.*

SCENE III.

Another Part of the Same.

Enter BIRONE, *with a paper.*

Bir. The King he is hunting the deer; I am coursing myself: they have pitch'd a toil; I am toiling in a pitch — pitch that defiles. Defile? a foul word. Well, sit thee down, sorrow! for so, they say, the fool said; and so say I, and ay the fool. Well proved, wit! By the Lord, this love is as mad as Ajax: it kills sheep; it kills me, ay, a sheep. Well proved again o' my side! I will not love; if I do, hang me: i'faith, I will not. O, but her eye! — by this light, but for her eye, I would not love her! yes, for her two eyes. Well, I do nothing in the world but lie, and lie in my throat. By Heaven, I do love, and it hath taught me to rhyme, and to be melancholy; and here is part of my rhyme, and here my melancholy. Well, she hath one o' my sonnets already: the clown bore it, the fool sent it, and the lady hath it: sweet clown, sweeter fool, sweetest lady! By the world, I would not care a pin if the other three were in. Here comes one with a paper: God give him grace to groan!

[*Gets up into a tree.*

Enter the KING, *with a paper.*

King. Ay me!

Bir. [*Aside.*] Shot, by Heaven! — Proceed, sweet Cupid: thou hast thump'd him with thy bird-bolt under the left pap. — In faith, secrets!

King. [Reads.] *So sweet a kiss the golden sun gives not*
To those fresh morning drops upon the rose,
As thy eye-beams, when their fresh rays have smote
The night of dew that on my cheeks down flows:
Nor shines the silver moon one half so bright
Through the transparent bosom of the deep,
As doth thy face through tears of mine give light;
Thou shin'st in every tear that I do weep:
No drop but as a coach doth carry thee;
So ridest thou triumphing in my woe.

Do but behold the tears that swell in me,
And they thy glory through my grief will show:
But do not love thyself; then thou wilt keep
My tears for glasses, and still make me weep.
O Queen of queens, how far dost thou excel!
No thought can think, nor tongue of mortal tell.

How shall she know my griefs? I'll drop the paper.
Sweet leaves, shade folly. Who is he comes here?

Enter LONGAVILLE, *with a paper.*

[*Aside.*] What, Longaville! and reading? listen, ear.
[*Steps aside.*

Bir. Now, in thy likeness, one more fool appear!

Long. Ay me! I am forsworn.

Bir. Why, he comes in like a perjurer, wearing papers.

King. In love, I hope. Sweet fellowship in shame!

Bir. One drunkard loves another of the name.

Long. Am I the first that have been perjur'd so?

Bir. I could put thee in comfort: not by two that I know.
Thou mak'st the triumviry, the corner-cap of society,
The shape of Love's Tyburn, that hangs up simplicity.

Long. I fear these stubborn lines lack power to move.
O sweet Maria, empress of my love!
These numbers will I tear, and write in prose.

Bir. O! rhymes are guards on wanton Cupid's hose:
Disfigure not his slop.

Long. This same shall go.—
[*He reads the sonnet.*

Did not the heavenly rhetoric of thine eye,
'Gainst whom the world cannot hold argument,
Persuade my heart to this false perjury?
Vows for thee broke deserve not punishment.
A woman I forswore; but I will prove,
Thou being a goddess, I forswore not thee:
My vow was earthly, thou a heavenly love;
Thy grace, being gain'd, cures all disgrace in me.
Vows are but breath, and breath a vapour is:
Then thou, fair sun, which on my earth do'st shine,
Exhal'st this vapour-vow; in thee it is:
If broken, then, it is no fault of mine.
If by me broke, what fool is not so wise,
To lose an oath, to win a paradise?

Bir. [*Aside.*] This is the liver vein, which makes flesh a deity;
A green goose, a goddess: pure, pure idolatry.
God amend us, God amend! we are much out o' th' way.

Enter DUMAINE, *with a paper.*

Long. By whom shall I send this?—Company! stay. [*Steps aside.*

Bir. All hid, all hid; an old infant play.
Like a demi-god here sit I in the sky,
And wretched fools' secrets heedfully o'er-eye.
'More sacks to the mill'! O Heavens! I have my wish:
Dumaine transform'd? four woodcocks in a dish!

Dum. O most divine Kate!

Bir. O most profane coxcomb!

Dum. By Heaven, the wonder of a mortal eye!

Bir. By Earth, she is not: Corporal, there you lie.

Dum. Her amber hairs for foul have amber quoted.

Bir. An amber-colour'd raven was well noted.

Dum. As upright as the cedar.

Bir. Stoop, I say:
Her shoulder is with child.

Dum. As fair as day.

Bir. Ay, as some days; but then no sun must shine.

Dum. O, that I had my wish!

Long. And I had mine.

King. And I mine too, good Lord!

Bir. Amen, so I had mine. Is not that a good word?

Dum. I would forget her; but a fever she
Reigns in my blood, and will remember'd be.

Bir. A fever in your blood? why, then incision
Would let her out in saucers: sweet misprision!

Dum. Once more I'll read the ode that I have writ.

Bir. Once more I'll mark how love can vary wit.

Dum. *On a day, (alack the day!)*
Love, whose month is ever May,
Spied a blossom, passing fair,
Playing in the wanton air:
Through the velvet leaves the wind,
All unseen, 'gan passage find;
That the lover, sick to death,
Wish'd himself the heaven's breath.
Air, quoth he, thy cheeks may blow;
Air, would I might triumph so!
But alack! my hand is sworn,
Ne'er to pluck thee from thy thorn:
Vow, alack! for youth unmeet,
Youth so apt to pluck a sweet.

Do not call it sin in me,
That I am forsworn for thee:
Thou, for whom Jove would swear
Juno but an Ethiop were;
And deny himself for Jove,
Turning mortal for thy love.

This will I send, and something else more plain,
That shall express my true love's fasting pain.
O, would the King, Birone, and Longaville,
Were lovers too! Ill, to example ill,
Would from my forehead wipe a perjur'd note;
For none offend, where all alike do dote.

Long. [*Advancing.*] Dumaine, thy love is far from charity,
That in love's grief desir'st society:
You may look pale, but I should blush, I know,
To be o'erheard, and taken napping so.

King. [*Advancing.*] Come, sir, you blush; as his your case is such;
You chide at him, offending twice as much:
You do not love Maria; Longaville
Did never sonnet for her sake compile,
Nor never lay his wreathed arms athwart
His loving bosom, to keep down his heart.
I have been closely shrouded in this bush,
And mark'd you both, and for you both did blush.
I heard your guilty rhymes, observ'd your fashion,
Saw sighs reek from you, noted well your passion:
Ay me! says one; O Jove! the other cries;
One, her hairs were gold, crystal the other's eyes:
You would for paradise break faith and troth;
[*To* LONGAVILLE.
And Jove for your love would infringe an oath.
[*To* DUMAINE.

What will Birone say, when that he shall hear
Faith infringed, which such zeal did swear?
How will he scorn! how will he spend his wit!
How will he triumph, leap, and laugh at it!
For all the wealth that ever I did see,
I would not have him know so much by me.
Bir. Now step I forth to whip hypocrisy.—
[*Descends.*
Ah, good my liege, I pray thee pardon me:
Good heart! what grace hast thou, thus to reprove
These worms for loving, that art most in love?
Your eyes do make no coaches; in your tears
There is no certain princess that appears:
You'll not be perjur'd, 'tis a hateful thing:
Tush! none but minstrels like of sonneting.
But are you not asham'd? nay, are you not,
All three of you, to be thus much o'ershot?
You found his mote; the King your mote did see;
But I a beam do find in each of three.
O! what a scene of fool'ry have I seen,
Of sighs, of groans, of sorrow, and of teen!
O me! with what strict patience have I sat,
To see a King transformed to a gnat!
To see great Hercules whipping a gig,
And profound Solomon to tune a jig,
And Nestor play at push-pin with the boys,
And critic Timon laugh at idle toys!
Where lies thy grief? O! tell me, good Dumaine:
And, gentle Longaville, where lies thy pain?
And where my liege's? all about the breast:—
A caudle, hoa!
King. Too bitter is thy jest.
Are we betray'd thus to thy over-view?
Bir. Not you to me, but I betray'd by you:

I, that am honest; I, that hold it sin
To break the vow I am engaged in;
I am betray'd, by keeping company
With men like men, of [strange] inconstancy.
When shall you see me write a thing in rhyme?
Or groan for Joan? or spend a minute's time
In pruning me? When shall you hear that I
Will praise a hand, a foot, a face, an eye,
A gait, a state, a brow, a breast, a waist,
A leg, a limb? —

King. Soft! Whither away so fast?
A true man, or a thief, that gallops so?

Bir. I post from Love: good lover, let me go.

Enter JAQUENETTA *and* COSTARD.

Jaq. God bless the King!

King. What present hast thou there?

Cost. Some certain treason.

King. What makes treason here?

Cost. Nay, it makes nothing, sir.

King. If it mar nothing neither,
The treason and you go in peace away together.

Jaq. I beseech your Grace, let this letter be read:
Our parson misdoubts it; 'twas treason, he said.

King. Birone, read it over.

[BIRONE *reads the letter.*

Where hadst thou it?

Jaq. Of Costard.

King. Where hadst thou it?

Cost. Of Dun Adramadio, Dun Adramadio.

King. How now! what is in you? why dost thou tear it?

Bir. A toy, my liege, a toy: your Grace needs not fear it.

Long. It did move him to passion, and therefore let's hear it.

Dum. It is Birone's writing, and here is his name. [*Picking up the pieces.*

Bir. Ah, you whoreson loggerhead! [*To* COSTARD.] you were born to do me shame.—
Guilty, my lord, guilty! I confess, I confess.

King. What?

Bir. That you three fools lack'd me, fool, to make up the mess.
He, he, and you, and you my liege, and I,
Are pick-purses in love, and we deserve to die.
O! dismiss this audience, and I shall tell you more.

Dum. Now the number is even.

Bir. True, true; we are four.—
Will these turtles be gone?

King. Hence, sirs: away!

Cost. Walk aside the true folk, and let the traitors stay. [*Exeunt* COSTARD *and* JAQUENETTA.

Bir. Sweet lords, sweet lovers, O! let us embrace.
As true we are, as flesh and blood can be:
The sea will ebb and flow, heaven will shew his face;
Young blood doth not obey an old decree:
We cannot cross the cause why we are born;
Therefore, of all hands must we be forsworn.

King. What, did these rent lines show some love of thine?

Bir. Did they? quoth you. Who sees the heavenly Rosaline,
That, like a rude and savage man of Inde,
At the first opening of the gorgeous east,
Bows not his vassal head, and, stricken blind,
Kisses the base ground with obedient breast?

What peremptory, eagle-sighted eye
Dares look upon the heaven of her brow,
That is not blinded by her majesty?

King. What zeal, what fury hath inspir'd thee now?
My love, her mistress, is a gracious moon,
She, an attending star, scarce seen a light.

Bir. My eyes are then no eyes, nor I Birone.
O! but for my love, day would turn to night.
Of all complexions the cull'd sovereignty
Do meet, as at a fair, in her fair cheek;
Where several worthies make one dignity,
Where nothing wants that want itself doth seek.
Lend me the flourish of all gentle tongues,—
Fie, painted rhetoric! O! she needs it not:
To things of sale a seller's praise belongs;
She passes praise; then praise too short doth blot.
A wither'd hermit, five-score winters worn,
Might shake off fifty, looking in her eye:
Beauty doth varnish age, as if new-born,
And gives the crutch the cradle's infancy.
O! 'tis the sun, that maketh all things shine!

King. By Heaven, thy love is black as ebony.

Bir. Is ebony like her? O wood divine!
A wife of such wood were felicity.
O! who can give an oath? where is a book?
That I may swear beauty doth beauty lack,
If that she learn not of her eye to look:
No face is fair that is not full so black.

King. O paradox! Black is the badge of Hell,
The hue of dungeons, and the shade of night,
And, beauty's crest, becomes the heavens well.

Bir. Devils soonest tempt, resembling spirits of light.

O! if in black my lady's brows be deck'd,
It mourns, that painting, [and] usurping hair,
Should ravish doters with a false aspect;
And therefore is she born to make black fair.
Her favour turns the fashion of the days;
For native blood is counted painting now,
And therefore red, that would avoid dispraise,
Paints itself black, to imitate her brow.

Dum. To look like her are chimney-sweepers black.

Long. And since her time are colliers counted bright.

King. And Ethiops of their sweet complexion crack.

Dum. Dark needs no candles now, for dark is light.

Bir. Your mistresses dare never come in rain,
For fear their colours should be wash'd away.

King. 'Twere good, yours did; for, sir, to tell you plain,
I'll find a fairer face not wash'd to-day.

Bir. I'll prove her fair, or talk till doomsday here.

King. No devil will fright thee then so much as she.

Dum. I never knew man hold vile stuff so dear.

Long. Look, here's thy love: my foot and her face see.

Bir. O! if the streets were paved with thine eyes,
Her feet were much too dainty for such tread.

Dum. O vile! then, as she goes, what upward lies
The street should see, as she walk'd over head.

King. But what of this? Are we not all in love?

Bir. O! nothing so sure; and thereby all forsworn.

King. Then leave this chat: and, good Birone, now prove
Our loving lawful, and our faith not torn.
Dum. Ay, marry, there; some flattery for this evil.
Long. O! some authority how to proceed;
Some tricks, some quillets, how to cheat the Devil.
Dum. Some salve for perjury.
Bir. O! 'tis more than need.—
Have at you, then, affection's men at arms.
Consider what you first did swear unto;—
To fast, to study, and to see no woman:
Flat treason 'gainst the kingly state of youth.
Say, can you fast? your stomachs are too young;
And abstinence engenders maladies.
And where that you have vow'd to study, lords,
In that each of you hath forsworn his book,
Can you still dream, and pore, and thereon look?
For when would you, my lord, or you, or you,
Have found the ground of study's excellence,
Without the beauty of a woman's face?
From women's eyes this doctrine I derive:
They are the ground, the books, the Academes,
From whence doth spring the true Promethean fire.
Why, universal plodding prisons up
The nimble spirits in the arteries,
As motion, and long-during action, tires
The sinewy vigour of the traveller.
Now, for not looking on a woman's face,
You have in that forsworn the use of eyes,
And study, too, the causer of your vow;
For where is any author in the world,
Teaches such learning as a woman's eye?
Learning is but an adjunct to ourself,
And where we are, our learning likewise is:
Then, when ourselves we see in ladies' eyes,

With ourselves,
Do we not likewise see our learning there?
O! we have made a vow to study, lords,
And in that vow we have forsworn our books;
For when would you, my liege, or you, or you,
In leaden contemplation have found out
Such fiery numbers as the prompting eyes
Of beauty's tutors have enrich'd you with?
Other slow arts entirely keep the brain,
And therefore, finding barren practisers,
Scarce show a harvest of their heavy toil;
But love, first learned in a lady's eyes,
Lives not alone immured in the brain,
But with the motion of all elements
Courses as swift as thought in every power,
And gives to every power a double power,
Above their functions and their offices.
It adds a precious seeing to the eye;
A lover's eyes will gaze an eagle blind;
A lover's ear will hear the lowest sound,
When the suspicious head of theft is stopp'd:
Love's feeling is more soft, and sensible,
Than are the tender horns of cockled snails:
Love's tongue proves dainty Bacchus gross in taste.
For valour, is not Love a Hercules,
Still climbing trees in the Hesperides?
Subtle as Sphinx? as sweet, and musical,
As bright Apollo's lute, strung with his hair?
And when Love speaks, the voice of all the gods
Makes Heaven drowsy with the harmony.
Never durst poet touch a pen to write,
Until his ink were temper'd with love's sighs;
O! then his lines would ravish savage ears,
And plant in tyrants mild humility.
From women's eyes this doctrine I derive:

They sparkle still the right Promethean fire;
They are the books, the arts, the Academes,
That shew, contain, and nourish all the world,
Else none at all in aught proves excellent.
Then, fools you were these women to forswear,
Or, keeping what is sworn, you will prove fools.
For wisdom's sake, a word that all men love,
Or for love's sake, a word that loves all men,
Or for men's sake, the authors of these women,
Or women's sake, by whom we men are men,
Let us once lose our oaths to find ourselves,
Or else we lose ourselves to keep our oaths.
It is religion to be thus forsworn;
For charity itself fulfils the law,
And who can sever love from charity?

King. Saint Cupid, then! and, soldiers, to the field!

Bir. Advance your standards, and upon them, lords!
Pell-mell, down with them! but be first advis'd,
In conflict that you get the sun of them.

Long. Now to plain-dealing: lay these glozes by.
Shall we resolve to woo these girls of France?

King. And win them too: therefore, let us devise
Some entertainment for them in their tents.

Bir. First, from the Park let us conduct them thither;
Then, homeward, every man attach the hand
Of his fair mistress. In the afternoon
We will with some strange pastime solace them,
Such as the shortness of the time can shape;
For revels, dances, masks, and merry hours,
Fore-run fair Love, strewing her way with flowers.

King. Away, away! no time shall be omitted,
That will be time, and may by us be fitted.

Bir. *Allons! allons!* — Sow'd cockle reap'd no corn;
And justice always whirls in equal measure:
Light wenches may prove plagues to men forsworn:
If so, our copper buys no better treasure.
[*Exeunt.*

ACT V.

Scene I. — Another Part of the Same.

Enter Holofernes, Sir Nathaniel, *and* Dull.

Holofernes.

SATIS *quod sufficit.*

Nath. I praise God for you, sir: your reasons at dinner have been sharp and sententious; pleasant without scurrility, witty without affection, audacious without impudency, learned without opinion, and strange without heresy. I did converse this *quondam* day with a companion of the King's, who is intituled, nominated, or called, Don Adriano de Armado.

Hol. *Novi hominem tanquam te:* his humour is lofty, his discourse peremptory, his tongue filed, his eye ambitious, his gait majestical, and his general behaviour vain, ridiculous, and thrasonical. He is too picked, too spruce, too affected, too odd, as it were, too peregrinate, as I may call it.

Nath. A most singular and choice epithet.
[*Draws out his table-book.*

Hol. He draweth out the thread of his verbosity

finer than the staple of his argument. I abhor such fanatical phantasms, such insociable and point-devise companions; such rackers of orthography, as to speak, *dout*, fine, when he should say, *doubt; det*, when he should pronounce, *debt*—*d e b t*, not *d e t:* he clepeth a 'calf,' *cauf;* 'half,' *hauf;* 'neighbour' *vocatur, nebour; neigh* abbreviated *ne*. This is ab-hominable, (which he would call abominable,) it insinuateth me of insanie: *ne intelligis, domine?*—to make frantic, lunatic.

Nath. *Laus Deo, bone intelligo.*

Hol. *Bone?*—*bone*, for *bene: Priscian* a little scratch'd; 'twill serve.

Enter ARMADO, MOTH, *and* COSTARD.

Nath. *Videsne quis venit?*

Hol. *Video, et gaudeo.*

Arm. Chirrah! [*To* MOTH.

Hol. *Quare* 'chirrah,' not 'sirrah'?

Arm. Men of peace, well encounter'd.

Hol. Most military sir, salutation.

Moth. They have been at a great feast of languages, and stolen the scraps.

Cost. O! they have liv'd long on the alms-basket of words. I marvel thy master hath not eaten thee for a word; for thou art not so long by the head as *honorificabilitudinitatibus:* thou art easier swallowed than a flap-dragon.

Moth. Peace! the peal begins.

Arm. Monsieur, [*to* HOL.] are you not letter'd?

Moth. Yes, yes; he teaches boys the horn-book. —What is a, b, spelt backward with the horn on his head?

Hol. Ba, *pueritia*, with a horn added.

Moth. Ba! most silly sheep, with a horn. — You hear his learning.

Hol. *Quis, quis,* thou consonant?

Moth. The third of the five vowels, if you repeat them; or the fifth, if I.

Hol. I will repeat them, a, e, i, —

Moth. The sheep: the other two concludes it; o, u.

Arm. Now, by the salt wave of the Mediterranean, a sweet touch, a quick venew of wit! snip, snap, quick and home: it rejoiceth my intellect; true wit!

Moth. Offered by a child to an old man; which is wit-old.

Hol. What is the figure? what is the figure?

Moth. Horns.

Hol. Thou disputest like an infant: go, whip thy gig.

Moth. Lend me your horn to make one, and I will whip about your infamy *circùm circà.* A gig of a cuckold's horn!

Cost. An I had but one penny in the world, thou shouldst have it to buy gingerbread: hold, there is the very remuneration I had of thy master, thou half-penny purse of wit, thou pigeon-egg of discretion. O! an the heavens were so pleased, that thou wert but my bastard, what a joyful father would'st thou make me. Go to; thou hast it *ad dunghill,* at the fingers' ends, as they say.

Hol. O! I smell false Latin; 'dunghill' for *unguem.*

Arm. Arts-man, *præambula:* we will be singled from the barbarous. Do you not educate youth at the charge-house on the top of the mountain?

Hol. Or *mons,* the hill.

Arm. At your sweet pleasure for the mountain.

Hol. I do, sans question.

Arm. Sir, it is the King's most sweet pleasure

and affection, to congratulate the Princess at her pavilion in the posteriors of this day, which the rude multitude call the afternoon.

Hol. The posterior of the day, most generous sir, is liable, congruent, and measurable for the afternoon: the word is well cull'd, chose; sweet and apt, I do assure you, sir; I do assure.

Arm. Sir, the King is a noble gentleman, and my familiar, I do assure you, very good friend. — For what is inward between us, let it pass. — [*To* COST.] I do beseech thee, remember thy courtesy; [*to* HOL.] — I beseech thee, apparel thy head: — and among other importunate and most serious designs, — and of great import indeed, too, — but let that pass; — for I must tell thee, it will please his Grace (by the world) sometime to lean upon my poor shoulder, and with his royal finger, thus dally with my excrement, with my mustachio: but, sweet heart, let that pass. By the world, I recount no fable: some certain special honours it pleaseth his greatness to impart to Armado, a soldier, a man of travel, that hath seen the world; but let that pass. — The very all of all is, — but sweet heart, I do implore secrecy, — that the King would have me present the Princess, sweet chuck, with some delightful ostentation, or show, or pageant, or antic, or fire-work. Now, understanding that the curate and your sweet self are good at such eruptions, and sudden breaking out of mirth, as it were, I have acquainted you withal, to the end to crave your assistance.

Hol. Sir, you shall present before her the Nine Worthies. — Sir Nathaniel, as concerning some entertainment of time, some show in the posterior of this day, to be rendered by our assistance, — the King's command, and this most gallant, illustrate, and learned gentleman, — before the Princess, I say, none so fit as to present the Nine Worthies.

Nath. Where will you find men worthy enough to present them?

Hol. Joshua, yourself; myself, or this gallant gentleman, Judas Maccabeus; this swain, (because of his great limb or joint,) shall pass Pompey the Great; the page, Hercules.

Arm. Pardon, sir; error: he is not quantity enough for that worthy's thumb: he is not so big as the end of his club.

Hol. Shall I have audience? he shall present Hercules in minority: his *enter* and *exit* shall be strangling a snake; and I will have an apology for that purpose.

Moth. An excellent device! so, if any of the audience hiss, you may cry, 'Well done, Hercules! now thou crushest the snake!' that is the way to make an offence gracious; though few have the grace to do it.

Arm. For the rest of the Worthies? —

Hol. I will play three myself.

Moth. Thrice-worthy gentleman!

Arm. Shall I tell you a thing?

Hol. We attend.

Arm. We will have, if this fadge not, an antic. I beseech you, follow.

Hol. *Via!* — Goodman Dull, thou hast spoken no word all this while.

Dull. Nor understood none neither, sir.

Hol. *Allons!* we will employ thee.

Dull. I'll make one in a dance, or so; or I will play on the tabor to the Worthies, and let them dance the hay.

Hol. Most dull, honest Dull. To our sport, away!

[*Exeunt.*

SCENE II.

Another Part of the Same. Before the PRINCESS's Pavilion.

Enter the PRINCESS, KATHARINE, ROSALINE, *and* MARIA.

Prin. Sweet hearts, we shall be rich ere we depart,
If fairings come thus plentifully in:
A lady wall'd about with diamonds!—
Look you, what I have from the loving King.
Ros. Madam, came nothing else along with that?
Prin. Nothing but this? yes; as much love in rhyme,
As would be cramm'd up in a sheet of paper,
Writ on both sides the leaf, margent and all,
That he was fain to seal on Cupid's name.
Ros. That was the way to make his god-head wax;
For he hath been five thousand years a boy.
Kath. Ay, and a shrewd unhappy gallows too.
Ros. You'll ne'er be friends with him: he kill'd your sister.
Kath. He made her melancholy, sad, and heavy;
And so she died: had she been light, like you,
Of such a merry, nimble, stirring spirit,
She might ha' been a grandam ere she died;
And so may you; for a light heart lives long.
Ros. What's your dark meaning, mouse, of this light word?
Kath. A light condition in a beauty dark.
Ros. We need more light to find your meaning out.

Kath. You'll mar the light by taking it in snuff;
Therefore, I'll darkly end the argument.

Ros. Look, what you do, you do it still i' th' dark.

Kath. So do not you, for you are a light wench.

Ros. Indeed, I weigh not you, and therefore light.

Kath. You weigh me not?—O! that's you care not for me.

Ros. Great reason; for, 'past cure is still past care.'

Prin. Well bandied both; a set of wit well play'd.
But, Rosaline, you have a favour too:
Who sent it? and what is it?

Ros. I would you knew:
An if my face were but as fair as yours,
My favour were as great: be witness this.
Nay, I have verses too, I thank Birone.
The numbers true; and, were the numb'ring too,
I were the fairest goddess on the ground:
I am compar'd to twenty thousand fairs.
O! he hath drawn my picture in his letter.

Prin. Any thing like?

Ros. Much, in the letters, nothing in the praise.

Prin. Beauteous as ink: a good conclusion.

Kath. Fair as a text B in a copy-book.

Ros. 'Ware pencils, ho! let me not die your debtor,
My red dominical, my golden letter:
O, that your face were not so full of O's!

Prin. A pox of that jest! and I beshrew all shrews!
But, Katharine, what was sent to you from fair Dumaine?

Kath. Madam, this glove.

Prin. Did he not send you twain?

Kath. Yes, madam; and, moreover,
Some thousand verses of a faithful lover:
A huge translation of hypocrisy,
Vilely compil'd, profound simplicity.
Mar. This and these pearls to me sent Longaville:
The letter is too long by half a mile.
Prin. I think no less. Dost thou not wish in heart,
The chain were longer, and the letter short?
Mar. Ay, or I would these hands might never part.
Prin. We are wise girls to mock our lovers so.
Ros. They are worse fools to purchase mocking so.
That same Birone I'll torture ere I go.
O! that I knew he were but in by th' week!
How I would make him fawn, and beg, and seek,
And wait the season, and observe the times,
And spend his prodigal wits in bootless rhymes,
And shape his service wholly to my behests,
And make him proud to make me proud that jests!
So persaunt-like would I o'ersway his state,
That he should be my fool, and I his fate.
Prin. None are so surely caught, when they are catch'd,
As wit turn'd fool: folly, in wisdom hatch'd,
Hath wisdom's warrant, and the help of school,
And wit's own grace to grace a learned fool.
Ros. The blood of youth burns not with such excess,
As gravity's revolt to wantonness.
Mar. Folly in fools bears not so strong a note,
As fool'ry in the wise, when wit doth dote;
Since all the power thereof it doth apply,
To prove by wit worth in simplicity.

Enter BOYET.

Prin. Here comes Boyet, and mirth is in his face.

Boyet. O! I am stabb'd with laughter? Where's her Grace?

Prin. Thy news, Boyet?

Boyet. Prepare, madam, prepare!
Arm, wenches, arm! encounters mounted are
Against your peace. Love doth approach disguis'd,
Armed in arguments: you'll be surpris'd.
Muster your wits; stand in your own defence;
Or hide your heads like cowards, and fly hence.

Prin. St. Dennis to St. Cupid! What are they,
That charge their breath against us? say, scout, say.

Boyet. Under the cool shade of a sycamore,
I thought to close mine eyes some half an hour,
When, lo! to interrupt my purpos'd rest,
Toward that shade I might behold addrest
The King and his companions: warily
I stole into a neighbour thicket by,
And overheard what you shall overhear;
That by and by disguis'd they will be here.
Their herald is a pretty knavish page,
That well by heart hath conn'd his embassage:
Action, and accent, did they teach him there;
"Thus must thou speak, and thus thy body bear:"
And ever and anon they made a doubt
Presence majestical would put him out;
"For," quoth the King, "an angel shalt thou see;
Yet fear not thou, but speak audaciously."
The boy replied, "An angel is not evil;
I should have fear'd her, had she been a devil."
With that all laugh'd, and clapp'd him on the shoulder,
Making the bold wag by their praises bolder.

One rubb'd his elbow thus, and fleer'd and swore
A better speech was never spoke before:
Another, with his finger and his thumb,
Cry'd "*Via!* we will do't, come what will come:"
The third he caper'd and cried, "All goes well:"
The fourth turn'd on the toe, and down he fell.
With that, they all did tumble on the ground,
With such a zealous laughter, so profound,
That in this spleen ridiculous appears,
To check their folly, passion's solemn tears.

Prin. But what, but what? come they to visit us?

Boyet. They do, they do; and are apparel'd thus,—
Like Muscovites, or Russians: as I guess,
Their purpose is, to parle, to court, and dance;
And every one his love-suit will advance
Unto his several mistress; which they'll know
By favours several which they did bestow.

Prin. And will they so? the gallants shall be task'd;
For, ladies, we will every one be mask'd,
And not a man of them shall have the grace,
Despite of suit, to see a lady's face.—
Hold, Rosaline; this favour thou shalt wear,
And then the King will court thee for his dear:
Hold, take thou this, my sweet, and give me thine,
So shall Birone take me for Rosaline.—
And change your favours, too; so shall your loves
Woo contrary, deceiv'd by these removes.

Ros. Come on then: wear the favours most in sight.

Kath. But in this changing, what is your intent?

Prin. The effect of my intent is, to cross theirs:
They do it but in mocking merriment;
And mock for mock is only my intent.

Their several counsels they unbosom shall
To loves mistook; and so be mock'd withal,
Upon the next occasion that we meet,
With visages display'd, to talk, and greet.

Ros. But shall we dance, if they desire us to't?

Prin. No; to the death we will not move a foot:
Nor to their penn'd speech render we no grace;
But, while 'tis spoke, each turn away her face.

Boyet. Why, that contempt will kill the speaker's heart,
And quite divorce his memory from his part.

Prin. Therefore I do it; and, I make no doubt,
The rest will ne'er come in, if he be out.
There's no such sport, as sport by sport o'erthrown;
To make theirs ours, and ours none but our own:
So shall we stay, mocking intended game;
And they, well mock'd, depart away with shame.
[*Trumpets sound within.*

Boyet. The trumpet sounds: be mask'd, the maskers come. [*The Ladies mask.*

Enter the KING, BIRONE, LONGAVILLE, *and* DUMAINE, *in Russian habits, and masked;* MOTH, Musicians, *and* Attendants.

Moth. "All hail, the richest beauties on the earth!—

Boyet. Beauties no richer than rich taffata.

Moth. "A holy parcel of the fairest dames,
[*The Ladies turn their backs to him.*
"That ever turn'd their backs to mortal views!—

Bir. "Their eyes," villain, "their eyes."

Moth. "That ever turn'd their eyes to mortal views!
"Out—

Boyet. True; "out," indeed.

Moth. "Out of your favours, heavenly spirits, vouchsafe
"Not to behold —

Bir. "Once to behold," rogue.

Moth. "Once to behold with your sun-beamed eyes,
"—— with your sun-beamed eyes —"

Boyet. They will not answer to that epithet;
You were best call it daughter-beamed eyes.

Moth. They do not mark me, and that brings me out.

Bir. Is this your perfectness? be gone, you rogue.

Ros. What would these strangers? know their minds, Boyet.
If they do speak our language, 'tis our will
That some plain man recount their purposes.
Know what they would.

Boyet. What would you with the Princess?

Bir. Nothing but peace, and gentle visitation.

Ros. What would they, say they?

Boyet. Nothing but peace, and gentle visitation.

Ros. Why, that they have; and bid them so be gone.

Boyet. She says, you have it, and you may be gone.

King. Say to her, we have measur'd many miles,
To tread a measure with her on this grass.

Boyet. They say, that they have measur'd many a mile,
To tread a measure with you on this grass.

Ros. It is not so: ask them how many inches
Is in one mile? if they have measur'd many,
The measure then of one is easily told.

Boyet. If, to come hither you have measur'd miles,

And many miles, the Princess bids you tell,
How many inches do fill up one mile.

Bir. Tell her we measure them by weary steps.

Boyet. She hears herself.

Ros. How many weary steps,
Of many weary miles you have o'ergone,
Are number'd in the travel of one mile?

Bir. We number nothing that we spend for you:
Our duty is so rich, so infinite,
That we may do it still without accompt.
Vouchsafe to shew the sunshine of your face,
That we, like savages, may worship it.

Ros. My face is but a moon, and clouded too.

King. Blessed are clouds, to do as such clouds do!
Vouchsafe, bright moon, and these thy stars, to shine
(Those clouds removed) upon our watery eyne.

Ros. O, vain petitioner! beg a greater matter;
Thou now request'st but moonshine in the water.

King. Then, in our measure, vouchsafe but one change.
Thou bid'st me beg; this begging is not strange.

Ros. Play, music, then! nay, you must do it soon.
[*Music plays.*
Not yet; — no dance: — thus change I like the moon.

King. Will you not dance? How came you thus estranged?

Ros. You took the moon at full, but now she's changed.

King. Yet still she is the moon, and I the man.
The music plays: vouchsafe some motion to it.

Ros. Our ears vouchsafe it.

King. But your legs should do it.

Ros. Since you are strangers, and come here by chance,
We'll not be nice. Take hands: — we will not dance.

King. Why take you hands then?

Ros. Only to part friends. —
Court'sy, sweet hearts; and so the measure ends.

King. More measure of this measure: be not nice.

Ros. We can afford no more at such a price.

King. Prize you yourselves? What buys your company?

Ros. Your absence only.

King. That can never be.

Ros. Then cannot we be bought; and so adieu.
Twice to your visor, and half once to you!

King. If you deny to dance, let's hold more chat.

Ros. In private then.

King. I am best pleas'd with that.
[*They converse apart.*

Bir. White-handed mistress, one sweet word with thee.

Prin. Honey, and milk, and sugar: there are three.

Bir. Nay, then, two treys, (an if you grow so nice,)
Metheglin, wort, and malmsey. — Well run, dice!
There's half a dozen sweets.

Prin. Seventh sweet, adieu.
Since you can cog, I'll play no more with you.

Bir. One word in secret.

Prin. Let it not be sweet.

Bir. Thou griev'st my gall.

Prin. Gall? bitter.

Bir. Therefore meet.
[*They converse apart.*

Dum. Will you vouchsafe with me to change a word?

Mar. Name it.

Dum. Fair lady,—

Mar. Say you so? Fair lord.—
Take that for your fair lady.

Dum. Please it you,
As much in private, and I'll bid adieu.
[*They converse apart.*

Kath. What, was your visor made without a tongue?

Long. I know the reason, lady, why you ask.

Kath. O, for your reason! quickly, sir; I long.

Long. You have a double tongue within your mask,
And would afford my speechless visor half.

Kath. Veal, quoth the Dutchman.—Is not veal a calf?

Long. A calf, fair lady?

Kath. No, a fair lord calf.

Long. Let's part the word.

Kath. No; I'll not be your half:
Take all, and wean it: it may prove an ox.

Long. Look, how you butt yourself in these sharp mocks.
Will you give horns, chaste lady? do not so.

Kath. Then die a calf, before your horns do grow.

Long. One word in private with you, ere I die.

Kath. Bleat softly then: the butcher hears you cry. [*They converse apart.*

Boyet. The tongues of mocking wenches are as keen
As is the razor's edge invisible,
Cutting a smaller hair than may be seen;
Above the sense of sense, so sensible
Seemeth their conference; their conceits have wings
Fleeter than arrows, bullets, wind, thought, swifter things.

Ros. Not one word more, my maids: break off, break off.

Bir. By Heaven, all dry-beaten with pure scoff!

King. Farewell, mad wenches: you have simple wits. [*Exeunt* KING, Lords, MOTH, Music, *and* Attendants.

Prin. Twenty adieus, my frozen Muscovits.—
Are these the breed of wits so wonder'd at?

Boyet. Tapers they are, with your sweet breaths puff'd out.

Ros. Well-liking wits they have; gross, gross; fat, fat.

Prin. O, poverty in wit, kingly-poor flout!
Will they not, think you, hang themselves to-night,
Or ever, but in visors, show their faces?
This pert Birone was out of count'nance quite.

Ros. They were all in lamentable cases!
The King was weeping-ripe for a good word.

Prin. Birone did swear himself out of all suit.

Mar. Dumaine was at my service, and his sword:
No *point*, quoth I: my servant straight was mute.

Kath. Lord Longaville said, I came o'er his heart;
And trow you, what he call'd me?

Prin. Qualm, perhaps.

Kath. Yes, in good faith.

Prin. Go, sickness as thou art!

Ros. Well, better wits have worn plain statute-caps.
But will you hear? the King is my love sworn.

Prin. And quick Birone hath plighted faith to me.

Kath. And Longaville was for my service born.

Mar. Dumaine is mine, as sure as bark on tree.

Boyet. Madam, and pretty Mistresses, give ear.
Immediately they will again be here

In their own shapes; for it can never be
They will digest this harsh indignity.

Prin. Will they return?

Boyet. They will, they will, God knows;
And leap for joy, though they are lame with blows:
Therefore, change favours; and, when they repair,
Blow like sweet roses in this summer air.

Prin. How blow? how blow? speak to be understood.

Boyet. Fair ladies, mask'd, are roses in their bud:
Dismask'd, their damask sweet commixture shewn,
Are angels vailing clouds, or roses blown.

Prin. Avaunt, perplexity! What shall we do,
If they return in their own shapes to woo?

Ros. Good Madam, if by me you'll be advis'd,
Let's mock them still, as well, known, as disguis'd.
Let us complain to them what fools were here,
Disguis'd like Muscovites, in shapeless gear;
And wonder what they were, and to what end
Their shallow shews, and prologue vilely penn'd,
And their rough carriage so ridiculous,
Should be presented at our tent to us.

Boyet. Ladies, withdraw: the gallants are at hand.

Prin. Whip to our tents, as roes run over land.

[*Exeunt* PRINCESS, ROS., KATH., *and* MARIA.

Enter the KING, BIRONE, LONGAVILLE, *and* DUMAINE, *in their proper habits.*

King. Fair sir, God save you! Where's the Princess?

Boyet. Gone to her tent: please it your Majesty, command me any service to her?

King. That she vouchsafe me audience for one word.

Boyet. I will; and so will she, I know, my lord.
[*Exit.*

Bir. This fellow picks up wit as pigeons peas,
And utters it again when Jove doth please.
He is wit's pedler, and retails his wares
At wakes, and wassails, meetings, markets, fairs;
And we that sell by gross, the Lord doth know,
Have not the grace to grace it with such shew.
This gallant pins the wenches on his sleeve:
Had he been Adam, he had tempted Eve.
He can carve, too, and lisp: why, this is he
That kiss'd away his hand in courtesy:
This is the ape of form, Monsieur the nice,
That, when he plays at tables, chides the dice
In honourable terms: nay, he can sing
A mean most meanly; and, in ushering,
Mend him who can: the ladies call him sweet;
The stairs, as he treads on them, kiss his feet.
This is the flower that smiles on every one,
To shew his teeth as white as whales-bone;
And consciences, that will not die in debt,
Pay him the due of 'honey-tongued Boyet.'

King. A blister on his sweet tongue, with my heart,
That put Armado's page out of his part!

Enter the PRINCESS, *ushered by* BOYET; ROSALINE, MARIA, KATHARINE, *and* Attendants.

Bir. See where it comes!—Behaviour, what wert thou,
Till this man shew'd thee? and what art thou now?

King. All hail, sweet Madam, and fair time of day!

Prin. Fair, in all hail, is foul, as I conceive.

King. Construe my speeches better, if you may.

Prin. Then wish me better: I will give you leave.

King. We came to visit you, and purpose now
To lead you to our Court: vouchsafe it, then.
Prin. This field shall hold me, and so hold your vow:
Nor God, nor I, delight in perjur'd men.
King. Rebuke me not for that which you provoke;
The virtue of your eye must break my oath.
Prin. You nick-name virtue; vice you should have spoke;
For virtue's office never breaks men's troth.
Now, by my maiden honour, yet as pure
As the unsullied lily, I protest,
A world of torments though I should endure,
I would not yield to be your house's guest;
So much I hate a breaking cause to be
Of heavenly oaths, vow'd with integrity.
King. O! you have liv'd in desolation here,
Unseen, unvisited; much to our shame.
Prin. Not so, my lord; it is not so, I swear:
We have had pastimes here, and pleasant game.
A mess of Russians left us but of late.
King. How, Madam! Russians?
Prin. Ay, in truth, my lord;
Trim gallants, full of courtship, and of state.
Ros. Madam, speak true. — It is not so, my lord:
My lady (to the manner of the days)
In courtesy gives undeserving praise.
We four, indeed, confronted were with four
In Russian habit: here they stay'd an hour,
And talk'd apace; and in that hour, my lord,
They did not bless us with one happy word.
I dare not call them fools; but this I think,
When they are thirsty, fools would fain have drink.
Bir. This jest is dry to me. — [My] gentle sweet,

Your wit makes wise things foolish: when we greet,
With eyes best seeing, Heaven's fiery eye,
By light we lose light: your capacity
Is of that nature, that to your huge store
Wise things seem foolish, and rich things but poor.

Ros. This proves you wise and rich, for in my eye,—

Bir. I am a fool, and full of poverty.

Ros. But that you take what doth to you belong,
It were a fault to snatch words from my tongue.

Bir. O! I am yours, and all that I possess.

Ros. All the fool mine?

Bir. I cannot give you less.

Ros. Which of the visors was it, that you wore?

Bir. Where? when? what visor? why demand you this?

Ros. There, then, that visor; that superfluous case,
That hid the worse, and shew'd the better face.

King. [*Aside.*] We are descried: they'll mock us now downright.

Dum. [*Aside.*] Let us confess, and turn it to a jest.

Prin. Amaz'd, my lord? Why looks your Highness sad?

Ros. Help! hold his brows! he'll swoon. Why look you pale?—
Sea-sick, I think, coming from Muscovy.

Bir. Thus pour the stars down plagues for perjury.
Can any face of brass hold longer out?—
Here stand I, lady; dart thy skill at me;
Bruise me with scorn, confound me with a flout;
Thrust thy sharp wit quite through my ignorance;
Cut me to pieces with thy keen conceit;
And I will wish thee never more to dance,
Nor never more in Russian habit wait.

O! never will I trust to speeches penn'd,
Nor to the motion of a school-boy's tongue;
Nor never come in visor to my friend;
Nor woo in rhyme, like a blind harper's song;
Taffata phrases, silken terms precise,
Three-pil'd hyperboles, spruce affection,
Figures pedantical: these summer flies
Have blown me full of maggot ostentation.
I do forswear them; and I here protest,
By this white glove, (how white the hand, God knows,)
Henceforth my wooing mind shall be express'd
In russet 'yeas,' and honest kersey 'noes':
And, to begin, — wench, so God help me, la!
My love to thee is sound, sans crack or flaw.

Ros. Sans '*sans*,' I pray you.

Bir. Yet I have a trick
Of the old rage: — bear with me, I am sick;
I'll leave it by degrees. Soft! let us see: —
Write "Lord have mercy on us" on those three;
They are infected, in their hearts it lies;
They have the plague, and caught it of your eyes:
These lords are visited; you are not free,
For the Lord's tokens on you do I see.

Prin. No, they are free that gave these tokens to us.

Bir. Our states are forfeit: seek not to undo us.

Ros. It is not so; for how can this be true,
That you stand forfeit, being those that sue?

Bir. Peace! for I will not have to do with you.

Ros. Nor shall not, if I do as I intend.

Bir. Speak for yourselves: my wit is at an end.

King. Teach us, sweet Madam, for our rude transgression
Some fair excuse.

Prin. The fairest is confession.
Were you not here, but even now, disguis'd?
King. Madam, I was.
Prin. And were you well advis'd?
King. I was, fair Madam.
Prin. When you then were here,
What did you whisper in your lady's ear?
King. That more than all the world I did respect her.
Prin. When she shall challenge this, you will reject her.
King. Upon mine honour, no.
Prin. Peace! peace! forbear:
Your oath once broke, you force not to forswear.
King. Despise me, when I break this oath of mine.
Prin. I will; and therefore keep it. — Rosaline,
What did the Russian whisper in your ear?
Ros. Madam, he swore, that he did hold me dear
As precious eye-sight, and did value me
Above this world; adding thereto, moreover,
That he would wed me, or else die my lover.
Prin. God give thee joy of him! the noble lord
Most honorably doth uphold his word.
King. What mean you, Madam? by my life, my troth,
I never swore this lady such an oath.
Ros. By Heaven, you did; and to confirm it plain,
You gave me this: but take it, sir, again.
King. My faith, and this, the Princess I did give:
I knew her by this jewel on her sleeve.
Prin. Pardon me, sir, this jewel did she wear;
And Lord Birone, I thank him, is my dear. —
What! will you have me, or your pearl again?
Bir. Neither of either; I remit both twain. —

I see the trick on't: — here was a consent,
Knowing aforehand of our merriment,
To dash it like a Christmas comedy.
Some carry-tale, some please-man, some slight zany,
Some mumble-news, some trencher-knight, some Dick,
That smiles his cheek in years, and knows the trick
To make my lady laugh when she's dispos'd,
Told our intents before; which once disclos'd,
The ladies did change favours; and then we,
Following the signs, woo'd but the sign of she.
Now, to our perjury to add more terror,
We are again forsworn — in will, and error.
Much upon this it is: — and might not you
[*To* BOYET.
Forestall our sport, to make us thus untrue?
Do not you know my lady's foot by th' squire,
And laugh upon the apple of her eye?
And stand between her back, sir, and the fire,
Holding a trencher, jesting merrily?
You put our page out: go, you are allow'd;
Die when you will, a smock shall be your shroud.
You leer upon me, do you? there's an eye,
Wounds like a leaden sword.

Boyet. Full merrily
Hath this brave manage, this career, been run.

Bir. Lo, he is tilting straight! Peace! I have done.

Enter COSTARD.

Welcome, pure wit! thou partest a fair fray.

Cost. O Lord, sir, they would know,
Whether the three Worthies shall come in, or no.

Bir. What, are there but three?

Cost. No, sir; but it is vara fine,
For every one pursents three.

Bir. And three times thrice is nine.

Cost. Not so, sir; under correction, sir, I hope, it is not so.
You cannot beg us, sir, I can assure you, sir; we know what we know:
I hope, sir, three times thrice, sir, —

Bir. Is not nine.

Cost. Under correction, sir, we know whereuntil it doth amount.

Bir. By Jove, I always took three threes for nine.

Cost. O Lord! sir, it were pity you should get your living by reckoning, sir.

Bir. How much is it?

Cost. O Lord! sir, the parties themselves, the actors, sir, will show whereuntil it doth amount: for mine own part, I am, as they say, but to pursent one man, — e'en one poor man — Pompion the Great, sir.

Bir. Art thou one of the Worthies?

Cost. It pleased them to think me worthy of Pompion the Great: for mine own part, I know not the degree of the Worthy, but I am to stand for him.

Bir. Go, bid them prepare.

Cost. We will turn it finely off, sir: we will take some care. [*Exit* COSTARD.

King. Birone, they will shame us; let them not approach.

Bir. We are shame-proof, my lord; and 'tis some policy
To have one shew worse than the King's and his company.

King. I say, they shall not come.

Prin. Nay, my good lord, let me o'er-rule you now.
That sport best pleases, that doth least know how:
Where zeal strives to content, and the contents

Dies in the zeal of that which it presents,
Their form confounded makes most form in mirth;
When great things labouring perish in their birth.

Bir. A right description of our sport, my lord.

Enter ARMADO.

Arm. Anointed, I implore so much expense of thy royal sweet breath, as will utter a brace of words.

[ARMADO *converses with the* KING, *and delivers a paper to him.*

Prin. Doth this man serve God?

Bir. Why ask you?

Prin. He speaks not like a man of God's making.

Arm. That's all one, my fair, sweet, honey monarch; for, I protest, the School-master is exceeding fantastical; too, too vain; too, too vain: but we will put it, as they say, to *fortuna della guerra.* I wish you the peace of mind, most royal couplement!

[*Exit* ARMADO.

King. Here is like to be a good presence of Worthies. He presents Hector of Troy; the swain, Pompey the Great; the Parish Curate, Alexander; Armado's page, Hercules; the Pedant, Judas Maccabeus.
And if these four Worthies in their first shew thrive,
These four will change habits, and present the other
five.

Bir. There is five in the first shew.

King. You are deceived; 'tis not so.

Bir. The Pedant, the Braggart, the Hedge-priest, the fool, and the boy: —
Abate throw at Novem, and the whole world again,
Cannot pick out five such, take each one in 's vein.

King. The ship is under sail, and here she comes
amain.

Enter COSTARD *armed, for* Pompey.

Cost. "I Pompey am, —

Boyet. You lie, you are not he.

Cost. "I Pompey am, —

Boyet. With libbard's head on knee.

Bir. Well said, old mocker: I must needs be friends with thee.

Cost. "I Pompey am, Pompey surnam'd the big, —

Dum. The Great.

Cost. It is great, sir; — "Pompey surnam'd the Great;
"That oft in field, with targe and shield, did make my foe to sweat:
"And travelling along this coast I here am come by chance,
"And lay my arms before the legs of this sweet lass of France."
If your ladyship would say, 'Thanks, Pompey,' I had done.

Prin. Great thanks, great Pompey.

Cost. 'Tis not so much worth; but, I hope, I was perfect. I made a little fault in 'great.'

Bir. My hat to a halfpenny, Pompey proves the best Worthy.

Enter Sir NATHANIEL *armed, for* Alexander.

Nath. "When in the world I liv'd, I was the world's commander;
"By East, West, North, and South, I spread my conquering might:
"My 'scutcheon plain declares, that I am Alisander." —

Boyet. Your nose says, no, you are not; for it stands too right.

Bir. Your nose smells, no, in this, most tender-smelling knight.

Prin. The conqueror is dismay'd. Proceed, good Alexander.

Nath. "When in the world I liv'd, I was the world's commander;" —

Boyet. Most true; 'tis right: you were so, Alisander.

Bir. Pompey the Great, —

Cost. Your servant, and Costard.

Bir. Take away the conqueror, take away Alisander.

Cost. O! sir, [*to* NATH.] you have overthrown Alisander the conqueror. You will be scrap'd out of the painted cloth for this: your lion, that holds his pole-axe sitting on a close stool, will be given to Ajax: he will be the ninth Worthy. A conqueror, and afeard to speak? run away for shame, Alisander. [NATH. *retires.*] There, an't shall please you: a foolish mild man; an honest man, look you, and soon dash'd! He is a marvellous good neighbour, in sooth, and a very good bowler; but, for Alisander, alas! you see, how 'tis; — a little o'erparted. — But there are Worthies a coming will speak their mind in some other sort.

Prin. Stand aside, good Pompey. [*Exit* COSTARD.

Enter HOLOFERNES *armed, for* Judas, *and* MOTH *armed, for* Hercules.

Hol. "Great Hercules is presented by this imp,
"Whose club kill'd Cerberus, that three-headed *canis;*
"And, when he was a babe, a child, a shrimp,
"Thus did he strangle serpents in his *manus.*
"*Quoniam,* he seemeth in minority,
"*Ergo,* I come with this apology." —

[*To* MOTH.] Keep some state in thy *exit*, and vanish. [*Exit* MOTH.

"Judas I am, —

Dum. A Judas!

Hol. Not Iscariot, sir. —

"Judas I am, ycleped Maccabeus. —

Dum. Judas Maccabeus clipp'd is plain Judas.

Bir. A kissing traitor. — How art thou prov'd Judas?

Hol. "Judas I am, —

Dum. The more shame for you, Judas.

Hol. What mean you, sir?

Boyet. To make Judas hang himself.

Hol. Begin, sir: you are my older.

Bir. Well follow'd: Judas was hang'd on an elder.

Hol. I will not be put out of countenance.

Bir. Because thou hast no face.

Hol. What is this?

Boyet. A cittern head.

Dum. The head of a bodkin.

Bir. A death's face in a ring.

Long. The face of an old Roman coin scarce seen.

Boyet. The pommel of Cæsar's faulchion.

Dum. The carv'd-bone face on a flask.

Bir. St. George's half-cheek in a brooch.

Dum. Ay, and in a brooch of lead.

Bir. Ay, and worn in the cap of a tooth-drawer.
And now forward; for we have put thee in countenance.

Hol. You have put me out of countenance.

Bir. False: we have given thee faces.

Hol. But you have out-fac'd them all.

Bir. An thou wert a lion, we would do so.

Boyet. Therefore, as he is an ass, let him go.
And so adieu, sweet Jude! nay, why dost thou stay?

Dum. For the latter end of his name.

Bir. For the ass to the Jude? give it him: — Jud-as, away.

Hol. This is not generous, not gentle, not humble.

Boyet. A light for Monsieur Judas! it grows dark; he may stumble.

Prin. Alas, poor Maccabeus, how hath he been baited!

Enter ARMADO, *armed, for* Hector.

Bir. Hide thy head, Achilles: here comes Hector in arms.

Dum. Though my mocks come home by me, I will now be merry.

King. Hector was but a Trojan in respect of this.

Boyet. But is this Hector?

King. I think Hector was not so clean-timber'd.

Long. His leg is too big for Hector's.

Dum. More calf, certain.

Boyet. No; he is best indued in the small.

Bir. This cannot be Hector.

Dum. He's a god or a painter; for he makes faces.

Arm. "The armipotent Mars, of lances the almighty,
Gave Hector a gift, —

Dum. A gilt nutmeg.

Bir. A lemon.

Long. Stuck with cloves.

Dum. No, cloven.

Arm. [Peace!]
"The armipotent Mars, of lances the almighty,
Gave Hector a gift, the heir of Ilion;
A man so breath'd, that certain he would fight, yea,
From morn till night, out of his pavilion.
I am that flower, —

Dum. That mint.

Long That columbine.

Arm. Sweet Lord Longaville, rein thy tongue.

Long. I must rather give it the rein, for it runs against Hector.

Dum. Ay, and Hector's a greyhound.

Arm. The sweet war-man is dead and rotten: sweet chucks, beat not the bones of the buried: [when he breathed, he was a man.] — But I will forward with my device. Sweet royalty, bestow on me the sense of hearing. [BIRONE *goes out.*

Prin. Speak, brave Hector: we are much delighted.

Arm. I do adore thy sweet Grace's slipper.

Boyet. Loves her by the foot.

Dum. He may not by the yard.

Arm. "This Hector far surmounted Hannibal, —

Enter COSTARD, *hastily and unarmed, and* BIRONE *after him.*

Cost. The party is gone: fellow Hector, she is gone; she is two moneths on her way.

Arm. What meanest thou?

Cost. Faith, unless you play the honest Trojan, the poor wench is cast away: she's quick: the child brags in her belly already, 'tis yours.

Arm. Dost thou infamonize me among potentates? Thou shalt die.

Cost. Then shall Hector be whipp'd for Jaquenetta that is quick by him, and hang'd for Pompey that is dead by him.

Dum. Most rare Pompey!

Boyet. Renowned Pompey!

Bir. Greater than great; — great, great, great Pompey! Pompey the huge!

Dum. Hector trembles.

Bir. Pompey is moved. — More Ates, more Ates! stir them on! stir them on!

Dum. Hector will challenge him.

Bir. Ay, if he have no more man's blood in's belly than will sup a flea.

Arm. By the North Pole, I do challenge thee.

Cost. I will not fight with a pole, like a northern man: I'll slash; I'll do it by the sword. — I pray you, let me borrow my arms again.

Dum. Room for the incensed Worthies!

Cost. I'll do it in my shirt.

Dum. Most resolute Pompey!

Moth. Master, let me take you a button-hole lower. Do you not see, Pompey is uncasing for the combat? What mean you? you will lose your reputation.

Arm. Gentlemen, and soldiers, pardon me; I will not combat in my shirt.

Dum. You may not deny it: Pompey hath made the challenge.

Arm. Sweet bloods, I both may and will.

Bir. What reason have you for't?

Arm. The naked truth of it is, I have no shirt. I go woolward for penance.

Boyet. True, and it was enjoin'd him in Rome, for want of linen; since when, I'll be sworn, he wore none, but a dish-clout of Jaquenetta's; and that he wears next his heart for a favour.

Enter a Messenger, Monsieur MERCADE.

Mercade. God save you, Madam.

Prin. Welcome, Mercade,
But that thou interrupt'st our merriment.

Mer. I am sorry, Madam, for the news I bring
Is heavy in my tongue. The King your father —

Prin. Dead, for my life!
Mer. Even so: my tale is told.
Bir. Worthies, away! The scene begins to cloud.
Arm. For mine own part, I breathe free breath. I have seen the day of wrong through the little hole of discretion; and I will right myself like a soldier.
[*Exeunt* Worthies.
King. How fares your Majesty?
Prin. Boyet, prepare: I will away to-night.
King. Madam, not so; I do beseech you, stay.
Prin. Prepare, I say.—I thank you, gracious lords,
For all your fair endeavours; and entreat,
Out of a new-sad soul, that you vouchsafe
In your rich wisdom to excuse, or hide,
The liberal opposition of our spirits:
If over-boldly we have borne ourselves
In the converse of breath, your gentleness
Was guilty of it. Farewell, worthy lord!
A heavy heart bears not a nimble tongue.
Excuse me so, coming so short of thanks
For my great suit so easily obtain'd.
King. The extreme haste of Time extremely forms
All causes to the purpose of his speed;
And often, at his very loose, decides
That which long process could not arbitrate:
And though the mourning brow of progeny
Forbid the smiling courtesy of love
The holy suit which fain it would convince,
Yet, since love's argument was first on foot,
Let not the cloud of sorrow justle it
From what it purpos'd; since, to wail friends lost
Is not by much so wholesome, profitable,
As to rejoice at friends but newly found.
Prin. I understand you not: my griefs are dull.

Bir. Honest plain words best pierce the ear of grief;
And by these badges understand the King.
For your fair sakes have we neglected time,
Play'd foul play with our oaths: your beauty, ladies,
Hath much deform'd us, fashioning our humours
Even to the opposed end of our intents;
And what in us hath seem'd ridiculous,—
As love is full of unbefitting strains,
All wanton as a child, skipping, and vain;
Form'd by the eye, and, therefore, like the eye,
Full of strange shapes, of habits, and of forms,
Varying in subjects, as the eye doth roll
To every varied object in his glance:
Which party-coated presence of loose love
Put on by us, if, in your heavenly eyes,
Have misbecome our oaths and gravities,
Those heavenly eyes, that look into these faults,
Suggested us to make. Therefore, ladies,
Our love being yours, the error that love makes
Is likewise yours: we to ourselves prove false,
By being once false for ever to be true
To those that make us both,—fair ladies, you:
And even that falsehood, in itself a sin,
Thus purifies itself, and turns to grace.
Prin. We have receiv'd your letters full of love;
Your favours, the ambassadors of love;
And, in our maiden council, rated them
At courtship, pleasant jest, and courtesy,
As bombast, and as lining to the time.
But more devout than this, in our respects
Have we not been; and therefore met your loves
In their own fashion, like a merriment.
Dum. Our letters, madam, shew'd much more than jest.

Long. So did our looks.
Ros. We did not quote them so.
King. Now, at the latest minute of the hour,
Grant us your loves.
Prin. A time, methinks, too short
To make a world-without-end bargain in.
No, no, my lord, your Grace is perjur'd much,
Full of dear guiltiness; and therefore this.—
If for my love (as there is no such cause)
You will do aught, this shall you do for me:
Your oath I will not trust; but go with speed
To some forlorn and naked hermitage,
Remote from all the pleasures of the world;
There stay, until the twelve celestial signs
Have brought about their annual reckoning.
If this austere insociable life
Change not your offer made in heat of blood;
If frosts and fasts, hard lodging and thin weeds,
Nip not the gaudy blossoms of your love,
But that it bear this trial, and last love;
Then, at the expiration of the year,
Come challenge me: challenge me by these deserts;
And by this virgin palm, now kissing thine,
I will be thine, and, till that instant, shut
My woful self up in a mourning house,
Raining the tears of lamentation,
For the remembrance of my father's death.
If this thou do deny, let our hands part,
Neither intitled in the other's heart.
King. If this, or more than this, I would deny,
To flatter up these powers of mine with rest,
The sudden hand of death close up mine eye.
Hence ever, then, my heart is in thy breast.
Bir. [And what to me, my love? and what to me?
Ros. You must be purged too, your sins are rack'd:

You are attaint with faults and perjury;
Therefore, if you my favour mean to get,
A twelvemonth shall you spend, and never rest,
But seek the weary beds of people sick.]

Dum. But what to me, my love? but what to me?

Kath. A wife! — A beard, fair health, and honesty;
With three-fold love I wish you all these three.

Dum. O! shall I say, I thank you, gentle wife?

Kath. Not so, my lord. A twelvemonth and a day
I'll mark no words that smooth-fac'd wooers say:
Come when the King doth to my lady come,
Then, if I have much love, I'll give you some.

Dum. I'll serve thee true and faithfully till then.

Kath. Yet swear not, lest you be forsworn again.

Long. What says Maria?

Mar. At the twelvemonth's end,
I'll change my black gown for a faithful friend.

Long. I'll stay with patience; but the time is long.

Mar. The liker you: few taller are so young.

Bir. Studies my lady? Mistress, look on me:
Behold the window of my heart, mine eye,
What humble suit attends thy answer there;
Impose some service on me for thy love.

Ros. Oft have I heard of you, my Lord Birone,
Before I saw you; and the world's large tongue
Proclaims you for a man replete with mocks,
Full of comparisons and wounding flouts,
Which you on all estates will execute,
That lie within the mercy of your wit.
To weed this wormwood from your fruitful brain,
And, therewithal, to win me, if you please,
(Without the which I am not to be won,)
You shall, this twelvemonth term, from day to day,
Visit the speechless sick, and still converse
With groaning wretches; and your task shall be,

With all the fierce endeavour of your wit,
To enforce the pained impotent to smile.

Bir. To move wild laughter in the throat of death?
It cannot be; it is impossible:
Mirth cannot move a soul in agony.

Ros. Why, that's the way to choke a gibing spirit,
Whose influence is begot of that loose grace,
Which shallow laughing hearers give to fools.
A jest's prosperity lies in the ear
Of him that hears it, never in the tongue
Of him that makes it: then, if sickly ears,
Deaf'd with the clamours of their own dear groans,
Will hear your idle scorns, continue them,
And I will have you, and that fault withal;
But, if they will not, throw away that spirit,
And I shall find you empty of that fault,
Right joyful of your reformation.

Bir. A twelvemonth? well, befall what will befall,
I'll jest a twelvemonth in an hospital.

Prin. [*To the* KING.] Ay, sweet, my lord; and so I take my leave.

King. No, Madam; we will bring you on your way.

Bir. Our wooing doth not end like an old play;
Jack hath not Jill: these ladies' courtesy
Might well have made our sport a comedy.

King. Come, sir, it wants a twelvemonth and a day,
And then 'twill end.

Bir. That's too long for a play.

Enter ARMADO.

Arm. Sweet Majesty, vouchsafe me,—

Prin. Was not that Hector?

Dum. The worthy knight of Troy.

Arm. I will kiss thy royal finger, and take leave.

I am a votary: I have vow'd to Jaquenetta to hold the plough for her sweet love three years. But, most esteemed greatness, will you hear the dialogue that the two learned men have compiled in praise of the owl and the cuckoo? it should have followed in the end of our shew.

King. Call them forth quickly; we will do so.

Arm. Holla! approach.

Enter HOLOFERNES, NATHANIEL, MOTH, COSTARD, *and others.*

This side is Hiems, Winter; this Ver, the Spring; the one maintained by the owl, the other by the cuckoo. Ver, begin.

Song.

I.

Spring. *When daisies pied, and violets blue,*
And lady-smocks all silver white,
And cuckoo-buds of yellow hue,
Do paint the meadows with delight,
The cuckoo then, on every tree,
Mocks married men, for thus sings he,
Cuckoo;
Cuckoo, cuckoo,— O word of fear!
Unpleasing to a married ear.

II.

When shepherds pipe on oaten straws,
And merry larks are ploughmen's clocks,
When turtles tread, and rooks, and daws,
And maidens bleach their summer smocks,
The cuckoo then, on every tree,
Mocks married men, for thus sings he,
Cuckoo;

Cuckoo, cuckoo, — O word of fear!
Unpleasing to a married ear.

III.

Winter. *When icicles hang by the wall,*
And Dick the shepherd blows his nail,
And Tom bears logs into the hall,
And milk comes frozen home in pail,
When blood is nipp'd, and ways be foul,
Then nightly sings the staring owl,
To-who;
Tu-whit, to-who, — a merry note,
While greasy Joan doth keel the pot.

IV.

When all aloud the wind doth blow,
And coughing drowns the parson's saw,
And birds sit brooding in the snow,
And Marian's nose looks red and raw;
When roasted crabs hiss in the bowl,
Then nightly sings the staring owl,
To-who;
Tu-whit, to-who, — a merry note,
While greasy Joan doth keel the pot.

Arm. The words of Mercury are harsh after the songs of Apollo. You, that way: we, this way.
[*Exeunt.*

NOTES ON LOVE'S LABOUR'S LOST.

ACT FIRST.

Scene I.

p. 349. "—— a little *Academe*":—This is the old and the more correct form of the word derived from the Greek *Ἀκαδήμεια*. The modern word 'academy' was, however, in use in Shakespeare's day.

" "You three, *Birone*":—The original spells this French name, in all cases, "*Berowne*," which expressed, at the time, its proper pronunciation very exactly—both the *e* and the *o* having the long pure sound. (See the last paragraph of the *Introduction* to *Much Ado about Nothing*.) It was not necessary to make any remark upon this name, or its orthography, until late in the last century; the English title, which in this century became so illustrious, having until that time been pronounced as it is in this play. It has of late been the practice to print it *Biron*, sometimes with an accent on the *o*; but the combination *on* does not at the present time express the proper sound.

p. 350. "—— but *bankerout* the wits":—an old form of 'bankrupt.' The quarto has "but *bankrupt quite*," &c. I have no doubt that 'bankerout' and 'bankrupt' were pronounced exactly alike; the *p* being silent in the latter, (as in 'accompt,' 'contempt,' 'solempnity,' &c.,) and both the *ou* and the *u* having the second sound of *u*, like *oo* in 'shoot.' The *e* in 'banke-rout' is a superfluous terminal of the first word of the compound; and as such it was sometimes a syllable, sometimes silent, and sometimes omitted in the spelling of the word. 'Bankerout' should be retained only when the trisyllabic form is required by the rhythm.

p. 351. "—— from *common sense*": — i. e., from common knowledge; as we have, just below, "When mistresses from common sense are hid." As in general speech 'common sense' means a faculty of the mind instead of what it is, — '*the common* sense,' i. e., 'the sense common to mankind,' — this note is not without excuse.

"When I to *feast*": — The original has "fast" — a manifest misprint, left to be corrected by Theobald. It was also corrected in Mr. Collier's folio of 1632.

" "—— *and* that most vain": — The quarto has "*but*."

p. 352. "—— an envious, *sneaping* frost": — Sneaping = snipping = nipping.

" "That were to climb the *house o'er* to unlock the gate": — So the folio, except a transposition — "*ore the* house" — which destroys the rhythm of the line. The quarto has, —

"Climb o'er the house to unlock the *little* gate."

The alteration in the folio — the addition of three words and the striking out of one — is plainly the result of no chance of any kind. More important differences between the authentic text and some earlier one — such as the omission of several essential lines — can be justly attributed to the errors or the forgetfulness of transcribers, or the accidents of the printing office: this cannot: it is clearly the result of design. Why was the change made? As clearly, because the text of the quarto, which may or may not have been originally written by the author, did not express his thought. *Birone*, in justification of his ridicule of these literary pursuits, says, (according to the folio,) that they are untimely, that he likes not roses at Christmas or snow in May, and adds, 'so it is too late for you to study now: that were to climb over a house to unlock a gate,' or, in other words, 'you are beginning at the wrong end — doing boys' work at men's years.' But, according to the quarto, he says, 'I like of each thing that in season grows; *so* you, now it is too late to study, climb over the house to unlock the little gate': whereas it was not *so*, (that is, like *Birone*,) at all, but exactly *not* so. Therefore the construction of the sentence was changed by the addition of the first three words of this line, as in the text, and its numbers were brought within the alexandrine limits so frequent in these plays, by the erasure of the not very happy word 'little' in the quarto. The neglect to make the needful transposition of 'house' and 'o'er' is an easy oversight. Editors having failed to look for a reason for the difference between the two texts, and merely choosing between the two, have all hitherto given, and very naturally under those circumstances, that of the older copy; but Mr. Collier's folio of 1632 has "Climb ore the house-*top* to unlock *the gate.*" The importance of the *character* of this change of the text of the quarto, from a copy of which the folio was printed, is the chief reason for the particularity of this note. Like similar changes in the text of *Much Ado about Nothing*, it shows that though the quarto is the older edition, the folio is the higher authority. The line "So you to study," &c., is without punctuation of any kind in the original.

It is hardly necessary to notice the folio's misprint of "*fit* you out" for "*fit* you out," in the King's next speech.

p. 353. "—— against *gentility*" : — The law excluding women from the Court was dangerous, if not fatal, to gentle breeding, *gentilesse*. The correctors of Mr. Collier's folio of 1632, and of Mr. Singer's, not seeing this, read 'garrulity;' against which, beside, the law was not directed, although the penalty was fatal to it.

" "—— *shall* possibly devise" : — The quarto has "*can*."

p. 354. "She must *lie* here" : — Sir Henry Wotton unconsciously wrote the best comment on this phrase in a passage in one of his letters, first quoted by Reed: "An ambassador is an honest man sent to *lie* abroad for the good of his country" — a joke which has doubtless converted many a diplomatist to the faith of Dr. Johnson in the matter of puns.

" "—— this word shall *speak* for me" : — The folio has "*break*" — a palpable misprint.

" "—— no *quick* recreation" : — 'Quick' has here the sense of 'lively.' 'Quick' was synonymous with 'alive' in Shakespeare's time; and we still speak of the quickening of a child in the womb.

" "—— a man of *complements*" : — 'Complement' and 'compliment' were in Shakespeare's time spelled alike; and the former word was applied to an individual in a sense much akin to that radical one to which it is now restricted — completeness, or entire accomplishment: 'a man of complement,' was 'a complete man.'

" "—— the world's *debate*" : — 'Debate' — from the French '*debattre*' — had, until Shakespeare's day, and after, its radical meaning, 'to quarrel,' or 'to fight.'

p. 355. "—— *fire*-new" : — brand or bran new.

" "*Enter* DULL" : — In the folio, "*Enter a Constable*," &c.

p. 355. " —— his Grace's *tharborough*" : — The thirdborough was a minor parish officer in Old England.

" " —— the *contempts* thereof" : — 'Contempts' and 'contents' used to be pronounced alike. See Note on "familiarity will breed content." *Merry Wives of Windsor*, Act I. Sc. 1.

" " —— a low *having*" : — The folio has "*heaven*." The correction was made by Theobald.

" " —— or forbear *laughing*" : — Folio and quarto have "*hearing*." Malone merely says, "One of the modern editors plausibly enough reads *laughing*," and Mr. Dyce, approving the change, attributes it to Steevens, although 'laughing' is in Capell's text, 1768. But the change is not plausible: it is necessary. *Armado's* pomposity is known; and when *Longaville* exclaims "God grant us patience!" *Birone* asks, "[For what] to hear or forbear laughing [at what we hear?]" *Longaville's* reply, "To hear meekly, sir, *and* to *laugh* moderately, or to *forbear both*," compels the change; and beside, it required no patience to forbear *hearing*.

" " —— as the *style* shall give us cause to climb" : — The pun, intended, like all Shakespeare's, for the ear only, was more obvious to the eye in his day, when 'style' and 'stile' were spelled alike.

" " —— taken with the *manner*" : — A thief taken with his booty in his hand was said 'to be taken with the mainour' — from the French *main*, 'the hand.'

p. 356. " —— in telling true, but *so*" : — So folio and quarto. Hanmer needlessly read '*so, so*,' and has been very generally followed.

" " —— *ycleped*" : — called.

p. 357. " —— thy *curious-knotted* garden" : — The garden was so called from the curious knots into which the walks were twisted by the fantastically-shaped beds.

" " —— that shallow *vassal*" : — Mr. Collier's folio of 1632 has '*vessel*.' It is not improbable that this was the author's word.

p. 358. " —— taken with a *damosel*" : — This is the old form of 'damsel' — from the French '*damoiselle*.' The word 'damsel,' which appears in all current editions, except Mr. Knight's, was not introduced into the text until late in the last century.

p. 359. " —— *until* then, *Sit* down, Sorrow" : — The quarto has "'*till* then *set thee* down sorrow."

SCENE II.

p. 359. "The Park near ARMADO'S House": — There are no directions as to the Scenes in the original; and this was placed in *Armado's* house by Pope, who has hitherto been invariably followed. But *Moth's* speech, "Forbear till *this company be past*," shows that they stood in the park, not in the house. Throughout this Scene, with two exceptions, *Armado* is styled *Braggart* in folio and quarto.

"*Enter* . . . MOTH": — I have not the least doubt that the name of *Armado's* page is not *Moth*, but *Mote* — a "congruent epitheton" to one whose extremely diminutive person is frequently alluded to in the play by phrases which seem applicable only to Tom Thumb. That 'mote' was spelled *moth* we have evidence twice in one line of this play, (Act IV. Sc. 3,) which stands in the original, —

"You found his *Moth*, the King your *Moth* did see," —

also in the following from *King John*, Act IV. Sc. 1, —

"O heaven, that there were but a *moth* in yours," —

and, in fact, in every case in which the word appears in the first folio, as well as in all the quartos. Wicliff wrote in Matthew vi., "were rust and *mought* distryeth." Indeed, it seems far from improbable that the two words were originally one, and that 'mote' is not, as Richardson supposes, from 'mite.' For both 'mite' and 'mot [e]' are found in the Anglo-Saxon, in which language 'moth' is *moghte*; and the idea of smallness would naturally come to be expressed by a word which is the name of so well-known and so diminutive an insect. "*Moth*" is allowed to remain in the text, because the name of the insect having been sometimes so spelled in Shakespeare's day, (though generally *moathe* or *mothe*,) that may possibly have been the word intended, in spite of the spelling of 'mote' in this very play, — because it is sufficiently expressive of the Liliputian dimensions of the page, — and because, to displace what has remained so long in the text, when there is no absolute necessity for doing so, would be doing almost wanton violence. But whether the name is *Moth* or *Mote*, it is plain that the pronunciation was *mote*. See *Introduction* to *Much Ado about Nothing*, and the Note on "Peasblossom, Cobweb, Mote, and Mustardseed." *M. N. Dream*, Act III. Sc. 1.

p. 359. "—— dear *imp*": — This word really means 'scion,' and of old was applied to any child, though chiefly to boys.

" "—— my tough *seigneur*": — So the original, uniformly, when the word occurs in this play, excepting an omission of the first *e*, due to ignorance or carelessness. The French title is evidently intended. Malone changed it to 'senior,' thus destroying, at once, *Moth's* pun on that word, and an important textual trait of the play. He also erroneously stated that the original word is 'signior.' He has hitherto been followed in both respects without a question.

p. 360. "—— that an eel is *ingenious*" :— The folio has "*ingenuous*." The words were not distinguished by orthography in Shakespeare's time.

" "—— *crosses* love not him" :— Pieces of money were called 'crosses,' from the cross-like division by which the arms on one side were quartered.

" "—— the base vulgar [do] call three" :— 'Do' is from the quarto.

" "—— the *dancing horse*" :— This horse was famous over Europe for the strange feats that he had been taught to perform by Banks, his owner, whom his intelligence and un-horse-ly accomplishments brought under suspicion of witchcraft. Allusions to him are frequent in the literature of the time. His name was *Morocco*.

p. 361. "Most *maculate* thoughts" :— The folio has "immaculate," which *Moth's* rhymes below show to be wrong. The quarto is correct.

p. 362. "—— a ballad, boy, of the King and the Beggar" :— For this ballad, of King Cophetua and the Beggar-Maid, see Percy's *Reliques*, First Series, Book II.

" "*Enter* DULL, COSTARD, *and* JAQUENETTA" :— The original direction is, "*Enter Clowne, Constable,* and *Wench.*" It is hardly necessary to say that nothing derogatory was intended to *Jaquenetta* by this designation. *Piers Ploughman* says of the Incarnation, —

"And in the wombe of that *wenche* he was fourty weeks
And man by-came of that mayde, to save man kynde."

Long past Shakespeare's time any young woman, even of princely rank, was called a 'wench.'

p. 363. "—— for the *day-woman*" :— i. e., the dairy-woman. The etymology is considered uncertain; but only, it would seem, because there are so many similar words in the northern languages from which it might be derived — all of which are connected with the idea of a mother's suckling her babe. The word is still in use in Scotland.

" "With *that* face" :— The folio has "*what*;" but this is a typographical error for the word in the text, (which is found in the quarto,) as we may fairly presume from the existence of the phrase to a late date in England as a common repartee.

p. 363. "Come, Jaquenetta, away": — In folio and quarto this speech is assigned, erroneously, to *Costard*, with the prefix "*Clo*[wn]" — the mistake being caused by the identity of the initial letters of 'Clown' and 'Constable.'

" "—— more bound to you than your *followers*": — The original has "fellowes" — an easy typographical error for the word in the text, which is found in Capell's edition. The Braggart's *fellows* were not "rewarded" by him, "lightly" or otherwise: hardly, his followers; although, on giving *Costard* the "remuneration," (Act III.,) he says, "the best ward of mine honour is rewarding my dependants." This confirms the reading here adopted; for it shows both how lightly rewarded his followers were, and that he was somewhat sensitive upon the point.

" "—— to be [*too*] silent": — 'Too' is found only in the quarto.

p. 364. "Yet *was Samson* so tempted": — Thus the quarto. In the folio the words "was Sampson" are transposed, by accident, evidently, as we see by the next clause of the sentence, in which the characteristic precession of the nominative by the verb, appears in both copies.

" "The first and second cause": — See Touchstone's exposition of the Code of Quarrel. *As You Like It*, Act V. Sc. 4.

" "I shall turn *sonnets*": — The original has "son*net*," — an easy misprint. We still speak of turning tunes or turning sentences. Hanmer read 'sonnet*eer*,' and has hitherto been universally followed. But that form was not known in Shakespeare's day. If so great and unnecessary a change in the original word were to be made, we should read 'sonnet*ist*;' as in Bishop Hall's *Satire*, quoted in Richardson's *Dictionary*: —

"And is become a new found sonnetist."

ACT SECOND.

Scene I.

p. 365. "Good Lord Boyet": — In the folio this speech has two prefixes, "*Queen*" and "*Prin.*": the former at the commencement, the latter at the line "You are not ignorant," &c. *Margaret* and *Katharine* are called 1*st* and 2*d Lady*.

p. 366. "Therefore *to 's seemeth* it," &c.: — Thus the original. It has been hitherto changed to "Therefore *to us seem'th*," &c.

" "Of Jaques Falconbridge, *solemnized*."

The pronunciation *solémni-zed* obtained until after Milton's day. See the last Note but one on *The Tempest*.

" "Well fitted in arts": — The second folio attempts to make this line rhythmical by reading "in *the* arts;" but this huddles "glorious" into two syllables. If there is an error in the text, it is probably a transposition, and we should read,

"*In arts well fitted*, glorious in arms."

p. 367. "Here comes Boyet": — The quarto, followed by Mr. Collier, (of course,) and by Mr. Hudson, gives these words to a *Lord;* the folio assigns them to *Margaret*, who is in haste to change the subject upon which the *Princess* has begun to rally her ladies. Plainly an intentional and authoritative change this, and not a misprint.

p. 368. "Why, *will* shall break it; *will*, and nothing else":

It seems quite probable that Shakespeare, whose person and manner fitted him for the part, played the *King*, and, knowing that he would do so, made here a play upon his name similar to that in his 135th Sonnet: else the asseveration and reply seem somewhat forced. There is a tradition that he played royal characters. See *Life*, Vol. I.

p. 369. "'Tis '*long of* you": — English editors think it necessary to explain "this ancient idiom," as they call it; but 'it's all along of you,' in the sense of 'it's because of you,' is common enough in America; although among cultivated persons it is generally, if not always, used in the way of badinage.

p. 370. "—— *would I* yield unto": — The quarto has, "*I will* yield unto."

" "—— *in* my gates": — The quarto, "*within* my gates."

" "—— *fair* harbour in my house": — The folio misprints, "*farther* harbour," &c.

p. 371. "*Birone.* Lady," &c.: — This and the five following speeches are assigned to *Boy*[*et*] in the folio; but plainly through a mistake caused by the identity of initial letters; for the sixth speech has the prefix *Ber*[*owne.*]

" "Is the *fool* sick": — The folio misprints "*foul*," or "*foul*."

" "No, *point*": — A pun is intended upon the strong

French negative, *non, point.* It is noteworthy that it occurs twice in this play. See Act V. Sc. 2, p. 421.

p. 371. "Sir, I pray you," &c.: — Here the original has a stage direction, "*Enter Dumane,*" and below, at "what's her name," "*Enter Beroune.*" This is owing to the very small stage on which the comedy was played. Neither is supposed to have left the company.

"The heir of Alençon, *Katharine,*" &c.: — Here the original has "*Rosaline,*" who is *Birone's* mistress, and afterward, when he makes inquiry, "*Katharine,*" who is *Dumaine's.* In the first part of this Scene, we see that *Maria* is presented as in some way connected with the house of Falconbridge, and *Katharine* with that of Alençon. '*Roſaline*' and '*Katharine*' might be easily mistaken in old MS.; but the error is one which we naturally expect to find rectified in the folio. I learn from Mr. Singer's new edition, that this correction has been previously suggested in *Notes and Queries.* The difficulty occurred to Steevens; and Malone thought he settled it by showing that all the ladies wore masks; but he forgot that their lovers recognized them in spite of their masks. See the first three speeches of *Birone* and *Rosaline* at this interview.

" "I have heard — on your beard": — 'Heard' and 'beard' are now no more rhymes than 'heard' and 'board;' but at the time when this comedy was written they were pronounced alike. The same is true of 'jest' and 'beast,' some lines below, and of numberless other rhymes in this, and of some in every play of Shakespeare.

p. 372. "My lips are no *common,* though *several* they be": — *Maria's* meaning and her first pun are plain enough: the second has been hitherto explained by the statement that the several or severell in England was a part of the common, set apart for some particular person or purpose, and that the town bull had equal right of pasture in common and severell. It seems to me, however, that we have here another exhibition of Shakespeare's familiarity with the Law; and that the allusion is to tenancy in common by several (i. e., divided, distinct) title. Thus, — "Tenants in Common are they which have lands or Tenements in Fee-simple, fee taile, or for terme of life, &c., and they have such Lands or Tenements by severall Titles, and not by a joynt Title, and none of them know by this his severall, but they ought by the Law to occupie these Lands or Tenements in common and *pro indiviso,* to take the profits in Common." *Coke upon Littleton,* Lib. III. Cap. 4, Sect. 292. "Also if lands be given to two to have and to hold s.[everally] the one moity to the one and to his heires, and the other moity to the other and to his heires, they are Tenants in Common." *Ibid.*, Sec. 298; and see this Chapter *passim*. *Maria's* lips were several as being two, and (as she says in the next line) as belonging in common to her fortunes and to herself; but yet they were no common pasture.

p. 373. "Boyet is *dispos'd*": — *Boyet* quibbles: the *Princess* meant, 'inclined to wanton merriment.' Mr. Dyce was the first to show, in his Notes on Beaumont and Fletcher's *Wit without Money*, and in his first volume of Shakespearian Notes, that 'disposed' had this signification.

ACT THIRD.

Scene I.

p. 374. Theobald included this Act in the second, and began the third Act where the fourth begins in the original, the fourth at the beginning of the original fifth, and the fifth in the middle of Scene second of that Act, where the *King* and his courtiers return to the *Princess'* pavilion in their proper habits. His reason for so doing was, the disproportionate length of the original Acts, which is manifest to every reader; but so little was gained by the alteration, that, although he was followed for a time, the first arrangement was soon resumed, and has since been preserved.

" "*Concolinel*": — The original has here simply "*Moth.* Concolinel." The word is incomprehensible; and it has been generally supposed to be the beginning of some Italian song that is lost; though why, it would be difficult to say. The corruption is probably irremediable; but it has occurred to me that 'concolinel' might be a distorted direction for musical expression (as almost all such begin with '*con*') which had been ignorantly foisted into the text instead of the first words of the song. These, according to Mr. Collier's folio of 1632, were *Amato bene;* but Dr. Rimbault, whose opinion merits high consideration, thinks that Italian solos were unknown in Shakespeare's England.

" "—— bring him *festinately*": — hastily.

" "—— a French *brawl*": — A brawl or *bransle* was a dance, of which Marston gives the following very particular, and, I suppose, lucid, description in his *Malcontent*: — "'tis but two singles on the left, two on the right, three doubles forward, a traverse of six round: do this twice, three singles side, galliard tricke of twentie, coranto pace: a figure of eight, three singles broken downe, come up, meete two doubles, fall backe and then honour." Act IV. Sc. 2. 'Honour' — a common term for 'salute' — here, perhaps, means 'kiss;' for at this feature of the dance in question was launched much nasal thunder.

p. 374. "—— by turning up your eye": — The quarto has "your eye-*lids*;" but it is the eye and not the eye-lid that affected people raise; and the eye-lid, when raised, is lifted, not turned-up: yet in spite of this and of the authority of the folio, every editor hitherto has silently followed the quarto.

p. 375. "By my *penny*," &c.: — Folio and quarto have "*penne*."

" "—— the hobby-horse is forgot": — *Moth* waggishly thrusts upon *Armado* the first line of an old song, frequently alluded to in Shakespeare's day, and which Mr. Collier supposes to have been written on the omission of the hobby-horse in the May games. It is mentioned again in *Hamlet*, Act III. Sc. 3.

p. 376. "*Most rude* melancholy": — The corrector of Mr. Collier's folio of 1632 read, "*moist eyed* melancholy;" but had he considered the context, he would have seen that *Armado* calls melancholy rude because she, in his person, sighs in the welkin's face.

" "—— a *Costard* broken in a shin": — *Moth* cries "wonder," because 'costard' means 'head.'

" "—— no salve in *them all*, sir": — Folio and quarto have "no salve in *thee male*, sir." The correction was suggested by Tyrwhitt, and was also found in Mr. Collier's folio of 1632. In most MS. it is difficult to tell, except by knowledge of the word, a final *ll* from a final *le*, and the attributing the *m* to the wrong word completed this blunder.

" "—— is not *l'envoy* a *salve*?" — It was discovered in the last century that there was a "quibble" to be sneered at here; but how to get at it they hardly knew. Monck Mason says that "it operates upon the eye, not the ear;" and Farmer, who attempted to prove that Jonson told an untruth, in saying that Shakespeare knew a little Greek and a little more Latin, could "scarcely think that Shakespeare had so far forgotten his little school learning as to suppose the Latin verb *salve* and the English substantive *salve*, had the same pronunciation." It were to be wished that Farmer had shown as much knowledge of the pronunciation, or of the meaning of Shakespeare's English, as Shakespeare showed of the pronunciation of Latin. In

Shakespeare's day the *l* was pronounced in 'salve,' as it was in 'calf' and 'half,' and as many other letters were which were silent on English lips when Farmer wrote. He should have looked forward a few pages, and taken a lesson of *Holofernes*, or have come to America; and he would have learned that the English 'salve' and the Latin '*salve*' were enough alike in sound to justify *Moth's* pun.

p. 377. "I will example it": — These words and the eight following lines are omitted in the folio; the reason being that the preceding line and the fourth following both end in *ain*, and that the line, "The fox, the ape, and the humble-bee," is repeated three times. The printer on looking at his copy took the latter *ain* for the former, which he had put in type, and so went on after the second repetition of "The fox," &c.

" "—— by [*mak*]*ing* four": — The original has "by *adding* four;" but to add four to three would not have "stay'd the odds." The correction was made in Mr. Collier's folio of 1632. It is barely possible that 'adding' was written thoughtlessly.

p. 378. "And he ended the market": — 'Three women and a goose make a market.' *Old Proverb.*

" "—— I will enfranchise thee": — Mr. Collier's folio of 1632 needlessly reads, "*marry*, I will enfranchise." The *ch* in 'enfranchise' being soft at the date of this play, there was ground enough for the clown's punning blunder.

" "—— set thee [free] from durance": — Folio and quarto omit 'free,' which was found in Mr. Collier's folio of 1632.

" "—— mine *honour*": — The folio misprints "honours."

" "—— my *incony* Jew": — Warburton said "*incony* or *kony* in the north signifies 'fine,' 'delicate,' as a *kony thing* — a fine thing. It is related to the Scotch 'canny.'" Mr. Dyce confirms this. 'Jew' is used as 'fool,' 'wretch,' and 'dog' sometimes are, in a pleasant signification which is the converse of ironical.

" "—— the price of this *inkle? a penny*": — Inkle was a kind of tape. For "a penny" the folio has merely "*i. d.*"

p. 379. "There's thy *guerdon*: go. — Cost. *Gardon.*" — In the original *Birone* is represented as giving this French name for remuneration correctly, and the clown as mispronouncing it; — a trifling but characteristic distinction, neglected by all editors hitherto, except Mr. Knight, —

even by the careful Capell. It would not be worthy of particular mention, except to remind the reader that there are many hundreds of like restorations of the original text (aside from those of more importance) which are silently made for the first time in this edition. Farmer pointed out to Steevens this joke about 'guerdon' and remuneration in a tract, called *A Health to the Gentlemanly Profession of Serving Men*, by J. M.; but as that book was not published until the year in which this play was printed, and when it had been on the stage at least four or five years, it was J. M. who plagiarized — if there were plagiarism — and Farmer's intended detraction fails of its object.

p. 379. "*O!* this afternoon:" — *Birone's* constant use of the exclamation '*O!*' which is particularly noticeable in this interview, is plainly one of those caricatures of verbal tricks of the time in which this comedy abounds.

" "—— in print": — Costard means, 'punctually, exactly.'

p. 380. "This *senior-junior*, giant-dwarf": — The original has, "This *Siginor Junios* gyant drawfe," 'Junios' being in italic letter, — the invariable mode of printing proper names in the folio, which, save for the lack of proof-reading, was a careful, and, for the day and country, a handsome piece of printers' work. The reading in the text, which is now universally received, was first suggested in Theobald's edition, 1733. It is very ingenious, and is supported by the correspondent contrast, "giant-dwarf," and the fact that in *Dromio of Syracuse's* last speech in the *Comedy of Errors*, 'senior' is misprinted "*signior*" in the original. It is, however, not at all impossible that there is an allusion in the original text which has escaped detection, or is entirely lost. The double misprint and the capital and italic letter of the second word make an accumulation of errors in a brief space which should not be lightly assumed. Theobald supposed an allusion to *Junius*, a distracted lover in Beaumont and Fletcher's *Bonduca*, which, however, was not written until after this play appeared; Warburton thought Signior Junio to be an impersonation of youth in general; and Upton conjectured that Shakespeare "intended to compliment Julio Romano, who drew Cupid in the character of a giant-dwarf," which conjecture was considered "very ingenious" by Dr. Johnson!

"Th' anointed *sovereign*": — 'Sovereign' is here a trisyllable.

"Dread prince of *plackets*": — American women call,

and time out of mind have called, that aperture in their petticoats (upper and under) which extends from the waist about one quarter down the back of the skirt, the placket-hole; and it is not necessary to say here that 'placket' meant a petticoat, at least soon after Shakespeare wrote. But as there has been some disagreement among English commentators and antiquarians upon the point, and as Mr. Singer has been misled by Florio into saying that a placket was a stomacher, which explanation has been adopted without question by Mr. Hudson, it may be well to confirm what should need no confirmation, by one or two decisive quotations which seem hitherto to have escaped attention. In Breton's *Pasquil's Night Cap*, 1612, are these lines: —

> "Within this church an image was erected
> Which did the Lady Fortune represent,
> * * * * *
> *Within her lap* whole bundles did there lie
> Of earthly blessings and terrestriall joyes
> * * * * *
> Then all the blessings which *her placket* fill'd
> She seem'd to shake, and on his head distill'd."

See also the following passage in *The Miracle*, a Whig lampoon upon the pregnancy of James II.'s Queen.

> "The Message with hearts full of Faith were [*sic*] receiv'd,
> And the next news we heard was Q.[ueen] M.[ary] conceiv'd.
> * * * * *
> Pray Heaven to strengthen *her Majestie's Placket*,
> For if this trick fail beware of your Jacket."
> *Poems on State Affairs*, Vol. I. Part II. p. 185.

Here 'placket' evidently means the Royal 'petticoat,' the strength of which was all important in sustaining that which, as the writer insinuated, produced the appearance of pregnancy in the Queen. Mr. Dyce also quotes a passage from Crowne's *Sir Courtly Nice*, saying of Eve, that "she cuckolded her husband with the serpent, and then pretended to modesty, and fell a making plackets presently." Here 'placket' means that limited covering which barely complies with the demands of shame in the most primitive state of society. And finally, it seems that in spite of the derivation of the word by the lexicographers from the Dutch *plagghe* — a clout, or small piece of cloth — 'placket' was originally, or at an early period, a name for that which it is the chief office of the petticoat to conceal; and that this meaning was attached to it, more or less, for a long time. I refer the reader to the second clause of the exclamation, which is the occasion of this note, — to a speech of *Autolycus*, in *The Winter's Tale*, Act IV. Sc. 3, in which he talks of pinching a placket, — to a speech of *Edgar's* in *King Lear*, Act III. Sc. 4, — to a passage in Marston's *What You Will*, Act II. Sc. 1, in which 'apple-squire,' which we know was a cant term for a kept-gallant or pimp, is used as synonymous with 'page of the placket,' — to one in *The Comicall History of Francion*, fol. 1655, Lib. I. p. 9, — and to one in Middleton's *Any-thing for a Quiet Life*, Act II. Sc. 2, in which the word is derived "*a placendo*, a thing or place to please." Vol. IV. p. 448. Ed. Dyce.

p. 380. "A *witty* wanton": — The original has "a *whitely* wanton." The text is from Mr. Collier's folio of 1632. It is plainly correct; for *Rosaline* was in no sense whitely. We are told again and again that she was the darkest of brunettes, and also that she was witty, — which needs no telling.

ACT FOURTH.

SCENE I.

p. 382. "God dig-you-den all": — A rustic corruption of 'God give you good even all.'

p. 383. "*Break up* this *capon*": — To break up a fowl, was to carve it, cut it open; and *capon* is here used as an equivalent to *poulet*, which in French means both a chicken and a love-letter. It was justly considered by Douce as one of the indications of the French origin of this play.

" "—— which to *annotanize*": — The original has "*annothanize*," which has been universally and silently taken to be a corruption of 'anatomize.' But considering the form of the word in the original, and that the Latin phrase is explained and commented upon, I am quite sure that 'annothanize' is an *Armado*-ism for 'annotate,' which was in use in Shakespeare's time. Note, in either case, *th* used as *t*.

p. 384. "Thus dost thou hear," &c.: — These lines seem to be a poetical postscript to *Armado's* letter — one of the sonnets he proposed to turn. They succeed the signature in the original, without a prefix. Warburton thought them "a quotation from some ridiculous poet of the time."

p. 384. "—— a *Monarcho*": — This was a fantastic, half-crazed Italian, well known in London when Shakespeare first arrived there. He is alluded to in the literature of the time almost as often as Banks' horse. He thought himself sovereign of the world, and that all the ships in port belonged to him.

p. 385. "—— she that bears the bow": — *Rosaline* puns upon *Boyet's* question. 'Suitor' was pronounced *shooter* in Shakespeare's day, and here, indeed, is printed so. Just before (Act III. Sc. 1,) 'sue' is printed 'shue.'

" "—— both did hit [*it*]": — 'It' is omitted in the original, by manifest accident.

p. 386. "—— by cleaving the *pin*": — In place of 'pin,' folio and quarto repeat "is in," of the line above. The correction was made in the folio of 1632. The "clout" was the white object which served as a mark, and which was held by the pin in the middle.

" "—— too much *rubbing*": — a term used by bowlers, Malone tells us, but not what it signifies.

" "—— o' the *to* side": — The original has "*ath to the* side," which, in all modern editions hitherto, has been changed to "*o' the one* side." This gives the sense, but by introducing 'one,' which does not exist in the text, and taking out of *Costard's* mouth a phrase which he meant to use, which was 'the to side,' i. e., 'the hither side,' an old, and though now obsolete or vulgar, a correct form of expression. It is of great antiquity, reaching back to the Middle English period, at least. Wycliffe's translation of the New Testament — made about 1380 — has, in Matthew vi. 24, "Noman may serue to two lordis | forsoth outher he schal hate the toon & loue the tother; outher he schal susteyne the toon & dispise the tother | yee mowne not serue to god & richessis." An Englishman and his wife, bred in the rural districts and very intelligent people, who were servants in my father's family, always said 'the to side,' and 't'e other side.'

" "—— how most sweetly 'a will *swear*": — The missing rhyme to this word seems to indicate the loss of a line which, in Mr. Collier's folio, is thus supplied: —

"Looking babies in her eyes, his passion to declare."

But the rhyme provided here, is, to me, sufficient evidence that it is entirely without authority. I am fully convinced that, at the time when this play was written, 'swear' was pronounced *sweer*, and that all words of, similar orthography had the same vowel sound, and that this can be proved, if indeed it has not been. I have yet to learn, however, that the question has been raised by any writer upon the language.

Scene II.

p. 387. "—— ripe as a *pomewater*": — a species of apple, not known in America, I believe.

" "—— a buck *of the first head*": — A buck of the first head was a buck five years old, and a 'pricket' was a stag of the second year, as we learn from a passage cited by Malone from *The Return from Parnassus*, 1606.

p. 388. "(Which we *of* taste," &c.: — Folio and quarto omit 'of,' the need of which was pointed out by Tyrwhitt.

" "And *raught* not": — and reached not.

" "—— to humour the ignorant, *call* the deer," &c.: — Folio and quarto have "*call'd*," and Rowe interpolated two words, and read, "*I have* call'd," in which he has hitherto been followed, except by Mr. Singer, who reads "I *will call*." But the real misprint is trifling. The Pedant asks the Parson to hear the epitaph, and to consent to call the deer a pricket, to humor the ignorant.

p. 389. "—— affect the *letter*": — i. e., affect alliteration. Shakespeare has another hit at this affectation in the Prologue to *Pyramus and Thisbe*. *Midsummer-Night's Dream*, Act V. Sc. 1.

"Whereat with blade, with bloody, blameful blade,
He bravely broach'd his boiling, bloody breast."

" "Or pricket *sore*, or *else sorel*": — A sorrel was a stag of the third year; a 'soare' or 'sore,' one of the fourth year, as we are told in the extract from *The Return from Parnassus*, referred to just above.

" "—— how he *claws* him with a talent": — 'Talon' was often written 'talent' in Shakespeare's day, and so pronounced. 'Claw' was used in the sense in which we use 'tickle' in the adage, 'Tickle me and I'll tickle you.' As, for instance, "there is nothing maketh the seruant more insolent and glorious than the ouer great gentlenesse of the master: you know well the prouerbe,

'Claw a clowne, he will thee scratch,
Scratch a clowne, he will thee claw.'"

Guazzo's *Civile Conversation*, 1586, fol. 171 a.

" "—— if their sons be *ingenuous*": — So the original, which has hitherto been changed to '*ingenious*,' because the two words used to be spelled alike. But *Holofernes* had not forgotten *Ingenuus puer*.

p. 390. "Master Person, — *quasi* pers-on": — The name for the rector of a parish, now rapidly passing out of use, was originally 'person,' as we see by Chaucer's *Persones Tale*: 'parson' is a comparatively modern corruption; the derivation being from '*persona ecclesiæ*:' see Butler's *Grammar*, 1633, p. 3. This passage is one of two in this play which are interesting and valuable as contemporary records of pronunciation. It shows that the combination *p e r s* and the word 'pierce,' as well as the words 'on' and 'one,' were, in Shakespeare's time, pronounced alike. The passage is printed thus in the original, with one of those errors in the prefixes, which are common in this Scene: —

"*Jaq.* God giue you good morrow, M. *Person.*

Nath. Master Person, *quaſi* Perſon. And if one should be perſt, Which is the one?

Clo. Marry, M. Schoolemaſter, hee that is likest to a hogſhead.

Nath. Of perſing a Hogshead," &c.

Plainly from this, either 'pierce' was then pronounced *purse*, as *p e r s* would be now, or that combination was pronounced as 'pierce' is now. But to decide with confidence what was the sound of *per* and *pier* when this play was written is very difficult — almost impossible. That simple unaccented vowels had their pure sound two hundred and fifty or three hundred years ago in numberless instances in which they have lost it, there seems to be no reason to doubt: but it is equally certain that if this were the result of a general rule, the rule had exceptions; and with regard to the pronunciation of diphthongs, it is very difficult to determine either the rule or the exceptions. In the present instance *Falstaff's* speech, (*Henry IV.* Part I., Act V. Sc. 3,) "if *Percy* be alive, I'll *pierce* him," is in point; for the vowel sounds in the two italicised syllables were evidently alike; but this only shows again that *per* and *pier* were pronounced alike; and the question still remains, — What was their common sound? The following passages, and one quoted in the Note on *Falstaff's* pun, may answer it: —

"Heer with her faire and *pearlesse* eies, which *pearced* have my heart."

Guazzo's *Civile Conversation*, 1586, fol. 210.

From this it appears that the first syllables of 'peer-less' and 'pier-ced' were pronounced alike. In Butler's *English Grammar*, Oxford, 1633, is an Index of "words of like sound which have different writing," &c., in which are these enumerations: —

"PEACE, *pax*: PEAS, *pisum*.
to PEARCE, F. *percer*, *penetro*: PIERCE, of *Pierre* [*Peter*] PEERES, *pares* or *magnates*.
a PIEL or rine, *cortex*: to PIEL, *decortico*, unde PILLED: a PEEL, to set bread into the oven, *pala*, F. *paelle*. a PIL, *pillula*.
a PIECE, *pars*, F. *piece*: yet where a PIECE dooeth signifie a kind [*species*] (whether it be put absolutely, or with its *genus*) it is, for difference, written with *e e* vouel; as a PEECE of ordnance, &c., &c.
to PEEP or look out: to PIEP as chicken dooe, *pipio*."

There is, therefore, evidence of the best kind, that immediately before the writing of this play, and within ten years after the publication of the folio edition, the diphthongs *ea* and *ie* had the sound of *ee* — that is, the pure, long sound of *e*; and particularly that the vowel sound of 'pierce,' or (according to the variable orthography of that day) 'pearce,' meaning to penetrate, was like that in 'peers.' It, however, is somewhat against this conclusion, that the proper name *Pierce* is sometimes pronounced *Purse* in New England. For instance, the eminent Cambridge astronomer is called by his friends Benjamin *Purse*, although his name is *Peirce*. It is also to be considered that the orthographies *person* and *parson* were both used when this play was written, and that the latter and a pronunciation conforming to the modern force of it have prevailed: 'clerk,' too, which was written *clearke* and *clerke*, was also written *clark*; 'Derby' was sometimes spelled *Darby*; and both these words, though spelled with *e*, have now in England the broad sound of *a*. Nor can we disregard the large class of words (such as vermin, serpent, desert, serve, sergeant, merchant) in which *e* had also, until a comparatively recent date, the broad sound of *a*. This pronunciation I suppose to be attributable to the fact that these words first came into the language with the Norman French sound of *e*, i. e., our name sound of *a*, which was corrupted to the broad sound of that letter, and has finally passed into the *u* sound of *e*.

p. 390. "—— good old Mantuan": — Not Virgil, but Battista Spagnolus, who wrote toward the end of the fifteenth century, and who was also born near Mantua. His Eclogues were much thought of by the pedants of the day. The lines about Venice are an old proverb, and are to be found in Florio's *Second Fruits*.

p. 391. "—— the '*tired horse*": — Another reference to Banks' horse, which was attired with ribbons and gay trappings.

" "—— the *intellect* of the letter": — i. e., the address,

that which gives intelligence of its destination. Folio and quarto misprint 'writing,' in the next line, "*written*."

p. 392. "—— I do fear *colourable colours*":— This common phrase of the time seems to have meant 'specious or plausible appearances.'

" "—— if *before* repast":— The folio has, "*being* repast."

Scene III.

p. 393. "—— and so say I, and *ay* the fool":— i. e., *confirm* the fool in what he said. Here and just after, "it kills me, ay a sheep," the old copies of course print "*I* the fool" and "*I* a sheep;" that being the way in which 'ay' is always spelled in them. The pun is patent, even did *Birone* not pat himself on the back with, "Well proved, wit!" but all editions hitherto have lost it by printing 'I.'

" "[*Gets up into a tree*":— The original stage direction is, "*He stands aside;*" but *Birone's* position is evident from the text. See remarks in Vol. I. on the date of the corrections in Mr. Collier's folio of 1632.

" "The *night* of dew":— Mr. Collier's folio of 1632 has, "The *dew* of *night*," which is plausible only: the King's night of dew is not only opposed to "the fresh morning drops," but expressive of his gloom during the absence or indifference of his mistress.

p. 394. "—— like a perjurer, *wearing papers*":— The allusion is to part of the punishment of a convicted perjurer, who wore on his breast a paper stating his crime.

" "The shape of Love's Tyburn":— Mr. Singer says that this is an allusion to the sometimes triangular gallows of Shakespeare's day.

" "Disfigure not his *slop*":— Loose breeches were called 'slops.' Folio and quarto have '*shop*,' which Theobald corrected. A MS. correction in the Earl of Ellesmere's copy of the folio of 1623 gives '*shape*,' which is adopted by Mr. Collier, and approved by Mr. Dyce. But 'slop' better suits *Birone's* jeering vein.

p. 395. "—— which on my earth *do'st* shine":— Thus the folio: the quarto has "do*est* shine," and "exhal*est*" at the beginning of the next line. The mark of contraction came into the folio by accident no more in the former case than in the latter; and it should be retained, or the spelling of the quarto adopted, unless we would remove from these works all chronological traces. In Shakespeare's day 'dost,' (i. e., 'do-est,') and 'didst,' (i. e., 'did-est,') were passing from their dissyllabic to their monosyllabic form. Both appear in the former shape in our translation of the Bible. "Therefore when thou *doest* thine alms," &c. (*Matt.* vi. 2.) "Wilt thou kill me as thou *diddest* the Egyptian yesterday?" (*Acts* viii. 28.) The contracted 'dost' appears to have had the pure sound of *o*, not that of *u* in 'dust.'

p 395. "By Earth, she is not: Corporal, there you lie": — Thus the original, except a comma for the colon. Theobald read, "she is *but* corporal," (i. e., corporeal,) because "Dumaine was a young lord," and "had no sort of post in the army," in which he has been followed by all editors except Mr. Knight and Mr. Collier, although the latter accepts this meaning of 'corporal;' the former approves Douce's explanation, that *Birone*, who had before called himself a "corporal of Cupid's field, applied the title to his friend in the same sense." But *Dumaine* quite surely *had* a post in the army. The editors and commentators forgot that when the ladies recount the vows and proffers of their misled lovers, (Act V. Sc. 2,) *Maria* alone says that *Dumaine* "and his *sword*" were at her service. Besides, *Dumaine* said nothing in the speech on which *Birone* comments to imply that his mistress was more than corporeal. The novel on which this play is founded would doubtless explain why *Dumaine* is called corporal, and why he only is made to talk of his sword.

p. 396. "—— is *ever* May": — The folio misprints "every."

" "—— from thy *thorn*": — Folio and quarto have "*throne*" — an easy misprint, as 'thorn' was spelled with a final *e*. It was corrected in *England's Helicon*, 1600.

p. 397. "Thou, for whom," &c.: — Thus folio and quarto. Pope read "Thou for whom *ev'n* Jove," &c., and Mr. Collier's folio of 1632, "*great* Jove." The quantity and accent proper to 'thou' make any addition to the line superfluous.

" "—— my true love's fasting pain": — Both Mr. Collier's and Mr. Singer's copies of the folio of 1632 read "*lasting* pain." This is plausible; but, as Mr. George Hammersley, of Philadelphia, pointed out to me, *Dumaine's* was a *fasting* pain: as he says in his Sonnet, —

"—— my hand is sworn,
Ne'er to pluck thee from thy thorn."

p. 398. ["*Descends*": — The original has no stage direction here. It is noteworthy that *Birone* does not say 'Now I *descend*,' but "Now *step* I *forth*," which betrays the poet's consciousness that, although he imagined the character to be in a tree, the actor who played it would be on the same plane with the others. See the examination of Mr. Collier's folio of 1632, in the *History of the Text*, Vol. I.

p. 398. "You found his *mote*": — It has been before remarked that the original has "*moth*" in both instances, and in all others in which 'mote' occurs. It cannot be but that the words were pronounced alike. See *Introduction* to *Much Ado*, &c., and Note on "*Enter* ARMADO *and* MOTH," Act I. Sc. 2.

p. 399. "With men like men," &c.: — Folio and quarto omit a word in this line — 'strange' being found first in the second folio. Malone, who has been almost universally followed, read "*moon*-like men" — an ingenious alteration of a text which needs no emendation. *Birone* tells his friends that after all their vows and pretences they are men like other men — no less inconstant. Soon after he says, —

"O! let us embrace.
As true we are, as flesh and blood can be."

" "What *present* hast thou there?" — that is, what 'presentment — matter to be presented.' People of all ranks brought presents to kings, it is true, but not folded up in letters.

p. 400. "—— we deserve *to die*": — It must be remembered that theft, as well as murder, was formerly punished with death.

p. 401. "—— nor I *Birone*": — Because this name here rhymes with 'moon,' and because Mr. Fox said Tou*loon* in the House of Commons, it has been concluded, without sufficient reason I think, that Bir*oon* was the pronunciation of the name in Shakespeare's time. Infinite and ridiculous were the affectations of the elegant folk of Mr. Fox's day. Perhaps due investigation might have convinced the editors that 'moon' was pronounced *mown*, and 'month' or 'moneth' *mownth* or *mown-eth* when this play was written.

' "O *wood* divine": — The original has "*word*."

" "—— and the *shade* of night": — Folio and quarto have "*schoole* of night." The word in the text, which was found in Mr. Collier's folio of 1632, is the best emendation which has been offered — *a* having probably been mistaken for *o*, and *ol* for *d*. Theobald suggested 'stole,' Warburton 'scowl,' — a poor word, which has yet kept a place in the text hitherto, — and Mr. Dyce 'soil.' As the passage has been always punctuated — with a semicolon after 'night' — it is almost senseless. The paradox is, that "the badge of hell," being "beauty's crest, becomes the heavens well."

p. 402. "—— that painting, [and] usurping hair":— The conjunction was supplied by the second folio.

" "—— of their sweet complexion *crack*":— 'Crack,' meaning 'talk,' 'gossip,' is still in use in England, though. I believe, entirely unknown here.

p 403. "—— plodding *prisons* up":— Folio and quarto misprint "*poisons*."

" "Teaches such *learning*":— The original has "*beauty*" — a word with little or no meaning here. Mr. Collier's folio of 1632 furnishes the word in the text, which might be mistaken in MS. for 'beauty,' and which the two following lines show to be correct.

p. 404. "—— in the Hesperides":— that is, in the gardens of the Hesperides. There is no need of supposing that Shakespeare thought the Hesperides themselves to be gardens; although Robert Greene, *Master of Arts in both Universities*, did write in his *Orpheus and Eurydice*, of "the fearful dragon"

"That watched the *gardens* call'd *Hesperides*."

"And when Love speaks," &c.:— Mr. Singer well remarks, that few passages have been more discussed than this; and where all editors and commentators have found some difficulty to explain, it would, perhaps, be presuming to deny that any exists. But the sense which the passage directly and clearly conveyed to me before I had been informed that it was considered obscure, or suspected it to be so,— that when Love speaks, a harmonious drowsy hum of approval from the voice of all the gods fills Heaven,— still clings to me in spite of all ingenious glosses and attempts at emendation. Theobald, on Warburton's suggestion, read,—

"And when Love speaks the voice of all the gods,
Mark Heaven drowsy with the harmony."

And the change in punctuation by which Love is made to speak the voice of all the gods has been generally received. Steevens suggested, '*its* harmony.' Heath explained the passage as meaning, "Whenever Love speaks, all the gods join their voices with his in harmonious concert." Tyrwhitt suggested,—

"And when Love speaks (the voice of all) the gods
Make," &c.

Farmer, —

"And when Love speaks, the voice *makes* all the gods
Of Heaven drowsy," &c.

Charles Knight gives an explanation much like that of the present editor, and Mr. Collier, as usual, confines himself to recording the difference of a letter between the old copies.

p. 405. "—— that *loves* all men": — an idiom of the time for 'that all men love.'

ACT FIFTH.

Scene I.

p. 406. "—— witty without *affection*": — Here 'affection' is used for 'affectation,' 'audacious' for 'self-possessed,' and 'opinion' for 'self-conceit' — as we still say that a man is 'opinionated.' In this speech, as often before and after, *Armado* is spelled *Armatho*.

p. 407. "—— such rackers of orthography," &c.: — This passage has especial interest on account of its testimony as to the condition of our language when it was written. In his pedagoguish wrath, the Pedant lets us know that consonants now silent were then heard on the lips of purists, that compound words preserved the forms and sounds of their elements, and that vowels were pronounced more purely and openly than they now are. The change from the ancient to what may be called the modern pronunciation appears to have begun, among the more cultivated classes, just before Shakespeare commenced his career, and to have been completed in the course of about fifty years — i. e., from about 1575 to about 1625. I am fully aware of the difficulty of fixing limits to such changes, and of the show of reason with which it might be maintained that they have no limits; but as there were periods when our language had, from being Anglo-Saxon, become successively Semi-Saxon, Old English, Middle English, and English, so there was a time when the principles upon which rested the pronunciation for which *Holofernes* contends were no longer thought of, among that class of people to whom we look as the best speakers of a language, and when those which yet guide us became in vogue. With regard to the completion of this change, the following passages from Charles Butler's *English Grammar, or the Institution of Letters, Syllables and Words in the English Tongue*, 4to., Oxford, 1633, are decisive: in them will be found the very words which *Holofernes* cites.

"Another use of the letters is to show the derivation of a woord: namely when wee keep a letter in the derivative, &c. . . . Also when a letter not sounded in the English is yet written, becaus it is in the language from whence the woord came: as *b* in *debt*, *doubt*; *e* in *George*; *g* in *deseign*, *fleyme*, *reign*, *signe*; *h* in *Thomas*, *authoriti*, [See *Introduction* to *Much Ado*, &c.]; *l* in *salve*, &c., &c." (P. 3.) "*L* after *a* and before *f*, *v*, *k* or *m* is vulgarly sounded like *u* (or, with the *a*, like the diphthong *au*); before *f* as in *calf*, *half*; before *v* as in *salv*, *calvs*, *halvs*, &c., &c." (P. 18.) Butler was a Master of Arts of Magdalen College, and his Grammar is a curious and valuable contribution to the later history of our language.

But the isolation of the Englishmen of New England, and their consequent protection from exterior influences, caused changes in pronunciation, as well as in idiom, to take place much more slowly among them than among their brethren who remained in the mother country; and the orthoepy for which the worthy Pedant contends is not very far removed from that of the grandfathers and great-grandfathers of the present generation in the more sequestered parts of the Eastern States. The scholars among these, as well as those who had received only that common-school education which no Yankee is allowed to lack, did not, for instance, in Holofernian phrase, speak *coud* and *woud* fine, but pronounced all the consonants, *could* and *would*; they said *sword*, not *sored*; they pronounced 'have' to rhyme with 'rave,' not *hav*, — 'jest,' which used to be written *j e a s t*, *jeest*, to rhyme with 'yeast,' — 'pert,' which of old was spelled *p e a r t*, *peert*; and in compound words they said, for instance, 'clean-ly,' not *clen-ly*, and, correctly, 'an-gel,' 'cham-ber,' 'dan-ger,' not *ane-gel*, *chame-ber*, *dane-ger*. Their accents yet linger in the ears of some of us, and make the words of Shakespeare's pedagogue not altogether strange. It is true that this note assists neither to determine Shakespeare's text nor to illustrate his meaning; but, perhaps, for its subject's sake, it will be acceptable to those who love the language in which Shakespeare wrote.

p. 407. "—— it insinuateth me of *insanie*": — Folio and quarto have "*infamie*" for '*insanie*,' which Theobald corrected.

" "*Quare* chirrah, not sirrah": — We learn from this passage that at the time when this play was written it was becoming the fashion to pronounce 'sirrah' *shirra*, as it was to pronounce 'suitor' *shooter*. See Note on "She that bears the bow," Act IV. Sc. I. This corruption of *s* to *sh* before *u* or *i*, is like that of *d* to *j* before u, or letters which have its sound: as some folk think it elegant to bid one 'a *jew*,' because 'the *jews* are falling.'

p. 408. "The *third* of the five vowels": — Folio and quarto have "The *last*," which is an obvious error.

" "—— a quick *venew* of wit": — This fencing term was in constant use in the metaphorical sense of 'hit': as, for instance, "being driven [i. e., coquettish women] from their warde, they ly so open that they are soone venued." Guazzo's *Civile Conversation*. 4to. 1586. fol. 135 b.

" "—— at the *Charge*-house": — We shall probably be without an explanation of this phrase until we discover the story on which the play is founded. Steevens supposed it to mean 'free-school,' though it is difficult to conjecture why. Mr. Collier's folio has '*large* house;' but as the original has "Charge-house," with a capital C, the misprint is hardly probable.

p. 409. "I do beseech thee, *remember thy courtesy*; . . . — I do beseech thee, *apparel thy head*": — Difficulty has been found here, which has not been explained, and which Malone proposed to obviate by reading "remember *not* thy courtesy" — an interpolation which Mr. Dyce pronounces "absolutely necessary." But the obscurity has arisen from supposing both sentences to be addressed to the same person. The Clown, who was present as well as the Pedant, probably forgot the courtesy which the other remembered; and *Armado* reminds the peasant of his duty to his betters, and waives the civility on the part of *Holofernes*. We must constantly remember that these plays were written only to be acted.

In the next line the quarto has "*important*" instead of 'importunate.'

p. 410. "—— if this *fadge* not": — i. e., suit not.

" "—— dance *the hay*": — The 'hay' was an old English country dance, which seems to have been a very lively one, from the following allusions to it: "Their violent turning and wild whirling hayes." Davies' *Orchestra*. 1622. "With their winding haies, active, antique dances," &c. Chapman's *Widowe's Tears*. 1612.

Scene II.

p. 411. "He made her melancholy," &c.: — Five lines here are accidentally printed as prose in the original.

p. 412. "—— past *cure* is still past *care*": — Folio and quarto transpose 'care' and 'cure' in this old adage.

" "'Ware pencils, ho!" — Folio and quarto have "'Ware

pensals. *How?*" The emendation is by Mr. Dyce, who says that "how" is "merely the old spelling of '*ho*,'" and cites many instances in support of his opinion, which is much confirmed by the fact that two hundred and fifty years ago *o w* had, much more generally than it now has, the pure sound of *o*. He adds, that "'ho' is, of course, equivalent to *cease*, *stop* — a meaning which *formerly it often bore*"! Has it ceased to bear that meaning in England?

p. 412. "—— I beshrew all *shrews*": — 'Shrew' was pronounced *shrow* in Shakespeare's time, of which pronunciation we yet have remnants, for instance, in 'sew' and 'shew.' The quarto has, "I beshrow all *shrows*."

p. 413. "—— in by th' week": — instead of by the day; that is, firmly engaged.

" "—— to my *behests*": — Folio and quarto have "*device*." The text is that of the second folio, and both sense and rhyme justify it, great as the corruption is which it supposes.

" "So *persaunt*-like": — that is, so sharply, so keenly. The word, from 'pierce,' (formerly written *perse*,) was often so used. The original has "*pertaunt*," with the very easy error of a *t* for a long *ſ*. Hanmer read '*portent*-like,' and has been generally followed. Capell read '*pageant*-like;' and '*potently*' was found in Mr. Collier's folio of 1632. The last word affords a good sense, but it differs too widely from the original, and does not suit the caustic *Rosaline* so well as that in the text.

" "—— to *wantonness*": — Folio and quarto have "*wantons be*," which was corrected in the second folio.

p. 414. "—— mirth *is* in his face": — The folio omits 'is.'

p. 415. "—— as I guess": — This line is without a rhyme. It may be the first of a couplet, the second of which is lost, and which is not absolutely necessary to the sense; otherwise it is the third of a triplet; but the former supposition is the more probable.

" "—— his love-*suit*": — Folio and quarto have "love-*feat*" — an error for which the long *ſ* is chiefly responsible. The correction was found in Mr. Collier's folio of 1632.

p. 416. "—— turn away *her* face": — The original has "*his*," and in the next line "*keepers*" for 'speakers,' which is found in the quarto. In the second line of the *Princess'* next speech '*e'er*' appears for "ne'er," which is found in the second folio.

p. 416. "*Enter the* KING," &c. : — The stage direction of the original is, somewhat oddly, "*Enter Black moores with musicke, the Boy with a speech, and the* rest *of the Lords disguised.*"

" "Beauties no richer," &c. : — This speech is given in the original to *Birone;* but it was *Boyet* who "put *Armado's* page out of his part," as we learn from the *King* just before the ladies join their lovers on the return of the latter in their own habits. The use of the same initial letter as a prefix caused the mistake, which occurs again in the folio in this Scene, when *Costard* enters for Pompey. Theobald made the change, and all editors and commentators have acquiesced in it, except Mr. Collier and Mr. Knight. "Taffata" refers to the silk masks of the ladies.

p. 418. "—— vouchsafe but one change" : — The quarto has "*do but vouchsafe* one change." This is one of many variations between the two editions, which shows that the copy of the quarto from which the folio was printed was corrected by authority.

" "Why take *you* hands" : — The quarto has "*we.*"

" "Prize *you* yourselves" : — The folio omits 'you' — owing to the repetition of the syllable.

p 420. "Take that," &c. : — The folio has "Take *you* that."

" "What, was your visor made," &c. : — In the original this and many other speeches are assigned to the wrong characters. The errors of this kind are so numerous in this play, and so easy of correction, that it has been very rarely necessary to point them out particularly.

" "—— *kingly poor flout*" : — It would have seemed quite unnecessary to point out that this expression refers to the *King's* lame retort at parting, had not "*killed by* poor flout," which was found in Mr. Collier's folio of 1632, been received with some favor, and had not Mr. Singer thought it necessary to read "*stung by* poor flout."

p. 421. "*Qualm,* perhaps" : — Plainly 'qualm' was pronounced *calm,* which gave the *Princess* an opportunity for her jest; for *Longaville* would surely not tell his mistress that she "came o'er his heart" like a *qualm!* Thus 'quote' was pronounced *cote,* and so printed, and sometimes *coat.* See also Note on *qui, quæ, quod. Merry Wives of Windsor,* Act IV. Sc. 1.

" "—— plain *statute-caps*" : — An Act of Parliament passed in 1571, for the benefit of cappers, enjoined, that all persons, *with the exception of noblemen* and a few others, should, on Sunday and other feast days, wear woollen caps entirely of English make, under a penalty of ten groats. Strype's *Annals of Queen Elizabeth.*

p. 422. "—— command me any service to her" :—Thus the folio: the quarto has, lamely enough, "any service to her *thither?*" — which Capell first adopted. He has been universally followed hitherto, the editors also reading, "Where *is* the Princess?" in the second line above, and thus obtaining three lines of poor blank verse. But they forgot that the speeches here are in couplets or alternate rhymes. If the quarto were ever right, which there is no warrant for believing, the difference from it is evidently the result of design. With the next line begins the verse and the rhyme.

p. 423. "—— when *Jove* doth please" : — The quarto has "*God.*" It is possible that the change was made in accordance with the statute 3 James, touching the use of the name of the Creator; but the heathen gods are much appealed to in this play.

" "He can *carve*, too" : — See Note on "She carves," *Merry Wives of Windsor*, Act I. Sc. 3.

" "—— as *whales*-bone" : — The teeth of the walrus, which used to be called the whale, furnished an inferior sort of ivory. Previous editors have noticed that *whales* is a dissyllable, though they have strangely failed to see that the same is true with regard to many other similar words in Shakespeare's earlier plays.

" "Pay him the *due*" : — The folio has "*dutie*," and just below, both folio and quarto have, "this *mad* man," — both evidently errors of the press.

p. 424. "—— [*My*] gentle sweet" : — Folio and quarto have no word in the place of 'My,' which was inserted by Malone. The second folio — no better authority as to a lost word — reads, "*Fair*, gentle sweet," which gives a much less musical line, and a collocation of epithets which *Birone* would be less likely to apply to *Rosaline*.

p. 425. "—— thy keen *conceit*" : — The analogically proper pronunciation of this word was in vogue when this play was written, and made it a perfect rhyme to 'wait.' The diphthong *ei* had then almost invariably the sound which it still preserves in 'freight,' 'obeisance,' &c.

p. 426. "—— spruce *affection*" : —Thus folio and quarto; but all modern editors, Mr. Collier excepted, read 'affec*tat*ion,' although 'affection' was the form most commonly used in Shakespeare's day : — just before, Sir *Nathaniel* says, "witty without affection." Besides, if we read 'affect*a*tion,' we must pronounce *hy-pér-bo-lés;* whereas Shakespeare used that word as a trisyllable, *hy-pér-boles,* as we see by this line in *Troilus and Cressida,* —

"Would seem *hy-per-boles.* At this fusty stuff."

It should be remarked also that affection has not our modern trisyllabic pronunciation, but one similar to that which such words have in French verse — af-fec-*ti-on:* thus it rhymes with os-ten-ta-*ti-on.* This pronunciation of words ending in *tion* is not uncommonly found in the literature of Shakespeare's day.

p. 426. "Sans '*sans*'": — The French word '*sans*' was in common use in the polite society of Shakespeare's time; but, like many others that have enjoyed the same favor, it failed to become domesticated. *Birone,* who had just forsworn "taffata phrases" for "russet yeas and honest kersey noes," has yet, as he says, "a trick of the old rage."

" "—— Lord, have mercy on us": — This was written on the doors of houses infected with the plague; and the plague spots were called 'the Lord's tokens.'

p. 427. "—— you *force* not to forswear": — 'Force' seems to have been used of old for 'weight,' metaphorically in the sense of 'consequence,' 'consideration;' and thus "you force not," means 'you think it of no consequence.'

p. 428. "—— by th' *squire*": — i. e., square, — from the French '*esquierre.*' *Boyet* knows all his royal mistress' whims and peculiarities; or, in an old English phrase which has died out here, 'he has got the length of her foot.'

" "—— you are allow'd": — As we say, 'you are privileged.'

p. 429. "You cannot *beg* us": — The custody of idiots and the management of their estates could be granted by the King to whomever he thought proper; and so persons then were 'begged' for fools with the same intent with which nowadays they are sometimes sent to lunatic asylums.

" "—— but to *pursent* one man": — The original has "*perfect,*" which, though hitherto retained, is plainly a misprint, and an easy one, for 'pursent,' (spelled with a long *ſ,*) which the Clown uses just before. 'Present' was specially applied to the assumption of character on the stage.

" "—— worthy of *Pompion* the Great": — In the previous speech the original has "Pompion," here "*Pompey,*" which seems manifestly an error. The Clown does not know "the degree of the Worthy," but mistaking his name for 'pompion,' ['pumpkin,'] he supposes him to be a "poor man."

p. 429. "Where zeal strives to content, and the contents": — These two lines are as in the original. The poet, had he lived now, or at any time when agreement in number was absolutely necessary, and had no rhyme been required for 'presents,' would have written "and the con*tent*." Much difficulty has been found in the passage, and it has been subjected to many alterations, in one of which, 'them' for 'that,' in the second line, I was once disposed to concur. But no change is necessary. The *Princess* in the preceding and two succeeding lines, is her own commentator upon this expression of the mischievous pleasure which she has in bathos.

p. 430. "Abate a throw at *Novem*": — 'Novem,' or 'Novemquinque,' was a game of dice; so called from the important throws being nine and five.

p. 431. "You lie," &c.: — This first interruption is given in the original to *Birone*, as the first also is in the masking interview in the early part of this Scene; the mistake being due to the identity of the initial letters in the names *Birone* and *Boyet*.

" "With *libbard's* head": — This refers to the *masquine*, which Cotgrave defines (1611) "the representation of a Lyon's head, &c., upon the elbow or knee of some old-fashioned garments." The caps for the knees and elbows in a suit of plate armor were also frequently wrought into the shape of a lion's or leopard's ('libbard's') head.

" "—— it stands too right": — It must be remembered that Alexander's head was awry.

p. 432. "—— the painted cloth": — Painted cloth was a cheap sort of hanging, used generally in halls, instead of arras; and, like that, was adorned with representations of classical or scriptural subjects. It is several times mentioned in these plays, and occurs in almost every remaining inventory of household goods made in Shakespeare's day. See some in Halliwell's *Life of Shakespeare*.

" "—— sitting on a close stool": — Tollet pointed out that in the arms assigned to the Nine Worthies in Leigh's *Accidence of Armory*, 1597, Alexander is made to bear, "geules, a lion seiante in a chayer, holding a battle-ax argent." By preserving, as *Costard* did, the pure sound of the last *a* in 'Ajax,' the nature of his pun will be made apparent. The pole axe was so called from its Polish origin: its handle was short.

p. 433. "A *kissing* traitor": — One meaning of 'clip' was to embrace, to throw the arms about; and hence Judas Maccabeus clipped is called a kissing traitor. We are told that the old Scotch guillotine, the Maiden, "clipped its victim about the neck;" and, doubtless, it hence received its name.

" "A cittern head": — The heads of stringed instruments were of old generally carved grotesquely into human or bestial forms, as they sometimes now are; and the same fashion prevailed with regard to the other articles mentioned afterwards.

p. 434. "A *gilt* nutmeg": — This, from frequent allusions in the literature of the time, appears to have been a common gift; why, it is impossible to say.

" "[Peace!]": — This exclamation, and the words "when he breathed," &c., in *Armado's* second speech below, are found only in the quarto.

p 435. "[BIRONE *goes out*": — In the original, "BEROWNE *steppes forth*." Since Capell's edition, it has been the universal practice to make *Birone* whisper *Costard*, who is kept on the stage, — a very clumsy arrangement, as well as inconsistent with the original direction. This direction shows, that although no entrance is marked in the original, *Costard* (whose exit is there directed when the *Princess* says, "Stand aside, good Pompey") comes running in, crying, "The party is gone," &c., after *Birone* has put him up to the trick. Mr. Collier's folio has, in the latter place, "*Enter* COSTARD *hastily, and unarmed*."

" "—— she's quick": — See *Costard's* next speech and the Note on "quick Birone," in the early part of this Scene.

p. 436. "I go woolward": — To wear wool next the skin was a milder form of the hair-shirt penance.

p. 437. "—— a *nimble* tongue": — The original has "*humble*," a word without meaning here. Theobald read 'nimble,' which was found also in Mr. Collier's folio of 1632, and which the context shows to be correct; for the *Princess* adds, '— and *so* (that is, because a heavy heart bears not a nimble tongue) excuse me for *coming so short* of thanks.'

" "The extreme *haste* of time," &c.: — The original has, "*parts* of time," an evident corruption. The correction, which is Mr. Singer's, is justified by the sense of the three following lines, as well as by the ease with which the old *h*, with a bow below the line, might be mistaken for *p*, and the likeness between *r* and *s* in MS. at any time.

p. 437. "—— my griefs are *dull*": — The original has "my griefs are *double*." The correction was made in Mr. Collier's folio of 1632; and the reply which the line elicits from *Birone* fully justifies the change.

p. 438. "Full of *strange* shapes": — The original has "*straying*," — a palpable misprint.

" "As *bombast*, and as lining": — 'Bombast' being the material which was used to stuff out dresses, the word was used to signify any filling or puffing out. Thus, "so that they have to bombast their bellies with good store of meate." Guazzo's *Civile Conversation*, 1591, fol. 187 b. "Studie should rather make him leane and thinne, and pull out the bumbast of his corpulent doublet." *Ibid.*, fol. 190 a.

" "—— *in* our respects": — The original has "*are*," which Hanmer corrected.

p. 439. "And what to me," &c.: — The five succeeding lines in reply to this question are repeated afterward almost in terms, and with amplification, by *Rosaline*. Various editors have suggested that they should be omitted altogether; and it is evident that they are the first draft of the thought, and by oversight were not struck out when the play was augmented; the parting tilt between these two wits having then been made the close of the conference.

p. 440. "—— for *thy* love": — The folio has "for *my* love."

p. 441. "—— their own *dear* groans": — Mr. Collier's folio of 1632 has "*dire* groans," which is a very specious alteration; but see the first line of Act II. Sc. 1 of this play: —

"Now, Madam, summon up your *dearest* spirits."

King Henry IV., too, calls his son his "dearest [i. e., his greatest] enemy." The use of the word in this superlative sense was common.

p. 442. "And lady-smocks": — This and the next line are transposed in the original. The first 'Tu-whit' is also omitted in *Winter's* stanzas. Theobald made the necessary correction. The structure of the stanzas requires both changes.

p. 443. "—— doth *keel* the pot": — To 'keel a pot' was to cool it by stirring the boiling contents with a ladle.

END OF VOL. III.

CPSIA information can be obtained
at www.ICGtesting.com
Printed in the USA
LVHW110800120522
718525LV00003B/24

9 783375 003074